ᴅᴀʀᴋɴᴇss ᴏꜰ ʟɪɢʜᴛ

(Darkness Series Book #1)

STACEY MARIE BROWN

Copyright © 2013 Stacey Marie Brown

All rights reserved.

ISBN: 978-0-989131-2-3

Edited by Chase Nottingham (www.chaseediting.com)
Cover Design by David Farrell at Woulds & Shoulds
Cover image copyright Shutter Stock

*For my friends, family, and my mom for always supporting and
pushing me to follow my dreams.*

ONE

What a terrifying mess this night turned out to be. I hadn't even wanted to come, but I'd lost a bet with Ryan. It was only one night. One stupid dance. How bad could it be?

Aren't those always the fateful, last words?

I scanned the decorated gym. Cheesy cardboard cutouts and paper streamers dangled from the ceiling. Red and black balloons and huge paper mache masks tried to cover up the basketball hoops and the school mascot painted on the walls. It didn't make the gym look any better, nor did it take away the slight stench of sweat and dirty socks.

"You really thought this would be fun?" I looked at my two friends, Ryan and Kennedy.

Ryan shrugged. "It's our last year. I thought we should at least come to one of these things."

"You're regretting your idea about now, aren't you?" I crossed my arms, a smug grin playing on my lips. It quickly turned to a grimace when the music changed into an obnoxious pop song.

"Oh, yeah." Ryan sighed deeply.

"Come on, guys, let's make the best of it. We got all dressed up." Kennedy's soft voice barely carried to me. This was so typical Kennedy, always trying to see the positive in everything.

Kennedy wasn't the girl who got noticed, especially by the boys in school. I could see the true beauty in her porcelain skin. Ryan always teased how Kennedy was the sweet one, I was the salty, and he was the spice. We had been friends since junior high, when people became cool and uncool. I don't think I have to say in what group we landed.

"I promise you, if we can leave, I'll wear my sweats with ruffles on them if it makes you happy," I said.

"First, I know there is no way you would own anything with frills on it. Second, if you did have sweats with ruffles, you would have found a way to have worn them tonight," Kennedy replied, adjusting her glasses on her nose.

"True." I nodded.

"You guys want something to drink?" Ryan motioned to the beverage stand.

My heart thumped faster. The gorgeous Ben Harris stood in line. I was not the type of girl who crushed on the popular guy, but Ben was different. We'd sat next to each other in class, and I'd gotten to know him.

"I'll go get them," I said quickly.

"Uh-huh." Ryan smirked. "I bet you will."

"What?" I tried to sound innocent. It didn't work for me. They knew me too well. "We're only friends."

"Uh-huh . . . sure," they said in unison.

I waved them off and headed for the refreshment stand. "Whatever."

I stood behind Ben for a couple of seconds and gathered my wits before tapping him on the shoulder. I smiled. "Hey."

Ben's face lit up upon seeing me. "Ember." His smile made me feel a strange, nauseated giddiness inside. "I didn't know you were coming. I thought you said you didn't come to these things?"

I shrugged. "I lost a bet."

"Well, I'm glad you did." His eyes ran over my body. "You look good . . . I mean beautiful."

I wasn't used to compliments, especially from cute, popular guys. Looking away, I gripped my fingers together, twisting them anxiously. "Uh-t-th-thank you. So you do. I mean, so do you . . . look good, I mean."

There was my astounding wit I wanted to use—gone to hell.

He smiled. "Thanks. Maybe you would like to dan—"

"Ben. There you are," Kallie Parson cut in and stood in front of me. She was everything you pictured a popular cheerleader to be— tall, blonde, and beautiful. She was not shy about flaunting her perfect body in a skintight, dark blue, sparkly dress.

"You're needed at the DJ stand right now for the announcement of the Valentine's Cupid Couple."

Ben glanced at me, then back to Kallie.

"Go, sweetie. Hurry!" She shooed him toward the stage.

He finally nodded. "I'll see you later, Em." He turned and disappeared into the crowd.

Kallie swung around and acknowledged my presence. Her eyes skimmed over me and examined me from head to toe before landing of my face. She then burst out laughing. "Awww, how sweet is that? You think he likes you . . . the popular boy falling for the misunderstood, freak girl."

She'd been after me for months now. It had become an all-out attack involving months of cruel jokes and verbal abuse when Ben and I had been partnered for an assignment in English class.

Ben was gorgeous and at the top of the food chain in our school. He was the basketball star and every girl's wet-dream. Kallie tried daily to claim him as hers. After years of my thinking he was a stuck-up, rich guy, he turned out really nice and shy. The more friendly we got, the more Kallie was set on obtaining him and crushing me.

I shook my head. "Wow. That was so blatantly sad."

"You're calling me sad? You should look in a mirror," Kallie replied, her eyes blazing. "I didn't know they let witches and freaks come to school dances. Isn't it against your pagan religion or something?"

This wasn't the first time I got comments about brooms, black cats, or other clichés about witches. With my unusual looks and the odd things that happened around me, weird comments and insults were the norm. "Do you have any idea what you're talking about? Or has your dress squeezed out your last surviving brain cell?"

Kallie stepped closer to me. "Jealous? Don't be mad because your dress looks like a hand-me-down from the Walmart dumpster."

I clenched my teeth. I should not let her get to me.

"Why don't you, plain Jane, and the gay Teletubby over there go home and play on your Ouija board?"

My repressed anger was reaching its crescendo. Tormenting me was one thing, but my friends were off limits. Rage I normally tried to keep on a tight leash started to break free. The darkness living deep inside me and that I kept concealed from the world stirred. Trying to find its way out of a cage, it was like a monster I couldn't control. "Look, I couldn't care less if you like me or not, but don't you dare talk about my friends like that," I threatened.

"Or you'll what? Hit me with your voodoo magic?" There was amusement but also a touch of fear in her smile. She was scared of me—most of the school was.

A wave of uncontrollable emotion gripped me. I heard a cracking from above; a single spark fell from the ceiling. All I could focus on was my deep-seated fury. "Shut-up." My voice broke through my gritted teeth. "You know nothing about me."

"I know you're deluding yourself into thinking people actually like you." Kallie sneered. "And your friends are as weird and insignificant as you are."

8

Blistering anger uncoiled and catapulted from every cell in my body. "Listen, you pathetically-trite anorexic bitch . . ."

The lights above my head started to explode, drowning out the rest of my words. Kallie screamed as sparks and glass rained on us. Students and teachers shielded themselves from the showering debris. Lights flickered on and off, causing a strobe light effect in the gym. Then, everything exploded.

I stared around in shock as crepe paper and cardboard decorations turned to fireballs before disintegrating into ash as they hit the floor. Balloons popped like machine guns. Glass and metal whined and moaned, cracking under the pressure. Chaos took over order and reason. Everyone screamed and ran in every direction. Sounds and movements were so muted to me it felt like there was thick glass between myself and everyone else.

People pushed past, knocking me off balance. The back of my legs hit an overturned chair, and I crashed to the floor, my elbows and back taking the brunt of the fall. Pain zipped up my arms and back. Students kicked and tripped over me as they fled the gym. I curled myself into a protective ball to absorb the trampling herd, and my eyes caught the glitter of reflected light.

The disco ball tore from its tether. Falling, it smashed to the floor with a thunderous roar and shattered into a thousand pieces. Fragments of mirror flew like slivered missiles. A sharp pain flashed across my forehead. Warm blood spilled from the cut and trickled down the side of my face. I covered my head, protecting the rest of my face from the tiny pieces of glass and plastic launching at me from the falling wreckage.

two

Fire engines wailed in the distance. Broken glass and debris dug into my arms and legs as I lay crumpled on the gym floor. Blood dripped from my forehead and arms. I groaned, sat up, and looked around. The gym was empty. Everyone, including the teachers and the chaperones, were gone.

Cringing, I forced myself to stand. I looked around at the remains of the Midnight Masquerade. I probably should have been more upset the dance was ruined. I wasn't. What really bothered me was deep down in my bruised bones I felt what happened was somehow my fault. I didn't know how or why I knew it, but I did. This wasn't the first time something similar had taken place.

I limped slowly toward the gym doors. My body, especially my backside, felt like it had been thrown down a ravine and stomped on. Sore and bleeding, I hobbled outside. Crowds of students huddled in groups as the ambulances and fire trucks screeched to a halt in front of me. I recoiled from the swirling bright red and blue emergency lights.

"Are you all right, miss?" A woman in an EMT uniform moved in front of me. I stared at her. The repetitive flickering of the lights in and out of my vision caused my head to ache more. "Miss, are you okay? Let's get you checked out. Those cuts look deep." She grabbed my arm and steered me toward the back of the ambulance. I needed to find Ryan and Kennedy. I knew they'd be worried, but the blood trickling into my eyes persuaded me to stay where I was.

The EMT was in the middle of cleaning and bandaging me when I heard a deep voice come out of the darkness. I recognized the figure walking toward, me immediately. "Shit," I mumbled. There was nowhere to go.

"Ms. Brycin," Principal Mitchell said as walked to me. "May I speak with you?" It was not a question or an option. I nodded, making the EMT frown as she tried to place the bandage on my forehead. She roughly taped the cut and nodded to show I was clear to go.

I walked wearily to the tall, substantial man whose form seemed to loom above me. "So, Ms. Brycin, can you tell me why the school exploded, and you seem to be right in the middle of it yet again?"

"I-I don't know what you mean, sir."

"Oh, I think you do." He looked at me as if he expected me to produce a bomb out of my pocket, along with my evil plans and a cliché sinister laugh. My stomach dropped. Thinking it about yourself was one thing—to be accused to your face was another. I returned his gaze and tried to hide my unease from draining into my features.

"Do you think I had something to do with this?"

"That's what I'm planning to find out," he replied. "The first several incidents that occurred, I naively chalked up to flukes and coincidences. Those days have long since passed." He glanced behind and motioned someone forward. "Sheriff Weiss would like to question you again, Ms. Brycin."

My insides fell even further. Sheriff Weiss had been called out for every "incident" thus far. He, along with Principal Mitchell, felt I had something to do with the school's electrical explosions, and they were determined to find the proof and lay it at my doorstep. Neither liked me much. The feeling was mutual.

A smug smile grew tight on the sheriff's lips as he stepped forward. He wasn't a big man, but his sharp features, gray hair, and rigid stance made him seem threatening. He had a no-nonsense,

I'd-rather-throw-you-in-jail-and-ask-questions-later philosophy.

"So, Ms. Brycin, what can you tell me about the explosion this time?"

"I don't know if I'd call it an explosion."

"Oh, really? What would you call it, then?"

"An extensive light outage?"

As I predicted, he didn't seem to appreciate my sense of humor, and it only made him angrier. "You think this is funny, Ms. Brycin?"

"No, not at all, sir."

"They will be inspecting the electrical wiring in the building, and if it looks remotely like someone has tampered with it, you are the first person I am coming for. You got that?" His voice was stern and chilly. I nodded quickly in response.

Students huddled around us and appeared to be listening in, their eyes widening as they watched the drama unfold. Embarrassment and anger heated my body. I hadn't gone anywhere near the damned wiring and lighting. I didn't know a thing about them being tampered with, so why was I being treated like a criminal? And, worse, why did I feel like one? I had been living most of my life pretending I was normal, that I wasn't slowly going insane. That veil was getting thin. Maybe I had finally, completely cracked, and one of my other personalities was a high-wire gymnast with a degree in electrical engineering.

"I will be calling your stepfather. I shouldn't have waited this long, but tomorrow Principal Mitchell and I will be meeting with you and your stepfather at the station. I will find the proof this time, Ms. Brycin. You will be caught."

I swallowed nervously. I understood how serious and true he was to his word. He walked away, leaving me standing there surrounded by my gossiping classmates. I needed to get away. I took off in the opposite direction to escape from all the watchful eyes.

Not wanting to be seen, I slipped behind the gym and immersed myself in the dark shadows. I slumped against the brick wall, struggling to keep my legs from giving out. I wanted to go home and crawl under my blankets and feel the security of my room. To know my stepfather, Mark, was there to shelter me. I longed for the days when I was little and Mark would keep me safe from the bad men and monsters. Somehow, I knew these incidents were not something Mark could protect me from.

As if on cue, a dark figure with piercing blue eyes slipped in and out of the shadows. I stiffened; the familiarity of them hit something deep in me. *No, not now!* I squeezed my lids shut. *It's not real. It's not real.* I chanted to myself. *This is really not a good time to be crazy.* I opened my eyes, and my gut twisted. The figure still stood there, its eyes locked onto mine, beckoning me. Then, they faded away.

For years I had been hearing voices and seeing things which shouldn't exist. But they weren't real. They couldn't be. It was only my mind showing me again I was one card short of a full house. I was about to turn and head back when I heard a low laugh bounce off the walls.

"Ember." My name floated off the surfaces around me, and my stomach lurched as I tried to find the source of the whisper.

"Who's there?"

A chuckle swirled about as a blurry figure stepped from the deep shadows. Only his deep blue eyes were clear. He moved slowly toward me, his eyes clinched mine, making my chest tighten.

"Cinaed," he whispered, his voice low and rough. I didn't understand what he said, but strangely there was something familiar about the word and his beautiful voice—like it was from a dream. "At last." He advanced through the darkness reaching my side quickly.

Fear cemented my feet to the ground. Even though he was right in front of me, my eyes couldn't seem to understand or make out his shape. It was like he didn't fully exist. I focused on the only

13

steady part of him—his unreal blue eyes. Without a sound, he moved in closer, his gaze never leaving mine.

"I have been watching you for a long time," he said. "You have grown into a beautiful woman."

"W-Who a-are you-u?"

"The better question to ask yourself is who you are?" A slow smile spread over his lips. "You have to stop closing your mind to me." His breath grazed my neck and caused my body to tingle. "You look so much like your mother."

"H-How do you know my mother?" The question shot out of my mouth before I even realized it. His statement seemed strange as I knew I didn't look anything like my mother. I might have taken after her in personality, but looks-wise I had always assumed I took after my biological father.

My mom was petite, with a tiny, curvy frame, long, thick auburn hair, and sparkling brown eyes with orange flecks. I, on the other hand, was tall, about five feet nine and more athletic than curvy.

The only thing I did have was my mom's thick hair, but mine was jet black and layered past the middle of my back. Ever since I was born, my hair also had dark red streaks running through it. Everyone assumed I put the color there, and I let them believe it. I got tired of explaining it was some strange quirk in my genes.

It was my eyes, though, that drew the most attention—but never the kind I wanted. Not only were they large and prominent, but I was one of those rare people who had two different colored eyes. Mine weren't any ordinary colors either. One was a strange, bright yellow-greenish color which illuminated like a cat's eyes. The other one was pale blue-lavender, outlined with electric dark blue and purple. Both pretty—separately. Together on one face, they caused strange looks and comments.

How I loved the comments. As if I didn't know they were different colors. One of these days, I was going to respond with, "Oh, how embarrassing. Did I leave the house with my eyes not matching again?" With my pale skin, black hair with red streaks, my different-colored eyes, and my tall build, I could never blend in.

"I know many things about you." His hazy frame moved in a little closer. "You are meant to be with me. You cannot fight who you truly are, *mo chuisle mo chroi*." His voice was so beautiful I wanted to close my eyes and float away in it. "You are not like them, Ember. Your mind and heart know it. You simply have to accept it." He studied me for a moment before he continued. "I am risking much by coming to you like this, but I had to see you tonight. You are becoming harder to hide from her. Soon, when you finally come into yourself, I will no longer be able to conceal you. I want you to be prepared."

"Hide me from whom? What are you talking about?"

"Em?" Ryan's voice drifted from around the building. "Are you out here?"

I jerked my head in the direction of his voice. I could see Ryan's face popping past the corner of the gym. When I turned back, I was alone. My eyes frantically searched everywhere around me, wondering why and how the person, or whatever it was, had vanished into thin air. I inhaled deeply as fear and logic made my mind reel with shock. *Where did he go? Who was he? What the hell happened?*

Ryan came toward me. "There you are. Kennedy and I have been looking for you."

Panic overwhelmed me. I drew in tiny gasps of air. I really was going crazy, wasn't I? This hallucination was way beyond having any reasonable explanation. I would be considered certifiable, and this time Mark wouldn't be able to stop it. My pulse hammered, and my body felt like it was on fire. The tingling sensation running over my skin remained, telling me I hadn't dreamed up the strange figure—unless my imagination was that good.

"Hey, are you okay?" Ryan leaned against the wall next to me. His soft brown eyes were full of concern. He had a sweet round face and dimples when he smiled. Ryan was a few pounds over what would be considered stocky. His outfits and dark hair were always styled perfectly. When I met him five years ago, I instantly liked him. His warm, comfortable aura made me want to hug him like a big, sweet teddy bear, but this bear had a sarcastic bite.

"Yeah, I'm fine. I only needed some air."

"You're a bad liar." He nudged my shoulder with his. "I heard the sheriff and the principal cornered you. The whole school is talking about it."

I sighed. "Of course they are."

"Come on, let's go home." Ryan put his arm around me. I nodded and let him steer me toward the parking lot. As Ryan and I walked away, I took one last glance over my shoulder. In the deepest shadows I could see glowing blue eyes staring back at me.

ᴄʜʀᴇᴇ

ೞ

"I'll call you guys tomorrow," I said, jumping out of Ryan's beat-up Nissan as it stopped in my driveway. Throwing a quick, last wave over my shoulder, I raced toward my front door. I unlocked it and stepped into the house. Double locking the door behind me gave me a false sense of safety. No lock or door could keep out the things haunting me, but the sound of the lock clicking still comforted me.

It was too early for Mark to be home from his poker night with the boys, so the house was dark and quiet. There were no streetlights where we lived, and the closest neighbors were over three miles away. We had moved to Olympia, Washington, five years earlier. Both Mark and I had fallen in love with the ranch-style house the moment we saw it as the property edged the Capitol State Park. I loved that trees constantly surrounded me, keeping me calm and at peace. But on this night, the woods felt like it had eyes watching me through a wall of glass separating us.

Going through the house, I turned on every light. Mark would yell at me for wasting energy, and normally I would have felt the same. Right then I didn't care. I wanted to feel comforted and safe, and illuminating every dark corner helped.

Making myself tea, I began to settle down. My bruised, achy bones longed for a warm bath. I headed for the bathroom. Undressed, I stood in front of the mirror, peeling the bandages from my arms. My stomach clenched as I peered at my cuts, or really the lack of them. Dried blood was crusted along my arm, around a healed wound. I grasped my forehead bandage and yanked it, a startled cry escaping my lips. My forehead bore a scab that should have taken days to achieve.

Numbness blanketed my body. I had always healed fast, but this was even faster than normal for me. I let out a crazed laugh. Turning around, I ignored the bathtub and stepped directly into the shower. Once I was in my pajamas and in bed, under the warmth of my comforter, my lids closed, sinking me into sleep.

Fire ripped through them with devastating speed and accuracy. The people fell to their knees with tortured cries, and the flames wrapped around them like snakes. I looked down on them. Children clung to their parents in fear. I felt nothing for them as power filled me while watching them wither in agony. Buildings collapsed behind them as my flames consumed their town. The people were not my target; they were obstacles in my way.

"Ember, stop!" My mom was there in front of me, her face full of anguish and fear. "You don't want to do this. This isn't you."

A slow smile spread across my face. "But it is."

I woke with a start. It was still the middle of the night, and sweat matted my hair to my forehead. The dream evaporated the instant I opened my eyes, but its essence continued to grip my chest, making it hard to breathe. Feeling unsettled, I swung my legs over the side of the bed. I stood and walked to my mirror, my glowing eyes reflected back at me. I turned around, pulling my sweatshirt up. My fingers begin to trace the markings. Celtic knots and symbols twisted and merged in thin, loopy, black lines down my back. Seeing them made me feel calmer, as if it was an anchor to my mom.

My tattoo wasn't a delicate, little butterfly or some tiny, sweet flower. No, my tattoo reached from my neck to the lower part of my back, curling around my side. After I lost my mother, I had an intense dream. When I woke up, I had sketched the symbols from my dream and ended up designing the tattoo which was now part of me. It gave me strength, which I needed after losing her. Mark hadn't been terribly pleased about me getting it, but he accepted it as something I had to do. He understood it made me feel she was always with me.

As I looked at the beautiful, haunting design, something nagged at me from the bottom of my soul, trying to tell me something. Whatever it was, it was just out of my reach.

FOUR

The next day went from bad to worse. Between the incident at the school being in the local paper and the gossip mill running overtime, Mark was enlightened about every little detail, true or not, before he returned home from his ritual Sunday morning run and coffee shop stop.

"Ember?" His voice reverberated throughout the house.

Uh-oh . . . I know that tone. Think he might have found out about last night?

"Ember Aisling Devlin Brycin! Get your butt up now!"

Yep.

I sighed and rolled out of bed. My head and my body still ached but not from the non-existent wounds. My discomfort was more like I had worked out really hard the day before. I felt exhausted as I shuffled into the kitchen.

"So when were you going to tell me about this?" Mark threw the newspaper he was holding onto the counter with the headline facing me: "Mysterious Explosion Lights School Masquerade Ball."

"Seriously?" I rolled my eyes. "It wasn't even an explosion."

Mark looked levelly at me. His look told me I was walking a very thin line.

"What?" I sighed and then shut up. I knew better than to push him further. Mark Hill was the only family I had left. Even if technically he wasn't blood, he was the only father I had ever known. He was a slim, tall, good-looking man who still received plenty of attention from women, especially because of his kind, blue eyes, warm smile, and slightly silvering blond hair. He kept in shape and enjoyed running marathons, which I considered the act of a truly demented person. But he seemed to really enjoy them.

"When were you going to tell me about this non-explosion, then?" he asked.

"When I woke up."

Again, he looked less than amused. "So instead, I get to hear it from every gossiping biddy in the coffee shop, saying not only was there some blast at the dance last night, but my daughter was the only one questioned by the police."

"It's not like I was trying to keep it from you. When I got home, you weren't here, so I went to bed. Then, I wake up to you yelling at me!"

"I'm sorry, Em." He looked down at the paper again. "But to hear this news involving you from a bunch of prattling, old ladies first was extremely upsetting. You are my daughter. I want to protect you no matter what. I didn't have a clue what they were talking about."

I was in the middle of explaining what had happened the previous night when the phone rang. Mark grabbed the receiver. "Hello?" There was a pause, and his lips twisted into a frown, making my pulse quicken.

Oh, shit.

"Good morning, Sheriff. How may I help you?"

Shitshitshit!

I tried to swallow the lump growing in my throat as Mark's face became grimmer. I had "temporarily" forgotten the sheriff wanted Mark and me to go to the station later in the afternoon to meet with him and Principal Mitchell. This was the kind of morning where I wished I hadn't bothered to get up.

Mark got off the phone, and I anxiously waited for his words.

"Sheriff Weiss wants to meet with us at four-thirty today," he said. It was hard to decipher his mood when he spoke in this tone. He turned and looked out the window. The silence in the room grew to an ear-piercing level.

"Mark?" My voice was soft. I didn't know if he'd heard me, so I repeated his name. Finally, he broke out of the trance captivating his thoughts.

"Be ready to go by four." He rubbed his forehead. "I need to go for another run. I'll be back soon." He pivoted and was out of the house before I could even respond.

For the rest of the day, I felt like I was awaiting sentence. In a way, I guess I was. Mark's usual laid-back attitude was anything but, and it got even worse when we walked into the police station.

Humor was my default, especially in stressful situations. Trying to lighten his blackening mood, I asked Mark if he had handcuffs, so he could walk me in like the criminal I was. He smiled at my joke, but not like he normally would. The summons was upsetting him more than he let on. His body was defensive and stiff. Mark was angry with the police and the principal for accusing me of such a ridiculous thing, but I felt his anger was an act of denial that his daughter could really be the problem.

"Do they have any proof?" he yelled out to no one in particular on the ride downtown. "How in the hell can they blame you for faulty wiring? Shouldn't they be questioning the electrician?"

We were shown into Sheriff Weiss' office. It held all the basics: an old desk piled with manila files, an 'eighties-style, black phone blinking continuously, a desk lamp, several chairs, and a banged up file cabinet in the corner.

Sheriff Weiss sat behind his desk and Principal Mitchell already occupied one of the chairs opposite the sheriff. Being under the florescent lights of the police station made the reality of what was happening fill me with dread.

"Mr. Hill, Ember, thank you for coming in," Sheriff Weiss said. Both he and Principal Mitchell stood and reached out to shake Mark's hand. They each gave me a short, curt nod.

Sheriff Weiss motioned for Mark to sit in the only available chair. Guess I was standing. This meeting seemed to have little to do with my input anyway; they had already made up their minds about me. I wanted to be invisible, so I pushed myself against the wall, hoping I'd blend in with its chipped, off-white texture.

"I really don't understand why you called us here. I can't fathom how you've come to the conclusion my daughter had anything to do with last night," Mark declared.

"I'm not saying she did. I have a few questions." The sheriff's patronizing tone wasn't lost on Mark.

Mark's demeanor hardened. "Let's cut the crap, Sheriff." He leaned forward. "We all know you didn't call us here because you think she's innocent."

Weiss pressed his lips together and sat back in his chair. "You're right, Mr. Hill, I do think she knows more than she's letting on, and I do believe she's somehow involved." He shot me an accusatory glance. "Do I think she was alone in this? No, it's far too complicated and complex for a girl her age to pull off by herself."

"Excuse me? A girl my age? You think it's too 'complex' for me? Are you serious?" I shot off before I could stop myself. Mark gave me a look which made my mouth shut with an audible click. It often got me in trouble. My brain and my mouth didn't always communicate when my buttons were pushed. I definitely got this from my mom. She could be a hothead, reacting first, thinking

23

later. Mark loved and hated that about her. He loved her passion, but sometimes it would come out at inopportune times—kind of like this one.

A slight smile formed on Weiss' mouth, like I had proven his theory and he had baited me into a confession. He didn't understand I couldn't admit to anything even if I wanted to. There was nothing to confess except a guilty feeling.

"What proof do you have?" Mark asked. "I'm furious about how this whole thing has been handled. You are treating my daughter like a criminal. Do you have *any* proof besides your insane theories about how she climbed into the rafters and messed with the lighting?"

"Mr. Hill, what the fire investigation team came up with was inconclusive, but they haven't ruled out foul play yet," Principal Mitchell stated.

"So what you're saying is you have no proof?"

"Proof or not, these explosions aren't a new occurrence. They mysteriously began around the time your daughter starting attending my school. And she has been at the center of every single episode." Principal Mitchell leaned forward in his chair, tapping his fingers on the desk for emphasis. "I will not put the other students, most of whom I've known their whole lives, in harm's way simply because you think your child is innocent!"

The tension was becoming unbearable. Sheriff Weiss held up his hand to calm the principal. "Mr. Hill, how many of these 'electrical incidents' has Ember told you about?"

Mark looked surprised. "Well, there was a small one a couple years back, and one at the beginning of the school year, I think, and then the one last night." Doubt crossed Mark's face. "Why?"

My innards twisted. I knew exactly where Weiss was going with this.

"Three, huh?" A condescending smile twitched on Weiss' lips. "Mr. Hill, what if I told you since the day your daughter started in the school system five years ago, we have been called out there six times? Six times, Mr. Hill, and that is not counting the metal shop incident. For the record, the school never had anything similar incidents before she started. Circumstances and common sense makes this event pretty cut and dried to me."

Mark looked at me, dumbfounded. "What are you talking about? What metal shop episode?"

I had hoped he would never learn about what happened there. It was something I tried to block from my mind. On that day, we had been sculpting with iron. I should have tried to get out of the project. Ignoring my intuition, I continued. I knew better, but I hadn't wanted to explain why I couldn't touch the metal.

Ever since I was very young, I had this strange allergy to certain forms of iron. My skin would itch and buzz, and I would feel really sick. The purer the iron, the more tired and worse I felt. Thankfully, most things nowadays weren't made with pure iron. I guess I had hoped in metal shop it would be different, or I could ignore the symptoms.

The moment the blowtorch got close to the metal, I knew I made a huge mistake. The odd feeling arose in me, and my organs felt like they were vibrating and tearing apart. The torch exploded in my hand, burning a hole in the ceiling. The chunk of iron flew across the room and hit a kid in the head, knocking him out. It was declared an accident, but I could see the speculation and doubt in every face afterward. I never had a partner in shop class again.

"What's he talking about, Em?"

I avoided Mark's gaze, ashamed of the embarrassment and pain I was causing him. It didn't change the fact I couldn't tell him anything. The only things I could say to him would send me straight to the funny farm.

"So there were other times you didn't tell me about." All I could do was nod. "I see," he said.

He didn't see. He didn't know how far things had progressed and how real my hallucinations had become.

I limited how much I told Mark about my crazy experiences, and now it was coming back to bite me in the ass. I watched his face as his emotions went from anger toward Weiss and Mitchell, to disbelief, back to anger, and then to disappointment in me. Seeing uncertainty in his eyes tore me apart. Because I hadn't told him the truth before, he doubted me now.

The sheriff leaned back in his chair, pulling a file toward him. "Also, the incident yesterday isn't the first time something like it has happened at a school your daughter attended, right, Mr. Hill?" There was a smug glint in his eyes. "I see two similar incidents happened at a school she attended in California. She was asked to leave after half of the building burned down. It was even recommended she be placed in a psychiatric hospital. Now, tell me, Mr. Hill, can you really not see the connection between your daughter and these occurrences?"

An icy sensation trickled down my spine. The truth was right in front of his eyes. Mark could no longer deny I was crazy.

"So what is your plan for me, then?" I whispered.

"Well, Ember, the sheriff and I have been talking, and we both agree it would be best if you're in a different environment for a while," Principal Mitchell replied.

"You're kicking me out of school?"

Principal Mitchell pulled some pamphlets from the leather briefcase sitting at his feet. "This is what I'm talking about." He handed the material to Mark.

"You want my daughter to go to juvie?"

"That's not exactly what Silverwood is, Mr. Hill. It is a facility for troubled teens, those in trouble emotionally or with the law."

"We think such a move is in her best interest and for the other students who go to Olympia High," Weiss stated firmly.

My mouth went dry. I was paralyzed and speechless. Observing all of the conversation, I was powerless to do anything about what was unfolding.

"You can't do this! You have no proof she did anything. You conclusion is wrong!" Mark threw the documents down onto the desk.

"I was trying to be considerate of Ember, Mr. Hill. I could expel her from my school. I have that right. We have statements from several students, parents, and even a teacher, who all feel their safety is threatened if she continues at Olympia High."

"What?" I spat. My outburst was ignored.

"I am providing a compromise. If she attends Silverwood, temporarily, and her marks remain satisfactory, she will graduate in June like planned. On the other hand, you could take her out of school completely. The online GED will take six months. Most colleges won't bother with her application, if she is planning on going to college, that is. It is really up to you." He thought for a second and then added, "It's only for a few weeks, Mr. Hill, and then we will reevaluate Ember's progress. If everything's good, she can come back and resume her classes." Principal Mitchell sat back in his chair, looking like he should get a gold star for being such an agreeable guy. I still wanted to deck him.

"This is bullshit, and you know it. Ember is not a threat to anyone." Mark looked like he wanted to punch Principal Mitchell, as well.

"Think what you like, but I have to consider everyone at the school, not only Ember," Mitchell shot back. "I'm sorry, but Ember is no longer welcome at my school, at least for the time being."

No one breathed; the air was ripped from the room, holding the room in tense silence.

"Ember, why don't you go get some coffee," Mark's taut voice shattered the silence.

"What? No . . . not if this has to do with me."

"Ember," his voice warned. "Let me talk to the sheriff and Mr. Mitchell alone for a moment, okay?"

I bit my lip to keep me from vocalizing any more protests and nodded. I pulled myself off the wall and headed out of the room, not caring if the door shut harder than it should have.

ꝑіⱱε

The waiting room held a generic coffee vending machine. I absently plopped quarters into the slot, my mind reeling with what had just happened. A few people mingled or sat around the room, but my attention immediately fell on a guy sitting in the corner. A hoodie covered his head, and a beat-up paperback book in his hand blocked his face from view.

My skin tingled, and the hair on my arms stood on end. My body went on high alert as if to warn me of danger. I watched him out of the corner of my eye as I got my coffee from the machine. He continued to read his book, seemingly oblivious to me. But for some reason, I felt he was aware of every inch of space around him. This strangely intrigued me, but of course, it had been well proven I wasn't right in the head.

I sat on a chair near him and picked up a magazine. I tried to focus on the scalding, cheap coffee in my hand and the gossip magazine in my lap, but my attention and my eyes wandered back to him. Not seeing anything but his fingers, which were curled around the well-worn book, I couldn't tell how old he was. From his body language and his form, I guessed he was in his early twenties.

There was something familiar about him, which was odd. I was pretty certain our paths had never crossed. I would remember meeting him; his presence was not something I'd forget. He didn't seem to fit in the room. Even though he had to be well over six feet tall, he seemed to take up even more space than his physical form.

He shifted in his seat, making some instinct in me kick in. I jumped up defensively, spilling half my coffee. Every head turned my way—every head except his. He didn't even flinch. The entire room watched me with curiosity and apprehension while his attention stayed locked on his book. My face flamed as I realized he had only shifted and was not springing to attack me.

Babbling out a lame excuse, I wiped up the coffee I'd spilled. Eventually, people went back to their own businesses. I sat again, watching him cautiously through my lashes. It felt similar to being in a cage with a wild animal, which tested its limits before it would bite me. It was normal to react during sudden movements or a commotion, but he didn't. He seemed to be making a point of not looking at me, and it aggravated me more than it should have.

Returning my focus onto my reading material, I couldn't stop my eyes from continuously slipping over the top of the magazine. My relentless desire to see his face sent my eyes slinking back to him over and over again. The more I watched him, the more he seemed to stir in his seat. He knew he was being watched, and part of me wanted him to look up and catch me, so I could see his face.

"Look up," I mumbled.

His head shook slightly underneath his hood as if he said, "Not a chance, girlie."

Chagrin flushed into my cheeks. *There was no way he could have heard me. No one could have. I was being silly.* Shaking his head had nothing to do with me. It was probably something he was responding to in his book. I still felt flustered, unnerved, and oddly hurt.

A police officer entered the room and approached the hooded mystery guy. "Okay, you're free to go, Mr. Dragen. You know the drill. Sign the forms, and you can leave."

The officer's familiarity with the guy should have been a red flag. It was clear he had been here before, probably more than once. But if this didn't send a warning, the clank of metal on metal as the officer leaned down and unlatched the guy's wrist cuffed to the chair certainly did. *Why was he manacled in a public area of the jail? What did he do?* This is what they called public safety?

I noticed several things when he got up: his movements were so smooth and quick I almost didn't see the transition. Also, I had been wrong about his height. He had to be at least six-four, if not taller. The extraordinary strength and confidence exuding from him eclipsed everything else in the room.

He shifted his head back into his hood, making it impossible to see his face clearly. That, of course, made me want to see him even more. My hands balled into fists; the desire to reach under his hood and lift up his face overwhelmed me.

As he passed, he cocked his head enough so I could see a hint of his chin and mouth. His lips twisted, curving into a terrifying, malicious smile I somehow knew was meant for me. A chill crept over me, and I didn't move until he and the officer disappeared from the room. When he was gone, I sighed and dropped my face into my hands.

"Ember?" Mark's voice made my heart leap into my throat. The last few days had left me even more jumpy than normal. From the stony look on his face, I knew this day would not be improving. "Let's go home," he said and started walking before I even got up from the chair.

It was dark by the time I stepped out to the parking lot, and only a few dimly-lit streetlamps guided me to the truck. Mark was already behind the wheel with the engine on, waiting for me. I picked up my pace, knowing the trouble that lay ahead of me.

Halfway across the lot, my skin prickled again, and an eerie feeling of being watched whispered at the back of my neck. I scanned the parking area and stopped dead in my tracks. A gasp caught in my throat.

Across the poorly lit lot, leaning against a motorcycle, a pair of electric-green eyes looked back into mine. Even though he was hidden by the shadows, I knew it was the guy from the waiting room. The way his eyes glowed reminded me of my own. I had never seen anyone else's like mine who wasn't somebody I had dreamed up or hallucinated. To see another breathing person whose eyes illuminated was a bit startling.

I quickly turned away, running for the truck, feeling his gaze burn into me. Shivers ran through my body. I didn't know why he was in the police station cuffed to a chair. It could've been for something minor, but for some reason, fear filled me knowing he knew my face.

SIX

Mark and I were silent on the way home. I sat back, letting some of the tension in my shoulders leave, glad to be out of there. The night was exceptionally dark. Only a sliver of light from the waning crescent moon broke the blackness along Delphi Road. The country road didn't have streetlamps, and the truck's headlights did little to keep the shadows at bay. Mark slowed at the approaching stop sign. A strange feeling came over me. The hair on my arms stood on end. Chills skirted down the back of my neck as I checked out the dark, murky forest around the truck.

Loud, piercing roars came from behind us. About half a dozen motorcycles surrounded the truck. The unlit street kept me from seeing the detail of the bikes or the riders, but I knew from the deep rumble of the engines vibrating around the truck they were classic Harleys. The road was long and dark. It would be difficult for a group of motorcyclists to be behind us without us seeing their headlights or hearing them before they were on us. So why hadn't we seen or heard them approach? The question was forgotten as one of the riders pulled up on the passenger's side and turned his head to me. I sucked in a gulp of air. Electric green eyes locked onto mine.

Something deep in my gut stirred as we held each other's gaze. Finally, he turned away. The black, gleaming motorcycles shot off, leaving me with cold chills blanketing my flesh. I couldn't explain what I felt, but fear didn't seem to cover it.

"That startled me. They came out of nowhere," Mark mumbled. All I could do was nod.

Ten minutes later, Mark pulled the truck into the driveway, turning off the ignition. He sighed heavily and sat back.

Uh-oh . . . here it comes.

"Sheriff Weiss is convinced you had something to do with the electrical explosion."

"I kind of got that." I looked down, playing with the zipper on my coat. "What do you believe?"

He sighed again and rubbed his face. "I want to trust you, Em, but I'd have to be blind and a fool to continue to ignore what is going on." He sat quietly for a moment before he spoke again, his voice softer. "I'm really trying here. I really am. I don't know what to do anymore. I wish your mother were here. Then again if she were, I don't think we'd be in this situation." His voice broke, but he quickly cleared his throat, covering the escaped emotion. "I can't imagine you having anything to do with something like they say, but we *have* been here before."

I saw the blocks begin to stack against me. The first time your daughter is accused of trying to burn a school down may be easier to ignore. A second time . . . not so much. I bit my lip and looked out the window into the dark forest next to the house. He was right. We had been here before.

I was asked to leave school after a part of my junior high in Monterey burned down. They had accused me of having something to do with its demise. Between the fire and my mom, Mark felt it was time to leave. He had wanted to get back into field research for the forestry service for a long time. Mark had gotten a job in Olympia right after I had been kicked out of the school in Monterey. It was a great opportunity for him and an even better reason to depart. Moving here gave us a fresh start, leaving the rumors, gossip, and bad memories behind.

"I thought moving away would help. I thought things were better here, but they aren't, are they? You've been lying to me this whole time." Mark stared out the windshield. "With what happened to your mother . . . we stopped your medication and therapy too soon."

Therapist, shrink, counselor, whatever you wanted to call them, I had seen them all. Teachers, doctors, and family friends thought I might have some psychological problems after finding my mother's dead body. She had died a little over five years ago.

Died . . .

That word always made it sound as if she had simply passed away. The word *murdered* got trapped in my throat, making me want to throw up. To think of my mom being killed was too much, and the visual of her shredded beyond recognition still haunted me. I woke up screaming from night terrors on a regular basis. Her killers still hadn't been caught.

Since that day, I wanted to curl up in a ball and cry until I no longer felt the emptiness inside, letting my attachment to reality disappear altogether. However, those options were simply an express ride to *another* therapist, *another* diagnosis, and *more* medication . . . and me being institutionalized. The last was something I was trying to avoid at all costs. Mark sent me to a dozen therapists and counseling groups after my mom's death. None of it helped. I still heard voices and still saw things which weren't there. *Schizophrenic* was one term many doctors used. I became really good at hiding the truth and making a show of taking my meds, before secretly flushing them down the toilet. They all patted themselves on their backs at my miraculous recovery. As good as I got at covering the truth, in reality I was only getting worse.

"What?" I looked at Mark. He pressed his lips together. A muscle in his jaw twitched. "Seriously? Is that what you think?" My voice raised an octave. "I blew up my school because I missed a therapy session? You really believe I did these things? I hate school, but I didn't blow it up!"

"Ember . . ."

"No!" My face heated with anger. "I can't believe you're using

Mom's murder and my therapy against me," I burst out. "There was a time when you were on my side and believed me. I guess I can no longer count on you, either." I threw open the truck door and slammed it behind me. I stomped up the porch and into the house, thankful I had my keys in my pocket. Nothing ruins a good exit more than when it's locked.

As I slammed the front door, I saw Mark still in the truck with his head on the steering wheel. Guilt and remorse tugged at my gut, but my pride made me continue to the safety of my bedroom. I slammed that door, too. Even if he didn't hear it, it made me feel better.

Mark entered the house as I changed into my sweats and quickly turned off my lights, hoping he'd think I went to bed, even if it was only six in the evening. I didn't want to deal with him right now. I didn't want to be with anyone right now, including myself, though I couldn't seem to get away from me so easily.

Sleep seemed highly unlikely. What sounded good was a kickboxing class. This not being possible, I grabbed my iPod, shoved the ear buds in, and turned it on full blast. I walked to my desk, turning on the small lamp. Messy piles of half-finished sketches covered the top. Drawing, painting, sculpting, and writing poetry always helped release any pent-up emotions. Something I needed right then. Grabbing my sketchpad, I sat drew, the pencil moving swiftly across the paper.

About an hour later, I heard a knock on the door. I plucked one earpiece free.

"Em, I made soup and sandwiches, if you want some."

I hesitated, my heart softening, but my pride and stubbornness overshadowed everything.

"I'm not hungry."

I felt he wanted to say more, but he didn't. After a moment, he walked away.

The happenings of the day continued to roll around in my head as my hand absently moved across the page. The TV blared from the other room. Mark was watching the sports channel, but I wondered how much he was paying attention. I was sure he was going over every word Weiss and Mitchell had said. I bit my lip stopping the tears wanting to come.

I looked down at my sketchpad. My mind had been on other things as I drew, so I really didn't think I was drawing anything particular. Through the abstract lines, a pair of eyes stared back at me. I immediately recognized them. Even without the piercing green color, there was no doubt whose eyes I had sketched. *Why in the hell did I draw his?* I put my head in my hands. I couldn't handle analyzing one more thing right now. I was so tired of being scared and feeling lost and alone. I leaped up, switched off my lamp, and crawled into bed, feeling drained and exhausted.

I stood in a shadowy forest of oak and ash. Wind ruffled through the dense trees, making them creak and moan. A gust rippled over my skin, and I drew up my hood and pulled my dark cloak closer to my body. Flames danced rhythmically in front of me. I huddled closer to the fire, feeling its warmth and strength, as it rose higher. The sun met the horizon, and darkness slithered in around me.

Anxiety tapped nervously on my neck. Something out there was coming for me, and it was getting nearer.

A warning crept into my body, and I felt eyes on me from all around, as if the trees themselves were staring at me. The branches swayed, creating bended, gnarled skeleton shadows. An unnerving guttural growl echoed over the wind. Fear slithered down my spine. I spun around, searching frantically for the threat.

They were coming for me. I had to run.

A deep, menacing laugh ricocheted off the rock walls beyond the trees. I whipped around again, a scream catching in my throat. Electric green eyes were only inches from my face and looked directly into mine, dancing with menacing glee.

"Time to join your mother."

I gasped as I woke, my legs and arms thrashing. Sweat soaked my tank top, making it cling to my chest. Chills clutched my spine, as I got my bearings and tried to calm myself. Leaning over, I turned on my nightstand light. The darkness created too many gloomy corners and shadowy figures, which my imagination wanted to make into monsters. I rested my head against my headboard.

Why were the eyes in my dream the same color as the guy's from the police station? He had unnerved me, and the fact he had been out on Delphi Road only made me more uneasy. Had he followed me? Did he know where I lived, or did he happen to live out here, as well? He wasn't merely passing through town—he was too familiar with the police officer. They let him go, so he couldn't be too dangerous to society, right? Maybe he forgot to pay a parking ticket, and I was making way too much of this. But then, why couldn't I get rid of a nagging fear in my gut?

Jumping at every creak the house made, I threw off the covers and grabbed my iPod from my desk. Playing music would help break the silence and relax me. I perched myself on top of my desk and pried the window blinds apart to look out into the night. The moon broke through the clouds as the fog slid through the trees. I was trying to relax and get in rhythm with the soothing music, but chills continued to prickle my skin. The feeling of being watched crept over me again.

I was about to snap my blinds together and go back to bed when something moved in my peripheral. A pair of green, cat-like eyes stared right back into mine from the forest. I jerked. Fear clamped down and strangled the scream wanting to bubble out. I blinked and the eyes were gone.

I only imagined it. I repeated in my head as the therapists had conditioned me to do when an "episode" happened. I did a running jump to my bed so nothing underneath could reach out and grab my ankles. I wrapped myself tightly in my duvet and kept the lights on, drifting in and out of sleep for the rest of the night.

SEVEN

On Monday, I took advantage of not having to go to school and spent most of the morning catching up on the sleep I hadn't gotten the night before. By noon, I finally dragged myself out of bed, mostly because my stomach was growling so loud it sounded like bears were waking up from hibernation in my gut. It was threatening to start gnawing on itself, so I finally gave in.

It was strange not to be at school. I could picture Kennedy and Ryan sitting at our normal table at lunch, one person short of our three-pack. My heart twisted at the thought. Unless Principal Mitchell had a change of mind, I would not be eating lunch with my friends in the foreseeable future.

I sighed and lugged my body down the hallway toward the kitchen. Mark sat at the breakfast bar, working on his laptop as I lumbered into the room. He was obviously doing a "work at home" day. At least we didn't have to go out in the torrential rain assaulting the windows.

"Morning . . . or afternoon, I guess," I mumbled, feeling awful about our conversation the night before. I had many sleepless hours to go over the situation and see what a brat I had been. Although I was still upset, I hated hurting Mark. I knew he was trying his best. He didn't ask to be a single parent of an orphaned girl. But he had me, for better or worse.

40

It made me miss my mom so much my heart ached. I longed for her laugh, her smile, the way she made everything better. We had been really close. For so long, it had only been the two of us. I longed for our talks, especially since talking about boys or girl stuff with Mark was not particularly comfortable for either one of us.

"I was wondering when you'd get up," Mark said breaking into my thoughts.

I poured some coffee, thankful he had kept a pot going for me. "Yeah, I didn't sleep well last night."

Mark pinched his lips together. He looked like he wanted to say something. An awkward silence filled the room when he said nothing. Glancing around, I noticed some eggs left on the stove for me. My throat tightened. I grabbed a plate from the cupboard. He pointed to the microwave. "There's some turkey bacon in there."

"Thanks," I replied, but I knew he didn't hear me. My voice couldn't get above a whisper without it cracking with emotion.

Quiet hung in the air before Mark started again. "I set up a meeting later this afternoon with Mrs. Sanchez, who runs the facility at Silverwood."

I kept my back to him and only nodded. More silence. Eventually Mark got up with a heavy sigh. He moved into the living room and tuned into the sports channel. I turned back to my plate of bacon and toast. As hungry as I was, my stomach was contorted with sadness and guilt. I forced the food down.

After I finished, I controlled the impulse to retreat to the safety of my bedroom and went in with Mark. We sat in awkward muteness, staring at the television. When the program went to a commercial break, Mark turned off the TV.

Oh boy . . .

"Em, I'm sorry for what I said last night. It was wrong, and I didn't mean to insinuate you had anything to do with the incidents." He hesitated. "You and I have always been able to talk, but I have to say it's harder now. It was much easier when you

41

were a little girl, but you're technically an adult. I've known for the last couple years we were heading into areas that weren't going to be comfortable for either of us. But yesterday was different . . . I wasn't ready for it. I don't know what to do here, kiddo. The sheriff is committed to finding and punishing who caused the explosion, and you seem to be the scapegoat."

"I'll put on a bell and start chewing on some paper."

"I do believe you, you know? I don't think you are a part of what happened."

"Thank you."

"But . . ."

Why was there always a "but"?

"But . . . there is something going on with you. I'm really worried. I know how hard it's been for you, losing your mother in such a way. I can't imagine how tough it was going through what you did."

I looked down. "I know nothing has been easy for you either."

He didn't say anything for a while. I thought I'd said the wrong thing, but when I lifted my gaze, tears glistened in his eyes.

"Some days I feel like I'll be all right, and other days it hurts so much I can't even breathe. I miss her beyond words, but it's nothing compared to you. You've lost your mother, who was also your best friend . . ."

"You did, too."

"I know, but losing a mother is a different kind of loss, especially your mother," he said, his eyes still glistening. In that moment, I saw how lonely he was. He thought "until death do us part" meant when they were old and gray, and he would go first. "I worry about you, Sunny D."

I smiled. He hadn't called me that in a while. Devlin was one of my middle names. Mom told me it was from my biological father's family. I had never been an overly cheerful little girl, always choosing sarcasm and biting wit, even at six years old. So Mark found it amusing calling me *Sunny D.*

"I'm fine, Mark," I lied. "I'm dealing with a lot lately."

He studied me. "Okay." His expression made it clear the topic was not going to be dropped, only suspended for now.

Mark decided to go for a run to clear his head. I knew how he felt. The forest behind our house called to me. So while he went running, I left to clear mine under the canopy of the trees, which protected me a bit from the relentless rain. I loved it out here. There was something about nature which instantly calmed me and made me feel complete. I sat on a rock and ignored the wetness soaking through my jeans. I picked up a leaf, tracing its veins.

A whisper floated with the wind.

"Ember . . ."

My head snapped up at the sound of a voice.

"Ember."

A crawling sensation crept down my spine when I realized I heard the voice in my mind, instead of out loud.

My eyes darted around the forest and the canopy. The air shimmering between a break in the trees grabbed my attention. Like ocean waves, the air danced and bobbed between the trees with increasing urgency. It twisted and rolled until a tall, broad, gorgeous man with piercing blue eyes stood there. A high pitch noise escaped me as I stared at him in fear. He was dressed in black leather pants and a black fitted shirt, which hugged every muscle to perfection. He was the vision from the dance, but this time I could see all of him clearly. And, wow, even though I was scared to death, I could appreciate the man's breathtaking looks and toned physique.

He appeared to be in his mid-to-late twenties, although there was something ageless and ancient about him at the same time. If his black hair and alluring smile didn't bring me to my knees, the magnetic energy resonating off him did. It seized me and turned my senses into an overcharged battlefield. I was mesmerized, terrified, and aroused by him all at the same time. As he stepped closer, I jerked back. I stumbled over a rock and fell to the ground, scrapping my arm. I tried to choke out a cry.

His voice fluttered through my mind again. *"I'm not trying to scare you, Ember. I came here for you."*

I scrambled to my feet. "How do you know my name?" I hadn't thought about how he knew it until now. "Who are you?"

"You've been familiar to me since your birth," his voice slid into my mind. *"As for who I am, I am someone who's been waiting for you for a long time."*

"H-How are you doing that?" My voice was barely a whisper.

"How am I doing what?" His words entered my head. From the smile, he knew exactly what I was talking about. Not that I noticed his deliciously beautiful lips.

I kept my voice level and low. "Speaking in my head."

"That's not important. What's essential right now is you." He spoke out loud now, his voice captivating.

"Me?" I asked. "Why me? What do you want? Who *are* you?"

Without even seeing him move, he was now only inches from me. "I am Torin." He said his name with honor and pride. Taking my hand, his lips brushed against my knuckles, sending butterflies to duke it out in my stomach. *Okay, Em, now you are letting your hallucinations name themselves and touch you.* At eighteen, I still had imaginary friends. Hot ones, granted, but still . . .

His hand came up and gently cupped my cheek. I felt protected and oddly safe. "This may be the last time I can appear to you in person. I must keep you safe for as long as possible."

"What? You're not coming back?" Panic pitched my voice higher. Why did I care? He was simply a figment of my imagination. But he felt so much more than that. He felt so comfortable, so familiar.

"*No mo chuisle*, not like this. It is too dangerous. But keep your mind open for me." He leaned down, kissing my hand again. "Sweet dreams, Ember."

With a parting kiss, he stepped back and disappeared into the forest.

I stood there blinking. Then, like someone had flipped a switch, reality flooded back. Fear, confusion, and a sensation like withdrawal rose and plummeted, colliding with everything inside me. My body shook. I felt emotional and raw.

I walked back to the house in a daze. As real as it felt, I knew my brain was inventing Torin. I had stayed at a mental hospital for several weeks after my mother had been murdered. The doctors there said minds are capable of unbelievable things. People who suffered through tragedy and wanted to escape from the harshness of reality would create entire worlds more actual to them than the real one. The doctors told me I was probably creating these people and creatures to hide from the loss I felt from her death. That had to be what was happening. Torin could not be real. He couldn't . . .

EIGHT

Kennedy and Ryan had called me a dozen times since the previous day. As much as I loved them, I didn't feel like talking to anyone. I should have known they would not put up with my silence for long. They came over after school, before Mark and I left for our appointment at Silverwood.

They hugged me and made me feel better, as they went through all the emotions I had gone through—shock, anger, and even a little grief. They couldn't believe what had happened and how I was being treated.

"This is so not fair. You didn't do anything. They don't even have any proof. This can't be legal," Kennedy exclaimed. "We should fight them. My mom could help."

Kennedy's mom had been a lawyer before she put her career on hold after Kennedy was adopted. Two years after, Mrs. Johnson got pregnant with Halley. There was no doubt they loved Kennedy, but I could tell she felt the difference between her and her sister. Deep down, she felt she didn't belong to them, not really. Something I understood.

I shook my head. "No."

"No?" Kennedy crossed her arms, looking confused.

"No," Ryan piped up. "She's right. I know what it feels like to be an outsider in this town, even though I was born and raised here." Sadness crept over Ryan's features. Because Ryan had come out in high school, dealing with all the discrimination and nasty comments on a daily basis, made me adore him more. At least his mom was supportive; his dad was still hoping Ryan was going through a phase. "Fighting them will only make it worse. You can't win against these people, especially against someone like Kallie Parson. I know."

I couldn't blame my circumstances on Kallie, but I had no doubt she was one of the people who made a statement against me and even less doubt she had her minions do the same.

I was used to girls like her. Growing up, I never had a lot of friends, and after my mother's death, I had even fewer. People tended to keep their distance, like they sensed something wasn't right with me. I also had an undeniable instinct to keep people at arm's length. Kennedy and Ryan were the first ones to really break through my walls. Even though there was still a lot I kept from them, they knew more about me than anyone.

When I first moved here, they had immediately taken me in, acting like we had been friends all our lives. It was something I never experienced before. We were kindred spirits in a way. The fact none of us felt like we really belonged drew us together.

Before they left, they promised they'd call or text me every day, and we'd spend the weekends together. I used to be fine on my own, but now I felt sick at the thought of losing them. They were my family. They were where I belonged.

When Mark and I drove to the facility, I was surprised how modern it was, with its wall of windows and solar panels on the roof. It looked nothing like the jail I thought it would.

We parked the car and headed through the large glass doors of the main building. Mrs. Sanchez greeted and showed us to her office. She was a little thing, about five-foot-two, but from the stern expression on her face, she was definitely feisty and not someone to screw with. She had short golden blonde hair cropped close to her head. It fit perfectly with her pantsuit, glasses, and strong, no-nonsense attitude.

"Welcome, Mr. Hill, Ember. Please have a seat." She motioned toward the chairs. I almost laughed at how quickly Mark did as he was told. She had the kind of authority adults, kids, and probably animals, obeyed. I liked her right away. I didn't get the vibe she was a bitch; she merely didn't put up with any crap. Tough but fair.

"Thank you for staying late and seeing us on such short notice," Mark said.

"No problem. I practically live here, and I know you must feel anxious and have a lot of questions before tomorrow." She settled into a chair behind her desk. "So Principal Mitchell has basically given me the rundown. In my honest opinion, I think it is a bunch of bull-honky; but he is settled on it, so there you go."

Except for my friends making me laugh earlier, she put the first genuine smile on my lips since this whole debacle began. Thank goodness someone else could see through the bullshit.

Mark seemed relieved as well. "Nice way of putting it. I wasn't so nice."

"Yes, well, I thought it would be improper to say what I really feel." A slight smile, but it quickly dropped and her face went back to her stern look. "We can't change their minds, so we must deal with the situation at hand." She opened a file and handed Mark and me some literature about the place. "We offer many different options here at Silverwood. We try to accommodate as many unique situations as there are unique people here.

"You will be here Monday through Friday, eight to four. There are no exceptions. Our rule is you check in and check out with a faculty member. We run a tight ship around here. We have to." Her face softened a little. I think she knew I didn't belong here.

"Rules don't mean you won't have fun at Silverwood. We have a lot of activities. You'll have classes from eight until noon, lunch from twelve to twelve-thirty, group counseling and individual counseling from twelve-thirty until two, then outdoor exercises and activities from two until four. We understand most of the kids who end up here don't learn the typical way, so we don't run our school program like ordinary schools. We do a lot of outside classes and projects, and we try to make the students know they belong and matter.

"Kids are here for many reasons. We run the gamut. A few simply come once a week to talk to one of our counselors. We have many who can no longer remain at home and live here permanently. Also, we have students who have committed crimes or struggle with drug or alcohol abuse problems. All ages and types. I don't feel we have any bad kids, merely misunderstood and mistreated ones."

I nodded my understanding.

She took us for a quick tour around the facility so I could get my bearings. The main room where I'd be was large, bright, and open. Glass windows lined the entire west side from top to bottom of the building, making use of the natural light. Through the windows I could make out some picnic tables and a basketball court that broke the line of the forest outside. Turning back to the room, I noticed there were no individual desks but instead there were long tables. Behind the tables, dozens of bookshelves sat in rows like a library. In the far end of the room were four high-topped counters lined with microscopes and other science equipment. Maps of every country hung on the walls around the room. It was not a classroom but a learning center.

Mrs. Sanchez walked us out to the parking lot and shook my hand. "Well, it was a pleasure to meet you, Ember. I think you will be happy here."

I wasn't sure how I felt, but at least she made me more comfortable in attending Silverwood. No matter what, the choice of me being here was no longer in my hands.

NINE

Wednesday was my first official day at Silverwood. Mark drove me to school to be sure I at least made it to the parking lot.

I looked out the truck's window at the facility. "Okay, I changed my mind. I don't care how long it takes, I'll get my GED or maybe do school online."

"Having a little *déjà vu* from the ghost of school-time past? You go through this every time you start a new school." Mark shook his head as we slowed to a stop in front. "You'll be fine. You're strong, Em. You won't let something get the better of you. You have too much of your mother in you."

"Wow, hello, manipulator."

Mark chuckled. "Guilty, but it's not any less true."

"Have I told you lately you are a cruel, cruel man?"

"Yeah, this morning when I tried to wake you." Mark got me up extra early so he could drop me at Silverwood and still be to work on time. I would arrive ahead of time, but I didn't mind. I wanted to get situated before the other kids showed up.

"Right." I nodded, then leaned over and kissed Mark's cheek. "I love you."

"Love you, too. Now go prove Sheriff Weiss and Principal Mitchell wrong." He pointed toward the school. "Remember I can't leave work till four-thirty. I have a meeting, but I'll come straight after."

"No worries. I'll start on my homework or something." I opened the truck door and slid out. "See you later."

Mark waved and took off. I turned to the front of the building, sucked in a deep breath, and slowly moved for the entrance.

As I reached the door, a motorcycle tore into the parking lot, making me jump. I whipped around and caught a glimpse of a guy in worn blue jeans, a black leather jacket, and scuffed boots. He passed too fast for me to see anything more, but something in my stomach twisted. I was a bundle of nerves anyway, so I ignored it and continued inside.

I checked in with Mrs. Holt, who gave me a rundown of how my classes worked. It reminded me a little of elementary school, since all the students were in one class and never changed rooms. Except here there was no main teacher. We were on our own and worked on subjects at our own levels. Responsibility for yourself was something they wanted you to learn. Several teachers and tutors went around working with each student and focused on individual trouble areas.

Mrs. Holt walked me to the main classroom. "I'll introduce you to Mr. Kemp."

I was confused when we approached a person whom I thought was another fellow student studying.

"Mr. Kemp?" Mrs. Holt tapped on the young man's shoulder. When he turned, I saw why I had been mistaken. He appeared to be in his early thirties. Dressed in jeans, t-shirt, and chucks, he was shorter than me, slim, with short, curly, dark brown hair and brown eyes. His face was happy and open. He was nothing like any teacher I ever had.

"Mr. Kemp, this is Ember Brycin, and it's her first day here."

"Oh, yes, Ember. Mrs. Sanchez told me about you. Welcome."

He shook my hand, looking at my eyes curiously. Mrs. Holt nodded at both of us and slipped out of the room. "And please call me Tim. We like to keep it on an even and personal level here."

"Thank you," I replied. He kept looking at my eyes. "It's okay. I know my eyes are strange."

"They are very unusual." His cheeks shaded slightly at getting caught staring at me so blatantly.

"Well, they match my personality."

Tim grinned and motioned to a chair. "Have a seat. Your last school sent your files, so we know what classes you were taking. Today we need to figure out your learning style and the best and most productive lesson plan for you." He folded his hands on top the table. "I know everyone hates being the new person, so we'll try to get you past it. We are big on everyone being equal here. No one's better than anybody else."

He got out of the chair and moved to the back of the room to retrieve the paperwork. I was left alone to watch the kids trickle in. At eight o'clock, eighteen students of various ages filled the seats. My hair and eyes invited stares, but I tried not to feel intimidated. Some of them had the street-tough "I can cut you" thing about them, and I had no doubt they could. There were a few who had the classic, druggie look—overly skinny, stringy hair, dark sunken eyes, who couldn't sit still in their seats and who bit their nails down to the nub. Three had the all-black, gothic emo-look, and another four were pretty average-looking, although I know looks could be deceiving.

There were no bells or anything telling me when class started or ended. But at noon, students stopped what they were working on, packed up, and left. I looked around, not sure what to do, but after several more people left, I followed suit. I put in my iPod and headed for the cafeteria.

Being alone never bothered me, and I think it's what made people at my old high school uncomfortable. Okay, it was one of many things making them uncomfortable. I could happily sit by myself and draw, but the average teenager didn't seem to understand that about me. It made me a target at school. I got a lot of things thrown at me and was whispered about behind my back. Because it didn't bother me only seem to cause them to be more uneasy.

I sat at one of the round tables dotting the lunchroom. The cafeteria was on the same west side as the main study room. Similar glass walls dominated the one side, letting in the hazy sunshine.

I was pulling out my lunch when a girl standing in the lunch line near me picked up a plastic fork and sprang on the goth-looking guy in front of her. I jumped back as they both crashed to the floor, sliding into my table, in a jumble of arms and limbs.

"What the hell you starin' at, you stupid freak?" the short but curvy Latino girl bellowed. She held the plastic fork at the guy's throat.

"Certainly not you, bitch," goth-boy hissed back at her as he tried to break the fork in her hand. Instantly, the security guards who walked around the school making sure people didn't do shit like this pounced on the two and tore them a part. They spat violent threats at each other as the guards dragged them in opposite directions.

Wow! Okay . . .

"She does that all the time. You'll get used to it."

I looked to my left to see who had spoken. A tall, lanky boy who couldn't have been older than sixteen smiled at me. He had sandy-blond hair with puppy dog hazel eyes. His skin was smacked by puberty. He had a sweet, boy-next-door face and an ah-shucks smile, which immediately made you feel protective of him, the way you would a younger brother.

"Keep your eyes down when you're around her, and you should be okay," he said. "She thinks every look in her direction is about her, like everyone is out to get her or something."

"Good to know. Thanks."

"I'm Josh. I'm in morning study with you."

"Ember," I replied. "I remember you. You were sitting by the window."

"I was." His smile widened.

"You stood out because you were one of the few who didn't look like they wanted to kill me," I added.

Josh laughed. "Don't let my charming looks fool you. I am terrifying. Okay, so maybe only in the World of Warcraft. But there I am feared." He looked away blushing. "I just proved I'm a dork."

"Don't worry. I'm one, too." I smiled.

"Probably not something which impresses the ladies, though, huh? The counselors are trying to get me to cut back on my gaming hours. They think I want to escape reality into a world of make believe where magic . . . elves, trolls, orcs, and druids . . . exist. Now I've officially said too much."

"That's okay," I said laughing. "Have a seat." I motioned to the empty spots around me.

"Thanks," he responded, planting himself on a bench. "So what's your schedule for the rest of the day?"

"After lunch I get my head probed. Then there is some outdoor thing . . . not sure what it is."

"Cool, we're on the same schedule." His smile got even bigger, which I didn't think was possible. "The outdoor thing is called O.A.R., Outdoor Adventure Rehabilitation."

"Exploring therapy. Great." I said dryly.

"No, that's the probing." He snickered as he pulled out a sandwich.

"We are talking about mental probes here, right?"

He grinned at me, stuffing the sandwich in his mouth. "Sure."

After lunch, Josh and I headed to our therapy session. We started in group therapy. Then, after about an hour, we went into individual therapy. Dawn, my assigned counselor, sat across from me for thirty minutes, thinking we were already progressing well with my treatment. I forced my lips into a smile and not a smirk. I was good at fooling people. I learned early on how to talk without really admitting or saying anything. I got used to hiding the strange happenings or things I saw. Finally, time was up, and Josh and I walked out toward the O.A.R. meeting spot.

"So what do we do in these outdoor activities anyway?"

"It varies. Last fall we helped landscape a retirement home close by or played 'Capture the flag.' It's all about team building and boosting our self-confidence. They also like us doing a lot of volunteer work . . . helping out the community, stuff like that. It's pretty cool. The couple who use to run it went to Arizona to be with their family. I'm not sure who will be in charge now."

Josh and I reached the designated spot, and despite the freezing temperature and misty rain, it was a beautiful site. It was a clearing in the woods with log benches circling a deep fire pit and a stage that sat not too far off to the side. There were more wooden benches lined in front of the stage, probably used for the summer and weekend camp programs.

By two o' clock, there were about fifteen of us waiting. I was looking around at everyone, wondering what they did to get here, when my skin started to tingle. A shiver rushed up my spine.

Someone moved in close behind me, trying to get through the throng of people. A burst of heat encompassed me, arousing any part of my exposed skin. It felt like heaven. I leaned back, longing to soak in more of the warmth. My neck craned as I looked for the source of the heat.

My heart stopped and my blood flushed cold as my eyes clasped onto the towering figure moving around me. I knew the form. It was not one you'd forget. His toned body couldn't hide underneath his baggy jeans, loose navy blue pullover hoodie, and a beat-up black leather jacket.

He seemed to be keenly aware of his body. Not in an arrogant or awkward way—but with an assured gracefulness. And even though there was a slight limp in his walk as if his leg had been hurt at one time, he still moved with a self-assured strut that made my heart thump harder in my chest. His presence demanded attention.

He turned to face us, and I couldn't help the small gasp escaping my lips.

When our eyes instantly locked, it was like fire shot through my frozen veins. Still shadowed under his hood, his eyes shone unnervingly bright, like someone left two lights on in a pitch-black room.

His face was not what people would consider classically handsome. He was too manly to be considered pretty. The term that came to mind was smoking hot. He looked like the disheveled, rough, bad boy with an animalistic quality, which drew me to him and scared the crap out of me. Two deep scars lined the left side of his face, cutting into the stubble growing along his strong, chiseled jawline. His disheveled light brown hair skimmed over the top of his shoulders.

My hands ached from wanting to reach out and touch him, to feel his hair between my fingers, but his face held such harshness it made me step back. My reaction didn't seem to go unnoticed. His eyes darted between the two of mine, and a whisper of a sardonic smirk crept across his features.

I couldn't believe I was face to face with the guy from the police station.

If he was shocked to see me, it didn't show. I was pretty sure he recognized me. The same hate I saw before at the station was there today. I couldn't fathom why he regarded me with such disdain, but I was used to people fearing or hating me for no reason.

Someone else stirred behind me. A tall, model-thin girl bumped my shoulder as she walked to where the guy stood. She smiled and squeezed his arm in the comfortable, familiar way you would with a close friend or boyfriend. He broke our eye contact as he turned and looked at her, giving her a small smile. I felt stupid for being surprised. Of course he'd have a hot girlfriend, if not several. Someone like him would not be single. And she was beautiful—breathtakingly gorgeous. She was dressed in black skinny jeans; a plain, white t-shirt with a scarf looped around her neck; sweater; and pristine, green and yellow checkered rain boots. She was what you'd picture on the cover of a GAP catalog, not at a school for troubled teens. There was something almost unreal about her, and she seemed at home in the forest even though her clothes screamed the opposite. She looked to be in her early to mid-twenties. She was a bit taller than me, with stunning long red hair, light blue eyes, and porcelain skin, all of which made me incredibly jealous.

Her eyes caught mine, and she smiled. I could have sworn the clouds parted, and I half expected bunnies and deer to come out of the forest to dance and sing around her. I didn't know if I liked or hated her. She was too pretty and sweet looking to be here. Her hair was unfazed by the dense mist swirling around us, which made mine look like an electrocuted poodle.

I glanced around and saw I wasn't the only one drooling on their boots. The unbelievably sexy couple enraptured everyone. I had to laugh watching the girls' (and maybe a few guys') eyes move salaciously over his body. The guys (and probably a few girls) looked dumbstruck and goofy, their eyes and pants bulging as they stared at her.

She took a step forward. "As you noticed, your old O.A.R. leaders are no longer here. We will be your new team leaders. My name is Samantha Walker and . . ." She turned to the guy next to her expectantly.

"Eli Dragen," he said reluctantly. His voice was deep and husky, sending vibrations through me. His eyes narrowed in disgust at me before he looked away again.

What the hell?

"We will be building community gardens," he continued. "Some of the food we grow will be used in our cafeteria, and the rest will be sent to a homeless shelter. We will be using compost from our kitchen here at Silverwood to help grow the plants. We need to build the planter boxes first. We'll be splitting into two groups, each one building five frames." When he spoke, I swore I heard a flutter of sighs from the girls, and, yes, definitely from a guy or two. The more the girls reacted to him, the more upset I got, which was stupid. I didn't know why I felt angry. I barely knew him, and it was clear he didn't like me, nor I him.

My thoughts immediately put me in check. What was I doing? This guy could be some creep who might have been watching me from outside my bedroom window a couple nights ago. He could have been stalking my house, wanting to kill me in my sleep. Okay, the last bit might be a little over the top but better safe than sorry, right?

There was no way I wanted to be with him. I started toward Samantha, when Eli's sharp voice filled the space. "You guys will be with me." He waved his hand around a group of people, which included me. His dislike for me was clear, so why would he pick me? He stared at me, his expression emotionless and hard.

The tough girl from the cafeteria stepped closer to Eli, her voice twirling like honey in a flirty, girlie tone. "But, I want to be in *your* group." I rolled my eyes. I had seen her stab a guy with a plastic fork at lunch. There was nothing sweet or girlie about her.

"Fine," he replied sharply. "Let's go."

ᴛᴇɴ

Josh and I followed the group across the street to a cleared area where remnants of an old garden remained. We stopped in front of a shed where barrels, hammers, drills, gloves, and other supplies were bundled in piles.

"Okay, everyone, grab gloves." Eli nodded towards the stack.

Right then, I saw something skitter deep in the shadows at the far end of the shed. The thing moved to the wall and scuttled toward the entrance. I squinted, trying to make out what it was. A large, brown rat stopped and turned to look at me.

"Ewww . . . gross a rat," a girl screamed.

I could have sworn I saw the rat's eyes narrow and glare at the girl. "I don't find you much to look at, either." The voice was tiny and gruff.

My breath caught in my throat as I froze with fear. *Holy shit.* I looked around. No one else seemed to be reacting to the fact a rat had talked. I turned back to the rodent.

A hazy glow surrounded it, and I found I was no longer looking at a rat but at a tiny woman, dressed in a long, green skirt and a white blouse. Her brown hair hung next to her face in two thick braids, and on her head was a tall, pointed green cap. She tilted her head and frowned at me, then turned and hustled out of the shed, in the direction of the forest.

Without a thought, I started after it, a knee-jerk reaction since I knew the rat-woman was only a hallucination. I needed to go back on medication.

I continued after her, and for as small and stocky as she was, she was insanely fast. "Wait," I called.

Adrenaline pumped through me as I ran after the little person, barreling through the old, dried-up garden. She stopped, and I came to a sudden halt as she turned and faced me. Her hands were on her hips, her stocky little frame all puffed up and angry. I could see her face more clearly now. The tiny woman was younger than I had first thought but still looked weathered and tough. Her eyes were squinty and lips were thin and pinched. Her hands were burly and thick and skin was coarse and cracked. She looked like she had worked extremely hard her whole life.

"Get out of my garden," a little, but strong, voice rang in my ears like sharp bells.

"Oh, Jesus," I mumbled to myself as I stared.

The tiny, homely woman stomped her foot. "Did you hear me? Get your tall, scrawny ass out of my garden."

"Em?"

My head jerked up to see Josh and the rest of the class standing behind him, looking at me like I had grown two heads. I continued to gape at him dumbfounded. Didn't they see the small person standing in front of me?

"Em, are you okay?" Josh's tone was full of wariness. I looked to where my hallucination had been, but it was gone.

I closed my eyes, sucking in a deep breath. "Yeah. Terrific."

When I reopened them, Eli's piercing eyes drew my attention. I couldn't make out the expression on his face, but it was intense and made me want to hide behind Josh.

Samantha joined the group, her gaze fixed on me. Something about her stare made me shift uncomfortably. "Let's leave the wildlife alone, shall we?" She smiled thinly and then turned to face the rest of the students. "Come on. Let's get to work. Grab some gloves and a hammer." She gathered the group, all observing me with wary expressions, but she soon distracted them with tools and plans for the new garden.

Eli maintained his stance, his scrutiny still focused on me. I looked down, trying to ignore the burning sensation his gaze seared into my skin.

My mind was reeling with the embarrassment of letting people see me splinter from reality. Hallucinations weren't new to me, but it had been awhile since I had been caught by other people while having one. No one knew right before my school in Monterey burned down, I thought I'd seen my awful math teacher turn into a troll with a huge, thick nose protruding from its hairy, ugly face. Dark, beady eyes gleamed as it watched me. It had felt so real, more real than anyone else in the room. It was a secret I kept locked deep down.

When I was younger, it was easier to brush off these oddities. My mom would laugh, telling the neighbors I had an overactive imagination and abundance of imaginary friends. I couldn't do that so easily now.

Eli turned away. "Today, we will be building the planter box frames. We only have two hours, so we better get started," he said, motioning to the stacks of thick boards. He rambled on, but after a while I tuned out.

"That also means *you*." Eli moved to me. It took me a moment to realize everyone else had moved on and was at work, but I stood staring at the spot where the tiny woman had disappeared. "Hey, *girl*, do you understand the words coming out of my mouth?"

My gaze snapped to his. "This *girl* has a name, you know?" I shot back. I was irritated by the way he had said "girl," like I was something off the bottom of his shoe.

"And what would it be?" He crossed his arms as he looked

61

down on me. "Please, tell me it's something like Tiffany or Brittany."

"It's Ember," I said as heat filled my cheeks.

"Ember." He repeated my name, and a slow smirk formed on his face. "Of course it is. Ember what?"

"Brycin."

He looked at me patronizingly. "Brycin, let's see if you can handle a hammer or if I should find something easier for you to do."

My eyes narrowed as we glared at each other. What was this guy's problem? What had I ever done to him? The other students had stopped what they were doing, sensing the tension and looked back and forth like it was a ping-pong match. I was waiting for someone to do a low whistle like you hear in all the standoff-scenes in the old cowboy movies.

I scooped up a hammer, gripping it tightly in my hand and stomped off toward the woodpiles. He scoffed in amusement as I walked away. I almost, *almost*, showed his face what I could do with the hammer, but I decided it might not help my case for getting out of here.

"All right, everyone, get back to work," he said and clomped away.

Josh leaned down and whispered in my ear, nodding to Eli. "Okay, that was weird."

"Yeah." It was the only response I could come up with as I grabbed a handful of nails, imagining it was Eli's face I would be hammering them into. At that thought, a smile broke over my face.

The two hours went by fast. Our team got into a good rhythm. The only thing bothering me was every time I looked up, Eli was staring at me, glaring actually. I tried to ignore him and concentrate on my work. My arms felt like they wanted to fall off, but I wouldn't stop. I didn't want to show him any weakness or let him know he could get to me.

After we'd returned our tools to the shed, Josh and I made our way back to Silverwood. He had a curious look on his face. "So, Ember, what's up with you and that guy, Eli? You two have history or something?"

"No, I never met him before." What I said was technically true. "I don't know what his problem is." I didn't feel like telling Josh about the police station incident. Plus this didn't even really count as having history with Eli, right?

"Really? Strange. I thought I picked up on some vibe there." His eyebrows furrowed, and he shrugged.

"Nope, simply some old-fashioned, predetermined dislike for me."

Josh smirked, looking like he didn't quite believe me. We got back to the main building, and Josh wandered off for the dorm. He was one of the students who could no longer remain at home.

"I'll see you tomorrow. And welcome to Silverwood. I'm glad you're here. You're already making things a whole lot more interesting." He gave a slight wave before disappearing down the hall.

I smiled, shaking my head, then turned in the opposite direction toward the classroom. I was exhausted. With no homework yet, I decided to spend the time relaxing and drawing until came.

As I walked into the main classroom, I stopped short. I instantly recognized Eli's body from the back as he talked to Samantha.

"What the hell was going on earlier?" Samantha demanded.

"Nothing you need to worry about," he said tartly.

Her blue eyes looked up at him in longing. "You sure?"

She was stunning, captivating, and beautifully feminine—everything a guy would want. Obviously, it was what Eli wanted. From the way she looked at him, there was no doubt she felt the same. They were stunning together; they had a bad boy/good girl stereotype thing going on. My chest clenched as I watched them. Why did I have to notice every perfect detail of his body, especially his ass and strong broad shoulders? Fury stormed through me, but I turned it on myself. I shouldn't be thinking this way about him. It was demented. He was scary and rude and clearly didn't like me, which was now reciprocated. I pivoted, wanting to flee the room. Instead I ran straight into Mr. Kemp.

"Hey, Ember." He smiled. "Where are you running off to?"

"I-I . . ." I floundered as I turned to look behind me. At the mention of my name, Eli's head snapped up and whipped towards the door, his eyes staring into mine like lightning bolts. My head felt a little addled as fear rose through me, which made me defiantly hold his stare. *Don't show fear.* The more intimidated I felt, the more stubborn I tended to get. Mark said I was headstrong and ornery, something I got from my mother.

"Ember?"

I turned back to face the teacher. "Sorry, Mr. Kemp, I was going outside and wait for my ride." I tried to move around him.

"Please call me Tim. It's freezing out there. Hang in here until then." His hand already lay gently on my back, guiding me again into the room. I let him direct me to the tables, where I sat in a chair closest to the door. I peered at Eli under my lashes. He stood with his arms crossed, watching me with disdain. *Seriously, what was his problem with me?* Sam tugged at his hand, eventually getting him to turn away. I tried to ignore them both as I took out my sketchpad from my backpack. I flipped through the sheets to find a fresh page.

"You are really talented. May I?" Tim motioned to my tablet. I shrugged, as if it was okay; it wasn't. Not too many artists like people looking at their drawings until they are ready to show them. It's like reading someone's diary. Sketching was release for me, and I drew things especially personal. However, I felt it rude to say no to him.

He commented frequently as he looked through my sketchpad, but he stopped on one page in particular. "Wow, this is really interesting. I don't know what it is. It has a haunting quality, as if you are looking into this person's tortured soul."

Tim laid the drawing on the table. I froze. Of all the drawings he could've picked, it was the one of Eli's eyes, the one I barely recalled drawing. At the time, I hadn't known his name or anything about him, but I felt his stare had burned a hole through my retina and my brain. I recalled how scared I'd been that night, the feeling of being watched, especially with those eyes staring from the shadows of the forest.

The same eyes on me now.

I tried to grab the pad away from Tim, when another hand from behind snatched it off the table and out of my grasp. It was like a car accident I couldn't prevent or turn away from. I sat helplessly, as Eli took my sketchpad, his eyes slowly recognizing his own. I don't remember breathing. It felt like time stopped.

I watched Eli's reaction as he took in the drawing, his gaze wandering down to the corner of the page where I always put a date. His reaction was so minuscule I thought I imagined it; but for an instant, his pupils thinned to a vertical slit. Or at least I thought they did. I blinked and his pupils were back to their passive, cold state.

Medication here I come.

"It's good." Tim motioned at Eli and Sam to look. As she approached, her body moved possessively close to Eli's.

"It's very good." There was a trace of warning in her voice as her head cocked to the side, undoubtedly recognizing whose eyes were on the paper.

Eli's glance slowly lifted from the sketchpad and caught mine. As we stared at each other over the ridge of the pad, it was as if we were having a silent conversation, although I didn't seem to understand the language. Looking away from him felt like tearing magnets apart. Even as my head turned, my eyes stayed on his until the last second, with my mind screaming: *Don't ever take your eyes off the enemy.*

"Yeah," Eli responded evenly and put the pad back down.

My phone buzzed in my pocket. It was a text from Mark saying he'd be there in five minutes. Relief washed over me. "Oh, I gotta go. My ride's here. Bye."

I jumped up with joy. Getting away from this strange, awkward situation and Eli's malice-laced stares was all I wanted. I collected my stuff and practically ran out the door.

Mark and I talked about my day as we headed home. "It was a lot better than I thought," I admitted. Nothing blew-up, which is always a plus, and there was a pleasant absence of nasty cheerleaders. Of course, I left out the part about my hallucinating in front of the entire class. Things like this would only upset Mark. He didn't need to know.

"Some scary people are there, but most seem like they've had a tough go of things," I told him. "If anything, it made me appreciate you even more."

"Remember your worst when I wake you up tomorrow morning."

"Not sure my appreciation will go that far."

"But I can't afford to lose another hand in the morning trying to get you up early."

"You know, Mark, a bus goes out there, which I could take instead. I might lose the cool factor of my daddy driving me, but I'm willing to sacrifice."

"No. You can't take the bus. We wouldn't want to lose your cool factor," he said. "I don't ask anything from you, like trying to get an education, or good grades, or even having some fun. All I ask from you is to be cool for my sake."

"I think you've taken all of the cool. None left for me." I shrugged dramatically. No matter my mood, Mark could always make me feel so much lighter and happier, letting my day become a humorous memory and not an irritation.

"Won't riding the bus take almost an hour more than if I drove you?" Mark asked. "I don't like the idea of you coming home in the dark."

"Mark, it's staying lighter later every day. I'll be fine."

"I'll think about it."

"You know I'm eighteen, I can legally . . ." I trailed off as I caught the warning in Mark's expression. "Shutting up now."

"Good choice."

ELEVEN

Wanting to hear every detail of my first day at Silverwood, Ryan and Kennedy planned to meet me later in the evening at one of our favorite hangouts. It was a hipster-type café, which played cool music, and local art covered the walls. Unfortunately, as of late, it seemed to be popular with the high school "in-crowd" as well. I assumed they went there to laugh at the funky outfits, the darkly twisted artwork, and the indie music.

When I arrived, I saw Kallie and her minions sitting at the front table by the window. I sighed deeply and kept my head up as I walked past her. There was no doubt she spotted me when I heard her say something, and the entire table turned to look and laugh.

Kennedy and Ryan sat at our usual table in the back. "Hey, guys." I pulled out a chair and plopped down.

Kennedy wordlessly pushed my already ordered vanilla latte to me.

"Thank you."

Kennedy had this knack for knowing exactly what you were feeling and what you needed. It was kind of strange how in-tune she was with everything around her. She was the one who had approached me on my first day of school five years earlier. I remember watching this tiny, fragile-looking girl, who was all of ninety pounds, with long, silky, brown hair and brown eyes framed by glasses come up to me at the lunch table. While the other kids seemed to stay away from me, she wordlessly took a seat next to me at lunch, acting like sitting next to me was something we did every day. Immediately, I felt comfortable around her, somehow sensing she, too, was different like me. Ryan had followed suit, and every day for a week they sat next to me without pressuring me to talk or join with them. Eventually, I let my walls down. We had been inseparable ever since.

"Sorry about the bitch infiltration." Ryan nodded towards the front window. "They came in after we did."

"Not your fault." I shrugged.

I started to tell them about my first day at Silverwood, when a shadow moved over the table.

"Oh, look who it is," Kallie mocked. "The wicked witch and her flying monkeys. How is the school for the mentally disturbed?"

"Better than the wicked bitch academy I recently left."

"Why can't you simply melt away with water?"

"And why can't you click your heels together and go back to Kansas?" Ryan shot at her.

She placed her hands on the table and leaned forward. "Is all this 'Dorothy talk' making you hot and bothered, Ryan? I'll bet you have a pair of ruby slippers you wear to dance around the house with Toto here." Kallie nodded towards Kennedy.

Like at the dance, I could handle her going after me, but my friends were off limits. My anger sprouted to elevated levels. My jaw set into a stony expression. Something came over me, and I felt a dark ferocity consuming my insides. I needed to get out of here.

I stood, knocking over my chair. "I would back off now."

Ryan reached for my hand. "Em, don't let her get to you. She's not worth it."

"Shut up, purple Teletubby," Kallie sneered at Ryan.

The lights in cafe flickered and buzzed over my head. A calm power oozed inside me. The lighting whined in protest as energy flooded through the wiring. A spark shot from one of the lights, breaking the dam holding them back. Tiny balls of fire rained down on the customers below.

Another burst of sparks exploded from the hanging lights. People screamed and scrambled to hide under the tables. I continued to stand there, a force building in me. I felt a connection to the bursts of energy. It wasn't electricity I felt in my veins but sparks of fire. Flames seared through my veins like it did in the wiring. One by one the lights blew, plunging the café into darkness.

"She's the one who's doing this," Kallie's shrill voice shot through the room, breaking the shocked silence. "It's her! She's a freak!"

It was dark with all the lights out, but I could sense dozens of eyes watching me, scared and suspicious. I did the only thing I could think of—I ran. It may not have been the wisest thing to do, but logic left me, and I reacted purely on instinct.

Within a few minutes, I was on the road in Mark's truck, stewing in my shocked, scared, and angry thoughts. Kallie was right. I was doing it—first at the dance and now at the café. There was no denying it; I was a freak.

It seemed I could cause things to explode when I got upset. Such a thing wasn't normal or even possible, was it? So—what did that make me? Was I some hybrid X-man, or was it simpler? Something was wrong with me. You'd hear about these people who could make things happen, and later you found out they had a tumor pressing on their brain. Whatever it was, I had the power to blow things up. I bit back the tears, alternating between mumbling to myself and screaming profanity as I drove along the highway.

I turned down the dark, winding, country road leading me home. My phone buzzed relentlessly with calls from Ryan and Kennedy. I needed to come up with some explanation before I called them back—if there was one. In my state, I found it hard to concentrate on the curvy route. Rounding the corner right before my turnoff, the headlights reflected off something in front of me. I squinted as a flash of light assaulted my eyes.

A polished Harley pulled onto the road, the metal of the bike reflecting my headlights. Something gripped my nerves as I recognized both the person and the black bike. His was followed by six more pristine Harleys of various models. The rumble of the engines hummed in my chest as the riders revved them to gain speed. I knew it was the same group who had circled Mark and me a few nights earlier. My heart pounded faster at the thought of Eli being only yards away. They quickly picked up speed, leaving my truck in the dust.

My road came and went, but I continued after the bikes. The impulse to follow Eli was too strong to deny. Why was he near my house? Was it a coincidence? Did he live out here, or was he watching me? There was no way he knew I was behind them and seeing where they went might give me a clue about who Eli was. I had to find out what was going on. I hit the gas, not wanting to lose them. The truck swerved and weaved through the twisty roads. I had barely got their taillights in sight, when red and blue lights flickered in my rearview mirror.

"Dammit!" I hit the steering wheel, pulling to the side of the road. I watched through my side mirror as a cop got out of the car and strode toward me. I recognized the officer instantly. "Oh, you've *GOT* to be kidding me!" I exclaimed, leaning my head back on my headrest, before taking it forward and banging it on the steering wheel. I swore that man was hiding in the bushes, waiting for me to cross his path. Reluctantly, I rolled down the window.

"License and reg . . ." Sheriff Weiss trailed off as he looked inside the window. I would have found Sheriff Weiss' expression humorous if it weren't for the fact his shock turned into complete and utter joy. "Well, well, if it isn't Ms. Brycin." His eyes danced. "We keep running into each other, don't we? You must really enjoy making my day."

"I really do," I retorted as sarcasm came flooding out.

"Do you know how fast you were going, Ms. Brycin?"

Keeping my head facing forward, I had a "let's get this over with" expression on my face. I didn't trust myself not to say something snarky, but he remained silent, waiting for my answer. Finally, I sighed. "I'm sure you are about to tell me."

"Sixty-five in a fifty mile-per-hour zone," he stated.

"See, you didn't need to ask me after all."

His lips pinched together in a thin, white line as he stared at me. "Have you been drinking, Ms. Brycin?"

"Does a bottle of tequila laced with heroin count? I also had some battery fluid . . . was that not a good thing?"

"Get out of the car."

I really needed to learn to keep my mouth shut. I sighed heavily, unsnapping my seatbelt. I opened the door and slid off the driver's seat to the ground. My eyes widened as he unhooked the handcuffs from his belt.

"Aren't you going to give me a breathalyzer test or something first?" I demanded. Even if I had been drinking, I knew I would have passed it. For some reason alcohol didn't affect me the same way it affected others. My tolerance had always been extremely high, especially compared to others my age.

"You see, I only need to suspect you are under the influence of drugs or alcohol to take you in." His smug expression was begging to be slapped off his face.

"So you're taking me in for having a caffeine-high?" I asked. "I confess . . . I'm a junkie. Lock me up."

"I plan to."

Something in his determined expression made my shoulders sag. I was tired of this man. He was making my life miserable, adding to the tremendous stress and exhaustion I felt already.

72

Abruptly, a motorcycle raced around the corner, heading straight for us. Like a deer caught in the headlights, I stood motionless and wide-eyed as the biker got within several yards of us before skidding to a stop. He flipped off the sheriff, then tore back in the direction from where he had come. Sheriff Weiss didn't think twice: he raced back to the cop car, turned on the siren and lights, and sped after the biker.

I stood in shock before a sly smile came over my face. In the darkness, I couldn't make out who was on the bike, but I had no doubt it was Eli or someone in his group who came back to distract Weiss' attention. Hurriedly, I climbed into the truck and drove away before Weiss lost them and decided to return for me.

Sighing with relief and happiness, I pulled into my driveway, jumped out of, and ran to the door. I slammed it behind me, feeling I was safely away from the fiasco that might have been tonight's ending. The one thing I kept thinking about was how Eli knew I needed help. When Sheriff Weiss pulled me over, I was behind the motorcycles and in Mark's truck. I didn't even have a car, so how would he have known it was me? It didn't make sense, although I knew in my gut it had been Eli who saved my butt.

TWELVE

Eventually I called Ryan and Kennedy back and mumbled some excuse about being freaked out the cops would show up, and I desperately needed to get away. They accepted my pathetic excuse, but I knew they didn't believe it. They weren't stupid or blind. They could see something was off, and it left me feeling even crazier and more alone.

I spent most of the night squinting at lamps, willing them to explode. When I wasn't trying to blow up lights, I was doing Internet research about how someone could cause electrical equipment to blow up. I did find lots of crazy-sounding people claiming they could control stoplights and turn on various appliances without touching them. They called it technopathy, the ability to control and manipulate electronics with the mind. Unfortunately there were no scientific facts included, merely a lot of people declaring they could affect electronics. The result: an incredibly horrendous headache. It was past three in the morning before I crawled into bed to catch a measly few hours of sleep.

I could barely keep my eyes open during school the next morning. At least I had Josh. At lunch, we sat together again. We seemed to find easy companionship with each other. In group therapy that day, it was his turn to share. I learned about his home life, and it made me feel sick inside. Being constantly beaten up and told you were nothing by people who were supposed to protect and love you was not an easy thing to get over. Most didn't. I hoped he'd be different. I already was protective of him, and, ironically, I felt like beating up anyone who would hurt him in any way. Josh made me happier when he was around; he was like my Ryan here at Silverwood, although a younger, taller, gawkier model.

When two o'clock came around, I wasn't sure if I was dreading or looking forward to O.A.R.

"Em, wait up," Josh called after me, his gangly body catching up. He was growing too fast for his motor skills to keep pace, leaving him awkward, clumsy, and self-conscious of his body. I smiled warmly at his approach. He was kind of a "dufus" but such a friendly, good-hearted guy.

"So do you think Mr. Attitude is going to give you anymore crap today?" he asked.

"I hope not. The last thing I need is another asshole on my back."

We arrived at the O.A.R. meeting point, and I felt a strange tingling sensation on my skin. Eli came from behind and brushed his arm against my shoulder; it was only a graze, but it sent a hot shockwave down my arm. I winced.

"You okay?" Josh asked.

I rubbed my shoulder. "Yeah, a spasm or something. This old lady's body is already creaking and complaining."

"Oh, come on, you're only, like, two and a half years older than me."

"Then you have two and a half years before you're creaking and moaning like this old, brittle biddy."

"Whatever you say, Miss Daisy," he said. He chuckled, causing me to giggle along with him.

Eli shot a cool gaze at us, his icy voice cutting through our laughter. "If you two are done, maybe we can get some work done today."

Samantha walked close to us, seeming to catch the tension in Eli's body. She followed his gaze to me. Something flashed in her eyes too quickly for me to really grasp before she pivoted and briskly departed for the garden.

Four o'clock came too soon again. Josh and I had laughed as we raced to see who could fill a wheelbarrow with soil and dump it the fastest. Once, we crashed into each other and ended in a heap covered in dirt. We giggled until our stomachs hurt. Eli didn't say anything, but he watched us with a permanent frown on his face, which only made us chuckle more. I would never want to admit it, but I was having fun and wished O.A.R. lasted longer.

I stood and brushed off my jeans. Everyone was putting away supplies and getting stuff together. Eli leaned against the garden shed, pulling his sweatshirt back on. He hitched up his t-shirt, exposing some of his toned, well-built torso. He had a man's body; nothing about him was undefined or still growing. A warm buzz danced through my own as I watched his muscles ripple and move under his skin. His entire left side was covered with a giant, looping Celtic tattoo. My eyes followed the thick, curving line all the way down to where it was cut off by his jeans. I longed to see more, to see how far down it went.

As if my wish had been granted, he stretched again, making the top of his jeans dip lower. My gaze greedily slid lower, following the muscular indention of his V-line. I gasped as a hint of hair captured my attention even more, locking my gaze on his raw, powerful body.

Eli's voice sliced through my reverie like a hot poker. "See something you like?"

I jerked my head up, briefly meeting his eyes and confirming, yes, he did in fact catch me checking him out.

I flushed so hot I could already feel the sweat coating my skin underneath my clothes. I glanced around to see if anyone else, especially Sam, was a witness to this. Thankfully, everyone

76

seemed to be doing his or her own thing. I looked back at Eli. A smirk played on his lips as his electric green eyes moved over me, making me blush more.

"No," I declared. "I was looking at your tattoo."

"Uh-huh."

"Whatever . . . think what you want." My embarrassment turned to anger quickly. "Seems your ego needs no help in believing what it wants."

He shoved off the wall. "And I thought you had a sense of humor."

In a blink, he moved so close to me I could feel his warm breath on my face. I froze. He looked back and forth to each of my eyes, his brows furrowing, as if he were trying to understand something. The glint in his stare turned my body to liquid. I was afraid if I moved, my bones would turn to mush, and I would be left in a puddle at his feet. We stayed like this for a few seconds as I tried desperately to gather my willpower. His eyes moved down my body, blanketing me in a wave of heat and desire.

Fear finally made words crawl from my throat. "See something you like?"

A small grin pulled at the side of his face as he stepped back. *Touché*, his eyes said.

I halted, realizing something amazing and unsettling had happened between us.

"Hey, Em, you ready?" Josh yelled from where our bags were.

"Yeah," I replied, my gaze never leaving Eli's. I felt something change as we stared at each other. It was as if I now understood the language his eyes spoke.

You want to challenge me? Eli's lips curled into a half smile.

My heart picked up speed, but I tried to keep the cool, nonchalant appearance on my face. *Bring it on.*

I had no doubt he understood because an eyebrow cocked in

surprise. I could have sworn, for a brief second, shock and alarm flew over his face.

This wasn't the same as what I experienced with Torin. Torin could communicate without looking at me. I couldn't hear Eli's voice speak directly into my head like I had with Torin. This was more as if Eli's eyes were conveying to me what he was thinking. I couldn't really explain it. It wasn't even humanly possible. But it was only the logical part of my brain freaking out; otherwise, I found it strangely normal and natural.

You really want to try it, little girl?

I smiled sweetly. *Oh, yeah.*

Fine, but you're going to be wishing you didn't. He gave a slight shrug.

We'll see about that. I gave him a smug smile of my own. I did not want to show him the true fear I felt. I turned and walked away, not at all sure what happened, but knowing something changed between us—something I might come to regret.

Josh and I were on our way back to Silverwood's main building when Tim found me. "Hey, Em, Mrs. Sanchez wants to see you in her office."

"Did she say why?" I asked nervously.

"Nope, sorry, but I don't think it's anything bad." He smiled and patted my arm as he walked away. He was one of those people who was always happy. People like that mystified me.

I moved to Mrs. Sanchez's office and knocked on her door.

"Come in," she said.

I opened it and stepped in. Mrs. Sanchez welcomed me from behind her desk. Even though it had been only a few days earlier, it felt like months since I sat in her office. "You wanted to see me?"

"Yes, sit down." She motioned to the seat in front of her desk. "Don't worry. It's nothing bad, not completely. I only want to see how you are doing. I've heard such positive things about you from

Tim. You know, Ember, I think the whole situation landing you at Silverwood is complete bull-honkey, but I can't say I mind you being with us. You are doing well, and people seem to take a natural liking to you."

I almost choked on the last part. In general, people *didn't* take a natural liking to me. If anything, it seemed like the opposite. Then, I thought of Ryan and Kennedy and some of my old friends from Monterey, few as they were. They were all in some way outsiders, like the people here, like me. Even if you didn't look like an outsider, it didn't make you any less of one. I came across as an average teenage girl—except for my eyes—but people sensed I somehow didn't belong. Here I did. In the land of outcasts and outsiders, I was home. Go figure.

Then, I felt a presence behind me and immediately stiffened. I knew before I looked who it was and that troubled me.

Mrs. Sanchez motioned to him. "Ah, Eli, please, come on in."

Eli moved into the room with an unsettling silence and swiftness. He didn't sit but stood behind the empty chair, as far away from me as he could possibly get.

"I asked you both in because Sheriff Weiss called me this morning, adamantly stating he is adding two days a week and weekends of community service to each of your sentences. Whatever the both of you did to this man, he seems determined to make sure your every waking moment is being controlled." She shook her head in frustration.

"What?" I exclaimed. "Are you kidding me?"

"I'm afraid not. You make him incredibly nervous, Ember, which I don't understand. You shouldn't have been placed at Silverwood in the first place. I'm not sure what it is about you that unsettles him so much. Unfortunately, he can extend punishment, even if you don't deserve it. If you fight it, he will say you are being uncooperative and make life here a living hell until you graduate. He can make sure your school files show you as 'troubled.' I want to be honest with you."

This was his revenge. After seeing how his mouth watered at the idea of locking me up last weekend, I shouldn't have been surprised. He was out to get me no matter what it took. He would do what he could to keep me under his thumb.

"Although you might be happy because, in the absence of the couple who used to operate it, I have convinced him to let you teach the ropes course for me instead."

Eli's voice was low but firm. "Marisol, I don't think it's a good idea."

"Why? I think it's perfect," she responded. "I need someone to run our Adventure Education Rehabilitation Course, and you need community service hours. It's a perfect fit."

Heat spread to my face, and a lump dropped into my stomach. *Are you kidding me?* This had to be some sick joke fate was playing on me. She wanted Eli and me to work together? We could barely be in the same place for a minute without venom shooting out of every word we uttered to each other. I felt Eli's gaze on me, making my pulse quicken and my insides twist and roll around, ready to choke off my air supply. "Y-You want me to run the ropes course with *him*? Are you sure?"

"I won't make you. You've had too many people force you into things, but I do believe you would be really good at this," she said. "And I have a feeling you and Eli will work really well together."

"May I speak to you alone, Marisol?" Eli said tersely.

Mrs. Sanchez frowned, then nodded. "Ember, will you kindly step out for a moment?"

I stood, my own rebuttal dying on my lips as I looked at Eli. His angry, determined face was the opposite of my humiliated expression. I flushed as I walked out of the room. Mrs. Sanchez's office had a long window next to her door. I situated myself so I could see what was happening, while not looking too obvious I was spying on them.

Watching Eli trying desperately to change Mrs. Sanchez's mind made something deep within my soul ache. The more she shook her head, the more adamant Eli became. I bit my lip, trying to keep back the tears. Why was I so upset? I didn't want to work with him any more than he wanted to work with me. Another gush of heat flooded into my face. By now I had to be purple. How dare he make me feel like this! Like clockwork, my hurt and embarrassment transformed into anger.

It was a few more minutes before Mrs. Sanchez called me back to her office. Eli sat in a chair with cool resentment, which sent chills down my spine. He kept his gaze on Mrs. Sanchez with a reserved hostility meant for me.

"I apologize. Eli and I had to work out a few details." I knew she was lying, and she knew I knew, but it was a lie everyone in the room was going to play along with. "I guess I should have asked first if you both wanted to run the class. I hoped, since it was either the ropes course or picking up trash on the side of the road, you'd be happy with this choice."

"I am. Thank you," I said as pleasantly as I could.

Eli scoffed beside me.

Mrs. Sanchez could not have missed the strange animosity between us. On the other hand, maybe it was her reason for doing it—thinking if we worked together, we'd work out whatever problems we had. I watched her, trying to decipher her motives, but her implacable expression revealed nothing. I would not let the jackass next to me control my life, and I certainly wasn't going to run and hide from him. He could glare and say snarky things all he wanted; I would merely smile more.

"I'm happy to do the ropes course," I said sweetly.

"Great. I'm so glad." Even now she didn't smile, but there was something warm in her voice and eyes that made you believe she really was thrilled.

The door to the office opened, and Mrs. Holt's head popped in. "Marisol, I'm sorry to interrupt, but there is someone here who needs to see you right now. It should only take a moment."

"Of course." She stood, all sixty-two inches of her. "I'll be right back." She walked out, closing the door behind her.

Eli continued to look forward. I exhaled my irritation, my anger growing. His head jerked my way, but at the last moment, he averted his gaze again. I leaned over my lap, propping my elbows on my legs, cupping my head in my hands. *I will not let him get to me. I will not let him get to me,* I repeated to myself. But I couldn't deny how one side of my body felt every molecule of his next to mine. Heat radiated off of him like a furnace, and I hungrily ate it up. Sighing again, I fiercely rubbed my temples. Why did this guy make me feel so baffled, frustrated, and emotional?

"Problem?" Eli's voice had a cruel taunting tone to it.

Picking my head up, I gave him a sharp look. "You're fucking kidding me, right?"

"I don't kid about fucking."

I flushed under his steady gaze. The last thing in the world I wanted was to show him he could embarrass me, especially with his sexual innuendos. I pressed my lips together, fighting back the heat rising in my body. "You may not, but I'm sure most of your girlfriends found it a joke," I shot back.

"Ouch." A ghost of a smile tugged at his lips. "So I'm gathering you have a problem working with me?"

I let out a bitter, crazed laugh. He was enjoying getting a rise out of me as if I were his personal voodoo doll he could needle. This guy could seriously provoke me. I sat up, looking him directly in the eye. "Listen, I'm not any happier about our situation than you, but I'm going to try to make the best out of things."

"I know a few ways you could make this situation better," he said, leaving me guessing at his meaning. My cheeks were already flushed from the earlier implication, and the imagery still rocketed in my head. I couldn't let myself linger on it for too long.

"What? Like running to Mrs. Sanchez and crying like a little girl?"

His face darkened as his eyes locked on mine. Dread and dizziness swept over me as I realized pissing him off was not the brightest idea. Not that I could help pissing people off, especially him. It seemed to come with the territory of being me.

He moved in closer, stopping only inches from my face. "I didn't run," he said through clenched teeth. "I skipped."

It took a second for his words to sink in, and then a nervous laugh bubbled up. "Wow, you really need to work on the skip of yours."

"How can you say that?" He moved back in his chair. "It was beautifully executed."

"You seriously have to be bipolar or something," I muttered, still confused by his changing moods.

The door opened, and Mrs. Sanchez came in. "I apologize. Now, where were we?" She went through all the details with us. Since it was still considered winter, they only had the ropes course on weekends. During the week, on Mondays and Thursdays, she wanted us to prep for the upcoming season by installing an obstacle course and a paintball area. In a few weeks, they would be hiring more people and switching to their summer schedule.

Mrs. Sanchez wanted us to stay late the next evening to go through some basic ropes training. "Jason is a professional trainer who prepares people to lead the ropes course. I've used him several times before. He's a great guy and is able to fit you in at the last moment. I understand my request is very quick, but I'm going to throw you two into the deep end and hope you can swim."

After she excused us, we both raced for the doors leading to freedom. But then I did something I wasn't expecting. Right as we came to the front of the building, I stepped in front of his path and blocked his exit.

"Truce?" I asked abruptly. "Till we get through this."

He stared down at me in silence, making my heart race. He looked like he was seriously debating with himself about whether he wanted to be civil to me. Finally, he nodded stiffly. "Truce."

I felt a weight which I hadn't even known was there lift off my shoulders. I sighed with relief. There was a peculiar buzzing which throbbed between us, making my heart beat faster. We were standing extremely close, staring at each other. Even the way he stood motionless intrigued me.

Was I *that* typical—drawn to the bad boy? Was ego all it was, a woman's tendency to think she will be the one to "tame" the beast? I hadn't thought I was that kind of girl, but obviously I was wrong. It seemed no matter how dangerous or scary he was, it only made me want to know more about him.

We watched one another skeptically, our eyes fixed on the other. Words were not spoken, but I felt I was on the verge of understanding his eyes again, like earlier. But it quickly dissipated as he jerked his gaze away from mine. Like a door slamming in my face, he became hard and aloof once again.

Chirceen

Mark looked relieved when I told him I had to stay late the next day and Ryan and Kennedy would be picking me up. I also told him I would be taking the bus in the morning. He nodded. Work was really starting to get hectic and stressful, so he didn't argue with me.

The next morning I was re-thinking this decision when I had to get up over an hour earlier than usual. I dragged myself to the bus stop, still half asleep, my coffee container in hand.

The day passed quickly enough. I felt a lot more comfortable and began to find a rhythm. It was a normal day, so for me that meant it was abnormal. It struck me as odd how Sam seemed to move away whenever I was near. At first I thought I imagined things, but when Eli did the same, I wondered if it could be more than coincidence. Was I seeing his version of a truce? *Yeah, he would be so much fun to work with.*

I walked into the lunchroom where we would be training for the ropes course. A guy with a bluish-black and red striped Mohawk and eyebrow piercings stood at the far end of the room. Tattoos covered both his arms and neck, but they were partly hidden by a t-shirt proclaiming "Rock the Rope." Mrs. Sanchez told us he was also an extreme sports enthusiast. Jumping out of planes with a snowboard and other insane stuff. I had tried bungee jumping and really liked it, but I was nowhere near an extremist.

I waved to get his attention. He looked to be in his mid-thirties but definitely had a young skateboarder-surfer vibe about him. He loped over to shake my hand.

"Oh, hey, I'm Jason. I guess you must be Ember? Cool hair." He smiled at me.

He stopped pumping my hand but continued to grasp it as he looked back and forth at my eyes, seemingly transfixed by them. He leaned so close I could see the tiny stud on his eyebrow ring. "Holy shit, man, those are the most freakin' unbelievable eyes I have ever seen. They're wicked!"

"Yeah, and if you get any closer to them, you might get a wicked view of my fist," a voice growled behind me. I spun around to see Eli leaning against the doorframe. His arms were crossed over his toned chest. He looked like he was relaxed and carefree, but I knew it was all a façade. I could see he was tense and ready to pounce. His green eyes glinted brightly.

Jason looked between us apologetically. "Oh, uh, sorry, man. I-I wasn't . . . I didn't know."

"Yeah, well, now you do." Eli pushed himself off the wall and lumbered to us.

My mouth was agape. "There's nothing to know. We're not together." I turned to Eli. "What the hell is your problem? Is being a jackass another one of your many hidden talents?" I glared at him.

"I won't deny I'm good at it, but it's definitely not one of my many *hidden* talents. Or so I've been told." His expression revealed nothing, but there was no doubt as to what he was hinting. My cheeks turned a deep shade of pink, and I quickly turned away. I didn't miss the smirk cutting across his face.

"T-that's not . . . I mean . . . I wasn't insinuating . . ." It usually wasn't easy to turn me into a stammering mess, but he seemed to do it effortlessly.

"What's wrong, Ember?" A cruel, smug smile tugged at the corner of Eli's mouth. "You don't strike me as the type who gets

86

thwarted so easily." Eli's bright eyes penetrated so deeply into mine it made me feel as if all my inner thoughts and feelings were being unveiled.

"'Thwart' suggests you defeated or outwitted me." My eyebrows arched in a mocking response, challenging him. A slow, unsettling grin spread over his face, but he stayed silent. "What's wrong, Eli? You don't strike me as the type who gets surmounted so easily."

You want to play vocabulary? Fine, bring it, I thought.

His eyebrow cocked, and I immediately wanted to slap myself. Oh, you idiot. *Why did you have to use that word?*

"It's a little early in our relationship for us to be 'surmounting,' but, hey, I'm game if you are. I'll even let you be on top." He looked directly at me, and a coy smile played on his lips.

Whenever I thought I had the upper hand, Eli seemed to be able to pull my legs out from under me, knocking me off my game. I grappled for any kind of thought not including images of this boy's naked body or his fingers against my bare skin. I shook my head, trying to rid my mind of the vivid images playing out.

He moved in closer, causing warmth to flare through me as he brushed my arm. He leaned and whispered in my ear, his hot breath slipped teasingly down my neck and spine. "I'll be waiting eagerly for a good retort from that wicked tongue of yours. I'm sure you will come back with some mind-blowing licks for me." He stepped away from me. Watching me flounder for words and the chagrin spreading over my cheeks only widened his smile.

He was toying with me. He enjoyed the power he got from watching me lose my defenses. Everything about him scared me, infuriated me, and intrigued me—an exceedingly dangerous combination. Absolutely nothing good would come of this. I needed to run in the opposite direction of anything having to do with Eli Dragen.

I really should have listened to my own advice.

The ropes trainer's mouth hung slightly open as his gaze flickered from Eli and me.

I cleared my throat. "Uh, sorry about this. Putting us in the same room should come with a warning label: Will cause a pain in the ass."

"O-kay . . ." He put on a polite smile. "Shall we continue?"

"Yes. Please continue, Jason." I turned back to him, letting my flirty smile out. Anything which would piss Eli off would make me happy. I smiled brightly. "What are you going to teach us tonight?"

"Oh, right. Yeah, man, come on over and I'll show you guys the basics, the safety tips, how you get in and out of the harness, and how to check the equipment properly." Jason waved us to the table piled with ropes and harnesses. For the next hour and half he took us through all the safety precautions and basic rope protocol.

"Okay, now I'm gonna have you take turns clicking each other onto the lead and adjusting the tension." He sprang toward the rope hanging in the room from end to end. Eli shot me an inscrutable look before spinning on his heels and going to the rope.

Speaking of adjusting the tension, I thought as I followed.

"Okay, Ember, I'll have you go first." Jason handed me line a clip. Eli stood with his legs apart, parallel to his shoulders and his arms crossed over his chest. The harness fit snuggly over his button-fly jeans. The weight of the harness pulled them down, exposing more of his hips and lower torso. As low as they dipped, I saw no hint of underwear. *No, don't go there.* I swallowed and shifted my gaze to the floor as I walked up to him.

My fingers nervously fumbled with the clip and front loop of his harness. I twisted my hand to get a better angle, and my knuckles brushed up against the exposed patch of his soft, toned skin. My hand and his body jerked back in response.

Embarrassment colored my face. His eyes held mine with a steady, critical gaze I couldn't really decipher before I returned my focus to the harness. I clipped him into the rope and adjusted the tension, then took several steps away.

"Awesome." Jason nodded approvingly. "Now, it's your turn, Eli."

I tried to calm my thumping heart as his eyes locked onto mine, the room becoming hazy and out of focus. Eli held the clip in one hand, and his fingers flicked the clasp open and closed as he stepped to me. With the other hand, he curled his fingers through my harness loop, purposely letting his thumb skim the space between my jean line and t-shirt hem. My skin burned where he touched it.

He yanked me closer to him, our bodies becoming aligned. My breath caught in my throat as he swiftly hooked the clip in the loop and gave it another strong tug to make sure it was secure. He stepped back and adjusted the tension of the rope, his eyes never leaving mine.

My body trembled. I hadn't realized I had stopped breathing until tiny, dark spots impeded my vision and the room decided to get a little unstable on me. I let go of my breath, hoping he wouldn't notice my reaction. From the fraction of a smile glinting in Eli's eyes, I was not so lucky.

I nodded at him. *Well played.*

He shrugged. *I thought so. Are you sure you really want to dance with me, little girl?*

I crossed my arms. *I've heard the Samba is enjoyable.*

He smirked. *You are out of your league.*

Don't underestimate me.

Tango it is then.

"Wow, awk-ward." Jason clasped his hands, trying to break the tension between Eli and me. Jason's voice snapped me back into the room, and I looked up, startled. I had almost forgotten he was there. That was a bad sign—a really bad sign.

We finished the rest of our training, and as soon as I was unhooked, I thanked Jason and bolted out of the room. My phone showed a text from Kennedy saying they'd be here at six-thirty, giving me ten more minutes. I walked outside, wanting to escape into the open air and hide in the dark shadows hanging from the building. My body still buzzed with adrenaline, and my skin where his thumb touched me zinged with heat. I leaned against the cement wall and closed my eyes, taking in a slow breath of cool air and trying to calm myself.

Someone barged out the front door of the building. My eyes flew open with a start. I froze as I saw Eli barreling toward the parking lot, his hand continuously running over his face and through his hair.

When he reached his motorcycle, he threw down his bag angrily, profanity hissing from his mouth. He leaned over his motor. He looked to be gathering himself together, his fingers digging into the leather seat. I didn't move a muscle, afraid he'd turn around and see me.

The front door creaked again as someone else pushed outside. "Eli?" A voice I immediately recognized as Samantha's echoed through the night air. "Eli?" She walked to him. I pressed myself harder into the wall, hoping I'd become part of it.

"What?" He sounded irritated.

"I waited for you."

His voice was clipped. "I didn't ask you to."

"I know." Her tone went from uncertainty to angry. "You never would because you don't want to need anything from anyone."

He pushed himself off the bike and turned to face her. "I've told you how I feel. I've warned you this is nothing more than what it is. I'm not looking for anything, but you continue to pursue it. You know full well what I'm like. I never deceived you."

Sam was silent for a moment. "It's her, isn't it?"

"I have no idea what you're talking about."

"Oh, please. It's so obvious. I have eyes. I can see what is happening." Her mood seemed to shift again, and a strange laugh escaped her. "I'm surprised at you. I know you've done the gauntlet of women, but I didn't imagine you'd go there. I mean you do know *what* she is, right?" Eli's jaw tightened, and he stared back at Sam without an ounce of emotion. "I thought that was one line even *you* wouldn't cross. She's one of *them*. Do you get it? You most of all can't forget what it means."

"I have forgotten *nothing*! I know what I am doing. I have a plan."

Samantha crossed her arms. "I'm starting to think there is more to it than that."

The tension was so thick I could feel it resonating off Eli and see its visible sonic waves crash into me. He turned away and grabbed his bag off the ground. "I've had enough of this conversation."

"Oh, did I hit a nerve, Eli?" She sounded hysterical. "What's wrong? Is wanting to screw an abomination too much for you?"

"*Enough,*" he roared. "You're out of line. Do not forget yourself."

Stumbling back at Eli's outburst, she bit her lip and shook her head slowly. "You really are a bastard," she whispered, turned on her heels, and ran inside. Eli watched her for a moment. Cursing under his breath, he shook his head and climbed onto his bike.

I let out my breath, not realizing I had been holding it. From that tiny movement, Eli's gaze shot in my direction, his blazing eyes finding mine in the darkness. As our stares locked, a light flooded the parking lot. Ryan's Nissan pulled up in front of me.

"Em," Kennedy yelled as she rolled down the window.

I closed my eyes, cringing. There was no doubt now as to the identity of the person eavesdropping—as if I had a choice in the matter. Without looking at him, I dashed to the car, desperately wanting to get away. Kennedy was trying to climb into the rear so I could have the front, and in my eagerness to get in, I flung myself into the front seat, pushing her headfirst into the back.

Ryan scoffed and then laughed as Kennedy's muffled squeaks sprang from behind us. "Jeez, lady, in a hurry?"

"Sorry, Ken." I turned to look at her. "I'm really ready to get out of here and hang out with you guys!"

"Oh, holy hotness, Batman!" Ryan's gaze was directed out the window at Eli. "I don't know why you'd want to hang out with us when you have playmates like him at school. Now, there's a Happy Meal I'd like to order."

Eli was straddling his glistening, black motorcycle. Hands wrapped around the bars and feet still planted on the ground, he started at me.

"Some playmates bite," I said.

"All the better." Ryan's eyebrows shot up and down.

Kennedy wiggled between our seats, trying to get a better view. "Wow . . ."

Ryan's reaction didn't surprise me, but seeing Kennedy stare at Eli with wide, unblinking eyes and a strange, confused look on her face made something twist inside me. I couldn't help but follow her gaze, even though I knew who she was looking at, and I found Eli staring back at her equally as intently.

"He's dangerous and very dark. Death surrounds him . . ." Kennedy mumbled.

I spun to face her. "What?"

She stared at Eli in a trance-like state.

"Ken?" I said louder.

She pulled her eyes away from him, shaking her head. "Sorry, there's something peculiar about him . . ." she trailed off. She realized we were all looking at her, and a deep blush covered her cheeks. "Nothing, just ignore me."

Eli's gaze seared intensely through the window as he looked back at me.

I turned to Ryan, feeling the intensity of Eli's stare. "Can we get out of here, please?"

"Sure thing, my salty M&M, but only if you tell me what is going on between you and Mr. Throw Me Up Against a Wall because I know there is something titillating happening there."

"Ryan, please." My eyes grew wild as he sat there, looking back at me with a sly smile. "Fine. Go, please."

He hit the gas and within seconds I was away from Eli's penetrating gaze. I sighed with relief. I didn't like him having such an effect on me. I took a deep breath and looked at my friends. A huge burden seemed to lift off me. I felt lighter and happier. My eyes misted up. I had missed them so much.

"Oh, no, missy. You are not going to get out of true confessions with those crocodile tears. Now talk." Ryan shook his head and smiled.

"There's nothing to talk about," I refuted, causing them to snort.

"Please." Ryan's glance had me withering in my seat. "There was more tension back at the parking lot than a southern woman's girdle at a bake sale."

I laughed and shook my head. "Nothing's going on, I swear."

"Hey, Pinocchio, remember who you're dealing with here. I can sense these things better than a clairvoyant on acid," Ryan replied. "Spill it."

I bit my lip. If I told them, then I was admitting there was something to tell, that there was something going on between Eli and myself. But if I thought I could get out of talking with these two, I was sorely mistaken.

Ryan was first. "So . . . the incredibly hot, bad boy who rides a motorcycle, his name is . . . ?"

I sighed, defeated. "Eli . . . is name is Eli."

"Eli what?" Kennedy sat forward in her seat, her chin settling on the back of my headrest.

"Eli Dragen."

Ryan coughed I thought they were going to fall out of her head. My insides tightened into a knot as I watched them.

"W-Wh-Who?" Kennedy stuttered.

"Eli Dragen."

"You do know who he is, right?"

"No."

"Ever heard of the RODs, the Riders of Darkness?"

"Yeah . . ." A nervous feeling settled in my gut.

"You know my dad works for the Gang Task Force. I've seen him looking at a file so I peeked. Eli Dragen is one of the names on the top of the list, along with his brother, Lorcan. They are both high-ranking members in the club. Seriously dangerous shit, Em."

I had heard the rumors about the RODs ever since I moved to Olympia. They were an infamous biker gang who lived on the outskirts of town. They were known to hang out at Mike's Bar, notorious for its underbelly clientele, seediness, and criminal activity. It was a place where law-abiding citizens didn't venture, and it was left for the biker gangs and outlaws who called it home.

Since nobody claimed to have met them, it was difficult to know if any of the rumors were true. The only thing I might be willing to believe is Eli had been in jail. Not only arrested but served some jail time. From my encounter with him in the police station, being chained to the chair, and from the familiarity between the cop and him, what Ryan said seemed within the realm of possibility.

It didn't surprise me Eli was part of the RODs. It terrified me though, especially when I thought of the creepy night I could have sworn I saw him outside my bedroom.

"I didn't take you for the kind of girl who goes out with *real* bad boy types. The rumors you hear about him and his brother. Dragen is definitely a name my father knows well." Ryan looked at me with his eyebrow cocked. "He's a guy who your mother warned you to stay away from and your father would be buying a bazooka for, not a shotgun."

I gulped.

"So now having the experience of seeing this guy in person, which is still causing me to orgasm,"—Ryan took a deep breath— "I'm even *more* curious about how our little Emmy is involved with the bad boy from the other side of the tracks. With a guy so bad and hot, what is the reason she is keeping it a secret from us?"

"I'm not involved with him."

"I don't buy it. Do you buy her porta potty potpourri, Ken?"

"Nope." Kennedy shook her head.

"Come on, guys, can we at least wait 'til we're home with food in our bellies before you berate me even more?"

"Fine, but you are not getting out of it." Ryan pulled into town. "I'm already placing bets on how long it will take you to get foliage burn or tree slivers on your back!"

"Ryan!" I looked at him, exasperated.

"What? You are going to be out in the woods with him for hours every day. I'm simply saying you should make use of what nature provides you." He shrugged, an impish smile playing on his face. "And don't tell me you haven't thought about how hot that guy would be in the sack?"

I looked out the side window.

"Thought so."

We went quiet before Kennedy's soft voice spoke from the back. "He's not my type, but there's really a presence about him, huh? Something you can't explain . . . a raw, sexual essence. A guy whose boxers you want to permanently on your floor."

Ryan and I turned slowly to look at each other our mouths gaped, eyes wide as saucers. Then I looked back at Kennedy. Ryan twisted the rearview mirror to get a better look at her.

"What?" Kennedy replied innocently, which sent us into a fit of giggles.

I smiled mischievously. "I don't think he wears any."

Their heads whipped towards me. We burst out laughing again, until tears poured down our faces.

An hour later we were sprawled on my living room floor, Chinese takeout containers between us as some brainless movie no one was watching played in the background, when Ryan broached the subject again.

"Holy crap, you are like a dog with a bone," I commented to Ryan.

"Or one with a boner."

"Ahhhh, Ryan." We groaned and laughed hysterically. It felt so good to smile and laugh.

"You're making a bigger deal of this than it is."

"I doubt it. I saw the way he looked at you."

"Yeah, it's called animosity."

"Right." Ryan winked at Kennedy. "Or, as I like to call it, sexual tension."

I finally gave in and told them parts of what had happened. I started with the police station, but I left out when I thought I saw him outside my bedroom window, my nightmares, and how his touch sent fire through my skin.

I also didn't tell them about what I had heard between Eli and Sam. There was something in their exchange that bothered me. It wasn't because they were obviously "friends with benefits," and Sam wanted more. That did upset me, especially how nonchalantly he talked about it, but there was something else troubling me. I didn't know who this other girl was, but the way they talked about her seemed strange to me: *"I'm surprised at you. I know you've done the gauntlet of women, but I could not imagine you going there. I mean, you do know what she is, right? I thought that was one line even you wouldn't cross. She's one of them. Do you get that? You, most of all, can't forget what it means?"*

What did she mean? I decided to push it away. I had to make myself not care. I wasn't going to get caught up in their drama. Hopefully, I wasn't going to be at Silverwood much longer. Principal Mitchell promised he'd reevaluate the situation at the end of the month. If I had any luck, Eli and all this crap, excluding Josh, would all be a distant memory.

I thought I would feel more relieved by the idea—I didn't.

Ryan and Kennedy stayed until Mark got home from his poker game. But even when I went to bed, thoughts of Eli's fingers running across my bare stomach kept me tossing and turning until I finally drifted off to sleep.

My bare feet pummeled the ground as I tore through the forest. Fear of something unseen behind me propelled dread through my veins, moving me faster. I broke through the thick brush, skidding to a stop as my feet hit the edge of the cliff. The sheer drop ended far below where a river snaked through the dense forest. Falling would mean death. I tried to scramble back; my feet slipped on the loose gravel, making me slide over the rim.

I was going to die.

I reached back, grabbing frantically for an exposed tree root. Sweat dotted my forehead as my hand caught hold.

Relief.

Groaning, I tried to pull myself back up.

"You look to be in need of some assistance, my lady." Torin stood on the cliff's edge above me, reaching out a hand for me.

"You're an observant one, aren't you?" Yes, even in peril I could still be a smart-ass.

Torin smiled and grabbed my wrists and pulled me up.

"Thank you." I nodded at him when my feet were secure on the ground again. My attention quickly turned to him. He was one of the reasons it was hard to catch my breath. Torin was dressed in black leather pants, a tight, black shirt, and black boots. His dark hair was tied neatly back at the base of his neck. I had forgotten how magnificent he was.

"You never have to thank me for saving you. Your life and safety mean everything to me." Torin squeezed my shoulders and brought me to him. "But I am at the Queen's command. For your protection, I can only come to you like this, in your dreams. We could still be found out. I should not even be risking your welfare to spend this time with you now."

"What are you talking about? The Queen's command? Are you British?"

"British? No, most definitely not."

"I don't understand."

"Listen to me, Ember. Word of your powers has raised some interest. You are no longer safe. Please . . . I am unable to say anything else, but I am trying to show you."

"Show me what? What are you forbidden to tell me?"

"You know," he said as he reached down and touched my heart. "Even if you are not aware, you do." My breath lodged in my throat, my heart pounding at his touch. There was something so natural and familiar about it. "You know in here."

FOURTEEN

My dreams continued through the night. They were filled with dark shadows and flaming red, cat-like eyes moving around me, pulling me into the deepest pit of darkness. I felt like I had barely fallen asleep when my alarm woke me up. My eyes were gritty and heavy as I forced myself out of bed, propelling my body toward the coffee machine before my lids fully opened.

Getting me up early on a Saturday was like poking a bear with a tiny stick. I was not a morning person. And it looked like it was going to be a caffeine-diet day.

"Good morning," Mark said in an annoyingly chipper voice, lifting his coffee cup toward me. Mark was a morning person.

"Right," I grumbled, heading to the cupboard for my coffee cup. Mark chuckled, knowing perfectly well how much I wanted to throw his perky, morning ass through the window.

"Oh, come on, Em. It's a great day. It's cold and overcast and you get to spend the day with a bunch of angry preteens."

Okay, now he was pushing my buttons. I whipped around and glared at him, which only made him chuckle harder. "Oh, someone is grumpy this morning."

"Wow, you really are pressing your luck, aren't you?"

"Oh, it wouldn't be a good morning for me if I didn't annoy you." He laughed, but he also knew to back off. He understood I was more of a night owl. As a kid, I would stay up until three in the morning drawing or reading, even if I had to be up at six am. Most people who knew me highly recommended to others not to make conversation with me until around 10 or 11 am.

"You used to be such a nice man."

"Yeah, before I joined your family." He snickered and handed me an empty bowl. I grabbed the cereal off the counter and sat with a thump.

I ate breakfast, staring out the window at the forest beyond our house. I watched the mist weave eerily through the trees, twirling and twisting like clawed hands, beckoning me into the dark woods. From the day we moved in, I felt like I was being watched, like the woods had eyes. Strangely this only drew me more. What was it about this forest? I couldn't explain why I was drawn to it. Knowing me, it was because it was creepy and dark. I was weird like that.

Mark looked at his watch. "You better get going. I'm going on my run. See you tonight." He kissed the top of my head and left the house.

"Really, it's someone like him who needs to be committed." I shook my head.

After I showered and dressed, I kind of sleepwalked to the bus stop. My body was awake, but my mind was still snoozing. I moved onto the bus like a zombie. I must have dozed because in no time I was at my stop.

As I walked down the aisle towards the exit, the guy sitting at the front looked up at me.

Torin's handsome face looked back into my frozen, shocked stare. *"Don't trust him."* His words came out clear, but for some reason, they didn't match the movement of his mouth.

"What? Don't trust who?"

I stared back in confusion. Then, Torin's features shifted and his face became chubbier. I watched, stunned, as Torin morphed, becoming an overweight man with glasses.

The man looked at me curiously. "I'm sorry. Did you need help with something?"

I jerked back. The pudgy man continued to look at me. I turned and ran off the bus.

The ropes course was twenty-five minutes from Silverwood, deep in woods, and no way to get there except by car. Mrs. Sanchez had told me Eli would take me the rest of the way if I got myself to Silverwood.

I needed to get a car—like, now.

I arrived at the school a little after nine. Eli was already there, leaning against his bike, reading a paperback, reminding me of the first time I saw him. He was so enthralled with his book he didn't seem to notice when I walked into the parking lot. I let myself take in his rugged beauty. His leather jacket was zipped all the way up to his chin, making me focus on the rough stubble along his jawline. My eyes moved to his lips as he rubbed his chin.

Dear God, he was hot.

The book was worn and old, and he held it so I couldn't see the front cover. I had to admit I was curious. What sort of books would he read? No genre seemed like it would be his thing.

I walked slowly toward him. His eyes never left the pages of the book, even when I knew he was aware of my presence. "Morning." My voice came out slightly squeaky.

His eyes flashed quickly to me, then back to the book. He continued to read for another moment before he dog-eared the battered book and stuffed it in his pocket. I humored myself, imagining it was a bodice ripper—a biker who liked romance novels. Now that I knew he was a part of the RODs, I couldn't help but look at him differently. I should run as fast and as far from him as I could, screaming the whole way. I knew I wouldn't. He was terrifying, even more so now, but there was something about him making me take another step forward.

"Sorry I'm late. The bus was running behind," I fibbed. The bus was on time. I was late, but he didn't need to know that.

He made a gruff sound in his throat. "You ready?"

"Um, yeah."

He threw me the only helmet he had.

"Hope you're not scared of motorcycles," he said as he swung his leg over the bike. He didn't say it because he was concerned. It was more like, "Tough luck if you are." If he thought or hoped I would be afraid, he had the wrong girl.

"Scared of a Harley-Davidson Dyna Super Glide FXD? Hardly." I hopped on the back and snapped the helmet strap under my chin.

He looked over his shoulder, his eyes wide in awe. "You know what model it is?"

"You sound surprised. Why? Because I'm a girl who knows about motorcycles?" I replied with a sly smile on my lips. "It's a 2003, Hundredth Anniversary model, right?"

He stared at me in disbelief for a few more seconds before turning around and shaking his head. Guys were always surprised I knew about motorcycles and automatically assumed it was because of Mark that I knew my way around a Harley. This was completely untrue and sexist. My mom was the one who had the love for Harleys. She had gone through a rebellious phase, dating many leather-clad bad boys on bikes. She might have lost her love for the biker, but she never lost her love for the bike. That love had been passed down to me.

"Hold on," he said.

I grabbed onto his waist and tried to ignore the raw electricity and heat I felt as our bodies pressed together. The chilly wind whipped at my face as he tore down the road. Nothing made me feel more exhilarated than being on a motorcycle.

Regrettably, driving so fast had us arriving at the location way too soon. His warm body had felt like heaven against mine. As soon as we separated, I felt a loss, both in temperature and in something more I didn't even want to think about.

Taking off the helmet, I looked around. Low and high rope challenges were suspended throughout the trees like spider webs. It looked like a strange version of the Ewok village from *Star Wars*.

There was a green storage unit a few feet away at the base of a large cedar tree. Eli walked to it and rolled up the door. It was filled with plastic bins and a huge blow-up air mattress.

He unzipped his jacket and threw it to the side. My eyes couldn't help but wander over him. He wore his usual button-fly jeans, a long-sleeved, white shirt under a dark green t-shirt that said *Team Leader* on the back. I ignored the quickening of my pulse as I watched him bend over a pile of harnesses.

Oh, holy hell.

"You want to grab something here, Brycin?" he asked, bending over again.

Um . . . yeah. Your ass.

Joining in, I helped collect the rest of the harnesses.

"Do I get one of those?" I pointed at his t-shirt.

He nodded and walked to where he had left his backpack. Pulling it out, he threw the shirt at me.

I held up the tee. It had a decal of a person on ropes with *Ropes Adventure Course* in the left hand corner. Like Eli's, it had *Team Leader* written in block letters across the back. I tugged off my jacket and hoodie and slipped the top on over my gray thermal.

Eli and I set up and checked everything before our group of pre-teens made their appearance. But nothing could have prepared me for the day that lay ahead. I wanted to be back in bed, under the safety of my warm comforter, instead of being glared at by bad attitudes behind twelve sets of eyes.

A.E.R.C. worked with different age groups and levels of troubled kids. Level 5 was the hardest, as they were already in juvie and extremely troubled. Level 1 was for those who were only beginning to show signs of problems; most had low self-esteem.

This morning's group was Level 3, which meant most had some real attitude problems. They ranged from age ten to twelve, and they looked like they wanted to be anywhere but here. Right then, I felt the same. When Eli took a step towards them, even the toughest looking kid gulped nervously.

"All right, we'll be going over some rules and safety tips with you. We want you to have fun, but if I see anyone pushing, fooling around, disregarding the rules, ignoring or disrespecting one of us"—Eli motioned to both of us—"you will find yourself dealing with me. I promise the experience isn't something you want." His tone sounded foreboding. "You got me?" Eli looked hard at each one of them. Terrified, they nodded in agreement. "What?" Eli took another step towards them; again he seemed to fill more space than occupied by his body. It was something you couldn't explain, but it was overwhelming and disturbing.

"Yes, sir!" the kids screamed.

"Yes, sir!" I echoed.

Eli turned his head to stare at me with a "what the hell" look.

"Sir, yes, sir?" I said hesitatingly, feigning meekness.

The kids laughed, and it immediately broke the ice as I had hoped it would. They needed to respect and listen to us, but they also needed to trust and like us for the day to work and become a positive experience for them. From the way Eli looked at me, I knew he understood what I was doing. A ghost of a smile formed on his lips before he crossed his arms. "That's right. You can call me sir or Eli. And if you refer to her as Fairy Princess all day, I'll get you pizza for lunch." He smiled wickedly, and the kids returned the conspiratorial smile.

Oh, you didn't do that, my eyes said to him.

I think I did.

Fine, but payback's a bitch.

Then, it won't be a far stretch for you.

I shook my head and smiled.

"Okay, Sir Eli, let's get these guys climbing!"

To my pleasure, the kids picked up on his nickname as well, which seemed to bother him enough to make me happy. Despite the annoyance of me being called "Fairy Princess" all morning, we worked efficiently and quickly together. We knew without saying a word to each other when to do something, picking up where the other had left off. I hated to admit it, but it looked like Mrs. Sanchez was right.

At lunch Eli followed through with his promise and got them pizza. The kids had lightened up a lot. They seemed to be laughing, joking, and talking about the experience with each other, except for one, a boy named Derek. He kept himself separated from the rest of the group. Something about him rubbed me the wrong way. I tried interacting with him a few times, but he would answer my questions with a shrug or a grunted word. At lunch, I decided to go where he sat alone, sketching, to try to get him to join the rest of the group.

"Hey, what are you doing over here?"

He looked up from his pictures depicting an assortment of beast-like monsters ripping people apart. *Hello, red flag.*

"I draw, too." I nodded at his sketches.

He bowed his head and continued drawing.

"Look, I understand about being independent and a loner. I am a loner, too, so I completely get that. But today is about being part of a team. It's about working with people you might not normally hang out or interact with or people you might not like too much. So today, I'd like you to try and get to know some of the others. Who knows? You might be shocked and meet someone you like. That's how some of my friendships have started."

He went on ignoring me.

"Derek?" I asked, trying to get his attention.

"Bitch, leave me alone," Derek shot out venomously.

"Excuse me?"

"*Bitch*, are you deaf?" he said louder.

Before I could react, Eli was there, pulling him off the bench by the front of his shirt. *Holy shit! How did he get here so fast?*

"Listen, I don't care what you do or say outside of here, but you will NOT disrespect her or anyone else while you are here. You got that?" Eli's voice seethed with anger.

I heard a barely audible mumble from Derek.

"What?"

"Yes," he yelled.

Without thinking, I walked to Eli and touched his elbow. It seemed to calm him. He let go of Derek and stepped backward.

"I think you're done for the day," Eli said.

My eyes widened. "Eli, no." He turned to look at me.

That *won't help him.*

He glared at me. *I don't give a shit.*

Eli, come on . . .

For a tense moment, I wasn't sure what he'd do. He exhaled before spinning on his heels. "All right, fine. Lunch time's over."

We were on the last course of the day. Eli led the group up through the trees on the ropes. The last event had them zip lining down to the ground, where I stood waiting for them on the giant air mattress. By now, almost all the bad attitudes disappeared, replaced by smiles and laughter, and it looked like some new friendships had developed.

A handful of squealing pre-teens already zipped down onto the mattress with gleeful laughter, when I noticed Derek watching the kid in front of him, Kevin, with unveiled hatred. Derek pulled something out of his pocket. Whatever it was, it glinted in the sunlight. Fear darted up my chest. While Eli and Kevin were distracted, Derek leaned over the rope.

Oh please, no.

Eli hooked the rope on Kevin. Before I could react, Kevin jumped off the platform.

"Eli, no!" I shrieked.

Eli's head shot up and looked at me in panic. My focus was on the kid. Kevin was screaming with joy as he sailed down the zip line, but his delight turned to utter fear as the rope snapped. His small body flailed wildly as he plummeted.

I screamed in horror, leaping off the mattress and running toward the falling boy. With everything in my body I wanted to reach him in time. I had to stop this from happening.

Energy surged inside me and suddenly I was closer to Kevin than should have been possible. His body was only a few feet from the ground when another rush of power ran through me. I dove for him, hitting the ground hard. His body stopped falling and paused in the air before floating into my outstretched arms. I stared at Kevin, his shocked expression mirroring mine.

I blinked as darkness seeped into my vision and quickly took me with it. The last thought I had before blacking out was I had stopped Kevin from hitting the ground—with my mind.

"Em . . ."

My ears took in my name, but my brain grappled to comprehend its meaning, letting it slip away again. The blackness called to me like an old friend, keeping my eyes shut. I longed to follow the soothing darkness into oblivion.

"Wake up, Brycin."

A husky voice gripped me, pulling me through the dark. I felt the sensations of someone touching my face gently. My lids slowly lifted, blinking against the bright daylight. My vision cleared to see a pair of unyielding green eyes. There was no hand on my face, but it still tingled with warmth. Everything flooded back to me, and I shot up into a sitting position, which I immediately regretted.

"Whoa, take it easy okay. You might be weak and dizzy for a bit." Eli steadied me.

"Is . . . is Kevin okay? Where is he?"

"Slow down. Kevin's fine. He's right here. We're more worried about you. You took quite a header onto the ground. You must have knocked yourself out when you caught him." Eli's tone was clipped and tight and his expression unreadable.

Instinct told me to play along, but the truth took over my thoughts. Could I actually control things with my mind? Years of incidents and denials flooded me. It seemed I was not only capable of pyrokinesis and technokinesis, but I may be telekinetic as well.

What kind of freak was I? Some science experiment? How was I able to do these things?

Crap on ash bark!

It was a funny phrase my mother would say sometimes when she got really upset. It seemed appropriate right then.

I stood and turned my attention to Kevin. "Are you okay?"

"Yeah, I'm cool." He nodded and smiled. There wasn't a scratch on him, but I could tell he was putting up a front for his friends. He, too, knew something wasn't right.

I smiled back, but it felt wrong. They all seemed to think I caught him. I did, but it was not the entire truth. I had watched his body stop and float before it settled into my arms.

I rubbed my face, my brain trying to take it all in. I felt weak and sick to my stomach. I shook my head, trying to make the images replaying in my head fly out of my ears.

My eyes landed on Derek. I thought he would look away with fear or have a guilt-ridden face, but he didn't. Derek held my gaze defiantly; a cruel smirk twisted his lips. Didn't he have a clue I saw what he did, or didn't he care?

Eli stepped in front of me, blocking my view of Derek. He grabbed my elbow where I was bleeding through my t-shirt. He pulled the sleeve up, revealing a large gash on my arm.

"Let's get a bandage on it," he said, sounding as if I were an aggravating nuisance.

"I'm fine," I replied but squeezed his arm to draw his attention to my face.

It was Derek. He cut the rope. My eyes looked intently into his as I tried to get my message across.

I know. Eli gave a slight nod. *I got it covered.*

I was so glad when the bus arrived to pick up the kids. The guard who had dropped them off earlier greeted us again. I couldn't recall her name, but she wasn't paying any attention to me anyway. She was looking and smiling at Eli like he was a cream-filled cupcake. I couldn't stop my eyes from rolling.

As Derek passed to get on the bus, Eli's hand clamped down on his shoulder and yanked him back. As much as Derek tried to hide it, panic and fear flashed across his face.

Eli turned to the guard. "I need to speak to you about this one."

If I was glad to see the kid's school bus arrive, I was even more thrilled to see it drive away. It disappeared around the corner with eleven kids going home and one on his way to juvie.

The moment the yellow vehicle disappeared, Eli abruptly headed for his bike. "Let's go," he said harshly.

I could feel the animosity oozing off him. At the moment I didn't have the energy to wonder or care what his problem was with me now. I simply turned and followed him to the Harley. I felt weak and overwhelmed. All I really wanted was to sleep.

Eli turned the bike around in the parking lot to start for the school but slammed on the brakes. My face and body squashed into his back. "What the hell?" I muttered into his leather jacket.

Eli's body was tense, and all his attention was on something in front of us. I peeked around him to see a tall, gorgeous man leaning against a railing in the parking lot. He smiled at me, but something in his eyes told me he was anything but friendly.

"What are you doing here, Lorcan?" Eli inquired.

The strain in his voice put me on edge. The name sounded familiar, but I forgot where I heard it.

"Not a very polite way to greet your brother."

Brother. Right. I heard the name from Ryan.

I could now see the family resemblance. Lorcan was a few inches shorter than Eli, and he had an oval face unlike his brother's angular facial structure, but those were the major difference between them. They shared the same color eyes and hair, but Lorcan's hair was cut close to his head. He looked to be older but still had to be in his twenties.

"I am not a very polite guy. Blame it on my upbringing," Eli responded.

Lorcan smirked, propelled himself off the railing, and sauntered toward us. I knew was in the presence of another Riders of Darkness member. I sucked my breath through my teeth. Running in the opposite direction was now looking like an extremely good idea.

"So are you going to introduce me to your *friend*, Eli?" Lorcan's eyes were locked on mine as he proceeded closer, like he was stalking me.

The desire to run and hide overwhelmed me even more. In an anomalous moment, Eli became my safety. He had always scared and unsettled me as if at any instant he would turn on me. But right then, Eli's body heat was like a security blanket that I wanted to wrap myself into, protecting me from Lorcan.

Eli glared at his brother. Through gritted teeth, he said, "Ember, this is my brother Lorcan. Lorcan, this is Ember." He hit the kickstand with his boot and swung off the bike.

"Ember, it's a pleasure to finally meet you." Lorcan reached out his hand to help me off the Harley. I instinctively jerked away from his grasp as I slid off the back of the bike.

"Finally?" I stepped away, putting distance between us.

"Yes, he's been keeping you from us."

"What do you mean? I haven't known him long."

My eyes darted to Eli in confusion, but his gaze was lost in the surrounding forest. I felt a strange sinking sensation. "What is he talking about?"

"You are important, Ember. To me, to Eli . . . but I'm afraid it's not in the way you are hoping."

"Lorcan," Eli growled. It was so deep and guttural it forced me back in fear.

"What is going on?" I demanded.

"Yes, Eli, what is going on?" Lorcan crossed his arms with amusement. "Maybe you can enlighten me on what you are doing."

"Lorcan, I'm warning you." Eli stepped closer to him. "Don't forget who is in charge."

"How can I forget, *little brother.*" Lorcan's voice was filled with abhorrence and anger.

"I think it's time you go." Eli stepped even closer to Lorcan and puffed up his chest.

Lorcan's eyes narrowed, but he averted his gaze. It was like watching animals in the wild claim their territory, and it was obvious who won this round. The authority Eli had over his brother was clear.

"Are you really willing to give it all up?" Lorcan spat at Eli. "Get your head on straight, brother."

He turned to look at me with disgust. "Take care, Ember. We'll be seeing each other really soon."

His voice sent chills shooting down my spine. He pivoted and in an instant disappeared into the forest. Eli and I stood in silence. There was little doubt as to an underlying threat in Lorcan's words.

FIFTEEN

"What the hell is going on, Eli?" My voice shook slightly. I hadn't noticed until then my body was trembling.

Eli rubbed his forehead as he looked at me. "Nothing. Don't worry about it. Lorcan is full of it. Forget about him."

"Forget? Are you joking?" I shrieked. "Tell me what is going on because none of this is making any sense." A muscle in his jaw twitched. The determination to remain mute on the subject was clear on his features. He wasn't going to tell me anything.

I let my shoulders sag. My energy was still low from the "saving Kevin" episode. I felt depleted by the day.

Closing my eyes, I willed myself to stay upright. When I opened them, Eli was studying me like a lab rat which was exactly how I felt. I let out a strangled laugh, and turned, and walked away from him. My security blanket had returned to its normal prickly state.

I needed to get away from him, from everything. I couldn't wait to get home. The walk to the bus stop would take forever. I was still in the middle of nowhere. It wasn't something I looked forward to, but it was my only option.

I wasn't watching where I was going as I hurried down the road. The sound of grinding tires slid over gravel as a Harley came to a stop in front of me. I jumped back with a startled yelp.

Eli's chiseled jaw protruded with arrogance under his helmet. "Get on," he said curtly, without even looking at me. Shock, anger, and frustration welled in me and caused me to stand there mutely glaring at him. "I won't ask you again."

"You're asking me? It was more an order," I spat back.

"*Ciach ort!*" He hit the handlebar with his fist. "Get on."

I crossed my arms. "What did you call me?"

Eli sighed deeply, sounding even more annoyed. My stubbornness kicked in, and I moved around the bike and continued to walk. I stomped through the puddles, my anger giving me strength as I plodded on. A muffled string of profanity came from behind me. My lips twitched into a satisfied smile, which quickly disappeared at the sound of a bike engine being cut.

Dammit!

"Brycin," he called, his voice low and strained. "Will you *please* get on the bike?"

"Why?" I whirled, but dizziness made my vision spin. Eli was there. His solid hand caught me as I stumbled.

"Because it's . . ." He paused and seemed to think better of what he was going to say. "Because you can barely stand."

"What do you care?"

He gave me a level look and stepped aside to make way for me. I wanted to protest, but I didn't have the energy or the desire. I let him walk me back to his motorcycle. He took off his helmet and pushed it roughly at me. I put it on without argument. I fastened the strap under my chin, feeling the warmth from his head still clinging to the inside of the helmet.

I climbed onto the rear seat. He mounted the bike and scooted back into me, my arms wrapping around him. As angry as I was, I found myself hyper-aware of his incredible physique pressing into mine. The intense heat from his body warmed mine, making me feel the need to sleep—or throw up—I hadn't quite decided yet. I only knew the closeness to Eli stirred contradictory feelings in me; he both unnerved and relaxed me.

Most of the way we rode in silence. I tried to stay awake but the hum of the motorcycle started to lull me to sleep. My life had changed today, and it left me feeling exhausted.

We came to a stoplight, and the sound of Eli's phone buzzing brought me out of my haze. He dug into his pocket, looking at the screen. There was a picture of a stunning, dark-haired girl blowing a kiss. She definitely wasn't Sam. Before I could stop myself, I blurted out, "Girlfriend?" My voice sounded more clipped than I wanted it to. It wasn't as if I cared if he had a girlfriend or *girlfriends*. Did I?

"Something like that." He shrugged as he stuffed the phone back into his pocket.

"Right . . ." I got his meaning and quickly looked away, bile rising in my throat.

We continued riding in silence until he steered off the road into my driveway. I slipped off the Harley and was unhooking the helmet when it hit me. *I never told him where I lived.* A meshed warning of confusion and alarm hit me.

"How did you know the way here?" My eyebrows scrunched down.

"Don't go walking into the woods or anything," he said, ignoring my question.

"What?" I looked at him, baffled.

"Don't. Go. In. To. The. Woods," he spoke slowly, as if to an imbecile. It made me want to hit him—excessively.

"Answer my question. How do you know where I live?"

"Just do what I say, please." He sighed again, sounding put out and extremely tired.

A guttural, agitated noise bubbled up. I shoved the helmet hard into his chest and started up the stairs to the door.

"Brycin?" I turned. "This changes nothing between us. This is only a truce for now."

I felt so zapped of energy, of pride, of emotion I merely nodded and turned back to the house. The roar of motorbike echoed through the air as he tore out of the driveway. I was tempted to throw my backpack at his head.

I unlocked the front door and let myself in. Dropping my book bag in the entry, I went straight for my room, fell onto my bed, and welcomed the sleep my body had been longing for.

"Wake up, mo chuisle." Torin's voice settled sweetly into my ear.

My eyes opened to him leaning over me. Air hiccupped in my chest as I took in his beauty and his proximity.

"Torin." I sat up. I felt the forest around me, how it was breathing and communicating. It was as if I were part of it, but it didn't scare me.

A red fox sat in a patch of grass nearby, staring at me. The familiarity in its huge, beautiful eyes tugged at something in my gut. It cocked its head and whined. The pain and longing in its gaze made my heart break. I had to look away.

"Ember, I need you to understand what I am trying to show you . . . what you are. Your powers cannot be hidden any longer. Others are now aware of your existence, and she will find out about you soon."

"Who will find out about me?"

A whimper came from the small fox as it stood. Torin's piercing gaze silenced the animal. It lowered its head and sat again.

"I am forbidden to say." Torin looked down, nervously licking

his lips. My gaze latched onto them. I imagined what it would feel like to kiss him, to have those soft lips on mine.

I really needed to learn to focus.

"Ember, I am trying to keep you safe, and the only way to do so is for you to be ready for what is coming. You know what you are capable of. Stop denying the truth. You are not one of them." His warm hand cupped my face. "Your mother did a good job hiding you, but she can no longer do that. She left clues for you. Clues you can and need to reason through."

The fox whined again, sounding more desperate. When I looked back to where it was, the fox was gone. When my head snapped back to Torin, I found he had disappeared, too. I was alone.

My lids cracked open, and I saw the sun was setting. I lay there, getting my bearings before I swung my feet onto the floor. Torin's face was still so vivid in my mind.

It was funny I had dreamed about a red fox. They had been my mother's favorite animal. She would go to Canada for weeks to study and take pictures of them. She had her articles and pictures featured a lot in *National Geographic* and with WWF. The fact they were in danger of becoming extinct made her crazy with rage. I guess dreaming about them was the same as dreaming about my mother.

Torin's voice replayed in my head. *"Your mother did a good job hiding you. She left clues. Clues you can and need to reason through."*

I stood and made my way to the door. Even if it were only a dream, my curiosity got the better of me. After what had happened today with Kevin and the incident with Lorcan, how could I keep pretending all these things didn't mean something?

As long as I could remember, I had had certain abilities—the way I felt the energy of nature when surrounded by it, the way I healed in record time, the way fire seemed to be attracted to me as much as I was drawn to it. It wasn't until after Mom's death did I think there was something wrong with me—these things weren't normal, that I was a freak. How could a mother not know something was strange about her child? She had to, right? Did she really leave clues for me like Torin said? But why? What was it that she couldn't simply tell me?

The only place I knew which had any important documents or ties to my past was the trunk at the end of Mark's bed. It was full of photo albums, old report cards, and other stuff my mom had saved that neither Mark nor I could get rid of. If she had been aware of my "talents," this was the only place I could think of which might hold some answers.

I opened my door, listening for any movement in the house. "Mark?" I shouted. "Are you home?" Silence greeted me in response. Maybe he was still at work.

Mark wouldn't care if I went into his room, especially to look at my mother's old photo albums and documents. He would have joined me which was exactly what I didn't need. I didn't want to be asked why I was going through them.

I snuck into Mark's bedroom. As I had suspected, he wasn't there. I knelt in front of the old wooden steam trunk. The lid whined in protest as I opened it. On top were several shoeboxes filled with my drawings and paintings. My heart stung as I pulled out one with "Mommy, I love you" in crayon across the top. I flipped it over to see my mom's handwriting: "Ember, 5 years old." I traced her handwriting with my finger, the pain in my heart growing. I placed my drawings aside and continued searching. There were several photo albums full of Mark and Mom's wedding and our camping trips. It hurt so much to see my mom's beautiful face smiling, laughing—alive.

I shut the books and moved on. Grabbing my baby book, I flipped through the pages. I had never noticed or cared before, but my baby book didn't start until I was at least a few months old. There were no pictures of me at the hospital or pictures of us coming home—nothing. That seemed odd. Most people take a video or pictures of every moment of their new baby's life. Granted, I didn't have a father who would've been there with a video camera, but you'd think someone would have been. No friends or even a nurse. If not, then wouldn't Mom take pictures when we got home? I also found it odd she didn't list any of my firsts—my first steps or my first words. It was like she didn't want any written record of me.

I was about to toss the album aside when I noticed a cut on the back of the leather cover. Sliding my fingers inside, I felt a soft piece of fabric. I tugged it out. It was a two-inch cut of cloth. The fabric was nothing I had ever felt before. It seemed as if it was made of something softer than fleece, cotton, and velvet all rolled into one. It was a beautiful yellow. It must have been from a baby blanket of mine. One I couldn't remember.

Something along the edge of this fabric caught my attention. I examine it, and a gasp escaped me. Woven into the cloth creating a border on the blanket was my tattoo design. It was the exact motif of symbols I had seen in my dream after my mother died and was the same design I had sketched and had tattooed on my back.

Thoughts tumbled around in my brain like clothes in a dryer. I found it difficult to breathe. My subconscious must have made me dream of the markings. Somewhere deep in my brain, I must have remembered the blanket. It was the only thing that made sense.

I didn't want to probe into old memories anymore, which only seemed to conjure more questions than answers. Returning the contents to the trunk, a paper slipped out of one of the albums onto the floor next to me. I picked it up. It was my birth certificate. Without knowing why, my heart pounded as my eyes ran over the document.

Name: Ember Aisling Devlin Brycin
Date of Birth: November 28
Place of Birth: Sedona, Arizona
Mother: Lily Brycin
Father: Unknown

So many things stood out that didn't seem right. First thing was my date of birth, which said November 28 but without a year. It was smudged beyond recognition. My birthday was October 23. Why would they have mistakenly listed my birthdate over a month later? And why didn't they fix the mistake, if it was one? The next was my place of birth. As far as I knew I never set foot in Arizona. Mom had never mentioned I was born there. I always thought I had been born in Colorado. We lived there until I was two, then moved to California. Why was my birthplace wrong? Everything on the paper, except my name and my mother's name, was incorrect or different from what I had believed was the truth.

The certificate only brought up more questions. It made no sense. Why had my mother lied? What else had she kept from me? They could have been simple errors, but something in me said there were too many coincidences in my life right now for these to be mere mistakes.

SIXTEEN

The next morning an old red 1969 Ford Bronco was parked outside my house. I stiffened with apprehension. Eli leaned against the car. "What are you doing here?"

He ignored my question. "You ready?"

I sucked in a deep breath. *Is it too soon to start on the future alcohol problem?* "Sure." I shrugged, tugging my bag higher on my shoulder. I was tired of trying to figure him out.

I climbed into the Bronco and watched his lean, muscular form swagger around it. His hair was still wet from his shower and slicked back off his face. I had to force myself to look away, a flutter stirring deep inside me as he climbed in. The smell of soap and something else I couldn't place filled the car. The flutter turned into a pounding. "Whose car is this?" I tried to distract myself.

"Mine," he replied.

"Till the police come for it?" I was only half teasing.

"You think I stole it?" He cocked an eyebrow at me. "I saved this baby from the car graveyard and fixed it up a bit. Put in an old diesel engine, so it runs off vegetable oil now."

I gave him a double take. "I've never met anyone who has done this in our age group. My mom had a car she changed over to run

121

off vegetable oil, too." I was astounded. "Sorry, I'm a bit surprised."

"Why? Because I care about the environment?"

"N-No . . . I . . . well, yeah, to be honest with you." I laughed, not sure why I was so amazed. He was constantly throwing me off kilter one way or another. "I'm impressed."

He shrugged, not seeming to care about my opinion.

"What about the Harley?"

He smirked as he pulled the Bronco out of my driveway and headed north. "I won the Harley off some guy at Mike's Bar, a guy who bet more than he could back." He didn't say anything else, making me extremely curious about the full story. I was sure it wasn't good or legal.

I had already heard of Mike's less than stellar reputation. Eli's part of that world. If he could hang out there and have enough authority at such a young age to ride off on another man's Harley-Davidson, I wondered how frightening Eli truly was. And I was alone with him. The idea sent a cold chill down my spine. Shaking my head, I forced the scary thought from my mind.

The sun nudged the thick fog, casting a warm glow on me through the windshield as we drove. I turned my face up, trying to heat the chill in my body. It felt so good to feel any kind of warmth.

"You miss living in California?"

My eyes flew open at the sound of his deep, rumbling voice. I was shocked by the sincerity of his question. "I do, a lot. I miss the area. I really miss my house."

Our old house represented my mom. When we were happy. When she was alive. I could still recall the sound of my mother's voice and the sweet smell of cinnamon and apples filling our home. Tears pricked my eyes as I thought of her. Realizing how vulnerable she made me feel, my stomach dropped in fear. I didn't like feeling weak or exposed to anyone, even more so with Eli. But it didn't feel like I was being forced to talk as I sometimes did with therapists or other people. It was more like I *wanted* to tell him these things, to finally open up to someone.

"I didn't want to come here, and at first I thought I would hate it. Most of the time, I think I still do. But, it's strange. In a way, I feel like I'm supposed to be here right now, you know? It's like I'm split between two worlds, and I belong equally to both or equally to neither."

Eli avoided looking at me but nodded slowly. "Yeah. I know."

"Are you from here?"

"No," he replied. I waited, but nothing more came. "So what made you move here?"

"My stepdad, Mark, was offered a job. It was a great opportunity for him, and I wasn't going to be the reason he didn't take it. I couldn't stand in his way." I left out the fact we moved here partly because of me accidentally blowing up my old school.

"What about your mom? How does she feel about the move?"

I looked down in my lap. "She wanted this for him."

He seemed to sense not to pursue it further, and he turned back to questions about Mark. "You and your stepdad are close, then." It was more of a statement than a question.

"Yes, we are. He's amazing and the only dad I've ever known. I was seven when my mom married Mark. From the moment she introduced us, Mark and I clicked, becoming instant family."

"And your real father?" he asked hesitatingly. "Sorry, forget that. I didn't mean to pry," he added. From the way he was looking at me, I must have had a "don't go there" expression on my face.

"No, it's fine. I mean, there's really not much to say. I've never met him. He's never wanted anything to do with me, and he ran off as soon as he heard my mom was pregnant. All I know is he's now living in New York somewhere with a wife and kids." I didn't elaborate, and he didn't ask anything more. I couldn't believe how much I was telling him anyway.

I was disappointed when Eli drove into the site. I was enjoying our talk without the claws coming out. I wasn't ready for it to end.

"So what about you?" I asked as we climbed out of the Bronco. "What's your story?"

"No story." Eli shrugged as he walked toward the ropes course.

"Wow, I have to say you are an incredible story teller. It was so detailed and descriptive. I felt like I was right there with you. I know you so much better now."

He stopped suddenly, and I almost ran into him. "Let's stick to the job."

"Oh, what? It's okay for you to ask me personal questions, but I can't ask you?"

"I asked . . . you chose to reply. It was your decision. You didn't have to," he said dryly. "I opted not to answer yours."

An aggravated scream built up inside me. Holy shit! This guy could cause me to become violent. Embarrassment, anger, and hurt cut through me. "You're a jerk, you know that?"

"So I've been told."

His retorts only riled me more. He started up the hill again, but I stayed put. Murder was extremely high on my "things I was most likely to do next" list. But I didn't really want to add the infinite amount of hours to my community service for homicide.

Eli sensed I was not following, so he turned. "What?" I continued to stare at him. I could tell he was getting as aggravated with me as I was with him. He breathed in deeply, calming himself. "What's the problem?"

"I don't think this is going to work." I motioned at both of us.

A mischievous grin spread over his face. "Do we already need to seek counseling?"

I didn't respond but turned around and started down the hill. I had enough of Eli's ping-pong moods to last a lifetime.

"Brycin, stop!"

When I didn't, I heard him let out a low, irritated growl. I could hear him moving behind me. Like lightning, I felt the warmth of his fingers skim the back of my arm. "Stop," he grumbled into my ear.

I paused. The feeling of his breath against my neck made me close my eyes in ecstasy. *Come on, Ember. Get a grip.*

I turned and looked at him, which was a mistake. His tall, amazingly built form made me lose my breath and feel hot all over. Suddenly finding my shoes fascinating, I tried to gather my strength. I wanted to stay mad, but I kept imagining myself throwing him down on the ground and devouring him. Oh, jeez, I'd never hear the end of it if I did come back with foliage burn on my back. *Damn you, Ryan, for putting those thoughts in my brain!*

His voice brought me back to reality. "You know I'm an ass, so did you really expect anything less?"

"No, you're right. I wouldn't want you to be anything less than the true asshole you are."

He smirked, his eyes glowing bright. They seemed iridescent at times. "All right. So back to work?"

"Yeah." I sighed, resigned. "Let's go." We walked in silence for a little bit, but like a dog with a bone, I couldn't let him get away free and clear. "So . . . are you ever going to *choose* to answer my questions?"

"You don't give up do you?"

"No. Haven't you realized it yet?"

"It's starting to become apparent." He let out a sigh. "So what exactly do you want to know?"

Everything, I felt like saying. "I'll start simple . . . family. I know you have a brother."

"Was there an actual question in there?"

"Okay, fine. Do you have any other brothers and sisters? Mother and father? Step-parents?"

"Those aren't simple questions."

"Yes, they are. Pretty cut and dried, nothing too tricky there. No, I don't have any other siblings, or yes, I do have other siblings . . . seems pretty simple to me."

"Then, no and yes," he said.

I stared at him, his murder being planned in my mind. If there had been a brick wall at this site, I would have been banging his head or possibly mine against it—repeatedly.

He sighed. "Lorcan's the only family I have left who is blood, but I have people whom I consider my family."

So Eli didn't have biological parents around either. Something I could relate to.

"Let's get to work." He made it clear this was as much information as I was going to get. Eli unlocked the storage unit, pulling out the containers of harnesses and ropes, and we unpacked the bins. I wasn't ready to give up learning more about him, even if I had to pull teeth.

"The night I first saw you, you were handcuffed to a chair. What did you do?" We had never talked about that night. I felt myself become nervous, though I had no idea why.

He looked at me over his shoulder. "Let's say my track record is pretty consistent."

"Is being a team leader at Silverwood a punishment?"

"One of many. Sheriff Weiss asked Mrs. Sanchez to find something for me to do. Keep me out of trouble."

"So I'm gonna take that as you have to be here as well." I was trying to get him to admit the real reason he was here—the fact he saved me from being dragged downtown on a bogus alcohol charge.

"Take what you want from it."

If I deck him, how many more community hours would I get? No matter—it would be worth it.

It was so odd. I couldn't get over all the coincidences that kept putting Eli and me in the same situation together. From the first night I saw him at the police station, he had somehow become intertwined in my daily life.

"You do something to piss off Sheriff Weiss?" Eli asked nonchalantly.

"Besides breathing?" I asked sardonically. "I had an interesting situation happen to me this past week. Sheriff Weiss pulled me over for speeding and was about to take me in on alleged drug or alcohol intoxication, he didn't care which one, when out of the blue this guy pulls up on a black Harley-Davidson, flips off the sheriff, and tears out of there. The sheriff felt the need to go after him more than stay and deal with me."

"Sounds like you were lucky."

"I was," I said dryly. It was pointless to hope for a confession. Never in a million years would he admit he had helped me. He did—I knew it without a doubt—but he would never confess it. "But Weiss always finds a way. That jerk is seriously out to get me." I shook my head. "I think his personal mission in life is to make mine a living hell. I can't wait 'til I can get out of this town."

"Yeah, me, too." His eyes darted to mine then back down.

"Wow, did we actually agree on something?" A surprised laugh came up from inside me.

"We should declare it a national holiday."

"I agree. Okay, we've agreed twice. Cue *The Twilight Zone* music, please."

"I would cue it, if I knew what it was."

"You don't know *The Twilight Zone?*" He stared at me with a blank expression. "Seriously, how have you never seen or heard of *The Twilight Zone?* It's a cult classic TV show. How can you not know about it?"

"I don't watch much TV."

"Yeah, but you still would have heard of it. It's embedded in American culture. The theme song in itself is iconic." I hummed the first couple bars of the tune. I was making a fool of myself, but I couldn't seem to stop.

Eli tilted his head, a seductive smile breaking out across his face. "I guess I'll have to watch it, then."

"Yeah, you could come over. Mark has the original on DVD." The words were out before I understood what I implied. "I mean, I'll give it to you so you can watch it . . . I-I mean if you want. You don't have to."

The grin on Eli's face became even more melt-worthy as I babbled, which only made me more frazzled. His eyes moved over my body. When they locked on mine, they were so intense and raw. I felt the air leave my lungs. I couldn't handle it. I turned away so he wouldn't see me blush. I busied myself to break the charged moment.

I absently reached for one of the lead lines hooked to a tree. Missing it, I stumbled back, colliding into Eli's chest. His arms went around me and kept me from falling. He pressed against my back. Through the layers of clothes, the lines of my tattoo ignited, drawing in the heat from his body. My skin buzzed and twitched like I'd had too many espresso shots. Every nerve inside me went on high alert as extreme emotions ping-ponged around.

He shuttered violently behind me and roughly pushed me away. With his body no longer next to mine, I felt strangely empty, and the feelings and sensations vanished. I was paralyzed, unable to move or breathe.

What the hell was that?

Pinpricks of ice trickled down my back. I turned around stiffly, my eyes locking on Eli's. His wide, green eyes reflected the same panic and the same questioning fear in mine. I knew he had experienced something as well. He briskly checked himself and erected his stonewall exterior again, his eyes becoming glinting slits of anger. They accused and blamed me, immediately putting me on the defense.

"What?" I sputtered, breaking the silence. My eyes narrowed. He continued to stare at me, searching my face. *"What?"* My arms flapped, exasperated.

His mouth opened as if he were about to say something but snapped shut. Rubbing his hand over his face and then up through his hair, he shook his head as if to clear his thoughts. He turned sharply and stalked toward the woods.

Shock, confusion, and fear left me standing there, bewildered. My brain was so befuddled I couldn't even make a decision on what to do. Anger sparked through me. *How dare he walk away like he did?*

My fury was covering what I really felt and feared, but before I realized it, I was storming after him anyway. I pushed away any thoughts telling me to stop. Finally, I spotted him through the trees, standing with his back to me.

"What do you want?" he snapped, without turning around.

"I don't know." I shrugged. "But something strange is going on. I know you experienced it back there as well . . . whatever it was."

He turned his head, looking at me as if I were crazy.

"Don't act like you don't know what I'm talking about. You know something happened . . . between us."

His body went rigid, and he swung around violently to face me. "I have no idea what you're talking about. But I can tell you one thing. Nothing occurred or ever will between us."

His tone told me the idea of being with me was the most insulting, disgusting thing that could ever happen to him. I stepped back hurt, chagrin flooding into my face.

"Th-th-that's not what I meant," I sputtered.

"Listen, whatever fantasy you have going on in that silly, little head of yours . . . isn't. So do yourself a favor and get far away from me. Leave the area if you have to."

It felt like someone slapped me. I took a step back. Rarely did I cry. My heart had hardened too much after my mother's murder. I wasn't prepared when my eyes filled with tears. I bit down on my lip. He would not see me cry. But I must not have been fast enough because instantly his eyes were searching mine.

Something flashed through his expression, but I couldn't make it out. He regained his composure and walked away again, grumbling to himself.

I didn't understand. Why did he hate me? It didn't make any sense. Every time I was near him, I wanted to laugh or cry or maybe crawl into a hole.

I leaned against a tree, which helped center me. Sucking in a rugged breath, I collected my thoughts. I didn't understand Eli's vast mood swings, nor what had taken place between us. He made himself perfectly clear how he felt about me and whatever was going on, so I would take his advice. I was going to stay far away from him, and when we had to work together, it would be work and work only. The end of this day couldn't come soon enough.

The throng of Level 2 teens kept us busy with little time to interact, which was a good thing. When we did speak, we stuck to business, and I tried to keep my distance as much as I could. It felt like I was swimming upstream the entire time, but I was determined to end the attraction I felt.

When the day finally came to an end without an incident, I was relieved. I let out a breath as I watched the group get on the bus and ride away, no longer our responsibility.

Mark picked me up that evening, wanting to take me to dinner and spend time together before he left for Tokyo. He had an important ten-day conference there and was taking off Friday morning.

We went to one of his favorite restaurants. It was a lively Mexican restaurant which served margaritas in glasses the size of fish bowls. He really enjoyed them, and we had a good dinner, laughing and joking together. Mark was always able to lighten my mood and help me forget about the world.

Once outside the restaurant, Mark threw me the truck keys. "Here you go, kiddo, guess you're old enough to drive me home."

"Technically I have been for two years now. Remember, I'm an adult . . . as much as you try to deny the fact."

"I have to deny it. The truth of you being an adult is much too frightening for me to even comprehend," Mark jested.

I smiled, climbing into the driver's seat. Putting the keys into the ignition, I froze. Green eyes stared at me from across the street. Under a street light, Lorcan stood, a smirk hitching up his lip.

"Ember? Are you okay?" Mark asked. My attention was fastened on Lorcan. "Ember?"

"What?" My eyes never left Lorcan's.

"He will lead her to you. You are no longer safe." Mark's voice now sounded completely unlike him. My head twisted to look at Mark. Where he had been sitting, Torin now sat, his unnerving blue eyes examining me. The shock of seeing Torin sent me reeling back, my head cracking against the driver's seat window.

"Run," Torin's voice said inside my head.

"Ember? What's wrong?" Torin reached for me, but the hand touching my arm belonged to Mark. He looked at me with concern.

"W-Wh-What are yo-you doing here?"

"What do you mean, what am I doing here?" Torin's voice was wary. It didn't sound like Torin, but it wasn't Mark's voice either. It was like a mix of the two.

I squeezed my eyes shut. My hands were balled so tightly I could feel my nails breaking the skin of my palms. When I opened my eyes, Mark sat there again, peering at me with apprehension. I had wanted to keep what was happening to me from him, but how could I now? He was watching his daughter's mind slowly crumble in front of him.

"What is going on with you? What happened?" he demanded.

"Nothing," I mumbled. "I-I . . ." What could I say? There really was nothing I could say to explain what had occurred, except I was certifiably nuts.

"They are happening again aren't they . . . the hallucinations?" Distress etched his face. "I can't watch you go through this again, Em. I won't do it."

"I told you. I'm dealing with a lot lately."

"Cut the crap, Em." His tone turned even more serious. "I really hoped the therapy at Silverwood was going to help. I wanted so to believe the hallucinations hadn't returned, and you were better. The school therapy is obviously not enough." He shook his head, looking angry. "I also know your night terrors are back as well. You may think you're hiding them from me, but you're not."

I had convinced myself I'd been good at concealing them from Mark for the past five years. But since my birthday in October, the night terrors became a lot more aggressive and frequent.

"Remember our pact when I let you stop going to the therapist and taking your meds a few years ago? We agreed if anything like this started again, you would go back on them." He looked at me. "I don't want you to go through all the pain again."

"Therapy is helping. I swear. Please give it more time. I promise I'm getting better," I whispered.

Mark sighed. "I will give you until I come back from Tokyo. If the school therapy isn't enough, and you aren't getting better, I will be talking to Mrs. Sanchez and your counselors to get their input on which medications would be best for you and then discussing what steps we need to take next. Okay?"

I nodded. There was nothing else to do. How could I tell him these unexplainable things were actually happening to me? He already thought I was unstable. Causing Mark any kind of pain made me sick.

Starting the car, I looked back at the space where Lorcan had been.

It was empty.

SEVENTEEN

The icy raindrops lashed my face, making me tighten my hood as I headed to the bus stop for school on Monday. Mark watched my every move that morning, waiting to see if I would lick windows or talk to the refrigerator.

I barely slept, my brain going over yesterday's events: the way my tattoo burned when Eli touched me; our fight and him warning me to stay away from him; Lorcan watching me outside the restaurant; and seeing my father turn into Torin in front of me.

I wrapped my arms around myself. The biting wind seeped through my jacket, causing my bones to ache. I bowed my head, battling the elements, while crossing the street to the bus stop. I almost fell asleep standing until the bus finally came. I climbed the steps slowly and pulled out my bus pass to show it to the driver. I stopped short, the pass slipping through my fingers, falling to the floor.

Oh, God, not again.

A small, disproportionate man sat in the driver's seat. He could not have been more than four feet tall and barely able to reach the pedals. Long, pointed ears protruded high on his oversized head. His skin was wrinkled, thin, the color of parchment paper, and oozed with lumps, sores, and knobs. He had an elongated hooknose, and his puny, dark, beady eyes glared back into mine.

"Move to the rear," he snarled. I couldn't budge. My legs were locked in place. "Hey, did you hear me? Either get on or off. You're holdin' up the bus."

His razor-sharp teeth gleamed, causing me to jump back, almost falling down the steps. When I looked up again, a tall, grumpy-looking *human* sat in the driver's seat, his long skinny legs tapping on the pedals impatiently.

I bit my lip. *This can't be happening again.*

"On or off?" the old man barked at me.

I stepped onto the bus, pushing through my fear. The driver yanked the handle, slamming the doors shut, and punched the gas pedal. I stumbled down the aisle and flopped in a seat.

The hallucinations were proof I was unstable. As the doctors had said, my mind was creating its own little world so I could handle all the things happening to me. I clearly wasn't dealing well with the possibility of being a fire-starter or someone who could manipulate and move elements with my mind!

Over the years, these hallucinations had been infrequent enough for me to brush them off as something else. But things had changed. When they happened now, they were so life-like and intense it was hard to tell what was real and what wasn't. The only thing keeping them separate and me grounded was the hallucinations were always strange mythical creatures. I had no idea why my mind chose fantasy characters to see. Maybe the stories my mother used to tell me before bed were coming back to me. Maybe it was another way to feel closer to her, to produce the world she used to spend hours creating for me.

I was relieved when the bus arrived at the stop closest to Silverwood. I hurried off the bus without looking at the old man. Already late for school, I detoured from the main path, cutting through the woods. It was a shortcut that hopefully wouldn't make me any later.

Darkness adhered to the thick canopy of trees. Mist swirled on the forest floor, clinging to ferns and mossy rocks. Crooked limbs weaved through each other, creating intricate spider webs of wood. Trampling through a dark, dense forest might have spooked most people or made them uncomfortable. It relaxed me.

The shortcut drove me deeper into the woods. It felt as if energy trickled into my legs, making them itch for movement, to run. I broke into a brisk jog, my backpack banging rhythmically against my back. I sailed through the forest, weaving around trees and bushes with ease. Dampness clung to my face and hair as the mist thickened under the cover of trees. All the things that had been happening to me were begging to be released. I pumped my legs faster. The pulse of the woods pounded simultaneously with my heartbeat.

Then, I felt something change. It felt like the drumming beat of the forest shouted a warning. Something was off. Wrong. Alarm nipped at my insides.

I slowed and came to a stop. A stronger feeling of dread gripped me. I was being watched. Spinning around in a circle, I eyed the trees surrounding me. Nervously, I swallowed, searching for the forest's once-vibrant sounds of life. Total silence enveloped me and was only broken by the thumping of my heart. The quiet was what really unnerved me. Not a single bird chirped, and not any of the other natural sounds of a forest whistled through the air. You never realize how comforting those sounds are until they're gone. All the time I spent in the woods, I never felt uncomfortable. But now I did.

A trickle of sweat ran down my face. I didn't know what to do. There was no obvious threat, but my gut told me something was different. My inner awareness was something I had gotten from my mom. Our gut feelings were eerily right on, like a truth detector or a warning system.

I was fairly certain there were no bears or other aggressive wildlife around this area, but the sensation of being hunted rang like a bell inside my head. Panic rose up, and I stumbled backward until I pressed against a massive boulder.

My skin tingled, and blood pounded in my ears. Whatever it

was, it was getting closer, edging slowly towards me. This was it. I hoped it would be an animal that attacked me. Yes, I'd rather die as a bear's Happy Meal than as some girl murdered by a deranged serial killer.

A branch snapped, breaking the silence. The sound came from the opposite direction from where I felt the threat. My attention flew to the sound, searching the perimeter in front of me. Out of nowhere, a massive figure appeared. I jumped back, squeaking out a startled yelp. "You scared the shit out of me." I put my hand on my chest as I caught my breath. I looked back to where Eli stood. His features were hard and cruel. Even though it was only Eli, something kept me from thinking I was entirely safe. "What are you doing out here?"

"Surveillance."

"You mean you're following me."

"If some girls did what they were told . . ."

"Not something I'm particularly good at."

"So I've noticed."

"Okay, besides you being an extremely creepy stalker guy . . . how did you know I was out here?"

Eli cocked his head, staying mute. A spine-chilling smile stretched his lips. There was something dark and unsafe about him, and something today reminded me of the first night I saw him. He was forbidding, cold, and let's be honest, straight out scary. What if he had hunted me in the forest? He might find it amusing to play with me as a cat would a mouse. There was no denying his predatory nature. I couldn't put my finger on it, but there was something about him that felt more animal than man.

"Think it's time you got to class," Eli said.

"And once again, you think I'm simply going to jump at your every command." I folded my arms. "I don't know what kind of girls you've dealt with before. Maybe Samantha obeys your every order, but I don't."

Suddenly, he was in my face. I took several steps back. "Samantha has to." Eli leaned down, his lips brushing across my ear. "You will eventually submit . . . and happily."

My breath hitched. I was locked in place as he moved around me, and heat blistered through my mind and body.

It had only been a few seconds before I turned to say something, which I'm *sure* would have been very witty, and he was gone. I pivoted as my eyes darted in every direction. *Where the hell did he go?* There was no way he could've walked away that fast.

It also hit me—I hadn't even *heard* him leave.

EIGHTEEN

The rest of the day didn't get any better. Actually, it sucked. The thing that should have put me in a good mood was Mrs. Sanchez calling me into her office and telling me Principal Mitchell was willing to reassess my going back to my old school at the end of the month—if I continued to walk a straight and narrow path. The community service would remain in play, so I would still have to come back after school on Mondays, Thursdays, and the weekends for the next several months.

I should have been thrilled at the prospect of returning to school with my friends, but the news seemed to only darken the cloud hanging over me. I felt more at home at Silverwood, but the idea I would prefer to stay in a school for troubled students rather than a normal high school with my friends kept my lips sealed.

Poor Josh tried so hard to get me out of my funk, but my mind wouldn't let him. I did my best to smother any more thoughts about leaving Silverwood, the bus driver, and Eli. I dreaded going out to the O.A.R. site, and Josh had to practically drag me there.

"Are you going to tell me what's going on between you two?" His chin jutted toward Eli, clearly not a fan of Josh's.

"Nothing."

"Really?" Josh looked down at me. "Come on, Em, you guys act like you hate each other, but the sexual tension is so thick you could choke on it. It's pretty obvious something is going on."

"I promise you. Nothing is going on with him," I said adamantly.

"Good," he replied as we walked to the site. "Because one, he has a girlfriend, and two, he is not the type of guy you should get involved with. Bikers don't make good boyfriends."

I didn't bother clarifying Samantha was more of a sex friend than a girlfriend. "You don't have to preach to the choir here."

"I think I do."

I gave Josh a side glance and was about to respond further when I felt the unique thumping within, warning me Eli was near. Until he touched my tattoo the other day, I never really thought about exactly where the warning was coming from. My whole body seemed to react when he got close to me, so I wasn't surprised I hadn't noticed it 'til today. It was slight, but I could feel my tattoo starting to warm.

"All right, today two of us will be taking the wheelbarrow to get the compost. The rest will stay here and shovel it into the planters," Eli addressed the group. "Brycin, you're with me."

I'm sure I looked elegant as I sputtered, "Huh? Me? Why me?"

He smirked. "Because . . ."

Ah, I was being punished for this morning. He knew I had to obey him here. This was his way of seeing me "submit." *Bastard.* I didn't like it one bit. I glowered at him, fighting every instinct to tell him off.

"Come on, Brycin. The compost isn't getting any less foul." Eli jerked his head for me to follow.

Josh snickered like this only proved his theory.

"Shut up," I grumbled, which only made him laugh harder. I approached Eli who threw two shovels into the wheelbarrow.

He nodded toward it. "It's not going to push itself."

The more my eyes narrowed, the more his glinted with merriment. I gripped the handles and followed him despairingly, muttering obscenities the entire way.

When we got to the rotten pile of food, it took everything I had not to gag. Eli pulled the shovels out, handed one to me, and without a word, started scooping the foul-smelling compost into the cart. Reluctantly, I did the same. I found myself once again watching Eli. His sculpted arms flexed, and his broad shoulders strained his t-shirt as he burrowed his shovel deep into the dirt.

There was no way I could deny it. I was attracted to him. Drawn to him. I shook my head. *Shallow, Em?* He was hot, but I knew nothing about him. I didn't even know how old he was. In some way, she seemed ageless.

"Stop staring at me, Brycin."

I quickly looked away, embarrassed. *Wait a minute, his back was to me. How did he know I was looking at him?* "Ummm . . . can I ask you something?"

"I don't know, can you?"

I sighed. "Can't you ever answer anything straight?" He turned and gave me a look saying I should ask him a question now if I was going to. "I'm curious about how old you are." I looked to the side, my eyes not able to meet his.

"Okay, wasn't expecting that one." He regarded me for a bit before answering. "I guess I would be considered around twenty-four or so."

"Huh? What do you mean considered?"

"I mean I'm twenty-four," he replied hastily, returning to shoveling. *Twenty-four. Six years older than me.*

"How long have you been in your motorcycle gang?"

"You sure are nosey today." He stopped shoveling and wiped his brow. "And it's a club, not a gang."

141

"I'm sure that makes all the difference." I snorted, and he gave me a severe look. I would not let him intimidate me. I would find out more about him, even if it frightened the crap out of me. "So how long have you been with them?"

"All my life. It's something I was sort of born into," he said. "But I became a leader when we arrived here."

"Where did you live before?"

He gave an exasperated sigh. "Let's say I came from a place far from here," he replied. "Now get back to work, Brycin."

There was so much I wanted to know about him, but I didn't dare ask. We fell back into a comfortable silence. The sounds of the shovel sinking into the earth and lifting the compost into the wheelbarrow drew me into a soothing trance as we worked. Besides my need to hear his voice, everything seemed to be okay between us for a while. We weren't at each other's throats, which would have been encouraging except we weren't talking at this moment.

I pulled my hair up into a ponytail to get it out of my face.

Eli drove his shovel into the compost pile, a glistening sheen starting to cover his forehead. "So . . . your tattoo . . ."

Those three words made the world halt around me. He was bringing up the exact subject I thought he would do everything in his power to avoid, denying it every happened.

"Yeah, what about it?"

"What is it?"

"It's only some symbols I sketched. It represents someone I love." I avoided talking about my mom. Every time I did, it felt like I was being stabbed in the heart again, so I turned the question back on him. "How big is the one on your arm?" I pointed to his shoulder.

"It's big. It goes around to my back and side and down to my thigh." He pulled up his sleeve, showing me a bit of his tattoo—inked lines wrapped around his biceps, slinking up to his shoulder.

From what I could see, it definitely looked like the same one I saw on his torso. My pulse raced. My fingers longed to reach out and touch his tattoo, to slide underneath his sleeve and trace the lines until they reached his back—or pull up his shirt and let my hand trickle down his abs. I gripped my fingers to stop them from acting on impulse.

Focus, Em!

"Does it mean anything?" I finally asked.

His tone and face were serious. "It's my gang tattoo."

"Right." I smirked, getting his jab.

"If you have a tattoo in this town, it's assumed you're in a tough biker gang. But let me give you a little advice. It helps if you do have a bike."

"I got a ten-speed. Does that count?"

"You are so badass."

"Hey, when I ring the bell, you should see them clear out of the way."

Our eyes connected. Heat steamrolled my veins, sending fire through me as something else traversed between us.

We worked harmony for the next two hours, going back and forth between the compost pile and the O.A.R. site, loading and dumping the fertilizer. We were both sweaty and I'm sure smelly. I was amazed at how comfortable I felt next to him, and strangely, the closer he was, the better I felt.

After school, Eli and I headed to the ropes course site. We didn't have to deal with kids during the week. On Mondays and Thursdays for the next two weeks, as a part of our community service hours, we had to set up the obstacle course and the paintball area for the summer schedule.

In the storage unit were old tires, different types of ropes, a balance beam, and other items used for the obstacle course. I liked that Eli didn't think I couldn't handle some of the heavier stuff because I was a girl. He treated me like an equal, even though I was sweating by the time we got to the climbing wall.

We were chaining some tires together when Eli stopped. His eyes darted around the forest as he sniffed the air. I should have found his actions peculiar, but the uneasiness I felt about his abrupt change in demeanor made any other concerns trivial.

I searched the area, looking for whatever Eli was sensing. "What's wrong? Do you hear something? Is something out there?"

"Shhh," he responded, not even looking at me. He crept toward the woods.

"Eli?" He ignored me, too focused on the forest in front of him. He disappeared into the throng of overgrown brush.

I trotted to the edge of the brush and looked around; Eli was still nowhere in sight. "Eli?" Nerves danced in my stomach. Warily, I stepped deeper into the thick of the forest. "Eli?" I repeated a little louder. I heard a strange, low growl and the snap of splintering wood. Then, silence.

I wasn't sure how long Eli had been away. Fear prickled my skin. My breath became short and almost stopped when a large, dark mass stepped out from the bushes. I screamed and turned to run. A large, strong hand grabbed my arm, pulling me back.

"It's me." Eli's deep voice immediately calmed my jumping heart.

"Damn it! You scared the hell out of me . . . again." I leaned into him, trying to catch my breath. "You seriously need to stop sneaking around. I thought you were some psychotic murderer!"

"I might be," he said, moving past me. I felt the chilliness of his mood. The easy-going feeling from earlier was gone.

"Where did you go?"

"I had to take a leak. I'm sorry. Did you want to watch?" I knew he was deflecting, but something about his mood kept me from pursuing it.

I turned to follow, then stopped short. The back of his t-shirt hung in torn, shredded pieces. "What the hell happened to your shirt?"

He halted, twisting his neck to look over his shoulder at the ragged cloth. An odd look flickered across his face. "Oh, I must have snagged it on a branch."

"That was some branch. Did it have a vendetta against your t-shirt?"

"Guess so."

"I hope you showed it who is boss."

"Yeah, I peed on it."

I rubbed my head. Of course there was an image that attached itself to his statement, and it wasn't a totally bad one.

"Think we can call it a day," Eli said, looking at his phone. "Come on." He motioned for me to follow.

"Where are we going?"

"Somewhere else." He hiked up a trail.

"Wow," I said quietly, taking in the amazing view. The setting sun cast a glow on the cascading waterfall as it sparkled in the distance. Crystal blue falls tumbled down the rocky surface, filling my ears with the soothing sound of rushing water as it connected with the flowing creek below.

I sat on the edge of the footbridge, my feet dangling. Eli sat next to me. I pulled out my thermos and took a drink. I automatically handed it to him, as if this was the most natural thing in the world to do. He took a swig and handed it back to me as we silently watched the gushing water plummet to the ground below. It wasn't until I took another sip that I thought about this little exchange between us. It felt extremely intimate and so natural, like it was an old habit of ours.

"This reminds me of a place my mom used to take me when I was young," I reflected.

He cleared his throat. "Your tone changes when you talk about your mom. You sometimes talk about her in the past tense. . ."

He left it hanging. My chest clenched. Most people, besides my two good friends, never picked up on my referring to her only in the past. Because he noticed and saw through me so easily, made panic churn inside. Feeling exposed, I looked down at my legs, watching them swing back and forth.

I had never told anyone the whole story except for the therapists Mark sent me to. They didn't count since I *had* to talk to them. Even with them, I had left stuff out. It wasn't something I wanted to talk about or wanted people to know. But there was something about Eli that made me feel he'd understand. Tragedy was interlinked with his life as well.

My chest constricted with heartache as I sucked in a staggering breath. "My mom was murdered six years ago. Exactly six years, one month, and eighteen days ago." A pain stabbed my heart. Saying it out loud made me realize how morbid it sounded—that I knew the exact number of days since her death.

"I was the one who found her." I gulped. It was a constant nightmare which clung to my soul and sucked it dry.

My heart twisted as I recalled the excitement I had felt, knowing she'd finally returned home from her research trip. "She had been gone for several weeks, the longest she had ever been away. I ran into the house calling for her, but there was no answer. I think deep down I knew something was wrong. I could feel it on my skin. I went through the whole house calling for her. Then I heard our dog whining from the backyard." I recalled Ray's high-pitched howl and how my stomach had dropped, twisting in trepidation.

"He never whined or barked unless he sensed something menacing, especially anything threatening my mother. That dog would have followed her to the ends of the Earth if he could. He had been abused so badly they didn't think he would live, but my

146

mother was not a woman who gave up on anything, especially animals. She stayed by his side day and night, feeding and nursing him back to health. She saved his life, but sadly, she could not save his eyesight. It had been too late, although it never seemed to slow him down. The love and dedication for each other was unreal. The fact he was a blind, black Labrador named Ray Charles only solidified my mom's sick sense of humor, something I definitely got from her.

"I could hear Ray's claws scraping hysterically across the glass door downstairs. I went downstairs to let him in . . ." My voice cracked as emotion flooded my memories. "There was blood everywhere." Images of bloody handprints and paw prints smeared and dripping across the sliding glass door flashed in my mind's eye. "It looked like dark, raspberry syrup had been spread across the glass. Ray threw himself at the door, trying to reach me, his paws splashing in puddles of blood, streaking more of the red liquid over the window.

"I don't remember moving forward or opening up the door, but I found myself on the patio. Th-there was this mass of something on the ground. The body was ripped apart . . . but I knew it was her." Bile instantly rose up as if it was reliving the moment again. Terror and grief still tore through me, shredding my heart as it ripped and clawed its way out. "I could pick out long, dark strands of hair tangled around the bloody mass. It was my mother's."

I breathed out sharply

"I remember hearing a scream pierce the air, sounding so agonized, so guttural and pained. It took me a while to realize it came from me." The vivid memories replayed in my mind like a movie. "Whoever did it really wanted to make a point. She had been torn into pieces, like she had been attacked by a bear or some wild animal. She was unrecognizable."

Eli stayed quiet for several minutes, as we watched the waterfall. "Your tattoo represents your mom," he said, more to himself than to me. His voice brought me back to the present.

I nodded. "I sketched these symbols from a dream I had one

night after her death." Every time a therapist forced me to recall that day, I became hollow. Empty. Dead. Eli's presence stirred raw emotions back into the wound, forcing me to choke back tears. "I got the tattoo so I could always have her with me. My mom, Lily was her name, was this free spirit, an independent, open-minded, sassy woman, with this deep love of the environment, especially animals. Her passion covered all animals, but her true love was foxes, especially the red fox. She had this unexplainable connection to them. She spent a lot of time with this specific skulk of foxes up in Canada doing research for a book."

I stopped when I realized I was rambling. When I looked up at Eli, he had a strange look on his face. "See, this is why I don't talk about it. It makes others feel awful and uncomfortable. What do you say to someone like me?" Eli avoided my gaze, his face blank of emotion. But I could see past the wall. "You know exactly how it feels, don't you?" I studied him.

When he told me earlier that Lorcan was the only blood family he had left, I figured it meant he no longer had his parents. But now I realized he, too, had lost them tragically. It was something you could sense if you had been through something similar. He was probably used to keeping it well hidden from others.

"You lost your parents, too?"

He stood up. Anger flashed over his face as he bristled defensively.

"I'm sorry," I said.

He grabbed me by the wrist, pulling me up. The cruelty was back in his eyes.

"Sorry?" He scoffed bitterly. "Fate is mocking me."

"What are you talking about?"

He moved closer to me. His eyes became distant and cold as they searched mine. The longer he looked, the more it seemed to incite wrath deep within him. His grip tightening on my wrist until my bones ached. I couldn't hold back a whimper. He released me and spun away.

"Why do you affect me?" he muttered. "I should hate you."

"Why?"

His response was to move toward the forest, retreating from my presence once again.

Later, instead of taking me back to Silverwood to catch the bus, which I figured he'd do, he drove me all the way home. The silent tension between us grew so thick that halfway there I debated about opening the door and diving out of the car to escape.

He had barely pulled up to the house before I was out of the car and running into the house.

NINETEEN

Tuesday and Wednesday passed by with little interaction with Eli. While he avoided me, Samantha seemed to go out of her way to make trouble. Her eyes were filled with looks of spite and malevolence. She probably sensed the strange tension between Eli and me and didn't like it.

On Thursday, when Eli drove us up to the ropes site after school, he did his best to remain true to his charade—pretending I was not there. The quiet drove me crazy because I could feel the hostility vibrating off him, the unsaid words hanging on him. Between the silence and the little sleep I was getting, I could only take so much of his bullshit.

I huffed, rolling my eyes. "So . . . it's going to be like this again?"

"Like what?"

I gave him a leveled look. "Like this." I motioned to both of us. "We go round and round. It's like our own warped version of 'Who's on First.'"

His lips twitched with a slight smile.

"Can I ask you something?" I was feeling bolder. Lack of sleep could do that. A smirk was the only response I got, which was enough for me to go ahead. "What is it about me that makes you

150

bipolar and so angry?" I stared at his profile, unflinching. He turned to look out the side window, his jaw strained as it clenched together in a tight line. "I know this charming personality isn't only for my benefit. I've seen how you are with others, but I know it comes on extra thick with me. So why do you hate me?"

There was a long silence after he parked the car. We sat in tense anticipation, neither of us moving for the door.

"I don't hate you." His voice was low and choppy. It almost sounded like he wished he did, and since he didn't, it was a huge nuisance for him. I stared at him, hoping he'd continue. He seemed to struggle with something, then shook his head and opened the car door. He grabbed both our backpacks and started for the site.

The strangled cry, which I wouldn't let reach my lips, howled inside me. I got out and slammed the door behind me, seething with indignation.

I had bared my soul, told him things I had never told anyone, and now I felt foolish for letting him in. *How could I be so stupid?*

My phone buzzed in my pocket. I pulled it out, looking at the caller ID. "Hey, Ryan, what's up?"

"Em, how's life on the chain gang?"

"Funny." A smile grew on my face from ear to ear.

"Kennedy already texted your dad telling him we're picking you up later today. He reminded us not to get you into too much mischief. So we were thinking a little B and E or robbing a convenience store. You know . . . a relaxing Thursday night."

"Oh, then it would definitely be a little breaking and entering, which always unwinds me after a long week," I replied.

"That's what I thought, but Kennedy was all for robbing a convenience store," Ryan exclaimed. "If they'll let you off for good behavior, where do we pick you up?"

"I'd be screwed if it was stipulated on my good behavior." I laughed. I gave him directions to pick me up by the parking lot near the waterfall.

"Sounds good. Oh, and guess what? To celebrate your impending release from the clink and the fact you will hopefully be back with Ken and me soon, I got us tickets for tomorrow night to Poisonous Mushrooms, the local band we've been waiting to see. So wear something hot . . . the sluttier the better. I heard that's an easy way to get backstage."

I had completely forgotten there was a chance of me leaving Silverwood at the end of the month.

"Then, *you* wear a slu . . ." My phone was snatched from my ear. "Hey!"

"Talk on your own time." Eli turned off my phone. "You can get it back later."

"Listen, you are not in charge here. You can't order me around!"

He lifted up his arms. "You wanna come and get it, then?" He nodded at the phone stuffed deeply into his front pocket.

I contemplated it. I seriously contemplated it. My eyes darted to him. *You are such a bastard.*

It's so hard being this good at something, his eyes replied.

Kiss my ass.

If you'd like me to start there.

I ground my teeth in irritation as opposing emotions rolled around in my stomach. The height of my maturity reared its ugly head. I stuck my tongue out at his back as he headed up the trail.

"I can think of many other uses for it than that," he replied, never even turning around.

I stood there, blinking in shock. *Does this guy have eyes in the back of his head?*

"You know, if you needed a ride home later, you could have asked." He turned to face me and walked backwards up the trail. A naughty, half-grin played on his lips, his voice was low and seductive. I wished every time I looked at him it didn't unnerve me

152

so much. Besides his "take me now" bad-boy looks, there was also something about him which both drew me in and terrified me.

"Yeah, but I prefer the rides that don't come with STDs."

Eli's mouth tugged at the corners as his eyes glowed with an evil mischievousness. "That would be the least of your worries." He turned, heading for the storage unit.

He seriously had to be bipolar.

I went the opposite way, walking in the direction of the obstacle course. It was safer to have distance between us.

Not until I was ankle deep in dirt and undergrowth was I able to calm myself. Blue skies opened up above my head, and an involuntary smile stretched across my face. It was colder today because there was no cloud cover, but seeing the sun made me want to crawl onto a rock like a snake and soak in every ray. Closing my eyes, I turned my face up to the warm sun, feeling my skin absorb the beams. I could feel myself slipping into a meditative state, becoming lighter as I relaxed.

I pictured myself as a leaf, fluttering in the wind. It felt so good to let go of all the stress and frustration. My eyes opened. Shock forced me to draw in a large gulp of air. Dozens of leaves were suspended in the air around me, floating in place. I knew I was capable of doing strange things, but it still frightened me. It was a clear sign I was not normal. I concentrated on an individual leaf, feeling the energy radiating from it. It floated back into the air. I opened my range, moving several more leaves at once.

Holy shit. I'm really doing this.

I heard a noise behind me. Whipping around, I saw Eli watching. The instant my concentration fractured, the leaves fluttered to the ground, some landing placidly on Eli's jacket. The look on his face made a chill creep into my body. The sun no longer felt warm on my skin. It was one thing to know something was different about me, but for someone else to see it was a whole other issue.

Picking a leaf from his jacket, he crushed it in his hand. His intense stare never wavered from mine. I expected shock, fear, or possibly awe, but he showed none of those reactions. The way he examined me was disturbing. I couldn't stay there another second. Grabbing my backpack, I ran for the trail.

"Where the hell are you going?"

I didn't respond but continued to hoof it down the hill. He never had the courtesy to tell me where he was going, so why should I?

"Brycin," he shouted.

Yeah, it doesn't feel so nice on the other side, does it?

I wanted time alone. I needed to think, so I proceeded to the waterfall. He would figure out where I went, I knew, but I was hoping it would give me some time. In all honesty, I didn't even know if he'd bother coming after me. At the moment, I didn't care.

When I got to the bridge, the sound of the water was soothing and comforted my soul. Dangling my feet over the edge, I stared at the water as it gushed down. Squeezing my eyes shut, I tried to focus on the sound of the crashing water, taking slow deep breaths.

Time became inconsequential to me. I lost myself to the revolving inquires in my brain.

Eventually I shivered with cold and became aware of my surroundings again. The sun was now melting below the horizon, leaving shadows in its wake. Ryan would be picking me up soon, and I couldn't let him see me like this. If Kennedy was with him, I had to be even more diligent. I swaddled my emotions tightly and placed them deep within. Forcing an easy-going smile on my lips, I reached around to grab my backpack. And stopped.

Several yards away, Eli leaned against a tree, his eyes gleaming through the dark shadows. Without question, I knew he had been there the whole time, watching me. Giving me space but keeping watch, making sure I was okay. Seeing his face made me forget all the warnings he had given me, the strange things that had happened between us, and that something told me I should run away from him, screaming.

154

I knew what I wanted. Needed. Without second-guessing myself, I got up and walked steadily to him, stopping only when I was a breath away from his lips. He didn't back away, but his expression was guarded, his eyes tracking my every movement. Without hesitation, I slipped my arms around his waist, leaning my head against his chest.

For a second he simply stood still, his body stiffening at my touch. I didn't let go. His heat only drew me closer. He let out a ragged breath, gradually wrapping his strong arms around me as he pulled me into a tight hug, laying his cheek against my head. We remained silent holding on to each other, pretending for just that moment the outside world didn't exist. His heart hammered against my chest, as mine slammed against his.

I felt safe, protected, and happy, and even though it wasn't true, I wanted to believe it was. We embraced for a long time, neither one of us letting go. Finally, I pulled back a little and whispered, "Thank you." He nodded as he let go of me, but he didn't move away. My mistake was looking into his eyes. They burned so intently I felt heat rise into my face. He made me want to do things I really shouldn't have been thinking about.

I stepped away, but his fingers curled around the front of my coat, pulling me back. I waited for an awkward, uncomfortable feeling to come over me. It didn't. All I could sense was heat blazing through my body. "Eli . . ." I weakly put a warning in my voice.

A grin hinted at his lips. He was aware I didn't really mean it. His roguish smile always caused my heart to jump up into my throat. I knew what it meant and felt helpless to stop it—I didn't want to stop it.

He bent slowly over me, giving me plenty of time to object. His hands still gripped the front of my jacket, tugging me closer, causing me to feel dizzy and breathless. His lips moved down to mine. I wanted to feel his lips so badly it was almost painful. His top lip barely grazed mine when a shrilling horn blasted through the air. We collided into each other as we jumped in shock.

"Oooowwww!" I reached up to my face. "My nose!"

"Your nose? You clocked my chin," he garbled as he put a finger into his mouth. "Oh, I think you made me bite my tongue." I laughed when he pulled his tongue out to inspect it. "You think it's funny?" He scoffed. "You are one seriously twisted girl."

The horn blared loudly again from the parking lot up on the hill. I looked up to where it was. Even though I couldn't see it, I knew the sound of Ryan's horn and knew he was waiting.

"No, none of this is funny." I became serious. "You're with someone else. We shouldn't be doing this."

"No, you're right, we shouldn't be." He looked off into the distance. "I also heard you're deserting Silverwood soon."

"How did . . . were you listening in on my phone call?" I demanded. Speaking of my phone, I remembered it was still confined deep in Eli's pants pocket.

He shrugged, still not looking at me.

"But I didn't say anything. How did you hear that?"

"I didn't. Mrs. Sanchez told me."

I looked at my feet. "Oh. Yeah, looks like I am leaving Silverwood." I kept emotion from my face. I was used to showing people I was okay when I wasn't.

"Good." He nodded to the parking lot. "You'd better go."

"Eli?" My eyes pleaded with him. All I really wanted was for him to ask me to stay, to tell me he had feelings, too. That would never happen. Another shrill blow of a horn from the parking lot cemented the feeling.

"Better run along, Ember." His voice twisted into a cruel, mocking tone.

My armor snapped back in place. "My phone." I held out my hand.

His eyes narrowed into glittering slits. He dug into his pocket, slapping the phone into my open palm. As I watched him walk away, it felt as if someone stabbed me in the stomach with a dull dagger and was wiggling it around until they ripped out my gut, piece by piece. Another honk of the horn brought me out of my pained trance. I moved up the hill toward the parking lot.

TWENTY

"Ember!" Mark yelped the next morning as he jumped back from the counter, coffee splashing out of my tipped-over coffee cup. "What is wrong with you? That's the second cup you've spilled this morning." He grabbed a towel to stop the spill from dripping onto the floor.

"Nothing."

"Em, come on. I've never seen you this jumpy. You are wound extremely tight this morning."

"I'm fine." I was so jittery at breakfast Mark tried to cut my coffee consumption after only half a cup, since the other one I poured ended on the floor. "What time is your flight again?" He had told me three times already, but nothing seemed to be registering.

He shook his head with a scoff. "It's still at one-forty-five. Remember, you are dropping me off at my office. I need to do a few more things before I go. I'll take a cab to the airport, which means you get the truck while I'm gone." He set his coffee on the counter. "You know, I hate saying this again, but remember our ground rules. No one in the truck besides you. And most important, there are to be no boys in the house while I'm gone, except Ryan. He's fine."

I laughed. No boy besides Ryan was likely to be in the house. "You do know I am eighteen, right?"

158

"Don't remind me," he said, sighing while putting his cup in the sink. "But my house, my rules."

"Wow, could you sound more like a typical parent? Very cliché of you."

"I never thought I'd be saying these things, either, but they really do work when you need them." He turned and looked at me. "I really don't like leaving you for so long and being so far away, especially right now."

"I'll be fine."

He sighed. "I still don't like it."

Fifteen minutes later, I parked the truck next to Mark's office building. He turned to me. "I want to remind you of my itinerary, so you will be able to clean up from that raging party you'll have while I'm gone. I will be back from Tokyo the Monday after next. Ten days is such a long time, but I will try to call every night. Okay? All the hotel contact information is on the fridge."

I knew it wasn't only me being on my own he didn't like, and it had little to do with boys staying out of the house. He was mostly scared that my state of mind might worsen. After the car episode, where I saw him turn into Torin, he'd been watching me like I was on the precipice above crazy town, about to teeter over.

"I love you, Sunny D, so much." He leaned over and kissed the top of my head. "Try not to get into too much trouble while I'm gone."

"I never make those types of promises." I hugged him. "Love you, too."

It did make me nervous he was leaving. Part of me was afraid without him here as my grounding base, I would flitter out into no man's land. I could feel in my bones something was coming. Something was going to change, and it terrified me.

The morning passed smoothly, but I felt restless and edgy. It only got worse when Josh and I got to O.A.R. Samantha addressed the group, her eyes landing frequently on me. "Today we have various types of seeds we'll be planting. Each container is divided into sections and has a tag already there stating what should be planted. Eli and a volunteer will also be bringing over some sets from the hothouse."

Girls' hands darted into the air to volunteer, but Eli's deep voice cut through the crowd. "Brycin." I thought Eli would have ignored me after our "near kiss." But just when I thought I had him pegged, he threw me another curveball, keeping me off-kilter. He had a gift for knowing exactly how to antagonize me. He turned, walking away, motioning over his shoulder for me to follow. I couldn't stop my heart from sputtering, even though I was still hurt and angry at how he left—like I had forced him to "almost" kiss me.

"Eli, are you sure you want her? I mean, wouldn't it be better if you took another guy with you? Better to help load?" Sam questioned. She tried to keep her tone level, but you could hear the panic weaving through her voice.

Eli whipped around, and his eyes pinned her to where she stood. Power and authority emanated off him. I could feel him communicating with her through his gaze. Her head bowed as she slunk back. It was clear she had overstepped her bounds.

"She can handle it," he said and spun, again walking toward the hothouse.

Oooo-kay . . . that was weird. I looked at Sam, her face blistering with rage. An overflowing fountain of her resentment was directed at me. I scurried after Eli.

"Are you ever going to talk to me again or not?" Eli approached me as I placed plants onto the cart.

"I'll pick the 'or not,'" I replied without looking up.

"So is it going to be like that now?" He mimicked my phrase from earlier. "This is about yesterday, isn't it?"

I didn't respond as I loaded more plants onto the cart, acting like the work took every bit of my attention.

"Maybe you could try getting over yourself," he replied, "and grasp that nothing happened. I had a moment of insanity, but it will never happen again."

It was like someone punched my gut. My anger flared quickly to the surface. "Excuse me?"

"I don't think I stuttered." Eli returned my glare. "I said nothing happened between us, and nothing ever will."

"You have *noooo* idea how grateful I am," I seethed as I shoved the cart. "And you know what? It's a little difficult to 'get over' myself when you're constantly in my way. How can I stay away from you if you won't let me?"

Eli sputtered. "In *your* way? Think you got it backwards, sweetheart."

"Fuck you!"

"Right here?" He crossed his arms. "That definitely wouldn't help your getting over me."

I needed to get away from him before I did something rash. I spun and took off without any real thought to where I was going.

"Brycin!" Eli yelled from behind me.

I kept going, having a feeling of *déjà vu* from every other interaction Eli and I had. Walking away from each other was all we seemed to know how to do—and we did it well.

Eli growled, "Damn it, woman, I swear you're going to be the end of me."

I stopped short and whirled, making him stumble back. "*I* am?" I laughed wildly. "You know what, Eli? I'm over this." I motioned between us. "It's the same cycle with you over and over. I think we make headway to becoming friends, and bam, you're back to being a dick again. One step forward and nine back."

His powerful eyes were fixed on me. I couldn't keep having these confrontations. I forced myself to back away. I shook my head, exasperated, and turned to walk from him again.

He grabbed my hand to stop me, but then quickly let it go. He let out an exasperated noise sounding more like a growl. "It's better this way. It's safer for you. You need to be as far from me, from here, as you can."

"What?"

He took in a breath. "Let me make this clear once and for all. I don't want to be friends or anything else with you." His voice curdled into a deep, soured anger. "Go back to your other school. You're not wanted here, *little girl.*"

The cold resignation in his voice made my heart plummet. His stony face looked down on me. Closing his eyes briefly, he turned and stalked off, towards the O.A.R. garden.

Wh-Wh-What? My head and heart screamed. I wasn't expecting the force behind his final rebuff. My emotions shifted so fast I couldn't keep up with what had happened. It was like he had drilled through my chest, ripped my heart out, and stormed off with it still beating in his bare hand. I wanted to call to him, and beg him to stop, but my throat was too thick and blocked my words.

Get it together, Em. You've known him for less than two weeks. You're not even friends.

Then, why did I feel like this?

Having opened up to him more than I had with anyone else, I felt the stab of betrayal. As turbulent as our relationship was, I had oddly come to count on him, and the sudden loss felt like a vast empty void. How did I let this happen? How did he slip over the wall I kept around myself? Why was it so easy for him to walk out of my life? And, more importantly, why did I care so much?

Man, I'm so screwed up!

There was no way I was going back to O.A.R. I couldn't face anyone. Most of all I couldn't face Eli, especially if he was unfazed by our interaction. I cut through the woods and headed for the parking lot, so I wouldn't run into anybody.

I was almost there when wariness crept down my back. I paused mid-step. My skin prickled. I was being stalked—again.

A loud snap and the rustling of leaves made me jump. I spun, feeling a pair of ice-cold eyes on me, but not knowing where they were located. I paused one more second, sucking in a deep breath before breaking into a run, fleeing as fast as I could. The ground crunched underfoot as I scrambled through the forest. Branches whipped across my face, slicing at my skin. My heart battered ruthlessly against my ribs, almost drowning the sound of something smashing through the brush behind me. Almost. Whatever was there, it was moving in closer, ready to jump out at me. I cringed in anticipation, preparing for the pain of the attack.

Adrenaline coursed through my veins, making my legs and lungs pump harder. Ahead I could see the parking lot through a break in the trees. *Almost there.*

A low snarl erupted behind me.

I wanted to laugh at the idiocy. It was so my luck to be this close to safety and not make it. I waited to feel hands or claws tearing at my body.

I broke through the trees and looked over my shoulder. There was nothing behind me. No rabid animal or deranged man ready to attack me, only the trees swaying peacefully in the wind.

I didn't stay around to find if this was something else I had simply imagined. I scrambled into the truck, locked the doors, and tore off down the road for home.

TWENTY-ONE

Without Mark around to comfort me or make me laugh, my mood was like PMS on crack.

I got ready for the concert, deciding against any of the outfits I would normally wear and went for something edgier. I pulled on skintight, black jeans, a pair of extremely sexy, sleek, knee-length, black-heeled boots, and a white tank top with necklaces of varying lengths I had made out of copper and recycled glass. I wore my hair down and loose. The braids from earlier made it a little more wild than usual. I grabbed my faux-leather jacket and headed out of the room.

I was walking a thin wire of sanity. I needed to have fun tonight. That didn't mean I didn't need some help to achieve it. I walked to Mark's liquor cabinet, and without wanting to think about the good and bad or the right and wrong, I searched for the best thing to help make the pain go away. I grabbed the tequila and took a shot straight from the bottle. I was a teenager who was going to make a lot mistakes, and tonight was looking one of those times. I pitied anyone who pushed me the wrong way. I was in a fighting mood. I'd fight, or I'd fall apart.

By the time Kennedy and Ryan came to pick me up for the concert, I was all over the place—mad to sad, frustrated to hopeless. Reckless.

"We better go. Ian just texted, sayin' the line's getting long. So let's get our butts down there now," Ryan said. Ian was Ryan's cousin. He went to a different school but hung out with us sometimes on the weekends.

Kennedy looked at me curiously, sensing something curious was going on with me. "You okay?"

"Yeah . . . sure . . . why not?"

She had an unsettled look on her face. "You seem different tonight. There's a strange darkness around you."

Kennedy always said odd things like this, but tonight it hit extremely close to home.

"I'm fine." I smiled.

"Okay or not, you look hot, girl." Ryan wiggled his eyebrows.

"Thanks. Now let's get going, before we have to wait to finally get in." I herded them out the door, trying to ignore my swirling emotions—and the darkness stirring in me.

"Ugh, I hate lines." Ryan nodded at the endless queue of concert goers wrapping around the block. "I didn't think this many people even knew about this band. It's going to take forever, and Ian's already waiting for us inside."

I stared at the queue The Poisonous Mushrooms were playing in one of the more popular clubs in downtown Olympia, but I was *not* going to freeze my ass waiting outside. I turned toward the back of the building. "Follow me, guys."

"What are we doing?" Kennedy asked wearily as I led them down a dark alleyway.

"Skipping the line," I replied, looking for the rear door of the club.

"How are we going to do that? Every door will be locked back here, and if you haven't noticed, I can't shimmy into a drain or through a small, restroom window." Ryan motioned to his body.

165

"Plus this outfit is to be seen and envied, not abused."

Finally, spotting the door I was looking for, I walked toward it. It was unguarded but locked. "We're going to walk right in."

I held up my hand for them to stop, not wanting them to see what I was about to do. I moved deeper into the shadows and stood close to the door. I had never tried my ability like this before, except on the leaves, but it had worked then. With the mood I was in, it would work now.

I concentrated on the knob, imagining my energy flowing into the lock, acting like a key. Heat rose within my body as my determination stayed focused on the door. The knob twisted, fighting against the latch. It creaked, and with a clinging pop, the lock snapped. I pulled at the door—it opened easily.

"Come on, guys." I motioned them forward. They moved in closer, their gaze shifting from me to the door. I shrugged. "Someone must have left it unlocked."

"This is wrong." Kennedy's eyes met mine, and something deep in them made me look away.

Ryan slipped past me into the club. "It's not like we're getting in for free, Ken. I paid for the tickets. We're simply getting out of standing in line."

Kennedy was still watching me. "That's not what I meant."

I always thought Kennedy was sensitive to people's moods because she was an observer, but now it felt different. Could she somehow feel or sense what I could do? Kennedy finally broke her eye contact with me and frowned, walking past me into the building. "Oh, yeah, tonight's gonna be fun," I mumbled and followed them inside.

About an hour into the concert, I was bored. Usually, I loved watching and listening to live music, but my mood left me restless and in need of some kind of outlet. My friends had given up asking me if things were okay and left me to wander around by myself.

I ambled along the catwalk while the music pulsated underfoot. Through the smoky veil of fog from a machine close to the stage, I watched the smiling faces of strangers beneath me, laughing and dancing in swarms. I knew I didn't belong with them; I didn't belong in their world. It was as if I watched a TV show, but I was the one who was make-believe.

I was leaning against the railing when the hair on my arms prickled, and an unsettling feeling crept over me. Deep shadows clung to the space around me, but I could feel something was there.

"Ember," said a familiar voice, causing me to jump. Samantha moved from the shadows, coming closer.

"What are you doing here?" I tried to hide the irritation in my voice.

"I love this band." For some reason, I felt her explanation was anything but the truth. "Funny running into you, because I wanted to talk." Sam's voice was so sweet that only from the forced smile she plastered on her lips and the cold look in her eyes did I see her true feelings.

"What about?"

Her unnatural smile grew even more malicious. "Eli," she began. "It seems as if you like to take things that don't belong to you." She stepped closer to me. "Don't think I will merely stand back and let it happen, especially from *you.*" Sam looked me up and down with blatant disgust.

The shock of her words and the tone left me speechless.

"I swear if I see you near him again, you and I will have more than words. And I promise I am not someone you want to mess with." A cruel smile pulled her lips up. "Besides you being young, stupid, and revolting, you two do not belong together can *never* be with him. He belongs with me, one of his own. You, sweetheart, are only a means to an end, and don't think for a second you are more. Stay away from him, or I *will* destroy you."

Her tone was so serene I had to replay her words in my head again to feel the true threat.

167

"You understand me?" She grabbed my jacket. At odds with her soothing voice, her sweet, beautiful face twisted into a beautiful ugliness. She was frightening and alluring in an exceptionally unearthly way. "Because I have no scruples about killing you."

My focus blurred, and instead of Samantha, I was staring at a beast with flaming red cat-like eyes. Its snout looked like a cross between a wolf and a panther, showing teeth as sharp as razors when its lips curled back into a snarl. A scream threatened to escape me, but as fast as the beast appeared, it vanished, leaving Samantha again in its stead. Her glare was so sinister I recoiled in fear.

"Do. You. Understand?"

I nodded, too stunned to do anything else.

She stepped back, patting me on the arm. "I'm glad we've had this talk. I feel so much better."

She was back to her usual pleasant sweetness, as if she had been talking about the latest fashion, not threatening my life. She walked past me and down the stairs, leaving me stunned, my brain still not really comprehending what transpired.

Holy shit! Can we say unstable? Was I the only sane one around here? I guess that really wasn't setting the standard very high.

The walls felt as if they were closing in on me. I slipped downstairs and out the door, gulping in the cool night air. I couldn't tell Ryan or Kennedy I was leaving. They would try to stop me, and I just wanted to go. I didn't want to worry them, so I quickly texted, *"Hey, sorry had to go home, not feeling good. Don't worry I got a cab. Call you tomorrow. Have fun."*

The night was clear, and the moon hung low in the sky. Walking seemed to help unclutter my head. As I strolled, my fear turned to anger. *How dare that bitch threaten me?* She was scary and a psycho, but I couldn't deny the guilt I felt. Even if Sam and Eli were only "friends with benefits" and not a couple, it still didn't make what happened between Eli and me right.

168

Such thoughts only made me walk faster, even more restless and angry with myself. I was so caught up in my thoughts, I didn't know how long I wandered or where I was.

"Hey!" A deep, raspy voice called to me from across the street. It was the kind of voice you pictured coming from a scary, rough, chain-smoking biker. I turned my head and saw my assumption was way off. Okay, he probably had a bike and was a little scary, but he was also hot. He was tall, with huge muscles, and his blond hair was clipped close to his head. He leaned against the door jamb of what I figured was a dive.

My eyes flicked up to the name of the bar. A small sign blinked, "Mike's Bar." It was the place where Eli hung out. Was he in there now? I had no doubt the place was dangerous. It seemed to be drenched in soulless, black shadows, and Eli was a part of it.

"Why don't you come over here? Promise I won't bite . . . yet," the guy flirted. There was a slight southern twang in his voice.

I couldn't seem to help myself. I walked across the road to the sleazy bar. It had this strange pull. Maybe it was the slim, slim chance of seeing Eli, but I knew nothing would stop me from going in, no matter the consequences. That's when I truly understood my feelings for Eli went beyond infatuation. He had already become a part of me, of my life, and I wanted to be wherever he was.

Oh, man, I am so in trouble.

"So, sweetheart, you gonna let me buy you a drink?" The man looked me up and down, his light brown eyes gleaming under the blinking neon lights. The power behind them was daunting. His neck was lined with scars, which I was sure had come from a knife fight of some sort. I had no doubt he had seen his fair share of them. The leer in his eyes made me nervous, but I couldn't seem to walk away. He was a lot younger than I first thought. He was certainly good-looking, but he was a terrifying kind of trouble— bad news all around. Exactly the way I seemed to like them lately.

"Sure," I responded as my brain screamed, *No!*

A crass smile crept across his lips as he winked. "Thought so."

He strutted into the bar, stopping to let me go before him. A very gentlemanly move in such a crass place. Inside was what I pictured a disreputable dive would look like. It was dark and dilapidated with a couple of pool tables in the back, a dartboard on the side, and an old TV flickering in the corner. A heavyset man with a stern face and balding head stood behind the bar wiping glasses. A smoky haze told me they didn't give a shit about the no-smoking law. The clientele didn't appear to be fans of any kind of law.

A couple of guys in back looked to be part of the Hells Angels motorcycle gang, which should have me walking straight out the door. But I seemed to be on a reckless mission tonight. The rest of the people in the bar were really dodgy characters, ones who had nothing more to lose. It was not a place for a girl to go unless she was as shady and tough as the guys there. No doubt I stood out like a beacon, asking for trouble.

Knowing the risk still didn't make me run for the door. Something kept me in the bar keeping company with a strange man. Was it because I was attracted to danger, or was it because something about this guy reminded me of Eli? I didn't know, but I couldn't seem to leave and didn't want to. This guy made me feel like I could forget all my pain. I was putting myself in a very, very dangerous position, but a part of me liked it. *What the hell is wrong with me?*

"What's your poison, darlin'?" The guy's eyes ran over my body again.

"Tequila," I responded.

"You don't fool around." His eyebrows shot up. "I like that." He turned to the bartender. "Hey, Mike, two shots of tequila and a beer."

While he ordered, I noticed everyone in the entire room was staring at me. The two guys by the pool table stopped their game and leaned against the table, looking like I could be their next snack. One of the guys, who struck me as the leader of the two, was short and fat with long, graying, frizzy black hair tied into a ponytail. He had bulging eyes and a nose like it had been broken several times. He reminded me of a really ugly pug dog. The other guy was his polar opposite—tall, skinny, and bald. He was extremely frightening to look at, with his hooknose and pockmarked face. I turned my head quickly back to the bar, not wanting to make eye contact with anyone else.

"Here you go, girlie." Mike pushed a huge shot of tequila at me.

I guess good ol' Mike didn't care about the underage drinking law either. We both slammed the shots back, and I almost choked as it burned my throat. It tasted more like battery acid, and by the looks of the clientele, I wouldn't be surprised if it was.

"Wooo-hooo," the guy screamed, his eyes dancing. "Feel the burn." The cheap alcohol immediately went to my head. He leaned against the bar, still looking me up and down intensely. "Damn," he mumbled. I went from feeling tough and sexy in my outfit to feeling naked and exposed. "You got a name, darlin'?" His southern drawl seemed more pronounced.

"Ember," I said, without thinking. I should have lied. From the way he looked at me, though, I had this feeling deep in the pit of my stomach he already knew my name before I even said it.

"Damn, Ember, you are a pretty girl. You got some unique eyes there."

"Umm . . . thanks."

"Hey," one of the bikers called from the back. "You gonna bring that sweet, young thing over here?"

"Sorry, boys, I'm really not into sharing." He didn't even turn to answer them. I don't know why, but my gut was telling me I was somewhat safer with him, even though my brain was saying something different. "See, darlin', there are some disreputable characters here. Not a place for good lookin', young girls like you." He went on undressing me with his eyes.

"I'd say it's even less my scene since I'm not legally supposed to be here. For some reason, I'm sensing the law is overlooked quite a bit here, and I've never been one to really follow the rules anyway."

"Think we got ourselves a wildcat here." A lewd smile played on his lips. "You are an interesting one, sweetheart, definitely my type. I can see now why the fuss. You have a boyfriend, darlin'?"

"I do," I lied, but Eli's image came into my mind. I rubbed my forehead, as if it would wipe away the vision as well.

"How would he feel about you being here with me?"

"He'd be absolutely thrilled. He was so worried I wouldn't fit in around here and now look at me, making new friends."

He almost spit out the beer he had swigged. "Oh, man, you're a feisty thing, aren't you?" He licked his lips. "Not like I expected any different from my boy," he mumbled.

"Expected what from whom?" My eyes narrowed. A strange feeling danced through me, as if I wasn't as much of a stranger to him as he was to me.

"Hey, Mike, two more shots," he said, ignoring my question. "I don't suppose you know how to play a little pool, do you?"

"Uhhh . . . a little," I replied. Mom had never really cared for the game, but Mark loved it. When I was young, Mark taught me pool so he would have someone to play with. I was good, but not great. In a place like this, I'd rather talk down my skill.

I cringed as he pushed another tequila shot at me. I wasn't feeling the effects like I thought I would, so I slammed this one back without hesitation. The ache in my heart wasn't numb enough.

He was about to turn and head to the pool tables when I realized I never asked his name. How odd. "So what's your name?" I demanded. This was a place where you didn't show weakness or fear.

He turned and smiled. "Let's make a little wager here. If you win, I will tell you my name. If I do, you will dump your man and run away with me."

"Funny, I don't see any real win in there for me."

"You'll see soon enough." He smiled seductively, his huge hand sliding around my wrist with force. A warning chill flickered through me. This guy was solid muscle and could snap my arm like a twig.

I stumbled as he led me to the back. "Hey, stop pulling me." I yanked my arm free, making him stop.

"Hey, West, looks like you can't handle your woman there. Why don't you let me take her off your hands?" The short, fat biker licked his lips, making my gag reflex kick in. "Woo-wee, she is young and firm. Ripe for the pickin'."

"I don't think so, McNamm. I don't share my toys," West replied.

McNamm approached us. Even though he was a foot or so shorter, he still tried to get in West's face. "Your mamma don't raise you right, then. Thinkin' about time you learn."

"I suggest you take a step away," West growled, his voice sounding extremely familiar, weirdly reminding me of Eli's. "She's mine." The possessiveness of his tone made me panic. To him I was no longer a person, only a piece of meat.

The tall, scarred Hells Angel sensed something was going to happen and stepped beside his buddy. "Don't be stupid, West. Thinkin' you better back off."

"Really, Pock? I think it's you two who are being stupid. But then, you guys were never the brightest bulbs in the pack."

McNamm was seething. Two against one, and I was the prize. I looked over my shoulder at the door. As soon as I thought about escape, I felt West's hand tighten around my wrist. The gaze from his light brown eyes burrowed deep into mine. Something about him made me no longer feel like fleeing. His hand slid over my shoulder and slipped in between the collar of my jacket to grab my neck. I knew he was doing it to show ownership of his property—me—for McNamm's and his partner's sake, showing they needed to back off. I still hated it. I was not someone who liked being

173

treated as property or being told what to do in any way.

Anger sprouted within me as I pulled away. His fingers lost their grip as they skidded across my neck, grazing my tattoo, which sent a vibration through the ink. West's hand jerked like he'd been stung, his eyes widening as he looked first at me then down at his hand. He quickly controlled his reaction. His face returned to neutral as he swung back to McNamm.

We weren't given the opportunity to dwell on what happened as McNamm stepped forward and poked West's chest. "What's it gonna be, dumbass? We wanna chance to play with her, or do we just be takin' her from you?"

West's huge frame moved quicker than I thought possible. He punched McNamm in the face, sending him flying to smash into the pool table. Pock pulled a knife and jumped on West, knocking me to the floor with them. My head smacked hard.

In the distance, the bartender screamed for the fight to stop, but it was past that. West and Pock rolled on the floor, grunting as they punched and shoved each other. Blood flew from their noses. A gnarled roar tore from West's lips as Pock's knife buried into West's gut, blood squirting out of the wound. It only distracted him for a moment before he pounced on Pock again.

I knew this was my best chance for escape, and now I wanted nothing more than to get away from there. I picked myself up and dizzily wobbled for the door, stumbling into every chair and table on the way. I was halfway there when I felt a hand on my shoulder, throwing me once more to the floor.

"Where'd you think you're goin'?" McNamm sneered. The smell of whiskey and beer was on his breath as he climbed on top of me. He grabbed my wrists with one hand, keeping me from hitting him.

Terror grew like weeds and wrapped around my lungs. "Get off me!"

"Shhh . . . you'll have a good time. If not, I know I will. I'm bettin' you're pure as the driven snow. This is gonna be a treat."

174

Fear engulfed me as I struggled against him. My panic was rising so high I almost didn't notice the deep tug of power inside me. Lights in the bar flickered. The bulb above my head sputtered and splintered. Shards of glass flew down on McNamm. "What the hell?" He twisted and looked up, grinding himself against me harder. A guttural cry escaped me. My hands flailed wildly, clawing at his face.

"Oh, you like it rough?" He sneered as my nails made contact with his face. "You lil' bitch." A burst of pain swept across my face as he hit me. Black dots spun across in my vision. My swollen cheek pounded with sharp pain. He groped for my pants, pulling down the zipper. I stiffened.

A light fixture popped across the room, reminding me what I was capable of. I forced all my emotion out of my body. The rest of the lights, the bottles, and the TV exploded, sending glass flying across the bar. I heard screams and chairs being moved as people dove under the tables. It rained glass, but the sparks were directed straight at McNamm, making him dive off me to find shelter.

Out of nowhere, West came flying onto McNamm, both of them crashing into the wall, sending cue sticks all over the floor. I scrambled to get one, but Pock jumped on my back, slamming my face into the dirty floor as he pushed all his weight on top of me. Tiny bits of broken glass cut into my cheek, spilling the warmth of oozing blood.

"I get my turn, too." He leaned down. "Hmmm . . . you smell good." His scratchy voice prickled at my ear, making my heart pound with dread. He moved and twisted so he could pin me better.

A cue stick lay several feet from me.

Occupied with getting under my layers of clothes, Pock's hand shoved into my jeans, rubbing my lower back before he shoved his fingers down farther. Through my jeans, I could feel his excitement poking into me. My chest heaved and chilled as cold fear dripped into every vein of my body.

I wiggled and stretched my arm as far as I could, but the cue stick was far beyond my reach. I let out a guttural cry as Pock's hand wormed around inside my pants. I focused all my energy on reaching the stick and concentrated on moving the object towards me. I had to get it. It was my only shot at getting away from him.

My mind locked on the object. I imagined it moving to me. A strong force filled my body, making my arms tingle with energy. The cue stick rocked back and forth. I tuned out everything around me. The only thing that mattered was having the stick in my possession. Suddenly, the smooth wood slid across the floor, landing in my hand. I blinked in shock, but my astonishment would have to wait.

I gripped the end and flung it back with all the power I could, smacking Pock full in the face.

"Ahhhh!" He grabbed his bloody cheek and rolled off me. I scrambled up and re-gripped the cue stick like a bat as I turned to confront him. "You fuckin' little bitch! I think you broke my nose!"

"And I'll fucking do it again. Don't think about touching me . . . ever." My own blood boiled in my ears, and my terror turned into sheer fury. All the anger and hurt I had felt today tore through me. My hands vibrated as I gripped the cue stick.

He lunged for me, and I reacted by swinging the cue with all my pent-up energy, cracking it across his head. The stick broke as it ricocheted off his head and half of it flew across the room. His body went limp and fell on the floor, unconscious. Blood spilled from his nose and the cut across his head.

"Everyone freeze!" a voice boomed from the doorway. Several cops with guns pointed at us inched into the bar. "You're all under arrest!"

At first, I felt relief from their presence, but then a hard lump settled in my stomach. Sheriff Weiss stood at the door with a gun pointed at me, his eyes glinting.

Shit!

Weiss looked pleased as punch as he took in the pool room. It appeared like a bomb had gone off in the bar. Glass and debris covered the floor, tables were broken and over turned, and the TV lay broken on its side halfway across the room from where it originally sat.

The best part for him was me. In my hands, gripped tightly, was a broken, jagged, bloody cue stick. The other half lay a few yards away from the bloody, beaten, unconscious man, the one I was standing over.

Weiss signaled for two of the officers to go after McNamm and West, while he and a younger cop moved to me.

"Why, Ms. Brycin, funny you being in the middle of this," he said smugly. "Not as if I'm at all surprised."

I gazed around confused, my body and mind still in shock.

"Miss, put the stick down," the other cop commanded.

I stared at him, my eyes wild and unclear. Couldn't they see I didn't belong here? I was a victim trying to protect myself.

"Please, put the stick down now, ma'am." The young officer's voice grew tight and demanding.

I let the stick drop from my hands. The sound echoed through the room as it bounced. Everything after was a blur of fear, adrenaline, alcohol, and shock. The only thing I remembered was the young cop coming to me, wiping the cuts on my face as the blood on my cheek dripped onto the floor.

Weiss moved in behind me. "You're under arrest, Ms. Brycin," he said as he slid handcuffs around my wrists. Numbness and shock kept me in a dreamlike state. I felt no pain.

It wasn't the first time I had been in handcuffs or been arrested, but those times usually came from my being attached to a tree, which was going to be bulldozed. Or at a PETA rally, which got out of hand. This was completely different.

"Sir, don't you think we should get her statement before arresting her? I mean this doesn't look like her type of place. I don't even think she's old enough to be in here." The young cop looked questioningly at his senior officer.

Weiss reminded me of those cops who were ten years past retiring. He was bitter, judgmental, narrow-minded, and cruel.

"Lambert, you being a rookie and all, will soon learn in this bar *no one* is innocent," he said coldly, "least of all this girl right here."

"You have the right to remain silent . . ." I tuned him out as he continued.

TWENTY-TWO

"Don't I get at least one phone call?" I yelled from my cell. "Or an oxygen mask?" The six-by-eight-foot cement block smelled like urine and body odor.

"Hmmm-hmmm," Deputy Officer Linne mumbled, not even bothering to look up from his magazine. I wasn't sure if he had heard my question or if a mutter was his automatic reply to everything. He seemed more interested in drinking his coffee and reading some cheesy gossip magazine than his actual job. I wondered if he was one of those cops who secretly watched soap operas and read trashy, bodice-ripping novels.

About an hour later, he decided it was time to get up and stretch, agreeing while he was up, he would give me my rights as a citizen.

"Okay, girlie, you get *one* phone call," he said. He opened the cell and motioned for me to sit at the desk. "The bar's not pressing charges, so you're free to go. But because you were drinking, we will only release you if someone drives you home."

Mark was in Japan for his conference. There was no way he was going to fly back only to take me home. He had done it plenty of times for my mother when protests had gone awry. What were my choices? Kennedy didn't have a car, nor would her parents let her use theirs at this time of morning. Ryan had a car. He could come get me.

179

Deputy Linne plopped the phone in front of me and returned to his gossip magazine. Picking up the receiver, my fingers shook as I punched in a number.

A groggy voice cracked over the line. "Hello?"

"Hi, it's me. I've kind of been . . . well . . . arrested, and I was wondering if . . . uh . . . you come and spring me out."

A long pause as the information sank in. "I'll be right there."

I hung up, smiling victoriously at the cop as he led me back to the cell.

"Okay, Miss Brycin, you are free to go." Deputy Linne motioned for me to come forward as he opened the door. "But we will need you to fill out some paperwork first."

I started to follow the deputy down the hallway when I heard Sheriff Weiss behind me. "Ms. Brycin, if you could hold on one moment, I'd like to speak with you."

I closed my eyes and swore under my breath. Of course he wouldn't let me go so easily. It wasn't his style. His personal vendetta would lap this incident up like cream. He was coming to claim his victory.

He walked around to face me. "Because that dump of a bar didn't press charges, doesn't mean you get off scot-free."

I was tired of his games. The more intently I looked at him, the more uncomfortable he got. My heeled boots gave me a few inches over him, and I used it to my advantage. His gaze darted away.

"It looks like you broke the terms to allow you back to the high school, Ms. Brycin, not that I thought with your track record you would. I knew you'd do something to screw it up. And wow, did you . . . being underage in a bar, getting into a bar brawl, destroying property, attacking a man and almost putting him into a coma . . . those are serious crimes!"

Serious crimes, really? Crimes, yes, but serious? How about attempted rape or murder? Now that's what you call serious.

He obviously wanted to scare me, but I still intended to clarify that the men had attacked me, and I was only trying to defend myself. I mean, come on. Those guys had years and pounds on me, but they were the innocents here? I knew, however, I'd be wasting my breath. Weiss was dying to put anything on me, even if he had to twist facts and turn two seedy men from the Hells Angels into the victims to do it. What a sad state of affairs when I was considered more dangerous to society.

"Is that all, Sheriff Weiss?" I said petulantly.

He stepped close, his voice low and threatening. "Listen to me. Every move you make . . ."

". . . I'll be watching you." I couldn't help myself as I completed his sentence, an old "Police" song. Quite appropriate actually.

It really wasn't a mystery why I always found myself in trouble.

Weiss' face turned a deep shade of purple. "I'm going to make your life a living hell. Don't think I won't. You put one little toe out on the road before the crosswalk light turns green, and you'll be back here in handcuffs before you can even blink."

The man really hated me. Was it only because he couldn't prove the stuff he thought I did, or was there something else about me causing him to feel such a deep-rooted hatred? I did know he would be true to his word, and he'd be looking for anything to get me for, even if he had to lie and cheat to do it.

I wanted to make another smart-ass remark, but my community service was already tripled. I kept my mouth shut and my eyes on his, which seemed to disturb him enough. He finally stepped back and motioned for his deputy to resume his role.

When Linne led me to the waiting area, my heart did a flip-flop. The bad taste in my mouth from my little tête-à-tête with Weiss vanished.

Against the wall with his usual relaxed confidence, leaned Eli. His eyes danced in guarded amusement as he looked around the jail's waiting room. A slight smile tugged at his lips as he watched the guy next to him get handcuffed to a chair. Eli's hair was messy and ruffled in this unbelievably hot way—straight out of bed—which, of course, made me think of his bed and him being in it.

Ember, focus.

I breathed in deeply and tried to put on a face which didn't show how much he made me nervous and my body tingle every time I saw him. Now that I had finally admitted to myself how I felt about him, I was afraid it was written all over me. I bit my lip as I nervously ran a hand through my tangled hair. I wasn't ready for brutal rejection this early in the morning.

Right then, he spotted me. Pushing himself off the wall, he moved toward me. His body was so incredibly fit it couldn't be hidden underneath his favorite worn-out jeans, which hung low enough that the top of his V-line peeked out from under his shirt. My eyes were in an all-out war. They fought with staying locked on his V-line and getting caught, or going up to his gorgeous face. The humiliation of him seeing me stare at *that* area again convinced me to move my eyes up. He wore an old, gray t-shirt, a navy blue hoodie, and some beat-up black combat boots. I wanted to dive into him—he was comfort, safety, and pure intrigue all rolled into one.

I needed to stay strong, but it didn't help when he studied me up and down with a look so primal, so raw, my blood boiled. I knew I looked rough and wild—a night in jail after a bar fight did wonders for my appearance. My black, knee-high heeled boots, tight fitting jeans, and red leather jacket only added to the image. The animalistic way he stared made me want to act on my desires.

"Miss, we need you to sign a few forms." A female deputy interrupted my carnal thoughts and motioned me to one of the windows. I nodded, keeping my eyes on Eli as I waited for him.

"Don't start," I warned as he walked to me.

"Whatever do you mean, jailbait?"

I sighed. "Yeah . . . it's gonna be a long day."

His amusement quickly became serious when he studied my

face. I turned my head away, trying to hide the cuts down the one side of my face and the black and blue bruise covering the other. Eli grabbed my chin and ran his thumbs over my wounds, making my body zing. "What happened?" His eyes were a mix of concern, anger, and speculation. I could see the wheels in his brain going through what or who could have done it to me.

I pulled my chin free of his grip and headed over to the discharge window. I couldn't tell Eli how foolish I had been, merely in the hope of seeing him or being close to someplace he might go had caused me to be a stupid moron. Eli stayed frozen in his spot, looking after me.

The woman glanced at Eli, and her stern expression softened. "Mr. Dragen, are you the one who is taking responsibility for her?"

"Yeah. Morning, Anita." Eli winked and smiled at the woman.

A slight blush fluttered over her mocha skin. "You can't seem to stay away, can you?" Anita's firm voice was all fluff and no bite. You could hear the teasing affection under it.

"Not with you here."

"Oh, you are such a tease." Anita swished her hand at Eli. I felt like I had entered an alternate universe. Eli being charming? Anita was the kind of woman who could make grown men huddle in the corner in fear. Here she was, as smitten as a schoolgirl. My head whipped back and forth from one to the other.

"I'm doing the picking up today." Eli nodded towards me. "What do you need me to do?"

Anita's eyes became annoyed and stern again when she looked at me but softened the second they flicked back to Eli. "You know the drill, honey child. I need to get your signature and information on these documents." Anita pushed a pile of forms and papers toward Eli.

Fantastic. I felt like it tied me even more to Eli. Yesterday, he didn't want me in his life, but when I needed him, he came running, no questions asked. After about ten minutes, we finished with the stack of forms.

"Bye, Anita, I'm sure I'll see you soon."

"You know I love your company, Eli, but try and stay out of trouble for a little while."

"Do my best," he said, smiling. He squeezed her hand as we turned to go. "You know, I've never been in here voluntarily before," Eli whispered in my ear as I collected my belongings.

"I find that so hard to believe," I said dryly.

"We should leave before Weiss feels my presence."

Eli herded me out the door. As we left, I looked over my shoulder. As if he actually had felt Eli's presence, Weiss stood watching us. He had assigned us together in the same facility, but seeing Eli pick me up from jail? I could see the wheels in his head turning with the misguided idea he'd found the co-conspirator in my shenanigans—that Eli might have been the one helping me with the school explosions all along. His logic was once again wrong, but it didn't matter. He would make the puzzle piece fit even if it didn't suit the picture. I sighed. Weiss had something against Eli as well, but seeing both of us here probably helped make his theories become concrete evidence to him. He would come after us with the determination of a pit bull.

"So are you going to tell me the reason you woke me up at five-forty-five in the morning to come bail you out of jail?" He reached into his pocket and dug out a package of baby wipes for me to clean the black ink off my fingers. Even a small gesture like that choked me up, and I longed to touch him. It was pointless to deny how I felt.

"Let's get out of here first."

He nodded as he opened the Bronco door for me, and I climbed in. "Where to, jailbait?" he asked as he shut his door.

"You're never going to let it go, are you? You know I am legal. I'm not really jailbait anymore."

"Oh, believe me, you are the embodiment of bait."

We drove for a bit before he pulled off on a deserted dirt road, close to the waterfall. He turned off the ignition, and we sat in silence for a while.

"I want to thank you for coming to get me." I stared at my hands, still partly stained with ink. "I'm indebted to you. I don't even know how to begin. I know you don't want to be friends with me anymore, but . . ." I couldn't finish.

A low grunt came from Eli, making my head snap up. His fingers pinched the bridge of his nose like he had an unbelievable headache. His sigh was heavily loaded as he leaned his head back on the headrest and stared out the side window. The mood in the car grew tense.

"Em, why did you call me?"

"Umm . . . I-I'm sorry I woke you. I know I shouldn't have. I just didn't know who else to go to. I promise I won't bother you aga—"

"Stop right there. I don't give a shit you woke me. I'm not mad you called. I only want to know why you did."

"I-I don't know. Mark's gone and . . . I don't know . . . you were the first person I thought of. It was automatic."

"Don't you find it a little odd?"

I returned my focus to my hands. "Maybe I thought you'd understand more than anyone else."

He grumbled, swinging the door open and jumping out of the Bronco. I followed shortly behind him. He trudged through the grass. "So as this person you automatically called and who sprung you out of jail without hesitation, I think I deserve to hear the story of why you were there."

"You mean the person who retracted his friendship from me? Which is amusing since we really didn't have one," I spat in heated humiliation.

We stood on opposite sides of the Bronco's hood as a volatile fury hummed between us. I was extremely stubborn, but I might have met my match.

185

"Fine," I hissed, turning away and took the trail leading to the waterfall. He tramped after me. I walked in silence until I got to the footbridge. The sound of the thundering water soothed me. I kicked one of the wooden beams supporting the bridge. "So where do you want me to start?"

"Try the beginning. It's usually a good place."

I was going to be revealing more than I wanted, but I was tired of lying to myself. Whatever his reaction, I would deal with it.

"Last night was a downward spiral from the moment you walked away from me," I whispered. I stole a glance at him, and quickly turned. There was no way I could look at him through this. I wouldn't be able to handle any rejection I might see in his eyes.

"I tried to drown the pain, but it wouldn't go away. And, man, did I try. I was so tired of being scared and alone. I left my friends at a concert. It felt claustrophobic, so I had to get away. I don't remember getting there, but I found myself at Mike's Bar." A low guttural sound came from him. "Please, let me get through this." I took a deep breath. "I know it was stupid, but I thought if there was even a slim chance of seeing you, of being near you . . ." I tapered off.

I took a deep breath. "There was a guy standing in front who called me over. I don't know if it was because there was something about him which reminded me of you, but I couldn't stop myself. I knew it was foolish and dangerous, but I didn't care."

"Are you kidding me? Do you know what kind of place Mike's is?" Eli's voice rose, sounding like a high-pitched howl. His body stiffened, and fury rolled off of him so severely I could see it.

"I already know how stupid it was, so save the lecture. It was probably all the shots of tequila I had last night, but I felt strangely safe with him. It was like he already knew me or something. He tried to protect me. It was the two Hells Angels who started the trouble."

The memories came rushing back. I shivered recalling McNamm's stinky breath as he straddled me and Pock's rough hands feeling their way down the back of my pants. I blinked away the tears threatening to flood my eyes.

"A fight broke out, and I had to defend myself. Weiss found me cracking a cue stick over one of the guy's heads."

After a pause, a smile twitched Eli's lips. "You took out a Hells Angel with a pool cue?"

"Yeah."

Eli laughed, shaking his head. He crossed his arms, looking at me with what looked like pride. "You really do scare the crap out of me."

I smiled, but the memories wouldn't stop flooding through my mind—the lights bursting, sparks going straight for McNamm, him hitting me across the face. My hands instinctively covered my face. I could still feel McNamm's fingers there and the cuts where Pock had crushed my cheek into the broken glass. Those would heal. But I remembered how they touched me, and how they ground against me. I looked up, realizing I stopped talking.

I became aware of the silence between us. Eli's amused face shifted, becoming cold and distant. "None of them touched you, right?"

I couldn't look him in the eye and lie, which is what I planned to do. I was awful at lying. I could've pretended Eli was asking about the bruises and cuts on my face, but we both knew he referred to something more important.

"Em?" he seethed. His voice was tight through his gritted teeth. "Did any of them *touch* you?"

"Look, it's over. I'd rather forget about it," I said.

Eli's silence made me finally dare to look up. He stood trembling, rankled by my dismissal. His eyes burned with rage. I had never seen them glow this bright before; they looked like an animal's eyes caught in the dark by a light.

"You're not telling me everything." He was barely able to contain any sort of appearance of calm. I stayed silent and averted my gaze, listening to him breathe deeply. "Ember, tell me."

"No. I told you enough. Let's call it even, so I can get out of your life like you want!"

"Tell. Me. What. Happened." Eli fumed, his body vibrating. His muscles twitched so fiercely it looked like worms were moving under his skin. My silence only aggravated him more, but something in my gut told me that telling him what happened or giving him names would be a mistake. "How could you be so foolish? It was just the stupidest, most idiotic, dangerous thing you could've done. You will never set foot in there again!"

"Excuse me?" I replied. "Are you telling me what to do? I'm so sick of people thinking they can. You don't own me. Nobody does."

"Somebody needs to. Not that you'd listen. You stubborn, pig-headed . . ."

"Pig-headed? That's rich coming from you, the most obstinate, opinionated, and ornery person I've ever met."

"Uh-oh, the three O's. I must be in trouble," Eli quipped. "How about this? You are insufferable, insolate, and infuriating!"

"Me, infuriating? You've got to be kidding me! I'm not the one with a multiple personality disorder who should be on a high dosage of lithium. I mean, talk about mood swings. Do you even know which mood or personality you are right now?"

His jaw clenched. "See any imaginary gnomes lately?"

I stopped my mouth falling open. "W-What?" I faltered under his stare. My worst fear was being thrown at me, but something about his words bothered me. "What a minute. How did you know I saw a gnome?"

"Uh . . . I was guessing." His eyes darted away.

"You're lying." He didn't respond. I stepped forward, hitting and shoving his chest. "Stop lying to me!"

Eli grabbed for my hands but missed. "I'm warning you, stop."

"Or what Eli? I'm curious, what will you do?" I hit him again, blind rage removing any reasonable thought. "What is your real story? Come on . . . let's hear it! Could you even tell me or would you have to kill me? How many monsters do you have in your closet?" I felt raw and naked, as if he could see all my darkest fears.

"You . . . have . . . no . . . idea," he said, his voice low and gritty.

"So give me an idea," I screamed, shoving him once more. It was like trying to push a cement wall.

"Em, stop!"

"Should I start calling you Dr. Jekyll and Mr. Hyde? Come on. Tell me the truth for once."

In a flash, Eli was on me, his hand feeling like sandpaper as it wrapped around my throat. Surprise and shock crippled my body as he pushed me against a tree, knocking the wind out of me. A gurgled noise escaped from the scream bubbling from the depths of my stomach. A fuzzy haze eclipsed my vision as tears filled my eyes. I twisted under his grasp, but his nails dragged against my neck's fragile skin.

"Truth?" His voice was strangled. "Is that what you think you want? I can tell you that you don't. Not really. And you certainly don't want to know mine."

My head buzzed as my lungs longed for air. I was waiting for my survival mode to kick in, to fight back. Instead, my gaze burrowed deep into his predatory, green eyes, which now had a strange glint of red in them. His eyes seized mine hungrily. Then, as if he'd received a slap to the face, he jerked back, releasing me. He looked down at his hands and snapped around, turning away from me.

My hands automatically went to massage my neck. The vulnerability of someone's hand clasped around my neck made me panic and sputter for air.

The weight of the tension between us silenced the surrounding forest. The trees held their breath in anticipation. "Damn you," he whispered. "How do you do this to me?" I wasn't completely sure he was talking to me. He looked into the woods, a deep growl vibrating through his chest. Then he took off through the trees.

I watched him go as my body slid down the trunk of the tree, and collapsed on the ground. My brain was so jumbled I couldn't think. My body shook with adrenaline as a cloud of heat engulfed me under my jacket, making it cling to my sweaty back. I tore it off, feeling suffocated and frazzled.

All different kinds of emotion erupted inside, making me agitated and fidgety. My neck stung. I touched the four raised scrapes he created down my neck. I swore I had seen red flames flash in his eyes, but I knew it was the extreme emotion making me hallucinate. All this was becoming so real.

I leaned my head back into the tree, digging both hands into the damp soil. Energy from the earth zinged through my arms and legs, making my body twitch with the need to move. I felt like a caged animal. I jumped up and walked. I shut off my thoughts and propelled myself through the forest. I wanted to scream, cry, or throw a tantrum, but I simply kept walking with a determination and stubbornness that didn't make sense to me. At least, it didn't until I was practically on him; then, I realized where and to whom my instincts had been taking me. I had done it before, only I hadn't understood it then.

I came up behind him, remaining silent. He knew I was there. Waiting for him to turn around, I felt absolutely no fear, not of him anyway. I felt . . . well, I wasn't quite sure what I felt, but I knew I had this undying need to break through to him. To show him no matter how much he pushed me away, I wasn't going anywhere, and he was just going to have to deal with it.

"Brycin." He said my name coolly. "I should know by now you will always find me." I continued to stand there, my stubbornness willing me to stay. He struggled to put his frustration into words. "What is it going to take? Why don't you go away and leave me in peace?" He turned toward me.

"I could say the same for you," I quipped, crossing my arms, trying to block his hurtful words.

A smile crept over his lips as he shook his head. "*You* don't really want me to."

Cocky and . . . true. Shit.

It was exactly the reason I stood there now. "You really don't want me to, either," I said, my voice quiet but strong.

Eli smirked as he faced me. "True."

Our eyes locked. The amusement fell from his face as his eyes burned with a ravenous hunger, making my body tingle dizzily. He moved to me with a steady intensity, stopping a few inches away. My breath locked in my lungs. Looking up at him, my eyes searched his. They swirled brightly with desire, no doubt mirroring mine.

"What about Samantha?" I whispered.

"Don't worry about Samantha," he said, bringing his hand up to my face. He softly slid his fingers over the scrapes, then moved up through my hair, brushing it back to expose my neck. I froze as his eyes lingered on the new wounds. For a second I feared he would turn and run again, but he stayed fastened on the cuts.

His fingers touched my jaw and slithered down, softly tracing the contours of my neck and the scrapes until he reached the top of my tank top. My eyes closed as I drowned in the pleasure of his touch. His other thumb swept gingerly across my bottom lip. My lips parted, catching his thumb and sucking it into my mouth. A soft moan came from his throat, making the yearning burn deeper in my body. My eyes fluttered open to see him staring down at me. For a brief time we stayed still, lost in everything we had left unsaid. Urgently, he slid his hands to cup my face. He concentrated intently on my lips as he lowered his slowly to mine, which ached for his touch.

A burst of electric shocks rippled through my body, sparking an intense passion that completely overtook me. There was nothing in the world I wanted more. Every touch was like fire. The taste of his lips spurred a divine hunger, an insatiable craving, an endless need for him. The kisses started slow as we took in the taste of each other, but their intensity swiftly increased as his tongue explored and tasted every inch of my mouth. I moved my hands through his hair as he breathed me in, his kiss bringing us closer. His hands dropped from my face and gripped my waist, pressing me in closer, and meticulously moved up my sides to my back.

His hands ran over my bare shoulder blade, and intense heat attacked and burned the lines of my tattoo, sending me reeling. Eli also jerked back in pain. I looked up at him. We could no longer pretend this wasn't happening. The raw power of his touch on my tattoo was too much to ignore. We both froze, breathing heavily. Then, without a word, Eli lifted the hair off my neck and flung it over my shoulder, exposing the lines of my tattoo the tank did not cover. I tilted my neck to the side, so he could see it clearly.

There was something about him seeing it that made my heart pound. It wasn't because I didn't want him to see my tattoo. That was too simple. It was something much deeper and poignant. He sucked in his breath as his finger hovered over the dark ink at the top of my neck. The instant the tips of his fingers stroked my flesh, my skin ignited into a flurry of heat, making me gasp. Eli ripped his hands away again, shaking off the zap. I felt heat, but it seemed to give him electric shocks when he touched it.

He reached out once more, causing a fever to crawl down the contours of my tattoo. The shock of his contact made me close my eyes. Eli held his breath as he caressed my skin. I knew it was causing him some sort of pain, but he didn't stop, and I didn't try to prevent him. The heat followed his touch like a shadow. He trailed down my neck until he reached my tank top strap. His fingers wrapped around the fabric and dragged it carefully off my shoulder, skimming my skin.

I bit my lip to keep myself from moaning in pleasure as his fingertips sent erotic chills over my skin. I reached around and unsnapped my bra, letting it fall. He went behind me and pulled the rest of my top down, revealing my bared back. I grew up taught not to be self-conscious of the human form. Not that we ran around naked, but nudity was not something I felt ashamed of. It wasn't embarrassment making me shake like a leaf.

Eli stumbled back. A guttural sound escaped his throat, making my blood go cold. I turned. His eyes were unfocused and distant. He was not the type of guy who got freaked out or showed it if he did, but he looked at me as if my head were about to spin around and pea soup would project out of my mouth. Covering myself, I reached for him. "Eli?" He scrambled away from me. "Eli? What's wrong? You're scaring me!"

He sputtered out a crazed laugh in response. "Scaring you?" I started to pull my top back on, snapping him out of his trance. "No, wait." He walked back to me. My heart thumped as he twisted me around again, his eyes drinking in every line of my tattoo. "No way," he whispered. "This can't be possible."

"What?" I demanded. "What's wrong?"

Eli spun me to face him. "Where did you get the tattoo? Who designed it?" His voice was hard, sending me reeling again. "Are you playing with me?"

"What?" My brain tried to catch up. Irritation flared in me as I tried to adjust to his shift in mood. I still desired his touch, to feel him on my bare skin, consuming me. I tugged up my tank top, not worrying about the bra I had let fall to the ground. It wasn't as if I had much need for it anyway.

"Your tattoo . . . when did you get it? Why this one?"

"Eli, what is going on? Why are you freaking out?" My voice shook with fear. "You know the reason I have my tattoo."

"Tell me again. The *whole* story . . . I mean everything."

"Why? What's going on?"

"Tell me the story," he demanded, ice coating his words. His tone told me this was extremely important, but I had no idea why. "And I mean every detail."

I gathered my thoughts. "A couple nights after my mother was killed, I had this extremely intense dream. I was walking in the woods. It was this beautiful, breathtaking place, with gorgeous ash trees, rolling hills, and streams that almost didn't look real. Even now, it's hard for me to explain . . . this place was indescribable, the most beautiful place I had ever seen. There were colors I could never imagine, and the forest throbbed with almost more energy than I could handle. I felt so at home there, and I knew this area like the back of my hand . . . as if I belonged." My head and heart still ached to dwell there, but I forced myself to move on.

"Someone whispered my name, and I turned around to see this person standing away from me. A hooded robe covered the face and the body, but I knew, I just knew, it was my mom . . . I could feel her. So . . . I walked up to her."

I shook my head as the memory of the dream, still feeling so real, played again in my mind. "She never showed her face, but she placed a necklace in my hand. It had these beautiful interweaving symbols on it, and she whispered, 'This is who you are. It will protect you.' Then, she turned away. When I looked up, she was gone, and I woke up for the first time feeling a little peace. It felt so real, so vivid." I paused for a breath. "I sketched the symbols from the necklace. I wasn't sure what they meant, if anything, but it simply felt right. It was my dedication to her and the only thing I have left which makes me feel close to her. It's as if she will always be with me, protecting me, forever a part of me. It makes me feel safe, even when everything around me is falling apart." Telling Eli these private painful thoughts made me feel exposed and raw.

"Holy shit . . ." He rubbed his hands over his face as he paced. Not quite the response I was expecting.

"What is going on?" I implored again. An odd expression flashed so quickly through Eli's eyes I wasn't sure if it actually happened. Something in me trembled. This wasn't the kind of look to make you feel good; it chilled me to the bone. "Eli?" I squeaked. "You're scaring me."

"You have no idea what this means?" His tone was tense as he spoke, ignoring my question.

"No . . ." My nerves tensed as I watched him pace. "Why?"

"I have to go . . . there are things I need to deal with."

"What? Are you kidding me? You can't just leave!" I sounded more desperate than I wanted to. "I-I mean you need to explain to me what's going on."

"I can't." He stepped back.

The thought of him leaving made me move closer to him. His expression hardened the closer I got, but it didn't stop me. Reaching up, I cupped his cheeks. They felt like fire against my hands. I paused, then brought his face to mine. He didn't move in to kiss me, but he didn't fight me either. When my lips met his, there was even more desperation this time around. A slow burn took over me, building until I almost couldn't stand it. My need for him was overpowering.

"Em . . ." He tried to break away. I kissed him harder. He attempted a pathetic struggle at first, then gave up, and kissed me back with complete abandon. The dizziness I felt made me finally see what all the fuss was about and how greatly girls had underrated making out. Eli kissed me so deeply I groaned, making him even more crazed. I retaliated by tugging on his lower lip. A carnal growl came from deep in him as he pushed me against a tree. This time I enjoyed it. The need was too great, and I knew where we were headed. I wouldn't do anything to stop it; I would be inciting it. I lifted his shirt, but he grabbed my hand.

"Stop," he said, stepping away.

"W-What? Why?" Hurt coated my words. I stood still, bewildered as I tried to catch my breath.

"I really have to go." He looked down and ran a hand through his hair, letting out an aggravated wail.

"Seriously? You're really going to leave me right now?" Hurt and anger flared within me as he kept silent. "You're not going to tell me anything?"

His face was hard, unemotional. He stayed silent.

"Fine." My words shot out like bullets. "Then, go."

"Em?"

"Go." I looked away, trying to hide the tears threatening to spill. Whatever it was he had to do, I knew he wasn't going to tell me, at least not right now. I looked at the ground, trying to hide my disappointment and hurt. Everything in me wanted to beg him to stay, but that was something I would never do.

When I looked up again, he was gone.

"I thought he would never leave," said a deep voice from behind me. I leaped around with a start. Lorcan stood there, a leer twisting his lips. "Not that I wasn't enjoying the show."

"What are you doing here?" A panicky sensation fell over me. "What do you want?"

"What I'm doing here and what I want is the same thing. You," he replied coolly. "But my little brother seems to want you in a whole different way, which I find nauseating." He picked up my bra from the ground and twirled it around his finger suggestively. "Think how he'd react if I played with his toy."

Terror gripped my gut, sending warning bells through my body. I recoiled. I was alone in the woods with a guy I didn't know well, who was dangerous and looked like he could easily kill me. The forest was thick, and the nearest person was probably miles away; we were truly isolated from the outside world.

"This is all so good, especially now I know who you really are. I think this worked out even better than I possibly could have imagined. The pleasant happenstance of it only makes it much sweeter. Oh, my pet, you are like the gift that keeps on giving."

I had no idea what he was talking about. It would have been easy to say it was the mutterings of a madman, but he was much too sane and confident. I meant something to him, but I simply didn't know what. It was nothing good—for me at least.

"Don't worry about watching your back, Ember, because I will be doing that for you." He moved his face close to mine, his features cruelly misshapen and sinister, his handsome face ugly and disturbing. "I'll be watching you all the time."

Then, he was gone.

ᴄᴡᴇɴᴄʏ-ᴄʜʀᴇᴇ

I didn't want to be alone, not after the veiled threat from Lorcan, so I called the gang. Eli had left me stranded in the middle of the woods, and so I sheepishly gave them directions. They came immediately with no questions asked. Those were being saved for later, so they didn't hound me right away. Instead, they curled up with me on the sofa, watching TV, and talking. It felt good having them here.

After an hour or so of them staring at my "war wounds," Ryan couldn't take it anymore. "Okay, M&M, I'm not trying to pressure you to talk, but we're worried about you. What the hell happened to your face?" Ryan's eyes were filled with worry.

"Uhhh . . . it's a long story." I lay back on the sofa pillow; I could barely keep my head up. I felt like shit all over. I would tell them what happened or most of it anyway. They were my best friends, and I didn't want to lie or keep things from them anymore. At the same time, there were some details I couldn't share with them or anybody.

Kennedy gave Ryan warning glances and gently lifted my head on her lap. She was like a mother bear, and today I was the cub. If it meant she had to growl, bite, or attack to protect me, she would.

She lightly brushed my hair off my face, which reminded me of my mom. It took everything I had not to fall asleep.

"Jeez, Em, you are burning up." Kennedy put her hand against my forehead. "You feel like you have a fever."

"It's really hot in here."

"No, it's freezing in here. I think you're sick." Kennedy gently rubbed my arm.

"Sick? But I never get sick . . ." I trailed off as another chill shook my body. I had experienced my fair share of headaches, cramps, and occasionally a hangover, but when I say I never got sick, I mean I had never gotten a fever, a cold, or the flu. I never had the chicken pox or any other childhood bug that every other kid seemed to get. I had never set foot into a doctor's office (therapists didn't count) or a hospital, not even to an eye doctor. When my elementary school was giving free eye exams to the students, my mom took me out of school. At the time I thought nothing of it, but now . . .

"Oh, Em, you are definitely sick." Kennedy tucked the blanket around me tighter. "Do you have a thermometer? I think I should take your temperature."

"No, I don't," I replied as a chill rushed over my body. Cold sweat beaded around my hairline. When you never got sick, you had no need for things like thermometers.

My mom had been against Western medicine, saying it only harmed the body. She didn't believe in the pill-popping cure. She was more into herbs and natural remedies, and Mark followed suit in parenting me. Whether he agreed with it or not, he never deviated from the way Mom wanted me raised. The only thing I fought her on was ibuprofen. That was a must. So what had caused me to get sick now?

Kennedy placed her hand on my sweaty forehead again, looking worried. "You are really, really hot." She turned to Ryan. "Will you run to the store?" Kennedy gave him a list of stuff to get and rushed him out the door.

I felt like I barely closed my eyes before he returned. "Holy cow, Em, you have a temperature of one hundred four degrees!" Kennedy exclaimed, looking at the thermometer. They propped me up, handing me a glass of water and a couple pills. I downed them and crashed back onto the sofa, falling sound asleep.

I was in a room the size of a football field. Striking dark wooden floors reflected the dozens of glittering hanging lights that dropped from the high, arched ceiling. It felt like being under a night sky. It looked like I was in a castle, but it was unlike any I had seen before. It was modern, but it had an Old World feel about it. I looked closer at the pendent lights. Flickering, rolling balls of fire were trapped within the glass balls, illuminating the room.

I sat on a sleek, fur-lined throne. An identical one was next to me, empty. A chandelier hung between the chairs. It looked to be made of millions of raw silk strands, illuminated from the inside, casting a bewitching glow over the chairs. There was a fire floating in the middle of the room on a huge metal plate. Glass windows lined one side of the room and revealed snowcapped mountains and a glistening lake. It was the most breathtaking place I had ever seen.

"Like it?" Torin's voice echoed through the room.

My head jerked to where it came from, and I gulped. Torin, with his leather pants and muscular arms, leaned against the doorframe not too far from me.

"Where am I?" I asked.

"We are in a castle. The throne room to be precise." Torin walked to me.

"The throne room?"

"It's where you belong. This is your rightful place. It is befitting for us together."

"Why would it be my rightful place?"

"It is in your blood, Ember. You and I were destined by the gods and goddesses to be together. It is why I could never stop looking for you. You are mine."

"I'm sorry . . . what?" I squeaked.

He shook his head. "I apologize. I should have known it was too soon for this discussion. I need you to focus on surviving first."

I didn't want to continue the conversation, but dread kept me from saying so. I had this strange feeling I wasn't going to like what I was about to find out. Better to live a while longer in ignorance. If I were dead, all other issues would be a moot point anyway.

"You need to stop thinking of these as mere dreams. I am real. With my limited ability, I am trying to prepare you for what is coming."

"All right. Let's say you are real. How are you able to come into my dreams?"

"They are not your dreams, Ember. They are dreamscapes I have made for us. All these places are not from your imagination but from true places I create from memory. When you fall asleep, I bring you into them. I know it is hard for you to think of this as real from the limited beliefs and thoughts humans have, but I assure you it is." He stiffened, then whirled, looking at the door behind him.

"Oh, no! She is coming to me now." He turned back and with one step was standing in front of me. He held the side of my face. "I have to go, Cinaed." He pressed his lips against my forehead. The beautiful world around me evaporated into darkness.

I woke up feeling the impression of Torin's lips on my forehead.

"I think your fever's gone." Kennedy's hand lifted away from my brows. I frowned at her hand, resentful it's what I had felt pressing on my forehead and not Torin's lips.

I was unsettled from the "dream" or whatever it was. Could it have all be real? Was Torin really coming to me in my dreams? But how was it possible? I shivered at the notion that something in me was not only different from everyone else but may not even be human. I couldn't think about it right now, or I would go insane. Funny how that was no longer my greatest fear.

The fever had broken. Whatever inflicted me was gone now, which calmed me. I didn't like being sick. Kennedy, still in mom-mode, took my temperature again and was happy to see it was back to normal.

I sat up, pushing all thoughts aside. "I want pizza."

"I think she's better," Ryan commented with a smirk.

An hour later, while I munched on the crust of my pizza slice, my brain worked its way back to Torin and what he had said about me being his. My thoughts drifted to Eli, recalling how his lips felt on mine, how his hands felt on my body.

Ryan's fingers waved in front of my face, and, he looked at me questioningly. "Okay, girl, what is going on with you?"

"The list is far too long." I rubbed my face, letting my head fall back onto Kennedy's lap. "Is the day over yet?"

"Not quite." Kennedy patted me gently. "Are you ready to talk about it?"

I groaned as Kennedy continued to stroke my hair. It felt warm and cozy, and I wanted to stay there and not have to deal with stupid sheriffs, dreams that might be real, or Eli's incredible lips and mood swings.

But life is a cruel bitch.

I sat up and finally confessed to them why I was in such a dilapidated state. I told them a lot of what had been going on, excluding or changing unexplainable bits, which seemed to take out a good chunk of it.

"You were in jail?" Ryan screeched. "This all happened after you left us at the concert last night?"

"Are you okay?" Kennedy's soft, concerned voice asked.

Ryan shook his head. "Wait. You and Eli Dragen? Do you understand that is huge? You are hooking up with the notorious Eli Dragen, the ultimate bad boy."

"Em, you're okay, right?" Ken put her hand on my arm. I nodded.

"Holy felon, Batman. You were in jail because you were in a bar brawl at Mike's? See, I told you, Ken. She is the *best* thing that ever happened to this town"—Ryan's teasing subsided as a serious look crossed his face—"and to us." I smiled as a warm buzz fluttered over me.

They demanded every detail of what happened with Eli. Again, I creatively edited what I told them and only gave enough detail to have them ask the least amount of questions. They already suspected Eli had something to do with my mysterious mood, but they didn't know how much had gone on between us.

My fingers twirled around the fringe of the blanket as Kennedy and Ryan discussed my encounter with Eli. My gaze shifted to the TV. The news was on, and above the reporter was a picture of two men whose faces were burned into my memory. I frantically grabbed the remote and upped the volume.

"Breaking news," the woman reporter said. "Two men who were found beaten to death this evening are reportedly members of the Hells Angels biker gang." My eyes widened. "The victims are Ronald McNamm and Frank Corman of the Washington chapter. Investigators stated they were arrested last night after a bar fight and released earlier this afternoon. Thurston County Sheriff's Department is actively investigating another biker club that lays claim to this area. There are no other details about the victims' violent deaths, but law enforcement suspect gang rivalries fueled these murders."

"Oh . . . my . . . god." I stared at the screen, in shock, acid dripping down my throat.

"What? What's going on?" Ryan looked around like we were about to be invaded by aliens, which from the way my life was going, wouldn't be out of the realm of possibility.

I numbly pointed a finger at the screen as the reporter regurgitated the same information. "Th-Th-That's them!" I jabbed my finger at the pictures of McNamm and Pock still on the screen.

"You mean the guys who you got into a bar fight with last night?" Kennedy exclaimed.

"Y-Yeah," I responded numbly. *Holy shit! Pock and McNamm are dead?* I sat with my mouth open during the rest of the story.

"Em?" Kennedy touched my arm timidly. I jumped off the sofa and almost fell when the room spun on me. "Take it easy, Em, you're still not well."

My heart pounded as I started to hyperventilate. I never told Eli the names, nor did I describe what they looked like, but that wouldn't stop him from finding out. I knew in my gut he was responsible for the murders. This was no coincidence. Did he really kill them because of me?

I remembered the vibrating hatred he had when he realized they had done more than strike me. The men hitting me had sent him into a rage, but knowing they had touched me had sent him over the edge.

So much had happened since then I had put his reaction out of my head. Was he capable of murder? Yes. I knew without a doubt he was.

What shocked me was it didn't cause me to be afraid of him. There was something about him which was predatory, feral, and dangerous. He was extremely animalistic, reminding me of how wolves act. He would do anything to protect his pack. Was I considered part of it?

Kennedy's eyes grew wide. "You're thinking it's Eli's gang they are referring to?"

"Yeah." I was seriously going to have to be careful around her. "But I never told him who did it . . . how would he know?" I rubbed my face roughly. He could've found out by asking Mike. "Holy shit! I did this. They were killed because of me."

"You don't know if that's true, but it's not your fault, no matter what happened. You didn't kill those guys, and you just admitted you didn't tell Eli," Kennedy said.

"It is my fault."

"No, it's not. Their deaths could be completely unrelated to Eli or anything involving you. Could simply be a coincidence, nothing more," Ken said firmly, making me believe it could be true—almost.

"Yeah, and I watch porn for the acting," Ryan said dryly. Ken shot Ryan a dirty look as I flopped my head onto the cushions, groaning.

"Great job, Ryan." Kennedy nudged him.

"Sorry, but denial's a bunch of BS. This is *so* about her!"

"Ry, you're really not helping," I grumbled through the cushions. I didn't know what to think or believe, but even worse was I didn't know how I felt about it.

"Still, even if Eli did do this, it is not your fault. He did it, not you," Kennedy said.

My overly attentive friends didn't leave my side until they had given me some chamomile tea to calm me and tucked me into bed. Whether I wanted them to be or not, they were going to be here for me. It felt good to talk and open up to them, even if it wasn't the full truth. That was something I didn't even know myself.

TWENTY-FOUR

On Monday, I parked the truck in the Silverwood parking lot. My stomach, an entangled mass of nerves, threatened to bring my breakfast back up. I hadn't talked to Eli since he abruptly left me in the woods Saturday morning. Sunday had been painful, stretching into an infinitely tedious, long day. I had to force myself not to look at my phone every other minute, but nothing seemed to occupy me enough to stop. I could feel a girly insecurity nipping at me, which only pissed me off more.

Now that I was about to face him, I wanted to run home and hide. I had no idea what to expect from Eli. I didn't really know how it was between us, and if I should mention my suspicions about McNamm's and Pock's murders. In all honesty, though, that wasn't even what made me the most anxious. I was more nervous about seeing him because of what had happened between us than I was he might have murdered two guys. What kind of person was I? Granted, they were lowlife scum who had attacked me and tried to rape me, but still, did they deserve to die?

My gut instinct said hell yes.

Those thoughts took a detour when I saw Eli's Bronco in the parking lot. Don't ask me why—I'd have to plead insanity or something—but when I saw the damn fiberglass top was off the Bronco, an overwhelming anger punched its way through my

206

nerves as I reached the gravel of the parking lot. My reaction was completely irrational I knew. It infuriated me he took the time to remove the top of his Bronco, kill a couple of people, and yet he still didn't have time to even text me?

I pushed my way through the doors and stormed down the hall. My nerves twisted even tighter at the thought of also seeing Samantha. I was afraid she would see my obsession with Eli written all over my face and know what happened. What would she do if she knew I kissed the guy she was involved with? This thought made me feel even more ill as I trudged into the classroom. I slid into an empty chair at the same table as Josh.

"Hey, Em." Josh's smile brightened. "This is your last week here, right?"

"Hey." I pulled my math book out of my bag and smiled at him. "No. I knew how much you'd miss me and that you wouldn't be able to function, so I decided to remain."

He blushed. "That goes without saying. But seriously you're staying here? Awesome." He paused, cocking his head to the side. "Wait, what happened? What'd you do?"

I laughed. "Let's say Christmas came early for the sheriff."

Josh nodded, understanding. "So you are here to stay."

"I am," I replied.

"Does your continuing here have anything to do with the scars on your face and neck?"

Like a flash of lightning, my mind recalled the way Pock shoved his hand down the back of my pants and how McNamm straddled me, grinding into me. I shuddered at the sickening memories.

"You okay?" Josh asked.

"I'm fine." I nodded and forced myself to smile. It felt fake and wrong on my lips. "I'm going through a lot lately." *That's an understatement.*

"If you stop trying to make Sheriff Weiss happy, you might find you have more time on your hands." Josh cocked his head at me, a smile playing on his lips.

"I know, but when I see his face and how happy he gets when he can add on more hours of community service, I can't seem to help myself. What can I say? I'm a giver."

Every step I took to the O.A.R. site in the afternoon was agonizing. I was determined to hold my head high. I would not let a guy make me feel stupid for my actions, and I most definitely would not allow myself to think the reason he didn't call me was because he was too busy beating someone to death or getting back together with Samantha. I would try to be mature about it all.

Yeah, sure. The inner me really wanted to kick him in the shins and call him a poopie-head.

Sam was my biggest fear because of her threat, and I believed she'd stay true to her word. I didn't want to think about if she found out what had happened between Eli and me.

I'm going to throw up.

I was barely at the trails when my body hummed, signaling Eli was somewhere close. It was as if he had his own ringtone or some kind of alarm to let me know he was near. I clenched my teeth, closing my eyes briefly, forcing all the insecure, panicky voices in my head to quiet down. I slyly scanned the group of students ahead for Sam. She stood not too far off, staring back at me. Her icy glare locked onto mine and told me all I needed to know. Rage, jealousy, and revulsion oozed from her narrowed eyes.

Oh, crap on ash bark.

I lifted the hood on my sweater to hide my face—like it would do any good—and looked away.

Eli unlocked the garden shed, and everyone gathered to claim the better tools. I hid behind Josh in line. Through my lashes, I watched Eli. He looked incredible, but the baseball hat he wore concealed his expression—not that he would show me anything if he didn't want to. He was good at that. *Could this incredible looking guy be a killer? Wasn't Ted Bundy supposed to be good-looking?*

I shook the questions from my head as I walked to the door where Eli stood. As Josh went to grab two shovels, I took the opportunity to peer up at Eli. From under his hat, his eyes found mine, causing the air to halt in my lungs. Any clue as to what he was thinking was absent from his face. If seeing me caused him any emotion, he kept it well buried.

Well, two can play at that game, I thought. As much as the power of his gaze weakened my knees, I would not show it. I would try—really, really hard.

"Hi," I forced out, keeping my voice steady and non-emotional.

"Hey," Eli replied as he flicked his chin up in a slight nod.

A pained expression twisted my face. Turning away from him, I tried to hide the emotions. I used to be good at concealing my feelings from others. I was not used to them being so near the surface. Breathing out, I forced my face to go blank.

The sensation of someone's eyes burning into me caused me to turn. I caught Sam's intense, narrowed gaze looking from Eli to me. Unlike Eli, her feelings were crystal clear.

Eli was trying to act like nothing had happened between us, or he was trying to forget that something did. Now his supposed "non-girlfriend" wanted to string my innards up in the trees like Christmas lights. My fear, my embarrassment, and my anger came bubbling up from deep inside. It came on so fast and strong it almost knocked me on my butt.

Twisting in the darkest pit inside me was another flood of emotions, an oozing blackness. It felt like tar, pulling and pushing me down into its dense confinement. Something shifted inside me. No longer frightened of being sucked into it, I surrendered. Comfort and a sense of peace replaced my fear. It was not a calming peace. This new sensation made me feel exceptionally powerful, strong, and indestructible. My focus became sharper. A strange smile curled my lips. Feeling sad and embarrassed was for the weak. I would show them how strong I really was.

"Em?" I heard Josh's wary voice next to me. "Your eyes? Th-They're black . . ."

I never had the chance to ask him what he meant when a firm hand clasped my arm and pulled me quickly away from the group. Eli showed no gentleness as he moved me deeper into the forest.

"Ow! Eli, what the hell?" I yanked my arm away from his grasp. I could already see a slight bruise forming in the shape of his hand around my bicep.

He scanned the thick forest and grabbed my arm again. "Not far enough," he muttered to himself as he tugged me roughly, plowing farther into the shrubbery. When he was content we were far enough into the woods, he stopped. He was silent as his eyes moved quickly over my body. I wish I could say it was in a way that would get my blood flowing, but the worried, critical way he examined every inch of me only made my blood turn cold. Whatever feeling of power I had experienced earlier disintegrated as dread began to prick at my skin.

"Eli?" I looked at him for an explanation. He didn't answer, just continued to stare at me. "Eli." I raised my voice. "What the hell is going on? Why did you pull me away?"

He held my gaze before looking down, mumbling. "This is not good."

"What's not good?"

"Nothing." He shook his head.

"Nothing? Really? That didn't seem like nothing. What's going on?"

"Really, nothing." He took off his hat, running his hand through his hair before replacing the cap on his head again. He seemed to do it a lot when he was frustrated.

His silence drove knives deep inside me. My voice was shaking when I finally spoke. "Did you kill those Hells Angels?"

"What?" He looked at me, startled.

"Tell me the truth, Eli. Did you kill them?"

"You mean those two lowlifes who attacked you?" His eyes darted between mine. "I heard they were killed by a rival gang."

"I'm certain I never told you who they were. H-How did you know?"

"There are things you're better off not learning."

I stared at him, my eyes narrowing as I mulled over his words. Even if Eli hadn't known the names of the men who attacked me, I had a feeling he'd find out somehow. There was war in Eli's eyes as he struggled to come up with an answer, which I hoped I would be able to stomach. I felt like Alice, who was about to fall down the rabbit hole. I didn't understand what was going on, but I knew there was so much more to everything than what I heard or saw.

"You can't imagine the things I've done in my past. I'm not a good guy; I won't ever be. I will never be someone who will bring flowers or candy or meet the parents. I don't do anything else normal guys do for girls. I'm not like them, not even close. There is no white horse and certainly no knight in shining armor in this story." His tone was ardent. "Does it make you want to run?"

I looked deeply into his eyes, searching his face. "No." It was the most honest I had been with myself all day. Nothing in me wanted to run from him.

A half-smile pulled on his lip.

A gust of wind blew my hair and rustled the leaves, reminding me the two of us were alone together in the middle of the woods. Anxiety tugged at me as I thought of what happened last time we were by ourselves in the forest. "So really, why did you pull me out here?"

"I wanted to get you alone," he said, stepping closer to me.

"Bullshit," I replied, my heart picking up speed.

His body pressed against mine. "You think I'm lying?"

"I think you're lying about a lot of things," I replied, feeling his body against mine. "What about Sam?"

"What about her?"

"By the looks she's giving me, I'd say you're clearly together."

"If we were, you'd be dead right now." He slid his hands up my neck, cupping the back of my head, bringing me closer to his lips. *Dead?* Somehow, when it came to Sam and her possessiveness over Eli, I believed it was true.

"Don't," I whispered against his lips with such little conviction it was laughable. His mouth met mine and again a zing of electricity raced through my body, making the hair on my arms stand on end. It made me feel alive. "You think you can use this pathetic tactic to distract me?" I mumbled against his mouth as we gasped for air.

"Yep," he said as he smiled wickedly and pulled me back into him. I couldn't argue with such extensive, in-depth logic.

Our kisses became deep and thorough. I couldn't seem to get close enough to him. His hands moved to the back of my head, crushing me into him even more, as if he couldn't get close enough either. He kept his hands there, and I knew he didn't want to venture anywhere near my tattoo. We both seemed okay with ignoring it. The way his tongue curled around mine and the way his lips pulled at mine, I was willing to ignore anything.

My hands had a mind of their own, running freely up and down his stomach. Those funny little buggers had discreetly found their way underneath his t-shirt and wanted to do more—a lot more. I had a sudden impulse to rip his clothes right off. Normally, the thought of "going further" would scare the shit out of me. With Eli, I couldn't seem to stop myself. I wanted him—badly.

"Eli?" A familiar, feminine voice rang through the air. We jumped apart, looking around for the intruder. He held a finger to my lips, telling me to keep quiet. I nodded. I envisioned Samantha stepping around the corner, catching us. What would happen if she did? I didn't want to find out.

"Eli? Where are you?" Sam's hard tone drifted over the trees.

He spoke with his eyes again. *Don't make a sound.*

I concurred. He had no idea how much I didn't want Sam to catch us.

"*A ghra?*" Her voice moved closer to us. "I know you're out here . . . *with her.*"

Somewhere deep inside me, I seemed to recognize her words. *My love?* Something possessive in me roared back: *He's mine!*

He turned his face to mine. I couldn't tell what Eli was feeling, but his eyes regarded me intensely.

"Eli, don't hide from me." Anger tightened her voice. "Don't lower yourself. Remember what she is. She is not one of us."

His lids lifted to look at me again, and for a brief second, I saw revulsion flicker through his eyes. I felt gutted. I gritted my teeth and stared back, trying my hardest not to show my feelings, but the image of me pounding both their faces—Sam first, then Eli—flittered across my brain. I stuffed my balled-up hands into my jacket, astounded at my violent, jealous thoughts.

I moved my body around his. He grabbed my arm; his expression remained neutral, but there was an unspoken question on his lips which I didn't want to answer. I yanked my arm from his grip and continued silently through the forest, away from him. Wanting to be alone, I wandered around the woods for a while, gratefully accepting the tranquility settling within me.

Eli was wreaking havoc in my life.

By the time I got back, O.A.R. was over. I hurried out of Silverwood to avoid dealing with Eli. I would drive myself to the ropes site. I had barely stepped onto the parking lot when I saw Sam leaning against Eli's car. Seeing me, she pushed herself off the Bronco and headed for me. I sighed, closing my eyes briefly.

This is not my week.

"You slutty, little whore." Her lips twisted cruelly. The sun hit her eyes and reflected a flaming red color, her pupils narrowing.

I should have been terrified, but instead I only felt exhausted and really, really annoyed. I took a deep breath, anger wrapping around my muscles. I was done—*so* done—with this bullshit. I strode toward her.

"Little?" I said. "If you're going to insult me, at least make me a big, slutty whore. Little makes me sound so incompetent."

"Shut up," she snarled. "Did you not think I was serious about my threat?"

"I think you were completely serious," I said evenly.

She sputtered at my response. "I warned you not to mess with me. But you couldn't stay away from him, could you?"

"Our friendship is really none of your business."

She blinked. My calmness unsettled her. I wasn't someone who usually got into fights, but I did inherit my mother's passionate temper. When I was little, kids used to tease me ruthlessly. One time I lost it, getting so mad I broke the nose of one of the boys who taunted me. Mom had been upset and alarmed upon hearing of this, but I could also see the secret pride she felt because I defended myself. I was usually too clumsy to be a fighter. I could walk into a room and fall on my face, but it didn't stop me from trying.

Sam looked too pretty and prim to get down and dirty; she didn't seem as if she could be scrappy. At the same time, there was something about her that told me I shouldn't challenge her.

When did that ever stop me?

"Do you know how easy it will be for me? Your kind is disgusting. You are scum. You shouldn't even be here."

"*Your kind?*" She had said this a few times now. "What are you talking about?" Heat rose in me. My temper was getting close to its breaking point. "What do you mean 'my kind'?"

She laughed, making her look wild and not a little bit nuts. "What you are is a disgrace. Trash."

"Funny. It looks like you were the one who got dumped."

Her eyes flashed red, and her irises seem to stretch vertically. I stepped back blinking in disbelief—did I really see that? In the same instant, she came flying at me.

"You stupid bitch!" she screamed. "You're the fool. He is only using you."

Still startled from what I thought I saw, I was startled by her attack. Her hand whipped across my face with a thunderous crack. Burning pain seared through my cheek. It was the same side McNamm had bruised, and this hit brought new pain.

Blood instantly pumped through the side of my face, making my eye pulsate as if it was going pop out of its socket. I reached up to touch my face, but stopped when I saw her hand coming towards me again. This time I wasn't caught off guard. I ducked, her hand grazing the top of my head as it swung over me.

The momentum threw her off balance when she didn't hit her target, allowing me to step away as she stumbled. It would have been a good opportunity to hit back, but I was still trying to avoid that. She was an instructor at the facility, and I didn't need any more community service hours. When her nails scraped the other side of my face, ripping at the tender scabs where shards of glass had been shoved into my cheek, any notion of taking the high road went out the window.

I swung up, hitting her in the gut. My hand crunched with pain as she doubled over. A low growl escaped from her throat, which seemed at odds with her angelic face.

I could hear a crowd behind me as Silverwood students gathered to see what was happening. Their voices and gasps rumbled together in my ears.

"Holy shit! Is that Samantha and Ember fighting?"

"Fight!" a girl yelled gleefully.

"Someone go get Mrs. Sanchez."

I had to tune them out as Sam's reflexes were too fast for me not to be completely focused on her. The darkness, which had come over me earlier, seemed to bubble happily to the surface, sharpening my focus. I felt calm, cool, and oddly giddy. A happy giggle ripped from me as she took another swing.

I barely had time to get out of the way. She was amazingly fast, but the fact she hadn't hit her target pissed her off even more and triggered another level of fury from her.

When she came at me again, my previous giddiness evaporated as her fingernails morphed into daggers headed for my neck. Her sharp nails sliced my skin as I fell back, kicking with my leg and getting her right in the stomach. Adrenaline put power into my legs I never knew I had. They slammed into her, sending her flying back onto the gravel several yards away.

Drops of blood splattered onto my shirt from where she caught me on my neck. I didn't feel any pain, although there was no doubt I would later. She jumped up and hurled back at me, her fists ready for their target. I rolled to my left, missing the force of the blow, but her foot and her fist caught my right side, clipping my hip and shoulder.

I twisted, getting my feet under me as I hopped up. She grabbed my leg, ripping through my jeans as she dug her nails in. The pain made me crumple to the ground. Rage hit me like a brick as I felt her fist come down on me again.

The darkness in me, which had been so patient, was done waiting. Playtime was over. I let myself go. I felt no pain, no fear. All other emotions were gone, and I was left with incredible power. Instinct took over. I got up, plucking her off me as if she was a mere bug and flung her to the ground.

She quickly recovered and leapt to her feet, and blood dripped from her mouth. Her face twisted into a hideous canvas of rage. She sprang, but I didn't move.

She was dropping down on me when I held out my hand. Her body stopped in mid-air, changed direction, and flew across the parking lot, landing on Eli's windshield with a crunch.

The impact made the glass shatter into a million pieces. Void of emotion, I watched as she stirred and twitched. I advanced on her, wanting to finish this fight—to finish her.

"Ember." A voice broke through my resolve. I turned my head, realizing I hadn't heard any sound for a long time, except for the noise of the fight. My focus had blocked everything else out.

"Ember, stop." The voice came to me again, but it still sounded faint and distant. I swung around to see someone standing not too far from me. The man's green eyes went wide as they looked into my face, but his mouth was set in a strong line. The tall, muscular man took a step towards me. I recognized this person as a possible threat, but not my biggest one at the moment. I turned back to look at the girl. The need to end her was still raging inside me. I moved toward her again.

"Brycin . . . stop, now," the voice commanded me.

I didn't want to listen; I wanted to destroy her. Yet as much as I fought to ignore the deep voice, there was a part of me that wanted to oblige it. As if a switch had been hit, the darkness left me, and I was overcome with emotion.

I turned, blinking. A heavy fog was lifting from my brain. "Eli?"

Eli let out a sigh of relief. "Come back to me, jailbait." His cocky smile filled me with warmth.

"Ember!" Mrs. Sanchez's voice ripped through my protective shield as she ran toward me.

Reality, logic, fear, and emotion crashed down breaking my security. The last tentacles of the darkness released me, throwing me back into reality. My legs gave out, and the world spun around me as I collapsed to the ground. Eli's hand was there cradling my head before it hit the pavement. His touch was the only sensation I comprehended before everything went black.

TWENTY-FIVE

I heard voices before I was fully awake. Sharp jabs of pain ruthlessly worked their way through every inch of my body. My lids lifted just enough to see I was lying on a cot in the nurse's office. Mrs. Sanchez paced the room frantically, while Eli sat calmly in a chair not far from me.

"Oh, my god, Eli, what the hell happened?" Mrs. Sanchez exclaimed. "I have a student who's been beaten to a pulp and a missing advisor who should be in intensive care. How did this happen?"

She moved back and forth behind the nurse's desk. "I expect fights to happen because of the kids who attend here. From their backgrounds, you know it might get dangerous and volatile. In all my years, though, I have *never* seen anything like this. I could have sworn Ember's eyes were completely black . . . obviously my imagination getting the better of me." She rubbed her temples. "But your windshield? I don't understand. There is no way Ember could have thrown Samantha with that much force. It's impossible. Tell me again what you saw?"

"Marisol, I got out there a bit before you did. I don't know what happened or how it started," Eli replied. I could sense the lie.

"Did you notice when Samantha disappeared? I looked up and she was gone."

218

"No, sorry. I had my hands full at the time."

"Yes. Thank you, Eli, for your help bringing Ember in," she said, pressing her lips together. "I simply can't get over this. Samantha seemed so sweet, and she was an instructor here, for goodness sakes. From what I heard, she was the one who attacked Ember first. Ember acted in self-defense. It all seems so odd to me. Why in the world would she want to attack Ember?"

"I don't know." Another lie.

"But you and Samantha are . . . close. I can't believe you don't know where she could have gone or what this was about?" The snappish tone in her voice showed Mrs. Sanchez didn't fully believe Eli. She knew this kind of fight usually was over a guy. "You are clear about the rules set in place here, right? We do not permit fraternizing with students."

"Yes, Marisol." Eli's tone was sharp and clear.

She nodded, looking relieved. "I still think we should call the hospital. I'm worried about Ember's injuries."

"No!" Eli shot from his chair. "I mean, the nurse checked her out and said she only had cuts and bruises. She'll be fine and will heal before you know it."

"Okay . . ." Mrs. Sanchez sounded unsure, but something about Eli's manner made her agree and forgo protocol. "I'm going to go speak with the rest of the students who were out there. If she wakes up, come and get me, please." She glanced at me, and I shut my eyes before she saw I was awake. "Okay, I'll be back as soon as I can get statements from the other students. Keep me updated on how she's doing." Mrs. Sanchez sighed and departed.

Eli leaned over the desk as the door shut, taking in a deep breath. "Shit," he muttered under his breath.

"People usually use bathrooms for that," I croaked.

He was at my side before I could blink. "Hey," he said softly, his hand brushing back some tangled hair from my face.

"Hey," I responded, soaking in the only pleasure my body felt. I

219

was afraid to move. I knew as soon as I did, I would find pain in areas I never knew I had. "You lied to her."

He smiled, knowing what I was talking about. "No, I didn't. She asked me if I was aware of the rules, and I said I was."

I gave a small snort, which caused pain to spike in my chest. I closed my eyes, not wanting to throw up.

"How are you feeling?"

"Like I've had the crap beaten out of me." I looked up at him again.

A slight smile curved his lips. "I'm thinking about signing you up for the WWF."

"The World Wildlife Fund?"

Eli scoffed. "Yeah, jailbait, the World Wildlife Fund. You can wrestle those scary panda bears to the ground." It took me a while to realize he meant the World Wrestling Federation. Okay, so I was a little slow. I tried to sit up and groaned with pain.

"Take it easy. I think you have some bruised ribs, but I'm pretty sure nothing is broken." Eli moved to the desk and grabbed a cotton swab and some ointment. Everything in my body felt liked it was cracked, broken, bruised, or cut. I touched my cheek and flinched. The swelling caused my left eye to only partially open. Dammit, I had almost gotten rid of my last set of cuts and bruises.

"You think you're hurt, you should see my windshield."

Everything that happened between Sam and me flooded back—things which shouldn't be possible. But I knew they had happened; they were too real to ignore. Without touching her, I had thrown Sam into Eli's car across the parking lot as if she were a mere rag doll. I knew I was capable of moving small stuff like leaves or a cue stick, but a whole person? There was no way I should have been able to do it—no possible way.

My mind flipped through the memories: Sam's eyes flaming like fireballs, her nails turning into talons, her face twisting into some beast-looking thing. I began to riffle through all the other incidents that had happened since I arrived in Olympia. Things I had tried to push aside and ignore began to pour into my consciousness in an unrelenting stream.

"What is going on?" I whispered hoarsely, even though talking made my jaw hurt like hell. The coldness gripping me needed answers.

"I'm going to finish patching up your wounds and get you home," he replied. "Not sure how, since I can't drive my car in its present condition."

"Don't act like you don't know what I'm talking about." My eyes cut into his. He looked away from me. "Eli?" I pleaded.

"This might sting a bit," he said, ignoring me. He knelt in front of me and patted my cheek with the damp swab, cleaning the deep nail scratches. I jerked and hissed through my clenched teeth. "Sorry, told you it might hurt."

I frowned, which made his eyes glitter with amusement. He moved to my neck and paused. The look in his eyes grew dark as he inspected the cuts there. Old, faded scratch marks and bruises lay beneath the new ones. A reminder of another moment we pretended didn't happen.

"What am I?" I asked quietly. "You know, don't you?"

A faraway look settled into his eyes as he absently ran his fingers along both the new and old lines on my neck. He looked up, our gazes connected, and even through the pain, I felt electricity pulsing through my body. My breath grew short and clipped as he continued to touch me. The truth was trying to break through, wanting to be free, to be heard. His soft, moist lips parted, as if he was going to speak.

A hard slam of a door from somewhere inside the school snapped us both back to the present. "All done." He moved quickly away from me. I looked away in disappointment. Whatever he was going to say, whatever he was going to tell me, was now gone. He headed for the door. "Marisol wanted me to get her when you woke up."

221

"Eli?"

His hand hovered above the door handle. Something had shifted; his body was rigid and defensive now. There was nothing I could say to reach him, to make him open up to me. I was smothered by pain and exhaustion. I fell silent as he opened the door and walked out. He didn't return.

After the commotion died down at Silverwood, Mrs. Sanchez offered to drive me home. As much as I tried to convince her I was okay to drive, she wouldn't have it. Eventually I gave in, knowing Mark's truck would be okay at Silverwood. Eli had left without a word to either one of us. I couldn't say it didn't hurt, but nothing about him was predictable or reliable—or unexpected. Mrs. Sanchez seemed quite confused by his disappearance and thought he might still be around until we saw the broken glass and twisted metal where his Bronco had been and the discarded remnants of his windshield left behind.

"Ahh, he must have gone to deal with his car." She nodded towards the empty space. "Or maybe he went to find Samantha." I bit my lip, looking at the ground. "This will give me an opportunity to speak with your stepfather."

"He's not home. He's on a business trip till next Monday," I uttered as I hobbled after Mrs. Sanchez to her car, gripping my ribs in pain. Everyone seemed bewildered I was even up and walking. I wasn't surprised, not anymore.

"What? Not until then? He leaves you alone for that long?"

"I am eighteen, and we have a very trusting relationship. I've never been quite the typical teenager."

"No, you are not." She smiled knowingly at me. "You are different from any other young lady I have met before."

As she drove me to my house, she used the opportunity to bombard me with questions. Most of them I couldn't answer with more than "I don't know." I could sense the aggravation building in her as I shrugged my shoulders and looked out the side window.

222

I'm sure she was hoping for more insight into the mystery of Samantha's attack and disappearance. I felt bad since I could provide some answers, but those wouldn't provide clarity, only more questions, so I kept my mouth shut. As we went, I felt a tingling sensation crawling over my skin, and I shifted my gaze to the dark forest rolling by at a steady pace. We were going too fast to see anything clearly, but I could feel something was out there. Something dangerous was calling to me—again.

At home, Mrs. Sanchez made sure I was settled in and even fixed me a cup of soup before she felt comfortable leaving. She also made me call Mark, but I only reached his voicemail. I was about to hang up when she grabbed the phone from my hand and left a long message about what had happened. I cringed, because it was not the sort of message you left a parent who was thousands of miles away. I had no doubt I would get a frantic phone call from Mark soon.

At first I was grateful when she finally left me by myself. That quickly changed. Memories and thoughts began to berate me, letting me stew in the unexplained and the impossible. Twisted, dark nightmares haunted me every time I shut my eyes. Even sleeping on the sofa with the TV on didn't stop them from coming.

My body was exhausted from trying to fight off another high fever that engulfed me, this one even worse than the one before. I went from having violent chills to burning hot and sweating through several layers of clothes. I wanted to sleep so I could heal, but my thoughts conspired to keep me awake. The memories of my fight with Sam were making me face all the other things I had pushed deep down—things I had kept in a tightly latched box, which was now too full to hold anything more. I had to grasp for air a few times, as fear sunk deeper into my chest.

The empty house only made matters worse. Every noise and creak had me jumping up and grabbing the steak knife I placed next to me on the coffee table. I couldn't wait for Mark to get home. I felt lonely without him here.

He called a few hours later, waking me from my restless, fever-induced sleep. He was frantic, as I knew he would. I assured him over and over I was fine and to not jump on the next plane home. I fudged on what happened a bit and made it sound like less of an incident than it was. The entire time I talked to him, I wanted to cry—cry because I missed him, cry because I felt scared and lonely without him, and cry because I knew I was lying to him. But most of all because I knew something wasn't right about me, even more than we kidded about. I didn't fit into this world somehow.

He could sense something was wrong, but I just kept reassuring him it was because I missed him. After I had him convinced enough I was okay, we said goodbye. My head pounded, and I felt like I was in a furnace. I needed sleep, which was easier said than done. After taking several ibuprofen tablets, a PM pill or two, and a whiskey shot for good measure, my brain finally relaxed around 4:30 am and let me drift.

Trees, flowers, and other vegetation that flourished wildly covered the green, luscious grounds rolling in gentle waves in front of me. The beauty was breathtaking and glistened under the warm sun in colors so intense I couldn't quite grasp them. I had been here before. I had dreamed of this place.

A voice floated into my ear. "It's beautiful, isn't it?"

I turned to see a man standing next to me. If this man was some brilliant figment in my dream or real as he claimed, it didn't matter. He was one of the most beautiful men I'd ever seen, especially in those tight leather pants.

"Torin."

"Miss me?" He gazed into my face. I found it almost painful to look at him. I realized with the thumping of my heart I had. I missed him the moment he left each time.

"Yes." The truth seemed to come out without my knowledge. His smile brightened at my reply, making my legs feel weak.

"I have missed you, too." He forced a smile as he touched my cheek lightly, but the pain and fear in his eyes were great. *"Ember, she is coming for you. I don't know how to protect you anymore."*

"Who is coming for me?"

"Remember, I will try to help you any way I can. I will do anything to keep you safe, mo chuisle." Torin leaned closer to me.

"But . . ."

He cut me off, cupping my face in his hands. Before I could protest, he kissed me deeply, sending sparks of heat and lust through my body, making me forget everything except the feel of his lips on mine. His hands followed the curves of my body, over the sides of my breasts, moving lower and lower . . .

My eyes shot open, a strangled gasp escaped my lips as I awoke with a start. My body tingled with pleasure and pain, feeling the ache of being unfulfilled. Through all the nightmares I was having, Torin was my only relief. I tried to recapture the dream, closing my eyes and desperately seeking a return to sleep, but I could not. I placed my head in my hands and let out a whimper. "Of course, I had to wake up then," I mumbled.

When I did fall back to sleep, the dreams were not of Torin but of fire and death.

Mrs. Sanchez had told me to take a few days off, so besides peeing and getting something to eat or drink, I didn't move off the sofa for the entire next day. I did feel better. The fever had gone down, and some of the bruising was already disappearing, but the scratches and cuts down my neck and cheek still really stung. It was making me extremely tired.

At least during the day, while resting on the sofa, my nightmares abated a little and let me sleep. I ignored my cell phone. The only call I wanted was the one number not showing on my caller ID.

I couldn't control my dreams, but when the night terrors started again, and I woke up screaming, I wouldn't allow myself to think about them. I would angrily roll over, punch my pillow, and try to go back to sleep, usually with my iPod on to drown the shadows clawing at my consciousness.

By Wednesday morning, the scratches and bruises healed enough so I wasn't in terrible pain. I was driving myself senseless with questions and fear. I used to enjoy being alone, but now it only left me with thoughts I couldn't handle, questions I couldn't answer, and questions I didn't want to answer. I tried my best to shut my mind from any thoughts except for what was in front of me.

I decided to return to school, thinking it would distract me. I regretted it the second I stepped on campus. I felt sick as I walked across the parking lot. Was Samantha back? Had she been fired? What about Eli? Would he act strangely around me? I wasn't strong enough to deal with him, yet at the same time all I wanted was to see him. For my own sanity, I desperately needed answers, and for some reason, I felt he could provide them.

I walked to Silverwood, immediately noting Eli's car was nowhere to be seen. Tiny pieces of glass were scattered across the parking lot, reflected in the sunlight. I turned away; the shards confirmed it definitely happened and wasn't some strange dream.

Josh came running to me. "Are you okay? You didn't call me back, and I've been so worried about you." His eyes moved over me. I guess he was checking to see if I was in one piece, to see if I had grown another head, or to see if merely by looking at me, he could tell if I had been bitten by a radioactive spider.

"I know. I'm sorry. I really wasn't up to talking to anyone."

Josh shook his head. "I can't believe I left right before it happened. So many people have told me about it, and all of it sounds completely outrageous. Did Samantha really attack you? Did you really throw her into a windshield?"

"Is she back?" I asked, ignoring his questions.

"No, she's completely disappeared. No call, no show. I heard Mrs. Sanchez tried to contact her, but the cell phone had been disconnected, and the address she gave was a fake." I looked down, my brain trying to absorb this information. Josh shrugged. "Looks like she and Eli got the hell out of town together."

My head snapped up. "What?"

"Yeah, he's disappeared, too. He didn't show up yesterday, either." Josh looked at me steadily. "But I guess it makes sense, you know, since they're a couple."

Heat filled my body, making me itchy and agitated. Maybe when he told me he wasn't "with" Samantha he meant it literally at that moment, not figuratively. Next time I would make sure I was clearer, because leaving a job and running off with a girl was certainly a boyfriend move.

The rest of the day didn't get better. I felt like I was at my old school again, where everyone whispered and talked about me behind my back. Once again, I was the freak. At least here I was a freak among freaks. *Great. I'm progressing.*

Mrs. Sanchez had cancelled O.A.R. the previous day because of Eli's and Samantha's disappearance. Today, nobody heard anything new, so we went there as we normally would. I was on my way when I heard someone calling my name. I turned to see Mrs. Holt running up to me. "Mrs. Sanchez asked me to give you these and tell you that you're in charge." Mrs. Holt placed a set of keys in my hand.

He's really gone. I sighed and left for the building site. It felt strange and wrong to go to the area and not have Eli there. I couldn't stop looking for him. I didn't expect there to be such a deep emptiness in me.

TWENTY-SIX

By Friday, Eli still hadn't shown up. I knew he wouldn't, but deep down I'd hoped. He was now the guy who disappeared with another girl. I shouldn't have been shocked. Even the voices inside my head were saying, *Told you so!* I'd already reached pathetic, but after days of secretly holding onto hope, I moved way beyond to plain pitiful. I had to escape these thoughts.

I need to be put out of my misery.

His absence caused a darkness to seep deep into me. People seemed to sense the change in me and gave me a wide berth while walking in the hallway. The gossip of how I threw Sam into Eli's windshield had spread like wildfire. The rumor mill took liberties with what happened, but nothing came close to the truth. People who hadn't been there thought the incident had been grossly exaggerated; others thought it had been understated.

No matter what they believed, they all seemed to fear me, and in a place like this it earned respect. The dark part of me relished those who had belonged in gangs or had lived on the street were now intimidated by me and saw me as the more dangerous one. But what I really tried to ignore was the voice in me that said they were right.

Saturday felt like a blessing and a curse. Mrs. Sanchez cancelled the ropes course because of Eli's disappearance and my injuries, which now had healed. For appearances, I kept a limp in my step. This meant I had more time alone with my thoughts. Too much time alone to allow my brain to dwell on things I didn't understand or know how to face. Even my writing and my painting didn't distract my mind from the mysteries haunting me.

I tried googling some of the things I'd seen and got nothing useful. The only things that came up were crazy people on blogs rambling about government conspiracies and X-Men theories. All this made me want to see Eli more. I felt certain he knew something—something about me.

Fortunately, Ryan and Kennedy were not the type to leave me alone for too long. They texted and called me relentlessly, trying to get me to go to a party in the woods with them tonight. I wasn't really in the mood, but at the same time I couldn't take sitting home alone anymore.

"Come on, M&M," Ryan begged. "What are you gonna do, sit home and wallow? I know you're hurting, but are you really going to let this loser guy get the better of you? Especially since it's not likely he's sitting at home wallowing over you."

"Wow, ouch." Truth was a nasty bitch sometimes. "That hurt."

"Honesty does, babe."

"Good manipulating," I said. "You really are good at it." He was right. There was no way Eli was at home moping about me. I needed to move on.

I was glad I let Ryan talk me into going with them. I needed a few blissful hours of simply having fun, letting everything else go. I was tired of being alone and scared. Blowing up things and throwing people into windshields with my mind could all be left at home tonight. So could my heartache over Eli.

I was pulling on my beanie and jacket when I heard the horn of Ryan's Nissan. I picked up my phone and house keys and paused, looking down at my cell. My annoyance spiked making me want to throw the phone out the window. All I'd be doing would be staring at it all night, and I didn't want that. I placed it on the counter and headed out.

Locking the door behind me, I ran into the cold night air. The thick fog clung to everything within its grasp. The moon emitted an eerie glow as it tried to penetrate the murkiness.

I hopped into the car. Kennedy was already in the backseat. Dance music cranked through the stereo, making the speakers sound like they were about to blow. "Ready, girl?" Ryan wiggled his eyebrows at me.

I gave him a short nod back. "Ready."

Ryan did a double take. "Jesus, what the hell happened to your face now?"

"I'll tell you, I promise, but can we have a good time tonight and let me forget everything for a few hours?"

"What are you guys talking about up there?" Ken yelled from the backseat.

"Nothing. We're talking about you." Ryan winked at me. "I'm telling her how you used to make out with your Orlando Bloom poster."

"Understandable," I replied.

"You dared me." Kennedy pulled herself up between the seats. "Oh, and by the way, your shoes and jacket don't go together," she jabbed back, looking at me winking.

"What?" Ryan looked down at himself in horror.

"Oh, thanks, Kennedy, now he's going to insist on going home so he can change." I threw up my hands, smiling to myself. This was exactly what I needed.

It took Ryan some major convincing that his outfit was fine before we finally got to the site. Grabbing our flashlights, we walked through the looming, dark forest. It was creepy, but I didn't feel uncomfortable. Trees felt like old friends. They would never hurt me, although I couldn't say the same for the people and things in the forest.

The music and the glow of the bonfire reached us before we found the party. The number of people already there surprised me. There must have been about eighty or more mulling around the fire, dancing, drinking, and talking while someone's iPod was hooked up to large speakers that were draining someone's car battery. It was a mixture of the different schools in the area and different ages. I didn't recognize most people, and for this I was glad.

"There's Ian." Kennedy pointed to a dark-haired, lanky boy laughing with a group of people not far from us. He was of average height and had the same dimples and dark, spiky hair as Ryan, but that's where the resemblance ended. Ryan was adorable, but Ian definitely made you look twice. He was striking with his Caucasian-Asian ethnicity; his large, almond shaped eyes framed his deep, dark brown, almost black pupils.

"Ryan. You're here, man," Ian called, heading over to us, "and your Angels!"

"Of course. You think I'd miss partying with you and pimpin' out my girls for some extra cash? Besides if I didn't come I'd have nothing to blackmail you with later when Aunt Vicky asks me what you've been up to!"

Ian gave Ryan a quick guy hug and pat. "Funny, that's why I do it, too."

"It's why this works . . . we both have too much shit on the other to ever rat each other out."

"Good plan so far," Ian said. Both of them smiled, showing their matching dimples. "But I have to admit I only invite you so you'll bring your beautiful harem."

"Yes, you should start paying me for this service."

"It's in the mail," he replied dryly and turned to Kennedy and me. "How are my favorite girls tonight?"

"Good," Kennedy said. I smiled, and the two of us gave him a quick hug.

"So who's ready for a drink?"

"Me!" The three of us raised our hands.

We followed him to where half a dozen coolers sat. I went down the row, trying to find something other than beer and finally settling on a chilled bottle of some kind of mixed vodka drink. I turned to head back to the gang when I stopped dead in my tracks.

On the other side of the fire, Eli leaned against a tree, casually drinking a beer. Firelight flickered off his profile in an alluring mix of shadow and light. He looked so dangerous and frightening but at the same time so unreal and strangely beautiful it gripped my heart. Dark shadows accentuated the heavy circles beneath his eyes. He looked exhausted.

Seeing him filled me with joy, then nervousness, then anger. What was he doing here? I looked around for his partner in crime, but I saw no sign of Samantha. I thought he'd gone, leaving Olympia in his rearview mirror. Here he was, though, drinking a beer like he fit in with this party of college and high school students.

It took a few deep breaths for me to liberate myself from that spot. He had yet to see me. I was about to go ask him what had happened and why in the hell he was even here, when my stomach coiled into a tight knot and my legs almost gave out. A stunning but trashy curvaceous brunette with a thin shirt emphasizing her extremely large boobs and jeans so tight I imagined they had to be painted onto her came purring up to Eli. It was the same girl who popped up on his caller ID when he drove me home several weeks earlier. She was far older than the average student here, and she oozed sexuality. The shadows blocked his face as he turned to her. Her arms slipped around his neck, pulling him into a passionate kiss.

I stared at them through the flames. I wanted to turn away but couldn't. Emotion boiled through me. The bonfire started crackling and exploding higher into the air. Anyone near it jumped back.

232

"Holy shit," I heard a voice exclaim. "Who's throwing alcohol on the fire?"

It was not alcohol causing the fire to swell. It was me—a dangerous cocktail of pissed off and hurt.

The commotion around me was enough for me to turn my gaze away from Eli. I turned and hightailed it away from the party, away from Eli and away from watching him kiss another girl. I didn't stop until I was deep in the throng of the towering trees.

I can't breathe. I can't breathe. Panic twisted through my lungs, and sharp pains constricted my chest. I gasped for air and bent over, putting my hands on my knees. Air slowly came back into my lungs. I sat down, leaning against a tree as my head spun. I was ashamed of myself. I was only just another stupid girl who knew better but still fell for him. *Dumb.* My mind tortured me with images of him and other girls, of him cupping their faces in his hands, his lips tasting theirs, him looking at them the same way I had seen him look at me. I banged my head against the bark. I guess I was the only one who thought we had this undeniable connection, this magnetic draw to each other, this unexplainable, even special electricity when we touched.

I was empty, lost in my heartache, when my internal warning system flickered. The mist hovered too close to the ground, making it hard to see anything. I felt someone's eyes on me. I picked myself up, gripping the tree behind me. It was time to return to the party. I would be strong and act as if I didn't care how much he had hurt me. I didn't need him. I turned to go and gasped. Eli stood in front of me with his arms crossed, blocking my way.

"Shit!" I yelped. "How do you keep sneaking up on me like that?"

"Maybe you should pay a bit more attention," he said aloofly.

"Yeah, maybe I should." I tried to move around him.

Grabbing my arm, he pulled me to a stop. "If you're trying to say something, say it."

I looked down at him grasping my elbow, then up to his face. "Take your hands off me." I clenched my jaw furiously. Studying me, he slowly removed his grip. I recoiled from him. "Don't ever touch me again."

"Is that what you really want?"

A short laugh erupted out of me. "You really think you're irresistible don't you? I'm not going to fall for whatever bullshit you're about to dump on me; I'm not *that* inane."

His brows furrowed. "What are you going on about?"

"Seriously?" I shook my head. "Why are you even here anyway?"

"To see you."

"Right." I wanted to go back to the party, but like a magnet, I was drawn to him. I couldn't leave. "I hate you," I whispered furiously, but it came out sounding more breathy and passionate than true hatred.

He looked at me so deeply it was as if he could read my mind. His fingers hooked into my belt loops and pulled me forcefully to him. My body pressed up against his, making me tremble. He tugged off my beanie and swept his hand up the nape of my neck, entwining his fingers through my hair. He gripped the back of my head and brought my face to his. My overwhelming need for him took over with dizzying intensity. Our lips fervently devoured each other, desperate and hungry.

No, I can't let him do this to me. He's sucking you back into his game. He's playing with you! It took several moments and a lot more shouting in my head to finally pull myself away. "No, stop!" I pushed him hard. Taken off guard, he stumbled into the tree.

"What the hell?" His eyes narrowed in confusion.

"Like you don't know? Seriously, how stupid do you think I am?"

"Rhetorical question, right?" The way I glared at him made the corner of his mouth twitch up in a smirk.

234

"I'm not going to let you treat me like this anymore." Fury dripped in my every word. I used to shake my head and laugh at girls like me. "Look, I'm aware you're a bit of a player. You've never made that fact a secret. But watching your tongue shoved down some girl's throat tonight was only icing on the cake after hearing you ran off with Samantha. I'm not going to be merely another girl you reel in."

"Em . . ."

"No," I said, cutting him off. "There is nothing you can say. I don't want to hear your bullshit excuses or cryptic, mysterious reasons anymore, or why you haven't called me, or why you happened to disappear the same time Sam did. The answers are pretty clear. I get it. Now, go away and leave me alone. You've been nothing but a headache. So run back to Sam or some other girl. I don't care. I couldn't give a crap about what you do anymore."

"Sounds like it."

Like fireworks, my anger burst into sparks, exploding fireballs that turned to ash. Cold anger controlled my voice. "Leave. Me. Alone." I took one step to go, but before I could blink, he pushed me against a tree, pinning my wrists above my head.

A sardonic look crossed his face as he towered over me. "You done now?" His breath was warm on my cheek. I glared back at him. "Good. Now, if you allow me to get a word in, you might hear some actual truths, instead of your delusional ramblings."

"Delusional? You assh—"

He placed his free hand over my mouth, cutting off my ranting. "Can you shut up for two seconds?" I stared back at him, not committing. He didn't look completely convinced, but he lowered his hand and sighed. *"Damnú ort!* I've never had to restrain a girl to get her to listen to me before."

"Maybe not to listen, but I'm sure you've restrained plenty of girls before." I struggled against him, trying to break free.

He leaned all his weight against me so he could get a better grip on me. I hated myself, because all I focused on was his torso against mine. It made me want to move in even closer to him. I was furious at my body and my heart, which yearned for him. My own body betrayed me. It would be marvelous if it would simply let me hate him.

"Stop fighting me," he said with a commanding voice. "Dammit woman, you are making me crazy." He looked away shaking his head. "And definitely in more ways than one."

We stared at each other. I struggled to keep my carnal thoughts under wraps. Eli shifted, looking away. My gaze drifted over his profile. He took my breath away, but he would only cause me pain. I had to look somewhere else.

His voice was soft, mumbling, and not unkind. "Em, I'm not trying to mislead you. I warned you I'm not a good guy, and I have a past proving it. But I won't apologize for it or for the girls I've been with."

"I don't want you to apologize. I only want you to let me go," I said, forcing myself to struggle against his hold. I was painfully aware of his body pressing into me.

He shook his head again, more in frustration than telling me no. "Listen. Yes, I left because of Sam, but it's not what you think."

"It never is."

"I told you before. I'm not with Samantha."

"Oh, really? Is she aware of this fact?"

"She is. She doesn't deal with rejection well, and unfortunately, you got punished for it."

"So what about your other girlfriend?" My voice sounded catty. "Jeez, Eli, you poor thing, you can't seem to keep them off of you, can you?"

"Yeah, and here I am out with the one I have to pin against the tree so she'll stay," he scoffed. "The girl you saw me with earlier was someone I hung out with for a bit. I haven't seen her in a while. It was what it was, and I never tried to deceive or delude her. She chose what she wanted to hear. I didn't know she was going to be here, and she kissed me before I could stop her. If it helps any, I pushed her away."

"It doesn't."

"I came here for you tonight." He saw my eyes narrow in suspicion. "Believe me or not, but it's the truth. Wait! If you saw her kiss me, then you would have seen me push her off."

"I didn't really stick around with a bowl of popcorn," I replied, turning my face from him. My rage tricked out of me, but the hurt wouldn't leave. "How do I know what you're saying is true? How do I know this isn't the same bullshit you regurgitate to all the other girls?" Pain ground into my heart at the thought of Eli's feelings being only lies.

"You don't." His eyes looked honestly into mine. "You either trust me or you don't."

How could I? I tried never to let people in enough to need them, so I could protect myself from the pain of loss. Here I was, however, letting the poster boy of the unstable into my life. My heart couldn't handle the agony of losing him, which seemed inevitable.

He shifted back, the pressure of his body against mine lessening bit by bit until we no longer touched. "Sorry if what you saw upsets you," he said quietly.

There was a lot that troubled me, like how acutely I missed the feel of his body pressed up against mine, or how with a touch, he could send unexplainable shockwaves through me. There were so many baffling things left unsaid between us. We were connected beyond what was normal. I knew he was like me, but somehow different, too. Our lives linked together the instant we met, no matter how much either one tried to deny it.

I averted my gaze. "We've had these indescribable moments, this instant bond. Then, other times it's like I disgust you, that there is something about me you truly and deeply despise. You know something about me . . . I know you do. So tell me, Eli . . .

what or who am I?" I looked up at him, my eyes pleading.

Anger and frustration pinched his expression as he ran his hand over his face and through his hair. He grunted and hissed under his breath, his hand smashing into the bark next to my head. Woodchips sprinkled down on me. I didn't flinch. He kept his hand up by my head, and leaned over me, his hair tickling my cheeks.

"Please," I entreated. "I know something's not right about me. I've known it my whole life. I've never felt like I belonged. But it's more, isn't it? Please, Eli, don't you think I deserve to know?" I asked, leaning my forehead into his.

We stayed like that for a few moments, our breaths falling in sync. Then I felt his head move against mine, nodding. "Yeah, you deserve to know."

Finally, I was going to find out what I was. There was a reason people said, "Be careful what you wish for." I suddenly felt the weight of that bit of wisdom. Did I really want to know? I knew it would change my life, but would it be for better or for worse?

Eli stiffened. He turned his head, scanning the dark forest.

The way he was acting made my nerves go on high alert. "What's wrong?"

He ignored my question and continued to listen for something I couldn't hear. All I heard was our breathing and the small sounds of the forest.

"No. It wasn't supposed to happen like this," he whispered so low I didn't know if I had heard him right. "Stay here. I'll be right back." Eli disappeared into the darkness before I could protest.

"What? Oh, you have got to be kidding me," I muttered to myself. "I swear if you're trying to get out of telling me, I'm going to kill you."

A crunch of broken twigs made me jump and caused my breath to catch. My voice quivered.

"Eli?"

A low, deep, menacing growl from the darkness locked my muscles in place. I wanted my brain to match the sound to an animal. A wolf or possibly a bear, but I knew it was neither.

Another beastlike snarl echoed through the woods, closer. My skin prickled as I felt its eyes studying me. I could hear the animal move through the dense brush, inching itself to me. Prowling. Stalking. I shoved myself off the tree and crept towards the direction of the party. I was too far away from my friends; even if I screamed, no one would hear.

A growl sounded from the direction I was headed. I froze. How did it move there so quickly? This thing was unnaturally fast, silent, and smart. It understood what I was doing and was blocking my escape. It rumbled again, stirring the underbrush. It was still too well hidden in the darkness to see clearly. I could barely make out an outline and its eyes. It was enough.

This can't be happening!

A cold sweat broke over me. A twig snapped. There was a moment of uncertainty. Neither of us moved. Air capsulated inside my lungs—the quiet before the storm. Then, it lunged, crashing through branches, heading right for me.

I spun and ran, darting in and around trees and through bushes. Loud cracks of breaking wood and foliage echoed behind me, like a bulldozer plowing through the forest close on my heels. My nightmares had become a reality, blending into this one true horror.

My heart pounded in my chest as my legs sprinted, trying to maneuver around the labyrinth of undergrowth. I heard it move to my right.

The thing is herding me.

As I looked over my shoulder to find it, my foot stumbled on a tree root, making me lurch forward. My hands flew out in front of me, trying to stop my fall. That's when I felt it. Blinding ripples of pain raged up my calf as the claws ripped through my jeans and lodged deep into the back of my leg, tearing into my flesh. Blood gushed as a mangled cry came up my throat.

The pain was so intense my mind went numb. I tried to keep moving, but sharp daggers ripped into my other calf, immobilizing me. Agony seized me. Falling forward, I slid on my face through the dirt. I was done and prepared myself for the full attack, knowing it would hurt, but it'd be quick.

Suddenly, the giant beast was hurled off me with so much force it sent me rolling into the bushes, my head slammed into a protruding tree stump.

Darkness engulfed me.

I don't know how long I lost consciousness. My brain was so jumbled it was hard to know which way was up. Opening my eyes briefly, I saw I was still deep in the bushes. A wave of nausea crashed over me. My head spun, and I shut my lids hoping it would stop.

A deep, menacing snarl erupted on the other side of the brush. I jerked with terror as the hazy memory of a beast with flaming, red eyes came back to me. If this thing came barreling through the bushes, there would be nothing I could do. I would die. I tried to prepare myself.

Then, another vicious growl ripped through the air. This one sounded different and farther off than the other.

Holy hell. There are two of them.

The snarls grew louder until the sound of two large bodies colliding with each other echoed through the forest. Jaws snapped, bones crunched, wood splintered as the two beasts tore at each other. This might be my only chance to escape before they remembered me and came for their dinner.

I forced myself to sit up. Pain ricocheted through my body, making me gag. I looked down and saw my legs gushing blood. I clenched my jaw to keep from being sick. Flesh, muscle, and veins were in shredded clumps, tumbling out of my calves. I was losing too much blood too fast. It wouldn't take long for me to bleed out. I had to stop or at least slow it.

As soon as this thought crossed my mind, a maple leaf-shaped plant slithered towards me. If I weren't already in a state of shock, this would have put me in one, but the warm pulse of the earth was keeping me calm. The leafy stems wound their long string-like stalks around my legs and cut off the flow of blood.

Was the earth trying to help keep me alive? Funny, when you were about to die the things which would normally terrify you don't. Deep down, I wasn't really surprised that we, the earth and I, could feel each other's pains and joys. I was grateful for its help and was comforted. I always figured I was a sensitive to the earth, someone who could feel the life sources around. But animated plants went beyond my simply being aware. Nature was protecting me, taking me in as one of its own and trying to heal me.

The plant tightened around my legs, causing spasms inside my body. There was barely enough time to turn my head before I vomited, heaving until there was nothing but bile left. All the energy I had, gone. I slumped back to the ground, squeezing my eyes together, while acid trickled down my throat.

No matter what, either because of some beast or from blood loss, I would not survive the night. I was thankful for the earth's help, but it would not be enough. I was going to die.

The beasts continued to combat in the distance, rattling the ground underneath me.

This is a dream. It has to be a dream. This isn't real. Wake up, Em, wake up!

I didn't. It wasn't a dream. But sleep was calling me. It wouldn't be long until I finally drifted off, never to wake again. Thoughts of Mark added to my pain. He lost my mother, which destroyed him. My death would kill him. I hated myself for putting him through more agony again. I also thought about my friends, especially Kennedy and Ryan. How worried they must be about me. How distraught they'd be knowing they were so close and couldn't help me. I never had friends like them before.

It was becoming harder for me to think coherently. A low buzz started in my ears, and it took me several minutes before I realized it was the woods, humming with silence. The beasts had stopped fighting, which meant one of them would be coming for me. I no longer cared; I welcomed it.

The bushes in front of me shifted. A guttural snarl broke the silence. It reminded me of the noise an animal makes when guarding its food. Time seemed to hold its breath before one of the creatures huffed, signaling defeat, and moved through the foliage away from me.

My consciousness slipped further away with every breath. No longer was I trying to hold on. Death was no longer scary to me. It would take all my pain away.

I let go.

It was like I was being lifted into the air. Maybe your soul really does move out of you and float away at the end. I forced my lids to open, to watch myself leave my body. Through the thin slits I could muster, piercing green eyes looked back into mine. They shone like stars. I wanted to float into them and stay forever in their brilliance.

My eyes got too heavy. Death, with his arms open, beckoned me to follow him. I went gladly.

TWENTY-SEVEN

You know the moment when you wake up before reality hits, and everything is perfect? Yeah, well, I didn't. Searing hot pain wrenched me awake as it tore through my body, making me convulse and spasm. I felt a red hot needle boring into my skin. Everything was blurry and jumbled. Voices seeped into my thoughts. Their words had no real meaning, but I strained to listen and make sense of them to distract me from the pain. The voices were my only tether to reality—without them, I felt as if I would let go and never come back.

"Hold her down. I can't do this when she's moving," said a man's voice I didn't recognize.

"Did you give her enough morphine?" I recognized the second deep, husky voice, but I couldn't quite grasp onto an image.

A woman was screaming in my ears. *Why are they letting her carry on like that?*

"I gave her another thirty milligrams. I can give her more, but because of what she is, her metabolism is going to burn through it faster than I can dose it out. The bigger problem here is the poison he put into her system from his nails. The toxin is like pure iron pumping straight into her bloodstream. A scratch can make her sick, but this much will most likely kill her. And she's lost so much blood . . . way too much. She won't be able to fight off the toxins and produce enough clean blood. She needs more units, but we don't have an ample supply in storage, especially the blood type she requires."

"But she has to be okay."

"The attack tore through several major arteries in her lower extremities. I'd estimate about seventy percent of her total blood volume has been depleted. That, on top of the poison in her blood stream . . . personally I'm shocked she's made it as long as she has," said the first man.

"When I found her, plants had wrapped themselves around her legs. I could feel the pulse. They were trying to save her."

"Then there is no doubt who she really is," the first man stated. "The odds are we will lose her, especially without more units. I really don't know what's going to happen. I'm working out of my realm here. All I know for certain is she needs blood . . . and quickly."

"Give her mine."

"Yours will kill her. It's not done. You know that. It's too risky."

"She will die anyway, right?"

There was a pregnant pause. "Yes," the man finally answered.

"Then we don't have a choice. It could help her fight the toxins. Point is we don't have her blood type, and I'm not going to let her die without a fight."

Silence followed. The only thing I could hear was the woman whimpering in the background.

"I don't agree with how Lorcan handled this, but being what she is, you do understand this will not end well? She will eventually be destroyed."

"I know," the second voice replied. "I knew the moment I saw her tattoo, if not the moment I first saw her. I am prepared for how this will end."

"Should we be worried about your judgment if the time comes?"

"Are you questioning me? You know I understand more than anyone. I know my priorities. Believe me. I will do what I have to do."

"I apologize," the other man replied, more soft spoken. "Okay, let's try it. It may not work, but we have no alternative."

"I understand. What do you need me to do?" He sounded more agitated as the woman continued to wail and moan.

"I'll hook you up to an I.V."

Jeez, will someone please shut that woman up. She's annoying as hell.

"I think she needs more morphine, Owen. She seems to be in a lot of pain."

Oh, listen to the man, Owen.

I felt a hand reposition my arm and soon after, a warm sensation came over me and silence filled my ears.

Oh, good, they finally shut her up . . . that feels soooo much better . . . ooohhh thaaat's niiice.

"Ember, open your eyes."

A sultry voice floated into my head and stirred me from a deep sleep. My eyes blinked open, and when I rolled over onto my side, a beautiful forest lay before me. Every leaf glistened in the sunlight, and fresh dew clung to the leaves. It was breathtaking, and I felt so warm and happy here. There was an instant emotional connection to it.

"Ember, mo chuisle, get up."

Pushing myself erect, I turned around to see Torin standing in the distance. My heart fluttered. He pivoted and walked into the

245

forest. I knew he wanted me to follow. But no matter how quickly I ran, Torin never let me catch up. A cool breeze stirred the leaves around me, sending chills over my skin as I delved deeper into the shadows. The branches curled and twisted into bony fingers. Heavy shadows hung over me, incarcerating me within their gloom. Panic consumed me when I realized Torin had disappeared. I picked up my pace, distressed I had lost him. I pushed through some brush into a clearing and halted.

Bodies were lumped in piles across the burnt meadow. Ash and smoke hung heavy in the air. Blood soaked into the grass, dying it a rich shade of burgundy. The sight of carnage and the smell of charred flesh bore down on me, making me retch. A stabbing pain sank into my heart. I was certain, without knowing why, I was responsible for the destruction in front of me.

"Ember?" Torin's voice spoke softly next to me.

"I did this." I fixed my gaze straight ahead as I spoke. "Didn't I?"

"Yes." He looked down on me, his eyes full of sadness. "You are capable of much worse. When the time comes, you must try to break free, Ember. Your life and everyone else's depends on it."

"What do you mean?"

Turning his body he pressed closer to me. "Things are about to change." He tucked a strand of hair behind my ear. I'm going to do everything I can to protect you. There is so much I wish I could tell you. Just know there is a spy and traitor among you."

"A spy? Who?"

Instead of answering, Torin brought his lips down onto mine and kissed me deeply. Eventually he pulled back. "I'm trying to show you." He kissed me quickly again before adding, "Don't trust them . . . nothing and nobody are what they seem . . . including you, my dear Ember." He turned away, fading into the trees.

"Torin, wait. Don't leave me."

His form shimmered and then completely disappeared. I felt myself dissipating and being pulled deeper into oblivion.

I drifted in and out of consciousness, but one thing I knew for certain in my gut was that Torin was real. Not even in my wildest fantasies could I have come up with someone like him. I had to deal with the fact some person could get inside my head and control my dreams. But I had bigger things to worry about.

My body was still too heavy to move. I was about to come up for air but my dreams grabbed me and pulled me back under.

My eyes blinked open to what looked like a makeshift clinic. It reminded me of movies I saw when the Red Cross used homes as hospitals for wounded men in war or disaster. It had several unoccupied metal-framed beds across from me, a large, standing screen that divided the room, and what looked like an operating table on the other side of the divider. The floor was covered with blood, discarded bandages, and an I.V. bag. What pulled my attention the most were the three men standing near me, their voices raging. One of them I recognized instantly—Eli. I didn't move, somehow knowing I shouldn't draw attention to myself.

A guy with long, surfer-blond hair hanging loosely around his beautiful face was yelling at Eli. "Why in the hell didn't you tell us what Lorcan was doing? You knew he was after her, and you know what Lorcan is capable of. You always protect him, but it only hurts us."

"I thought I could handle it. Lorcan has his issues, but he wouldn't do anything to hurt this family." Eli's voice was curled with certainty.

"Is that what you got from tonight? He went directly against both your orders!" the blond guy bellowed.

"Cooper, let's calm down. This went bad, but we have to deal with what's at hand," said the third man.

"Cole, this went more than a little bad. She nearly died. Now how useful would she have been to us dead, huh?" The guy named Cooper paused. "Because Eli can't step up to the plate, Lorcan almost killed our only way out of here."

Eli moved quicker than my eye could follow, slamming Cooper into the door. "Watch yourself. I won't tolerate your insubordination, either."

"Is it my insubordination that bothers you, or do my words hit too close to home? It's not a secret you have feelings for her."

"What?" Eli backed away from Cooper. "I don't have feelings for her. What I've done has been for us."

"Oh, please. I know you, and that girl has you completely undone."

"Enough!" Eli's voice rang with such ferociousness it shook the room. "If you have a problem with my leadership decisions, then challenge me."

Tension-filled silence fogged the room. Eli and Cooper stood only inches away from each other, neither one willing to back away from the challenge.

Cole yelled. "Okay, enough, both of you. Cooper, this is not the time or place. We need to focus on the fact that Lorcan and the others have disappeared. They are obviously going out on their own, taking things into their own hands, which means they will come back for her. We need to be on guard."

"I already know who is with him." Eli turned to Cole. "I could smell them out there. Dax purposely led me away, so Lorcan could get to her."

"Cooper, I will have you and Gabby set up watch." Cole sighed. "Have Jared join you. It'll be a good learning experience for him."

Cooper dipped his head in acknowledgment of the order and left the room.

"A war is brewing. Not only between Dark and Light, but between us as well." Cole sighed and sauntered toward Eli, his hand pushing back his shoulder-length, dark hair. The soles of his boots scuffed against the wood floor. "But you know, Eli, he's not entirely wrong. It has become apparent to all of us that she captivates you. I do understand why, but you must remember what she is to us. This is far too important to allow your feelings to get the upper hand."

"As I told Owen earlier, I know my priorities."

"I hope so, Eli, because there is too much riding on this," Cole said. "But what I promised you earlier, I still stand by. You have my word."

Eli clasped Cole on the shoulder. "It's all I ask."

TWENTY-EIGHT

I awoke with a jolt.

Looking around, I was unsure of where I was, even though something about the room felt familiar. My dreams had been so vivid; I almost could still feel Torin's lips on mine. I longed to go back there, but instead I tried to recall how I got here. The night, until Eli kissed some girl at the party, was clear. Everything after that was hazy and distant.

Memories skimmed the surface, but darted away the second I tried to snatch one. Obscured recollections buzzed around my head like angry bees. I couldn't hold on to any one of them long enough. But I knew they weren't good.

I didn't know what I was afraid of, and somehow, this made everything worse. Spasms shot up my leg, returning me to one uncomplicated thought—pain. I was extremely exhausted and sick to my stomach.

When the spasms finally eased, I pushed myself up into a seated position, so I could get a better look around the room. I was in a one-room cabin, which had been turned into an infirmary. There were six beds total, three on each side of the room. Each one was neatly made with white sheets, except for the bed I was in. My covers were hanging off the bed in twisted jumbles. Damp streaks of pink soiled the sheets underneath my legs.

A muddled memory of three guys arguing in this room was tangled with the present. Had it been real or a dream?

A voice popped into my head from the memory. *"Cole, this went more than a little bad. She nearly died. Now how useful would she have been to us dead, huh?"*

My world was sliding. Things I had no control over were about to tear my life apart. I wanted to go home. I felt scared and alone. I needed my dad. I sank into the pillows. Exhausted, I drifted off to sleep again.

As soon as I woke up, I realized I had one priority to be dealt with. I had to pee. I slipped off the blankets, my bare feet timidly touching the cold floor. My legs cramped and twitched as I stood. It took me a few tries before I was able to stand fully upright, but as I did, I slowly moved towards what looked like a bathroom.

"That's the closet," a voice said from behind me.

"Holy shit!" I spun around, my leg muscles protesting.

"Sorry, I should have warned you I was here." A man stood from the chair in a darkened corner. His slacks and buttoned-up shirt were rumpled, as if he'd been wearing them for several days. "How are you feeling?"

"Uh . . . okay, I think," I replied, stepping away from him warily.

"I'm Doctor Owen Donavan. Owen is fine. I guess you could say I'm the house physician. I operated on your legs." He nodded towards my calves, looking slightly surprised as I stood before him.

"Thank you." Under his analytical stare, I was keenly aware I was only wearing a guy's old t-shirt, which barely came to the top of my thighs. By the familiar, comforting smell, I knew it had to be Eli's.

Where was I? What happened to me last night? How did I end up in some makeshift hospital wearing Eli's t-shirt with my legs bandaged? The memories of the night before were slowly coming back. I remembered Eli had me pinned against a tree as we argued. I also knew I had been attacked but by what? I had no idea. I was groggy and my memory struggled with pinpointing the details of the actual attack.

"I'd like to check your vitals and see how your legs are healing."

"Umm . . . sure."

"I'm sorry. You wanted to use the restroom first." He straightened his glasses.

I hadn't realized I was doing the pee-pee dance. "Uhh . . . yeah that would be great."

"It's the door over there, on your right." He pointed in the opposite direction from where I had been heading. Hell, right now I would pee in the closet.

I quickly altered directions and ambled for the bathroom. It wasn't until I was washing my hands did I finally look at myself in the mirror. I rubbed my eyes and blinked. Something was off—different. I turned my head to one side, then the other. Several red, scabbed lacerations lined my face, overlapping the older white scars from before. My heart skipped a beat. Another glimpse of an image, and I knew the cuts and scrapes across my face had been extensive and deep. I had felt the blood gushing out of them as rocks, twigs, and other matter sliced my face as I skidded over them. Now they were scabbed and disappearing. I healed fast, but this was too fast, even for me.

I breathed deeply and attempted to smooth my hair, pulling at some of the longer strands. My hair shimmered and glowed unnaturally under the bathroom lights. Trying to ignore the panic rising, I continued with the inspection. I leaned toward the mirror. My eyes were their same odd colors. I was reassured, but they appeared brighter than normal, which made them that much more unnerving.

At first glance, my skin seemed to be its normal pale complexion. But on closer inspection, it also had a glow. My fingertips slid along the healing cuts on my cheek. One of them, which I looked at moments ago, was now almost gone. Looking down at my heavily bandaged calves, I was nearly hyperventilating as the enormity of all this began sinking in.

It hadn't hit me until right then that I shouldn't have been able to walk. I started tearing at the bandages. The thick layers of dressings and tape made it a frustrating exercise. As I ripped the last bit of gauze off my leg, I gasped. Stitches lined the back of both my legs and were encrusted with dried blood.

The sutured areas were red and tender, but from my recollection of the mess of veins and the shredded muscle and tissue torn from them only hours before, my legs should not have looked so good. They shouldn't have been this healed. I should've been confined to a wheelchair and in a tremendous amount of pain. Every nerve and tendon had been torn to shreds. The damage had been so severe I should have been looking at physical therapy for months, if not years. But here I was, a short time later, walking.

I fell back onto my butt, sitting on the hard floor. Trepidation turned my blood cold. I vomited into the toilet. This was all too much for my body and my mind to handle. As much as I had healed, I was still weak and nauseated. After throwing up twice more, I leaned against the wall, completely drained.

What was happening? Everything was becoming far too real. I could no longer assume everything I was hearing and seeing was simply my imagination.

Torin's voice from a far-off memory warned me: *"Nothing and no one are what they seem . . . including you, my dear Ember."*

I pulled myself off the floor, my legs shaking. I had to look again. Studying myself in the mirror, I tried to see who was really looking back. If I were not what I seemed, what was I? I didn't know exactly what he meant, but I had an overwhelming feeling what Torin had said was true. I felt dizzy again and leaned against the sink to steady myself. Holding my face to the light, I watched how my skin radiated incandescently. *Why was this happening to me? What was different? Why now?*

A memory from deep within my subconscious burst to the surface. I heard voices in my mind—Owen's, then Eli's.

"All I do know for certain is she needs blood and quickly."

"Give her mine."

My gut bottomed out, my subconscious understanding something way beyond what my conscious was willing to allow. The scene hadn't been a dream. I had Eli's blood in my system. Was that the difference? Why would his blood cause me to look like Tinkerbelle had just exploded into fairy dust all over me? What was he?

"Don't trust them . . . nothing and nobody are what they seem."

Ohmygodohmygod . . .

"Ember?" A soft knock on the bathroom door. "You okay?" Owen asked. I jumped, yelping, my heart slamming wildly against my chest. "Ember?"

"Y-yes, I'm fine," I stammered. "I'll be out in a minute."

More hazy memories emerged. What I thought were dreams weren't. Indistinct voices overlapped each other in my head.

"Don't trust them . . ."

"She nearly died. Now how useful would she have been to us dead?"

". . . but being what she is, you do understand this will not end well? She will eventually be destroyed."

"I knew it the moment I saw her tattoo, if not the moment I first saw her. I am prepared for how this will end."

I swallowed nervously, why did I feel I was "dead girl walking"? How well did I know Eli, really? There had been times I had felt so much abhorrence from him, as if it took everything he had not to hurt me. But why? Did he really want to kill me? I knew I hadn't done anything to deserve that amount of hatred, but it didn't stop me from feeling there was a real threat there.

I looked around the room, debating on what to do. A window over the toilet caught my attention.

I flushed the toilet and turned on the faucets to mask any sounds I might make. Daggers stabbed my still-mending legs as I climbed onto the toilet. I held my breath as I opened the window silently, listening for any signs of Owen or anyone else outside the door. Thankfully, it was a one-story house, so I slid through the open window and let myself drop to the ground. As I landed, I bit my lip and covered my mouth to stop myself from screaming in pain. Tears stung my eyes as I breathed in and out deeply, hoping the pain and dizziness would subside quickly. I shivered as cold air and light drizzle seeped quickly through the thin t-shirt I was wearing. I had no idea where I was, but I didn't care. I had to get out of there.

"Going somewhere?" A familiar voice came from behind me.

TWENTY-NINE

I whipped around to see Eli leaning against the side of the house. Rage emanated off him, especially from his eyes. He looked like he'd been waiting for me. How did he know I'd sneak out the window?

"How far did you think you'd get?"

There was no point in denying I was trying to escape—think that ship had sailed. Barefoot and half-naked, I stood staring back at him, terrified. Adrenaline rushed through my veins, making me feel antsy and hyper-aware of him. It was like I could feel him without touching him.

He shook his head and scoffed. "So you think making a break for it . . . no shoes and hurt . . . was the wisest plan? Think I wouldn't be able to find you?"

Icy dread consumed me as his words sunk in. It was true. I wouldn't have gotten far, and it was even more frightening because of that fact. "What do you want with me?"

A slow grin tugged at his lips as he looked me up and down. "I want many things." Heat sliced through me. I became overly conscious of the thin t-shirt I was wearing. I shut my brain down fast to all thoughts leading in that direction. He was trying to distract me, get me off kilter. I couldn't let myself show weakness. I twitched with the desire to bolt, but running would have been pointless.

"Are you going to go quietly back into the house?" His expression was stony again. "You've got two options. Either you save my back and the tiny eardrums of the local squirrel population by walking or you return over my shoulder and most likely muzzled. You're going inside either way."

"I'm not going anywhere with you 'til you tell me the truth."

"The truth?"

"Stop. I'm done with your bullshit." My anger flared. "What are you, Eli? Did you think I wouldn't notice something about you isn't right? That I look like a freakin' fairy with your blood in my system?" Eli stared at me in silence. "Yeah, I know what you did. Did you think I wouldn't find out about your little blood donation?" I tried to keep my teeth from chattering as I railed into him.

His expression darkened. Fury rolled off him. I was walking a thin line and knew it. Instead of waiting for him to throw me over his shoulder, I turned and headed for the entrance. He followed closely behind, ready for me to try to run again, but I knew when something was a waste of time and energy. I had to save mine and come up with an actual plan.

I opened the front door and almost walked straight into Owen and another man, someone who seemed very familiar to me. "Ah, our runaway has returned," said the man I didn't know. Power resonated off him. Instinctively, I knew he was the leader.

He looked to be in his mid-thirties and was a few inches shorter than Eli, but he was equally as toned and muscular. His hazel eyes glowed. He had chin-length shaggy, dark reddish-brown hair and a hint of a beard around his jaw line. His t-shirt and jeans fitted snugly to the contours of his body. He was exceptionally good-looking . . . of course, he had to be, right? It seemed you couldn't be in this little group unless you had a rockin' hard body and were unbelievably hot and rugged. His face had evidence that he, too, had been in a few scuffles. Like Eli, it seemed to suit him and made him even sexier.

All these boys were lethal. It really wasn't fair.

Seeing him up close triggered a fuzzy memory. I had met him before.

"We have not officially been introduced. I'm Cole," he said. At his name my memory flooded back.

"Nice to meet you, Cole," I said dryly as I moved around them, not responding to their reproachful glances.

To the right of the front door was the bed I recently occupied. Not knowing where else to go, I went there. I wanted to keep standing. It made me feel more prepared for whatever was coming, but my calves were already aching and weak. I sat down on my bed. My escape attempt would have been very short.

Eli came in, silent fury clouding around him as he shut the door and gave Cole a pointed look. Owen noticed and cleared his throat. "Let me examine her first."

"First? First before what?" The thought popped out of my mouth.

Owen came to my bedside. The resemblance between Cole and Owen was undeniable; no doubt they were brothers. Both had the same hazel eyes and reddish brown hair. Where Cole was rugged, powerful, and dangerous, Owen was clean-cut, reserved, and a tad nerdy. His hair was cut short and smoothed back neatly. Owen was good looking, but in a more unassuming way than the other two other guys. He was also a lot less muscular, not that he didn't have an attractive physique. You could tell he spent more time inside than the others, probably working in a hospital somewhere. For some reason I had this suspicion he worked hard to be unassuming, so he wouldn't stand out, but no matter how hard he'd try, he could never be plain or ordinary. I was sure he still sent plenty of patients' and nurses' hearts fluttering.

His eyebrows rose when he saw the torn and missing gauze on my legs. The room was unnervingly silent as Owen checked my legs, face, and vitals. He made strange grunts here and there as he conducted the examination, but it seemed Cole and Eli understood them, exchanging knowing looks between them.

"Well, Ms. Brycin, it seems you are healing nicely."

"Yeah, no kidding. It doesn't take a genius to notice I healed exceptionally fast, even for me." I was taking a leap here, and if this was all in my imagination, they could call me crazy. So be it. My gut told me I was right. "But now that Eli has bestowed me with some of his blood, I've become a super-freak. I mean, look at me. My glowing skin, hair, and eyes kind of tipped me off something was different. But I don't think it's only his blood that caused this, huh? There's something different about me." All three went completely still as they looked back at me. Tension grew so thick and volatile I had to force myself not to slink back in fear. "I want the truth."

"Ember, you were attacked, and you're highly emotional right n—"

"Don't," I cut Cole off. "Please don't act like you have no idea what I'm talking about or try and make me feel stupid or crazy. I now know I'm not. I've been trying to ignore things for too long." I took in a breath. "Tell me. What am I?"

"Ms. Brycin, I think it's best if you get some rest," Owen said in a calm, doctor-like voice.

"Good luck with that," Eli mumbled from across the room.

"I will not back down 'til I get some answers," I said, my jaw clenched in stubborn determination. "Tell me, now!"

"Ember, you've been under some serious emotional distress and have been heavily medicated," Cole exclaimed with a mix of forcefulness and calmness, as if he were trying to mollify me but really wanting to strangle me.

"Don't you dare try to pacify me. And don't you dare presume you can so easily distract or brush me off . . . or dismiss me as a foolish girl with delusions and an overactive imagination!" My knuckles were white as they tightly grasped the bedding. I wanted to tear it to shreds. "I'm not stupid. Don't treat me as such."

"We never meant to suggest you were stupid, Ember. I merely think you need to lie down and rest for a while."

"Did you think I wouldn't notice this?" I pulled at the ends of my glimmering hair. "Or this?" I pointed to the disappearing scrapes on my face. "And I wouldn't notice only hours after my legs were turned into shredded beef I can walk? Don't you think I haven't known deep down for a long time there's something different about me? That things happen around me I can't explain? That I see things which shouldn't be there or shouldn't be real? That I don't fit into this world no matter how hard I try?" It felt good for my fears to finally find a voice. "I've always somehow known it, and I know you guys don't fit here, either. So you might as well tell me what's going on now."

Eli shot Cole and Owen a smirk. "Told you."

Cole and Owen exchanged glances, communicating silently before Cole sighed and nodded reluctantly. He moved a chair close to me and sat.

"So you know, Ember, I never figured you for a fool or stupid. I assumed this would happen sooner or later," Cole stated coolly.

"Then, why?"

"Because once the truth is out, there's no going back, and you will wish you could," he replied. "There is also something you must understand. No one can learn the truth about us . . . no one."

Cole's look was so severe I had to hold back the hysteria gripping me. There was no reassurance from either Owen or Eli. Were they going to kill me? Did I just sign my own death warrant?

"There was one instance a *human* learned about us. She didn't live long enough to tell anyone else."

I gulped. Terror slashed my chest, making me dizzy and weak. My eyes darted around the room. The door and two windows were my only means of escape, and escaping was about as likely as them letting me walk out of this room. I was trapped.

Cole picked up on my fear. "We're not going to hurt you, Ember. You are safe for now."

I did not miss the not-so-subtle implication of "for now," but I didn't linger on it. Something else caught my attention.

"You said the word 'human' like you don't belong to that classification?" I forced a wobbly smile, still not sure if I was ready to hear the truth. "It sounds like you're implying you're not." None of them disputed my words. I looked between them and burst out laughing. "This is some kind of joke, right?" But their solemn expressions were unchanged. "Okay, I'll play along. So . . . what are you supposed to be?

Eli launched himself off the wall and was inches from my face before I could blink. His warm breath brushed my face. "This isn't a game, Brycin. This isn't going to be a cute little storybook you can close when you're done. You open this, and you're going to be letting things out you cannot possibly imagine. And believe me when I tell you this is no fairytale." A brutal smile formed on his lips. "You still ready to hear a bedtime story?"

There was no going back, but I could no longer ignore the truth. "Y-Yes," I forced myself to say through the fear.

"Even if it endangers your life?" he snapped.

"Are you threatening me, Dragen?"

"It's not a threat." His carnal grin made my pulse pound. It affected me on two disturbing levels.

"Eli." Cole shot him a warning look.

Eli stepped back, but the cold smile never left his face. How could he turn me on so much while scaring the living crap out of me? "So why does your blood affect me like this?"

"As you figured, we are not human, Ms. Brycin," Owen said calmly. "And neither are you."

If he hadn't said it so emotionless, I would have burst out laughing again. But Owen's reserved tone made me shiver. Only a tiny, nervous giggle escaped my lips. "Oh, come on. You expect me to believe you're being serious?"

"What do you think?" Eli replied. "You think we're just having a bit of fun with you?"

I knew they weren't. The truth I had been denying for so long was finally being said out loud. I was not human. "So, what are you telling me exactly?" I swallowed apprehensively; heaviness weighed down on me.

Cole cleared his throat. "The world is not always what it appears to be. There are things out there, things you truly should be afraid of . . . beings and creatures in any book. How much do you know about the Otherworld?" Taking my shocked look as ignorance, Cole started again. "Okay, how about mythology, particularly Celtic or Scottish mythology?"

"You're talking leprechauns and the Loch Ness monster?"

Eli frowned. "The Loch Ness monster was a kelpie who went insane and got caught without its glamour. But, yeah, I guess if you want to put it in layman's terms, kelpies and leprechauns are part of the Otherworld."

"Have you ever heard of the *Tuatha Dé Danann?*" Cole tilted his head as he spoke.

And, finally, there goes Alice down the rabbit hole . . .

I took in a sharp breath. I knew the name well. When I was little, my mom would tell me bedtime stories about the Otherworld, its beautiful land and magical Fae-folk of *Tuatha Dé Danann.* She would make up these incredibly detailed stories about the Court of Inner Light, called the Seelie, and the Court of the Outer Darkness, called the Unseelie. I would later pretend to live in this world and make believe I was a fairy at this magical court.

But I was a child, and those were only stories, right?

Eli noted my reaction and gave a slight nod. "So you've heard of it. I imagine from your mother, right?"

"Yes. She would tell me bedtime stories about it. Why?"

"They weren't bedtime stories. Fairies, Seelie, Sidhe, Fae, whatever you call them, are not some cute, little winged creatures sprinkling fairy dust on children," Eli scoffed. "They are elitist snobs who can be vindictive and cruel, especially that bitch of a Queen."

"Eli," Cole warned again. I could feel the vehement wrath stirring in Eli at the mention of this Queen. I could taste his hatred of her, and the revenge he so desired. He wanted her dead. It disturbed me that I could feel him so acutely. There had always been a connection between us, but this was beyond anything before.

"Okay . . . whoa. Hold on here." I held up my hands. "What are you guys talking about? Are you saying things like fairies, imps, and kelpies are real?"

"Yes, and creatures of which you have never dreamed, things you can't find in books or on the Internet."

"Oh, my god," I mumbled. Even though I had somehow known this, it felt different to have it confirmed. "It's actually real. I'm not crazy."

"I wouldn't say that," Eli quipped.

I smiled thinly. "No, I mean the things I've been seeing, like the goblin driving the bus . . . he was real?" Another loaded thought occurred to me. "Oh, shit. The rat in the shed was some kind of Fae creature."

"A gnome," Eli said.

I laughed, relief tumbling off my shoulders. My smile slipped quickly from my lips. "You made me feel crazy, like I was seeing things." My eyes narrowed at Eli. Looking at him brought more memories to surface. I remembered seeing him change. His eyes had shifted like a cat's, resembling the ones haunting my dreams, and his nails had grown into claws. The beast in the forest . . .

"You"—I pointed at the guys—"attacked me."

"No one in this room attacked you," Cole assured me.

"But one of your kind did?"

Cole nodded.

"What are you?" An image of a panther-like animal, which was blacker than night, with knifelike teeth and claws and red, cat-like eyes, came bounding into my head.

"Those in the Otherworld call us Dark Dwellers," Cole replied.

"Dark Dwellers?" I repeated the name out loud, panic crashing into me like a wave. "What is a Dark Dweller?"

"We are worse than any nightmare." Cole's biting response let me know this was all he was going to say on the subject. The fact they were dangerous was something I had known the moment I had crossed paths with Eli. By their name and the secrecy they ardently held onto, I knew whatever they were was even worse than I had first thought.

With every breath I tried to fight my instinct to run. "So are you Fae?"

"We are under the umbrella of Fae," Cole said coolly. "Fae is a general term for all things living in or from the Otherworld. It's like the term 'human,' but there are a thousand different species which fall under this, both Dark and Light."

"So what am I?"

"You are Fae," Eli responded.

Always helpful.

"You have some pure blood in you. F-a-e is a general term for everything in the Otherworld. F-a-y is an actual species of fairy, and they are the pureblooded fairies. The Seelie Court is made up of pure Fay. They rule most of the Otherworld now."

"So I'm a *fairy*?" The powers I had didn't seem like things fairies would do, but I guessed I was basing this on movies.

"You can have your own wand and everything," Eli mused. I shot him a dirty look.

"Breathe, Ember." Owen looked worried. "I know this must be overwhelming and frightening to you right now."

264

"You think?" I exclaimed. "You're telling me the Otherworld exists. That monsters and goblins exist. That fairytales and myths are real, and even more, I'm one of them!" I sucked in a deep breath. "On top of all this, I was almost killed last night by a so-called Dark Dweller, and for all I know, it might have been one of you. You *think* I might get a little worked up here?"

"You must try to stay calm," Owen repeated.

"Yeah, that's easier said than done." My voice came out lighter than how I truly felt. I was terrified; my world was crumbling around me. I wanted to laugh this off and continue being ignorant, but I knew better.

I wasn't human. I think I had known for a long time. It was something I had kept locked tight inside and never let myself think about or acknowledge, but it was something I somehow always sensed. Cole's earlier words came back to haunt me: *"Once the truth is out, there's no going back. And you will wish you could."* It was too late. There would be no going back now.

"I'm not keeping you in the dark about what we are simply for fun, Ember. It's for your safety . . . and ours. Keeping our secret is the most important thing to us. We cannot chance anyone finding out about us or about you, unless we choose for someone to know. Do you understand?" Cole looked sternly at me.

I nodded. "So . . . I'm from the Otherworld, too."

It really wasn't a question, but Cole confirmed it anyway. "Yes."

"Tell me. Exactly. What am I?"

They remained silent, and I could feel Eli's emotions without looking at him, as if he were sending his feelings over radio waves. I was aware of every move he made. A slight sigh or the grinding of his teeth felt like a scream. I rubbed my head; a throbbing pain pulsed in my temples. He had known this whole time what I was and said nothing. I looked between Cole and Eli. Something in their expression made me think they weren't telling me the whole truth.

"We will tell you exactly what you are. But there is something else we must speak of first," Owen said.

"Something else?"

"Yes. You see, you lost a lot of blood after the attack, and you were close to dying. As you've figured out, Eli donated his blood to save your life." I couldn't help my eyes from darting to Eli before returning to Owen. "What you are and what we are is different, and his blood seems to have changed you."

"I don't understand? Change me how?"

"In layman's terms, Eli's blood changed your DNA a bit."

"A bit?" Icy heat slithered down, and a wave of vertigo hit me.

"We don't really know how much it has affected you or if it's permanent. Physically, your reactions to the blood, like the glowing, should taper off in a day or so, but as for inside your body, we may never know the long-term effects. This is not something that has happened . . . ever."

"What do you mean this is not something that happens? What is his blood doing to me?"

"You would have died without it, but based on history, you should have died because of it. Blood is not exchanged between 'species.'" Owen made air quotes with his fingers. "So I have no reference as to how it will affect you or why you didn't die from taking in his blood. I could take a sample of your blood and test it."

"Yes, do it," I replied. I hadn't even learned what I really was, and now suddenly I was something else. I could feel the power of Eli's blood pumping through my veins, taking over my body. Instead of attacking the foreign invader, my body seemed to be welcoming it.

"I will try to find out as much as I can. But in the meantime, I need you to tell me everything you feel or any changes you notice."

I laughed. Changes? Everything about me had changed.

The morphine was wearing off. I could feel pain shoot through my legs, making me even more unsettled. Acid coated my tongue. My head pounded. I wanted to shut down and forget everything I recently learned, as Cole had warned me I would. I was a fucking fairy. As shocked and overwhelmed as I felt, there was a part of me that wasn't surprised.

My stomach convulsed, emptying anything in there. Vomit came pouring out all over the floor in front of me.

"Shit!" Cole jumped out of the way, while Owen was instantly at my side with a cloth, tending to me. The guys had the dirty job of cleaning up my mess.

My head was too heavy to hold up any longer. "Rest," Owen said softly as he guided my head towards the pillow. "Your body is in shock and is also reacting to the foreign blood in your system. It should get better after a while."

I curled into a ball, wrapping my arms tightly around my legs. Owen withdrew samples of my blood, before injecting me with more morphine. "This will help you sleep." I nodded in response and felt a pat on my arm. Owen and Cole slipped out of the room almost undetected. Damn, they were stealthy.

It was only mid-morning, but dark thunderclouds kept most of the light from entering the room. Any brightness made me feel nauseous, so I wanted to pull the blankets over my head and hide from the world—both of them.

I didn't even notice I was shaking until Eli put another blanket on me. "Get some sleep." He tucked the blanket tight around me and started to walk away.

I grabbed his hand. The last thing I wanted was to be alone. I was past caring that he was a threat to my life; it didn't seem to matter right then.

Stay with me. My eyes pleaded with him.

His eyebrows creased together, and a range of emotions fought for dominance over his features.

Please . . . I thought he'd pull his hand away and leave the room. But after a pause, he sighed and moved me over, crawling in beside me. He stayed above the covers, but wrapped his arms around me, fitting his body closely with mine.

I closed my eyes, as my body curled in perfectly with his, soaking up his warmth and closeness. We didn't talk. That could be done later. All I wanted was his warmth next to me his strong arms protecting me from the nightmares inside and outside my head. It was a lie but a lie I needed to believe.

My mind swam with dreamlike memories of red, burning eyes and claws slashing at my throat. Eli's arms tightened around me, and I realized I was whimpering. I couldn't seem to stop the nightmares from coming as sleep finally claimed me.

Later when I opened my eyes, I was alone. The gray afternoon light broke through the window, and rain pelted on the windowpane. I wasn't feeling up to par yet, but I felt ten times better than earlier. My mind was groggy and my body was limp, but this could have been from the morphine Owen gave me.

My thoughts fell back to all the things I recently discovered, especially that I wasn't human, but Fae. Did this mean my mom was also a Fae? Were the stories she told me true? Were they about the world she came from? Were the characters in her stories real? Did she have family? Friends?

Shit!

I sat up with a wobbly jolt, remembering Kennedy and Ryan had no idea where I was. I had simply disappeared from the party. They had to be freaking out. I needed to let them know I was okay—well, relatively okay—before they got the police involved. Maybe they already had. Not that Sheriff Weiss would lift a finger to find me, but I didn't want anyone to contact Mark. He would be thinking something awful happened to me and completely lose it, especially being in Japan and not being able to get back fast enough.

Oh, crap on ash bark. He was returning home Monday

afternoon. Tomorrow. He might even be getting ready to go to the airport now. He would've called me before he left. I had to find my phone. I looked around the room for any of my belongings. Oh, right, I'd left my cell on the counter at home.

Great idea there, Em!

I pushed the blankets off and swung my legs over the side of the bed. I stopped, sensing I was not alone in the room. My eyes darted around. Was I being guarded? Even though it was most likely Owen or Eli, warning chills tingled against my skin, screaming at me to flee. Somehow I knew it wasn't Eli; I could feel he wasn't close by. Plus, whatever Eli would do, he'd do outright, not ambush me. I knew that much about him. Whoever was here was creeping up on me, lying in wait for the perfect moment to pounce.

I launched off the bed and darted for the door. At the same time, several dark figures moved silently and quickly around me. They all wore dark clothes, and deep hoods covered their heads. Between the darkness and my drug-induced state, I couldn't make out any of them. Someone grabbed me from behind, immediately covering my mouth with a black glove. Panic worsened my suffocation. I tried to scream, but nothing came out. The person behind me pulled me tightly to his body, and a sharp pain ignited in my thigh. I twisted to see another covered head pulling a syringe out of my leg.

"You sure you don't want me to knock her out as well?" A woman's voice said to the guy behind me. There was something familiar about her voice.

"That won't be necessary," the guy replied. His voice was deep and vibrated in my ear. He gripped me tighter around the waist as my legs went limp.

"Bitch," I spat at the girl, which sounded more like "Vvlliittch."

"Oh, I think it's necessary," the woman replied.

Her fist came towards me at a speed my eyes could not grasp. A bone-crunching sound echoed off the walls. My head jerked and twisted, and rich blackness seized me.

Chirty
☮

When my lids fluttered open, I blinked a few times to adjust to the dim lighting. Pain and stiffness locked my muscles against the cold, stone floor. I turned my head slowly. Blood throbbed through my swollen face.

Man, I was done with getting my ass kicked. I mentally assessed the rest of my body. My calves were stiff and sore, but not hurting too badly. My mouth felt as if it had been stuffed with cotton. I was so dehydrated my tongue stuck like glue to the sandpapery dry patches in my mouth.

I looked around. Leaking stone walls surrounded me except for one wall which consisted of metal bars. A jail. I knew I was in a cave or deep underground as I could smell the dank, musty smell of dirt. It was cold, and the only light came from a single hanging bulb on the other side of the bars. A cool drop of water slipped off the rock ceiling and splashed onto my forehead.

Where the hell was I? And how did I become a prisoner in a dungeon? My brain spun with a million questions, and panic rolled in like a tsunami. My eyes darted frantically around for any clues as to where I was, who kidnapped me, how, why? None of these questions were answered. All there was around me was stone, impermeable packed-dirt floor, and bars.

I reached for a cross bar to pull myself up. As my fingers wrapped around the bar closest to me, pain shot through my arms, down through my core, reaching the tips of my toes. My insides felt like they were getting pulled out of my stomach. Something was sucking my energy away, draining me. With a cry, I managed to pull free and fell back to the ground.

What the hell was that? I lay there breathing in huge gulps of air. I felt exhausted and limp.

"Iron . . . it's fairy kryptonite," a male voice came out of the darkness.

I made myself sit up and scoot across the floor, pressing my back against the wall. A tall, shadowy figure moved slowly towards me. Squinting, I tried to make out the form. Familiar green eyes locked on mine, but these eyes didn't hold any of the feeling I had felt from the other pair. These were empty and cold—Lorcan.

"Pure iron drains you of your powers. It's my insurance in case you get a little unruly." Lorcan looked me up and down in a predatory fashion. There was something off about him, something that made me recoil against the wall.

"It doesn't affect you?"

"No, but then Dark Dwellers don't have many weaknesses. It only affects the pure Fays. Every Fae race has their weakness. Iron is one of yours."

Another ah-ha moment struck me. My "iron allergy" now made perfect sense. Why I got tired and weak when I touched it or was around it too long. All those years, my system had been trying to tell me what I really was.

In the dim light, Lorcan resembled Eli. I had to avert my eyes from him as the effect overwhelmed me.

"You look so sad. So pitiful. Quite tragic really," he mocked. "Wishing I was Eli?" He leaned against the bars, shaking his head. "You think Eli will come save you? What if I told you he's the reason you're here? He was the one who told us who and what you are. I guess he's not the nice guy you thought he was."

271

"I never thought he was a nice guy."

Lorcan laughed. "You're not as stupid as I thought, but this makes you even more foolish. He never cared about you. He was using you, getting closer so he could learn more about you. Whatever extra perks he could get from you were just for kicks. He may not be happy with how I handled this, kidnapping you from him. He'll be pissed for a second or two, but then he'll see my way is better, quicker." He gave me a look to show me how pathetic he thought I was. "Don't think for a minute Eli wasn't going to use you for the same thing. He was going to make a deal with the Unseelie King for you. The outcome would have been no different."

I swallowed. I would not show emotion. I would not give him the pleasure of seeing me react. I could no longer pretend what I had learned earlier from Eli, Cole, and Owen was only another strange dream. Everything between us had been a lie.

It seemed my whole life had been built on lies. Eli feigning interest in me was mere icing on the cake. Was it all an act? Memories of how he'd looked at me before we kissed and how his lips felt against mine caused my eyes to brim with tears. I commanded them to recede, my anger blanketing the heartache and pain.

There was another truth I had to deal with. Something my gut had understood the moment I'd seen Lorcan. "You're the one who attacked me."

"Yeah, sorry about that. I didn't expect you to move so fast. I got a little carried away." Lorcan shrugged.

"A *little* carried away? You turned my legs into beef jerky!"

"And look at you now, better than ever. You heal faster than I thought possible."

I briefly shut my eyes. Telling him about Eli's blood donation would be a bad idea. Knowledge was power, and he didn't need to have the upper hand. "Why do *you* want me?"

He crossed his arms. "Because of what you are, Ember."

I looked at him, my eyebrows furrowed as I took in what he said. "Because I'm Fay?"

"Is that what Eli told you? If it were only the truth." Lorcan sighed as he shook his head. "Eli lied to you. He obviously wanted to keep you unaware about what you *truly* are. I can only imagine it was for his benefit to keep you ignorant, but I think you have the right to know."

"Aren't you a sweetheart?" I glared at him. "So what am I?"

"You, Ember, are a Dae."

"A what?"

"It's true you are Fay but only partially. You are also half Demon." He cocked his head as he spoke, waiting my reaction.

I stared at him, my brain not excepting his words. "What are you talking about?"

"You have both pure Fay and Demon blood in those veins. Your very existence is an abomination and outlawed in our world." Lorcan's matter-of-fact tone made everything inside me turn upside down. "Don't you love it when you find not only your whole life has been a lie, and you don't belong to this world, but then you find out you don't even belong in the Otherworld, either?"

I shook my head, unwilling to accept his words. "I don't believe you. You're lying."

"Why would I lie to you? Unlike Eli, I have no motivation to keep the truth from you. I promise you I'm not lying."

Did Eli and the others know this? If so, why would they keep it from me? My mind reeled with confusion and conflicting emotions. "I-I still don't understand why you want me. What are you planning on doing with me?"

"To me you are a transaction, merely merchandise. Incredibly useful merchandise I will say," he uttered in such a way it made me stir uncomfortably. "But to others, you are a weapon, with unlimited powers."

273

"A weapon? Unlimited powers?" I was aware I may have certain "gifts," but to be used as a weapon? I certainly wasn't that powerful. Was I?

Lorcan, thinking I wasn't getting his meaning, continued. "Come on, Ember, I know you're brighter than you pretend." He looked at me with a patronizing expression. "Lights and electrical equipment exploring when you get upset? Flames erupting uncontrollably around you? A young boy stopped midair from falling to his death? Strength no human could possess? A body catapulted through a windshield using only the powers of your mind? Any of this sounding familiar?" He smirked. "And think . . . you haven't even begun to tap into your true powers yet. You are still powerful enough to start a war, though."

"A war? Why in the hell would I help you start a war?"

"I didn't say you would be helping me or you'd be willing." Lorcan paced, running his fingers across the bars, seeming to enjoy his lecture to me far too much. "The war is what someone else wants you for. The reason I want you is because you are the key for my group to get back into the Otherworld. You should count yourself lucky you are being kept alive right now. Daes were never allowed to exist. Breeding between Fay and Demons is outlawed, though it hasn't seemed to stop the Demons from trying, even when the Fay is unwilling."

"Y-You mean they rape them?"

"You catch on quickly," he nodded. "The reason it's outlawed is because the offspring are too powerful. They are not able to contain their power, which results in destroying everyone and everything in their paths and eventually themselves." Lorcan looked me straight in the eyes. "In the past, if a Dae was discovered, Seelie soldiers would hunt it down and make sure it was gutted and burned."

"So you are trading me to someone who wants to use me as a weapon, so you and your gang can get back into the Otherworld. Do I have this right so far?"

Lorcan nodded, his eyebrow cocked.

"Why can't you go back? What did you do?"

"Let's say there was a slight 'misunderstanding' that got us exiled from the Otherworld by the Queen."

"Misunderstanding?"

"It's not information with which you need to concern yourself."

"Of course not," I replied. It felt like cement blocks were being piled on me, one by one. All I could do was remain composed as a throbbing headache pounded against my temples from the overload of information. I'm sure the attack, the poison in my bloodstream, the lack of food and water all contributed. Over-exhaustion didn't help, either.

"This is far too important for us. We have been waiting almost two decades for this opportunity. I could no longer trust Eli to stay impartial," Lorcan stated. "He will eventually understand you are a small price to pay in the scheme of things."

I turned my face to him my eyes burning with tears wanting to be shed, but I would not allow it. He would not see me cry or beg. "You are a monster."

"Yes, I suppose I really am, but not the kind you mean." He shook his head. "You can put whatever label you want on me, but I'm doing this for my family. You cannot deny you wouldn't put your family first if you had to."

"You're willing to trade someone's life merely to get back to the Otherworld. I would never do that."

"Don't ever say what you would or wouldn't do. You have no idea what you are capable of, given the circumstances." A knowing smile curled his lips. "Don't be a righteous fool. It might come back to haunt you one day." His voice turned so hard and cold, forcing me closer to the wall. I never wanted to find out the circumstances it would take for me to be like him.

"I'll send someone in with some food and water for you." Lorcan turned and walked out. His footsteps receded down the hallway, echoing off the wall of the small chamber.

A shudder went through me. The only world I had ever known had been completely ripped away. I finally allowed a few tears to fall silently down my cheeks as my heart and my life fractured into a million pieces.

I drifted off into a light sleep, my cheek resting on the gritty wall. I woke to the sound of quick footsteps clicking on the hard earth floor. As they gradually grew closer, I drew my knees up to my chest defensively.

A slim figure dressed in dark pants and t-shirt glided into the room holding a plate of food and bottled water. Her red hair was pulled back in a tight ponytail. She looked as beautiful and angelic as I remembered.

"Samantha," I said, shaking my head. "Of course, I should have seen this one coming." It all made sense now, her random odd comments about "my kind" and her disgust of me, and the times I'd thought I'd seen her turn into a monster. Though, I sensed the real reason she hated me had more to do with Eli than what I was.

"No one ever said Daes were very smart," she said snidely.

"Yeah, but I bet it smarted a bit when this Dae had the extreme pleasure of kicking your ass." I smiled so sweetly I could feel sugar oozing from my pores.

"Shut up, bitch," she flared but quickly caught herself. A twisted smile formed on her lips. "Oh, gosh, all this yelling has made me so thirsty." She opened the bottled water, took a huge swig, and poured the rest onto the floor. "Oops!"

I watched the water puddle as my parched throat ached for relief.

"Oh, did you want this?" Her eyes were wide with false innocence as she returned the same sickly-sweet smile.

I bit my lip and held back any snide comment wanting to tumble out of my mouth.

"Good girl." Her voice was so condescending it took everything I had not to jump at the bars. "You can be taught." She screwed on the cap and threw what was left of the water at me. I grabbed it, draining it dry. It only wet my mouth and didn't take away the aching thirst.

"Sam, knock it off." A deep, distinct, raspy twang came from behind Samantha, and a large, muscular form sauntered up to my cage. I knew instantly whom the voice and body belonged to.

"Oh, my god." I put my head in my hands in disbelief. It was another piece of this crazy puzzle falling into place. I couldn't see the whole picture or how big and intricate it was, but piece by piece it was forming.

"You called, darlin'?"

I picked up my head from my hands and looked into West's glinting, soft brown eyes. I couldn't help the small laugh escaping me as I watched him lean against the bars with the cocky grin of his, looking the same as when I saw him at Mike's Bar.

"Again, I suppose I shouldn't be surprised. I should have known you'd be a part of this, too."

How many others had infiltrated my life in some way or another without me knowing? My life was becoming farcical. Was there any part of it true or real?

He winked at me. "Oh, don't be so hard on yourself, darlin'. You're playin' with the big boys, and let me tell you, you can hold your own. You were more than impressive, and I'll admit, quite easy on the eye."

"Ugh, disgusting." Sam motioned as if she might vomit. "Did all you guys get completely hexed by her or something?"

"Ah, Sam, green doesn't suit you."

"You think I'm jealous of *that*?" She pointed at me, her tiny little nose wrinkling in disgust. West looked at her with a lopsided grin on his face. *"Téigh trasna ort féin,"* Sam barked at him, throwing the plate of food she had brought against the wall and storming out. Sauce and bits of some kind of meat slithered down the wall to the floor with a plopping sound. I sensed whatever it was she said wasn't complimentary, yet it made West smile even more.

"Sorry about her. I'll get you another plate." He motioned to the food now in indefinable clumps on the floor. "Eli's always been a sore spot for Sam. She can't handle he's only thought of her as a sister and a pain-in-the-ass-psycho one to boot."

I frowned. "What do you mean? I thought . . . they were never together?"

West burst out laughing. "Eli and Sam? Not a chance. He wouldn't touch her. That one comes with a straight-jacket and a restraining order."

"No." I shook my head. "He left because . . . I saw them together . . ." My brain swam with every conflicting memory or image I had of Eli and Sam. I had always felt horrible because I had been *that* girl willing to let something happen with a guy who had a so-called girlfriend.

It was hard to readjust everything I thought hadn't been true. It never even entered my mind there wasn't *something* going on between them, but now in hindsight, I could see all the little clues validating what West claimed. Eli was always pulling away from her advances, treating her coolly. Eli had said their relationship was nothing more than what it was.

I always assumed it meant they were casual lovers, but nothing more serious. Was what I interpreted as a lover's quarrel nothing more than Eli trying to deflect her relentless pursuits? Sam was always the one who reached out to him. I don't remember ever seeing him initiating any touch. I rubbed my forehead in frustration.

"Eli is a complicated man, darlin', and unfortunately, you are a mere pawn in all this."

It felt like a knife was twisting in my gut. Yes, truth could definitely hurt. "Yeah, so I'm gathering."

"He's second in command. His duties come first," West said.

"Duties? Is that what you called it, or did it have some fun name like 'Operation Seduce' or 'Operation Lie, Lure, and Betray' or 'Operation Being a Typical Man'?" I retorted.

West sighed and leaned against the bars. "I'm really sorry for it, darlin'. The night we met I was doin' a little undercover work. Eli wasn't letting us get anywhere near you, and Lorcan decided to see why, so he sent me. You were more than I imagined. I liked you. You really surprised me, and believe me when I say I didn't have to pretend with you. I do wish it didn't have to be like this."

"Go away," I uttered, my voice low and tight. They talked about my life so nonchalantly. I suppose it was better than Sam who was giddy with joy about my demise.

"I'll get you some more food and water," he uttered, looking back at me once more before leaving.

ᴄᴛʜɪʀᴛʏ-ᴏɴᴇ

I leaned my head against the wall, taking in a deep breath. I hadn't had any time to really contemplate or try to understand everything I learned over the last day. It was so overwhelming and unbelievable; it was hard for my brain to wrap around it all.

Fay.

Demon.

How was I supposed to deal with this? I had so many questions, especially for my parents. Questions for a mother who was dead and for a father who ran out on us before I was born.

Perfect.

It made me sick to think I was a product of a rape. But my mother kept and loved me anyway. I longed to hear my mother's voice, to feel her arms wrapping me, reassuring everything was going to be okay. But the only thing surrounding me now was dank, damp, musty air and the thin cotton fabric of Eli's old t-shirt. I could still smell him on it, and I detested that it still comforted me.

I thought about Mark, wondering if he knew about me or if Mom had left him in the dark, too. Of course, if he had known about me, then he wouldn't have been so concerned about my sanity. He would have understood I was different and not in the "mental facility" way.

Then, with a stab of foreboding, I remembered it was most likely Monday by now—the day Mark was returning from his trip. I had no clue what time it was. He might already be home. What would he do when he found I had disappeared? He would fall apart. Losing both my mom and me would be too much for him. I needed a plan and needed one fast.

I was searching my prison for any kind of way out or a weapon when West brought me a plate of fried chicken and mashed potatoes with a bottle of water. I downed the water in three gulps. I was so hungry and knew I needed my strength. I eyed the food West handed me, highly doubting they'd poison me before they got what they needed. The smell made my stomach growl, and I dove into the food greedily. He left me alone while I devoured everything.

I was finishing when there was a commotion down the hallway.

My skin prickled as I stood cautiously, crowding into the far corner. Footsteps reverberated from the corridor, coming toward my cell. This time I recognized the intense feeling of power plowing into me from was coming. It was so strong it made me dizzy under its weight. My breath became rapid and shallow as my legs tried to hold me up. I slinked back, pressing myself against the wall, willing myself to blend in with the shadows.

An elegant, strong figure with brazen confidence swept into the room, making a cool breeze flutter over me. The tall woman stepped into the light, making me gasp. Beauty could not define who stood gracefully in front of me. Her hair was such a brilliant shade of deep red there was no way to describe it. The color didn't exist in this world. Her long strands were pulled back in a most elaborate design of braids, which fell to the middle of her back. With eyes of pale violet and alabaster skin, she was so perfect it made me want to weep. She looked young, but I knew it was only her shell. Power, confidence, and wisdom saturated her aura. She wore a long dress, which was more modern than I expected. The delicate fabric was the color of cream and flowed under the light as she moved.

Even though I had never seen her before, there was no question who the exquisite lady was. She looked in my direction with a cool, smug smile twisting her beautiful full lips.

"Ember," the Queen addressed me. My voice failed to find its way out of my throat as I continued to stare at her. "No point trying to hide yourself in the shadows. It's not like I don't know you're there or that I can't get to you." Her commanding voice caused goose bumps to run down my arms and legs. "I have no doubt you are aware of who I am."

My backside continued to mold itself to the wall as I watched her in silence. She was so ethereal it was painful to look at her. "The Q-Queen," I mumbled.

Lorcan had kidnapped me, so why was the Queen here? Lorcan said she had exiled the Dark Dwellers, and I already felt Eli's hatred of her, the strong desire for revenge, but there she stood. Somewhere in my gut, the truth was trying to reach my brain to make sense of the scene in front of me.

"Yes," she replied. "Now come closer."

Her words hovered over me. I stayed where I was, the shadows keeping me in a false bubble.

Irritation flickered on her face. "Come here now."

Again, a sensation fluttered around me. There was pressure and a commanding energy to it, but I could ignore it. She was trying to compel me, but it wasn't working.

She adjusted her stance and spoke again. This time her voice was sweet and kind and felt false to my ears. "Let me see you. Please."

I decided to oblige. She was only going to play nice for so long before she'd come into the cage and get me herself.

As I stepped into the light, she did something unexpected. She jerked away from me. Her eyes grew wide as air pushed through her teeth in a hiss, and for a brief second she looked tortured as she took in every detail of my face and body.

She quickly swung away, and when she turned back, her expression was hard and cruel. A pitiless look now hung in her eyes, and heated anger replaced the shock which had temporarily jolted her. But the image of what I saw, the fleeting moment when the Queen had looked at me with trepidation, was seared in my brain. She looked like she had seen a ghost—a ghost she feared.

"You look exactly like your traitorous mother and that filthy repulsive monster you have for father." Her voice was harsh and short. "You are nauseating to see."

Rage burned deep within me. The iron bars kept me from acting out. Even without touching them, I could feel their negative energy drooling at the closeness of my presence, hungry to consume my powers.

"Your mother was right to take you away because I would have killed you . . . and enjoyed it. At present, I am glad you survived." Her voice returned to its soothing, sweet tone, which made me even more nervous. "I have been looking for you for a long time, Ember. This time, though, I have other plans for you besides a painful death. You will be quite useful to me."

"How?" I croaked.

"You will be my greatest weapon to oppose the Unseelie King. It will be sweet justice using you against him."

Lorcan brazenly strode into the small space. The proud, wicked look on his face drove the knowledge from my gut straight to my brain.

Oh, God, no! "Lorcan?"

"And somehow you still appear surprised," he said, grinning.

"How can you do this? To your brother? To your family?"

Lorcan was instantly at the bars, pressing into them. "I am doing this *for* them." His eyes flashed red fire before turning back to the familiar shade of green I knew all too well. "Eli got too close and could no longer make the choices a leader has to. I was always supposed to be the First, not him, and certainly not Cole. I am the rightful leader, and I am willing to make sacrifices for the good of my clan. Not even our First is willing to do so. Cole and Eli are made from the same cloth. Spineless. But I have no problem doing what I need to do."

"You hate me that much?"

"You mean nothing to me. Your kind should be destroyed in both this realm and the other."

The Queen stepped to Lorcan. "I couldn't agree more, but first we need to finish my side of the deal before you can destroy her." She touched his arm, and calmness fell over his features.

"Of course, my Queen." Her influence rolled over him like a sedative. She could compel him, but not me. Why couldn't she control me? Was it because I was a Dae, or was it because of my strength of will? Was this why she hated Daes so much? She couldn't compel us?

I felt power in knowing the Queen couldn't control me. It gave me confidence as I walked closer to the bars.

"So, Lorcan, you really think making a deal with her will get you what you want? That she will simply let you back into the Otherworld? Are you so delusional you think it will happen so easily?"

"I think I'll be okay. It's you who needs to worry," he sneered and then turned to the Queen. "I am going to check on the progress of my other charge."

"Yes, yes, please go." The Queen waved him out of the room without even looking at him. Lorcan turned and gave me a disturbing smile, one that made my veins turn to ice. It was like he knew something I didn't and was enjoying it far too much. He pivoted and exited the room, leaving the Queen and me alone.

"Lorcan is not as clever as his brother. He's too eager for power and control, which has come in quite useful to me." She smiled coolly. "We all have our parts to play. Yours is to take the Unseelie King's domain and burn it to the ground. Taking away his hold on Earth will cripple him for good. We will start with his home base in Seattle."

"Burn Seattle?" I gaped. "I-I don't understand. I can burst a bulb or two but burn down an entire city?"

"You are a Dae, Ember. Destruction and murder runs in your veins."

"Lorcan said you used to kill Daes, but now you've changed your mind. Why me? Why now?"

"The 'why now,'" she repeated, "is because I finally found you. You were well hidden from me, though Lily knew she couldn't hide you forever. You are special. Once I got over your mother's betrayal, I realized what use you could be to me in executing my plans."

"Everything is set, my Queen."

My knees buckled. I knew that voice. It had comforted and spoken softly to me so many nights in my dreams.

Torin stepped into the room. He had only come to me twice in person. Those times felt so long ago and less real than my dreams of him did. I had almost believed he really was a hallucination, no more than a creation in my mind. But there he stood, real and even more beautiful than I recalled. His hair was slicked back neatly and tied with a leather strip. He wore his leather pants, but instead of his black shirt, he wore a long-sleeved, leather shirt with a chest guard engraved with the Queen's crest on the front.

He was a soldier of the Queen.

The whole time he had been coming to me, he had been working for the Queen. He had kissed me, made me feel secure. I felt foolish and betrayed by him, another person in a long list who deceived me. My heart felt sorrowful. He had felt safe to me, comfortable, like he'd always protect me. I bit my lip, forcing myself not to cry. But a tiny voice kept me hopeful. *If he's working for her, why didn't he turn me over to her before? Why did he try to warn me and keep me safe instead?*

"Oh, Torin, my beautiful boy." The Queen smiled at him, placing her hand on his chest. Something in me wanted to swipe her hand away. I felt possessive of him, which didn't make sense. Why did I feel like he belonged to me?

His eyes flickered quickly to mine and then away.

"Get our prisoner prepared, Torin."

"As you command." He bowed to acknowledge her order. He pulled out some gloves made of a strange, thick material as he approached and unlocked the cage. I hadn't notice until then a robe hung off his arm. Guess the thin t-shirt and underwear I was wearing wasn't appropriate for whatever they had planned for me.

My eyes met his with desperation and a need to understand. He shook his head slightly as his gaze slid to the Queen.

"Thought you might be cold," he uttered softly to me and held out the cloak. I nodded and let him help me put it on. This was all so surreal. The robe was soft and warm against my skin.

"Quickly. We are on a schedule," the Queen said curtly.

Torin nodded, looking down at his feet. "I am sorry," he mumbled so softly I barely heard him. His gloved hands removed a pair of handcuffs on his belt and latched them around my wrists.

A strangled cry slipped out of my mouth, and once again I felt my powers being sucked out of me. Iron cuffs. I sagged to the ground.

"I hope you realize it would be pointless and stupid to try anything, Ember. You are no match for me or my men. You would merely be wasting your energy."

I heard her words but didn't acknowledge them. I had no plan to fight him or anyone for that matter. I could barely keep my head up. My so-called powers weren't the most reliable things anyway. I had no clue what they really were or even how to use them. Since I

286

could barely stand on my own two feet without help, there was no way I could take anyone on, and she knew it. She was enjoying playing with me.

Torin lifted me like a baby, sweeping me out of the cage, down the hall, up a steep flight of stairs, and out of the cabin that had been my kidnappers' lair.

CHIRCY-CWO

Torin held me close, his breath warm on my head as he carried me. The initial shock of the iron had worn off a little. Now, I felt strong enough to stand but lethargic and empty. My powers were dormant.

It seemed as if we had barely stepped outside, when a strange sensation tingled over my skin, as if we had walked through electrified Jell-O. Suddenly, we were deep in the woods, high on a mountain. This must be a Fae trick to magically be teleported someplace else. There was no other way we could have gotten this far so fast.

Torin gingerly placed my feet on the ground, wrapping his arm firmly around my waist to keep me upright. Movement caused me to look up. Groups of people stepped out from the trees. Lorcan and Sam and a few others I didn't recognize assembled to my left. I noticed West was not among them. The Queen, a dozen or so guards, and people of her court stood to my right.

I was scared, but I was also angry. I hated feeling out of control or backed into a corner. She couldn't manipulate me like she could the others. "I will not help you," I said. "You cannot control me."

Anger flushed across her face, her eyes narrowing, but in an instant it was gone. She forced a smile and walked close to me.

"Oh, I can control you," she said, her voice hard. "And you *will* do as I say."

"No." It was the only word I could muster. The power emanating off her was hard to fight.

"We shall see." She nodded to Lorcan.

He whistled over his shoulder. "Dax, can you show Em her 'incentive' to cooperate?" Lorcan spoke loudly, addressing someone behind him.

From around a tree a tall, sexy man stepped out. His close-cut haircut and milk-chocolate complexion offset his structured jawline and full lips. I was so taken by his beauty I didn't immediately notice he was holding someone. As my eyes took in the person standing next to Dax, everything else was forgotten.

"Mark!" I screamed and instinctively moved toward him. Torin's arm held me back.

Mark was bound and gagged. Fright lit his light blue eyes as they bounced over everyone in confusion. Hearing me call his name, he looked up. His eyes became wide. He pitched forward trying to get to me. Dax had a firm grip on him and pulled him back. My panic only intensified when I saw the huge knife Dax carried in his other hand.

The Queen strode to Mark. "Oh, what a handsome man. He will be fun to play with." She slid her fingers down his face.

I seethed, struggling against Torin. "Don't touch him."

The Queen pressed her hand against Mark's chest. He hunched over. An anguished cry escaped from under his cloth gag.

"Stop. Please, stop!" I wailed.

"Are you ready to do what I ask?" the Queen demanded.

"You want me to destroy a city, killing innocent people, even children, to get the attention of this Unseelie King?"

"The humans killed us for centuries. They took everything from us first. They deserve this!" A flash of unrestrained rage flared.

She took a deep breath. "You are wasting my time. You will do this for me. You are mine now, Ember."

I looked at Mark, who was stooped over. His blue eyes, watering with pain, looked up into mine. He shook his head in a "no" movement. He didn't want me to do whatever it was he thought this lady wanted. He would rather sacrifice himself, even if he didn't know what for. I couldn't let Mark suffer for me—for what I was.

The few seconds of hesitation were too long for the Queen. Her hand slammed into Mark's ribcage. A tormented scream rang from him, making my knees go weak. He fell to the ground and huddled into a ball. The Queen motioned to Dax and then nodded at Mark as she moved toward me. "Torture him until she concedes."

Before I could get a word out, Dax kicked Mark in the stomach and then in the face. His body snapped back in an unnatural angle. Blood flew from his nose and mouth.

A sorrowful whimper seeped through my lips. "Please, please stop. I'll do anything you want." Tears trickled down my face. I looked at Mark again, agony distorting his features. Through the pain and the blood, I saw his bewilderment and confusion. I knew he didn't comprehend what was going on or how I was involved in it. There was nothing I could do to make it better for him.

Lorcan smirked. "Funny, I remember you saying something earlier about how you would never do what I did."

"That's not fair. This isn't the same thing." My voice was small and uncertain.

"Is it not?" He cocked his head. "I never said I'd be fair. I'm a little partial to getting what I want, so I made sure I had a little leverage. You're lucky it was only him. I could have added your two little friends into the mix."

Lorcan's smug smile made me want to attack him. Torin seemed to sense my intentions and tightened his grip on my waist. They knew who my friends were. I had no doubt they would go after them if I didn't comply. Lorcan was right. There wasn't anything I wouldn't do to keep my friends and my family safe. My choice made me feel disgusted with myself, but it really was no longer a choice. I would protect my family and my friends no matter what.

"Remember, Ember, I know how powerful Daes are, so if you do not give me everything you are capable of, your human father gets punished," the Queen threatened.

I straightened, wiping the tears from my face. "I understand."

She grabbed my arm, her long, delicate fingers digging into my skin. "Asim, come here." The Queen motioned to someone in her entourage. A boy who looked about twelve stepped out of the group. He was beautiful. His dark, tan skin was flawless. His chocolate brown hair obscured one of his large, dark brown eyes. I couldn't stop looking at him.

"My Queen." He bowed subserviently.

"Go ahead, my perfect boy." She nodded in my direction.

The angel-faced boy moved closer to me, making me nervous. "Wh-What are you going to do?"

"Asim is an amplifier," the Queen said. "Your powers are not fully developed yet. You need a little boost, and he enhances people's powers. He's been a great gift to me."

"You mean a slave," I spat. "He's only another pawn for you to play with. He's only a boy."

"Asim, do you feel used? Are you doing anything against your will?" She regarded him with a sweet, gentle smile.

"No, my Queen," Asim gushed. "It is an honor and privilege to be at your command." There was not a false word spoken from his lips. He meant every word. He probably grew up believing being a part of her court was the greatest honor in the world.

"See?" The Queen laughed. "Now, do not speak anymore. You're giving me a headache."

The Queen let go of my arm and turned to Torin. He still held me by the waist, his thumb absently rubbing my side trying to calm and comfort me. This did not go unnoticed by the Queen. "I don't think she will be going anywhere," she said firmly, looking at his hand again. Jealousy and possessiveness rolled off her.

Torin instantly dropped his hand from my waist, stepping back. "Yes, my Queen."

"All right, let us began. Torin, I trust you to keep an eye on her. Not a hand."

"Of course, my lady." He gave her a slight bow. Hearing his voice in person and feeling the heat from his body clinging to my robe made my head spin. How was he the same guy who had said he'd keep me safe no matter what—this man who was now holding me prisoner? At the same time, I still felt oddly comforted by him—that he would protect me.

The Queen turned away and strode to the edge of the cliff. Seattle loomed in the distance. She nodded to the soldier who was closest to me. He approached and with the same kind of gloves Torin had worn, unlocked my iron cuffs. My energy flowed back into me. It felt like stepping into a warm bath after a long day out in the snow. It was heaven.

Mark was barely conscious on the ground. Two of the Queen's guards pulled him up into a sitting position. He groaned as they sat him against a tree. Trails of dried blood streaked down his nose to the top of his lip. One of his bruised, cut eyes was swollen shut.

In the distance, a rumble erupted from the sky, followed by a strike of lightning.

The Queen smiled, clasping her hands together. "Perfect."

Bile tore at my insides as it gushed up my esophagus. I understood now. I knew exactly how she was going to use me as a weapon.

The Queen had picked this night on purpose. I couldn't start fires without a combustible agent, but I could affect them, down to the basic charge of electricity. I couldn't really control my powers

292

yet. She understood this. With Asim's help, though, my powers could devastate a city.

The Queen nodded to Lorcan. With a self-satisfied smile, Lorcan walked to me and cracked me hard across the face. I crumpled to the ground, my face burning with pain. Behind me, Torin said something nasty to Lorcan, but I couldn't understand a thing. My ears and head were ringing as they absorbed the blow.

Rage quickly boiled to the surface, my dark power eager to come out and play. I stood, wiping the blood from my lip with a snort. "You sure you're not Fay? You hit like a little fairy."

Lorcan promptly came back for me, his leg snapped forward and his foot dug into my stomach, shoving me backward onto the ground. My chest throbbed. It hurt to breathe, but I forced myself to stand again.

I knew this was the plan, to get me riled up, to conjure my powers to the surface, but I couldn't stop them now. They *wanted* to come out.

"Come on, Tinkerbelle, is that all you got?" Personally, I was done with the whole ass beating. When he swung this time, I was ready. He was still too fast. He hit my temple as I tried to duck. Fury hissed through me. Lorcan was prepping for another slap when he stopped. His eyes widened as he looked at me. My gaze shifted, focusing in on its target.

"Her eyes are turning black. Do it now," the Queen shouted.

Asim's hand clamped my bare arm. It felt like a bomb exploded inside me. All my senses were gone. I could no longer feel a separation between the rest of the world and my body. I was so full of energy I couldn't contain it.

The ground quaked beneath me. I felt another burst of energy in me, and a renewed surge of power ignited within me. The powers, which had been dormant, burst to the surface with exultance. They were awake.

Untamed power. Strength. Exhilaration. I craved more. I wanted more.

When Asim's hands pulled away, it felt like something was being ripped from me, making me feel empty and alone.

"No!" I cried out. *Don't leave me.*

My lids blinked open. I was on all fours on the ground. My ribs still ached from being kicked, and dried blood crusted my nose and the side of my mouth.

"Thank you, Asim. We will start again in a moment. I am sure Ember would love to see the brilliant work she's done so far."

My head snapped up. Everyone was staring at me. Their awe and fear could not be hidden. My breath tightened in my chest.

"Come here, Ember." The Queen motioned for me to join her on the cliff's edge. Excess energy sizzled in me, and electricity crackled from my skin as I moved to the rim.

The world stopped.

Seattle and the surrounding area were in ruins, engulfed in fire. Houses burned and hissed as flames consumed the city. One side of me felt exhilarated at the sheer, raw power; the other part of me was burning. The part connected to the earth could feel each tree and each organism dying in a tortured, flaming death, as if I were being charred from the inside out.

"Oh, God, no." My eyes fastened on the devastation. *This was my fault. I did this.*

The Queen looked over her shoulder at Asim. "Not so much this time, Asim. I have no doubt my message has been received, but I've always had the flare for the dramatic. We might as well have a finale. One finger should do it."

Everyone moved out of his way when he got close. I guess a touch from him was never a mere touch. Even though he was facilitating this annihilation, I felt sad for him. What a lonely life—never being able to touch or hug anyone.

He slipped up next to me without a thread of his clothes touching mine. As another bolt of lightning shot across the sky, he lightly touched a finger to my arm. My senses didn't leave me this

294

time, but it felt like I had taken about twelve shots of espresso and leaned against an electrical fence.

The moment he touched me, lightning split across the sky, hitting the Space Needle. Electricity encompassed the building, and with a loud crack, the jagged bolt sliced through the steel structure. The sound of groaning metal pierced the evening sky. A scream ripped from my lungs as I watched the city's most famous monument separated from its base and crumble to the ground. A tidal wave of debris rolled into the surrounding buildings, causing them to fold like houses of cards, devastating the area within a several mile radius of the icon.

My mouth dropped open with a silent scream.

"Now, that is a finale," Lorcan mumbled next to me.

What have I done? Thousands of lives . . . gone.

I knew the Queen would keep using me to destroy and kill, and there was nothing I could do. If I let her take me, I would belong to her forever or until she had done enough damage. Then, she would have me killed. This couldn't happen. I had to get away. I shot a glance over my shoulder at Mark. He was still unconscious. There was no way to get him out of here. But leaving him was not an option.

I felt irritated when Torin stepped into my line of sight. I was about to twist away, when his voice broke into my head. *"Ember, I have an idea. Pay attention. We don't have much time."*

Images poured into my brain, playing like a movie. I immediately understood what he was trying to show me. He wanted to cause a distraction to help me escape. It was a flimsy plan and had a slim chance of working, but it was the only one available. My bigger problem lay unconscious. I slid my eyes to Mark, then back to Torin. Torin tilted his head and shook it slightly. If he was thinking I would simply leave Mark behind, he was sorely mistaken.

"Guard, re-cuff her." The Queen turned her back on Seattle and addressed the same guard who had removed the restraints from me earlier. I knew this was my last chance. If she got those cuffs on me, I was done. I wouldn't be able to fight or get away. She would own my ass.

Panic soared through my veins. My powers were still skimming the surface, and it didn't take much effort to get them to answer my call, but I needed to be precise for this to work. I lightly touched Asim. My focus sharpened, and I sent all of my force to the electrostatic charge. Brilliant, white light sliced across the sky, hitting the tree near us. Intense heat and a loud snap fell upon the surrounding space, knocking everyone off their feet.

Fire isn't quiet. It has a frighteningly deep, steady humming sound as it devours everything in its sight. The noise, along with the commotion of everyone making sure the Queen was all right, was the perfect opportunity for me to escape. I pushed myself up and scrambled to Mark, ignoring the jabbing pain in my ribs.

"Go, Ember." Torin yelled into my head as he gestured frantically towards the forest.

"No, I'm not leaving him," I hissed.

"You cannot help him now. You're only condemning yourself. You will be of no use to him or yourself. Please, I'm trying to save you. Now, go!"

Mark's sweet, familiar face was turned my way, and his swollen eyes opened enough so I could see his blue irises. I knew Mark well enough to know what they were telling me. *Go. Save yourself.*

Torin moved in behind me. *"I will protect him, Ember, but you have to go. She will not hurt him. She knows he is too valuable to you. But you know if she gets those cuffs on you, you have no hope. You will be hers."* Torin's words hit their target. He was right.

Everyone was regrouping, getting ready to act. This was my last chance. It was the only way I could keep Mark alive. If she had me, she would kill him. Without me, she would keep him alive using him as bait. I nodded at Torin, then took my last opportunity to look back at Mark. *I love you,* I mouthed to him.

Torin grabbed me, pulling me back into him. *"Find Lars. He will help you. "* He gently kissed my head before pushing me away. I didn't hesitate. I shot off, leaped over the bushes, and disappeared into the thick, dark forest.

☧ʜɪꞃ☧y-☧ʜꞃɛɛ

My bare feet barely struck the cold, wet ground as I tore through the forest. I stumbled through the maze of trees and the foliage, gripping my side. It took everything I had to stay upright. I ached everywhere, but I couldn't stop. I didn't know how long or how far I ran. My mind turned off, and the woods became a blurred picture in my peripheral vision.

I ran until exhaustion made me clumsy. My foot hooked on a rock. I fell, sliding over the dead leaves and foliage to the edge of a cliff.

I bit my lip to keep from shouting as my ribcage screamed in agony. Sweat and tears mixed together as I inched backward, away from the ledge. I lay down, my cheek pressing against the damp earth. It took a moment for my eyes to register what I was seeing. A pitiful whimper left my lips.

Seattle was a charred ruin. It was unrecognizable—leveled.

Smoldering billows of smoke rolled and twisted into the sky. Ash fell from above like black snowflakes. The smell of gas, burning plastic, and smoldering wood assaulted my nose. I could hear the fire engines echo off the mountain. But what was worse was the sound of people screaming. The terrified, aching cries of people searching for their loved ones and watching their homes burn resounded in my ears. Thousands of innocent lives had been consumed by the destruction I created.

I threw up in the bush as another anguished cry tugged at my soul. *This was what I was capable of?* Seattle was no small town, and now it was destroyed.

The pain was too much to bear.

Torin had helped me escape because he knew the Queen was planning to start a war with the Unseelie King, to take Earth from him. Seattle was only the beginning. It was only a declaration of war. She planned to use Earth as her battlefield and me as her weapon.

I gazed across the watery sound at Seattle's scorched remains. The Queen wouldn't rest until she found me. I couldn't, I wouldn't, let it happen. I would not be a pawn in her game.

Torin's words repeated in my head: *Find Lars. He will help you.*

I had no idea who or what Lars was, but I trusted Torin. If he wanted me to find this Lars person, I knew it was for a good reason. He wanted me to fight the Queen, and I would fight. That bitch had my father, the only family I had left. I would battle whatever she threw at me to get him back.

I stood again, watching the last bit of sun reflect off the city. Everything had changed, but instead of being scared, I was ready. I had never fit in before, but now I found my place.

I was Fay and Demon. I was earth and fire. I was darkness and light. I was not a victim. I would become what I was meant to be.

A Dae.

And I would fight.

Thank you to all my readers. Your opinion really matters to me and helps others decide if they want to purchase my book. If you enjoyed this book, please consider leaving an honest review on the site where you purchased it. Thank you!

Want to find out about my next release in the Darkness Series? Sign up on my website and keep updated on the latest news! www.staceymariebrown.com

Fire In The Darkness
(Darkness Series Book #2)

Coming out in Fall 2013

It's been four weeks since Ember Brycin witnessed what her powers are capable of. What they're calling the Electrical Current Storm (ECS). It has turned the entire state of Washington into a third world country and Ember is the one who caused it. Something she'll have to live with every day.

Those people who were unable to escape either turned quickly into gangs or live in shelters. Ember, on the other hand, can't do either. With a price on her head and a Dark Dweller on her ass, she is constantly on the move.

Both Fae and Demons are hunting her—each for their own purpose—to use her as a weapon or a pawn in the war between the Unseelie King of the Dark and the Seelie Queen of the Light.

Em needs help but she doesn't know who to trust: Torin, the Seelie Queen's personal knight, who has sworn to keep Em safe? Or Eli, part of the Dark Dwellers, whom she has an undeniable, intense connection? No matter what she chooses she will probably lose—her life or everything and everyone she loves.

Acknowledgements

Writing a book is anything but easy. It involves years of blood, sweat, tears, banging your head against the desk, more crying, and some serious tantrums. That is just the writing part, turning it into a book for the public is even more laborious. However, I'd do it all over again, without hesitation.

Writing is also a very solitary activity, but publishing a book is not. There are "victims" you drag into it, whether they want to or not, who help so much through this long, sometimes painful, journey.

First and foremost to my mom, who is my best friend, sounding board, editor (I will admit I'm not the best speller), and cheerleader. You came into this unfamiliar with the fantasy world (besides *Harry Potter* books) and became proficient in the Fae/Demon world. You helped me look at things differently, question and solve those glitches in the story. There are not enough thank yous in the world to repay you. I love you more than anything and am so grateful you are my mother. Thank you for believing in me and always letting me follow my own road. You helped my dreams come true. Now get ready for book two!

To Linne, "L," for being my beta reader. Your insight and funny comments helped add so much more to the story. The Ember and Eli scenes seemed to get hotter with your input. Both you and Paul helped me see different views when I got too far inside my own head. You are amazing, and I am so thankful you have come into my life.

To Chase Nottingham, editor/proofreader extraordinaire. Thanks for making this book even better than before. I'm so lucky to have found you. (www.chaseediting.com)

To Clare and Dave, at Woulds & Shoulds, for your editing and design. You two are amazing! Clare, thanks for the hours of editing and helping me really shape this story and getting to what mattered. Dave, thank you for the endless hours editing and for putting up with my nitpicking and being a general pain in the rear about the cover. Your talent and patience is astounding. I am so grateful to you both for bringing my baby to life.

To Dawn and Lily, your love of fantasy and your friendship inspired me more than you know.

To my "Shut up and Write" writing group, thanks for making me shut up and write . . . well maybe not shut-up, but at least write!

To my family, a big thank you for the support and love. For all my friends scattered around the world, you are all constant inspiration to me. I love you all so much. (If you are not "named" in this book, remember there are two more books and future ones you might show up in! Good or bad—writer's revenge!)

And lastly to my nieces, Audrey, Kinsey, and Darcy, you girls are my light in the darkness.

Glossary

A GHRA: Gaelic for "my love."

CIACH ORT: Irish for "dammit."

CINAED/CIONAODH: Irish meaning "born of fire."

DAE: Beings having both pure fairy and demon blood. Their powers and physical features represent both parentages. The offspring of fairies and demons are extremely powerful. They are feared and considered abominations, being killed at birth for centuries by the Seelie Queen.

DAMNU' ORT: Irish for "damn you."

DARK DWELLER: Freelance mercenaries of the Otherworld. The only group in the Otherworld that is neither under the command of the Seelie Queen or the Unseelie King. They were exiled to Earth by the Queen.

DEMON: A broad term for group of powerful and usually malevolent beings. They live off human life forces, gained by sex, debauchery, corruption, greed, dreams, energy, and death. They live on Earth, taking on animal or human form, their shell being the best weapon to seduce or gain their prey.

DRUID: Important figures in ancient Celtic Ireland. They held positions of advisors, judges, and teachers. They can be either male or female and are magicians and seers who have the power to manipulate time, space, and matter. They are the only humans able to live in the Otherworld and can live for centuries.

FAE: A broad group of magical beings who originated in the Earth realm and migrated to the Otherworld when human wars started to take their land. They can be both sweet and playful or scary and dangerous. All fae possess the gifts of glamour (power of illusion), and some have the ability to shape-shift.

FAIRY (FAY): A selective and elite group of fae. The noble pureblooded fairies who stand as the ruling court known as the

303

Seelie of Tuatha de Danann. They are of human stature and can be confused for human if it wasn't for their unnatural beauty. One of their weaknesses is Iron as it is poisonous to the fey/fae and may kill them if there is too much in their system. Also see "Fae" above.

GLAMOUR: Illusion cast by the fae to camouflage, divert, or change appearance.

GNOME: Small humanlike creatures that live underground. Gnomes consist of a number of different types: forest gnomes, garden gnomes, and house gnomes. They are territorial and mischievous and don't particularly like humans.

GOBLINS: Short, ugly creatures. They can be very ill-tempered and grumpy. They are greedy and are attracted to coins and shiny objects. Will take whatever you set down.

KELPIE: A water spirit of Scottish folklore, typically taking the form of a horse, reputed to delight in the drowning of travelers.

MO CHUISLE MO CHROI: Irish phrase of endearment meaning "pulse of my heart." Can also mean "my love" or "my darling."

OTHERWORLD: Another realm outside of the Earth realm.

PYROKINESIS: The ability to set objects or people on fire through the concentration of psychic power.

SEELIE: The "Light" court of the Tuatha De Danaan meaning "blessed." This court consists of all the noble (pure) fairies and fae. They have powers that can be used for good or bad, but are thought of as more principled as the Unseelie. However, "light" does not necessarily mean "good."

SIDHE: Another name for the fae folk of Tuatha De Danann.

TECHNOKINESIS: The ability to move an object with the power of one's thoughts.

TEIGH TRASNA ORT FEIN: A Gaelic swear word with the approximate meaning of "Go screw yourself."

TELEKINETIC: The power to move something by thinking about it without the application of physical force.

TUATHA DE DANANN (or DANAAN): A race of people Irish mythology. They are the earliest fae/fairies.

UNSEELIE: The "Dark" fae of the Tuatha De Danaan. These are considered the un-pure or rebels of the Otherworld and do not follow the Seelie ways. They are nocturnal and have powers thought to be more immoral. They can also use their shell to seduce or gain their prey; however, "dark" does not necessarily mean "bad."

About The Author

Stacey Marie Brown works by day as an Interior/Set Designer and by night a writer of paranormal fantasy, adventure, and literary fiction. She grew up in Northern California, where she ran around on her family's farm raising animals, riding horses, playing flashlight tag, and turning hay bales into cool forts.

Even before she could write, she was creating stories and making up intricate fantasies. Writing came as easy as breathing. She later turned this passion into acting, living and traveling abroad, and designing.

Though she had never stopped writing, moving back to San Francisco seemed to have brought it back to the forefront and this time it would not be ignored.

When she's not writing, she's out hiking, spending time with friends, traveling, listening to music, or designing.

To learn more about Stacey or her books, visit her at:

Author website

www.staceymariebrown.com

Facebook

Author page: https://www.facebook.com/staceymarie.brown.5

Book page: https://www.facebook.com/DOLSeries

Twitter

@S_MarieBrown